THE
ACCIDENTAL
PEACEMAKER

To Bill + Susie
Best Wishes!

THE
ACCIDENTAL
PEACEMAKER

A Novel

by
George Lindamood

The Accidental Peacemaker

This book is set in Adobe Caslon. Caslon, a typeface originally designed by William Caslon I (1692–1766), has been faithfully reproduced for the electronic media by font designers at Adobe Systems Incorporated.

Book and cover design: Magdalena Bassett

In memory of
Victor R. Beasley, PhD
(1939-1999)

Author's Note and Disclaimer

This is a work of fiction. However, to give an air of immediacy to the story I have placed it in actual locations in California, Oregon, and Washington by using the names of real towns, streets, businesses, organizations, parks, and geographical features — but not in every instance. Some names have been changed for the sake of privacy and anonymity, and others are completely fictional because there is no real place that "fits." Bottom line: If you think it's real, it's probably not; if you think it's made up, think again. In any event, no disrespect or disparagement of any real locations, businesses or organizations is intended.

Some of the 'backstory' incidents that supposedly occurred before the time the story begins, which is 29 April 2014, are as real as news gets. My account of them has been taken from public news sources such as the online archives of the *Portland Oregonian*. The names of persons involved in those historical events are also as accurate as reported — that is, not fictional — but none of those individuals are "present" as characters in this story.

Again, this is a work of fiction. All of the characters who do appear in this story at the time of the story, late April thru early December 2014, are entirely fictitious, and any resemblance to actual persons, living or dead, is purely coincidental.

Withdraw into yourself and look.
And if you do not find yourself beautiful yet.
act as does the creator of a statue
that is to be made beautiful:
he cuts away here, he smoothes there,
he makes this line lighter, this other purer,
until a lovely face has grown upon his work.

So do you also:
cut away all that is excessive;
straighten all that is crooked,
bring light to all that is overcast,
labor to make all one glow of beauty
and never cease chiseling your statue,
until there shall shine out on you from it
the godlike splendor of virtue,
until you shall see the perfect goodness
surely established in the stainless shrine.

—Plotinus (205-270 CE), *The Enneads*

PART ONE

Endings and Beginnings

In my end is my beginning.
— T.S. Eliot (1888-1965)

1.

Up until six months ago, when he had innocently embarked on a solitary retreat to review and reinvent his life in an isolated shack near Klamath Falls, Oregon, very little in Walter's past forty-five years had prepared him for the bizarre situation he now faced. (Mac, the peripatetic polymath who served as his fishing guide and mental health counselor, had warned him that it was imminent.) On his left stood a ragtag cadre of AK47-bearing Muslim males, shoddily trained but brimming with the unbridled zeal of immaturity; on his right a pickup-load of heavily armed, slightly over-the-hill patriots from the Jefferson State Militia, self-appointed but committed to intervene whenever and wherever they deem it necessary to protect local property and persons; and himself, the would-be peacemaker, in the middle, supported only by his new fiancée Susan and her twenty-year-old Army linguist daughter Lucy, both minimally sheltered in the rustic cabin behind him, plus a lone US Marshal lurking in the bushes along the narrow path leading to a nearby house from which his neighbor and landlord Ted, (whose abduction was the stated objective of the Muslims' incursion) had been whisked away to safety only minutes before by a Federal government "Black Hawk" helicopter, and his paranoiac wife Lottie (whose past brutal transgressions had triggered—and nearly justified—terrorist *jihad*) had cut and run a few days earlier—but only after a parting display of defiance and ingratitude. If he had had the slightest premonition of *any* of that, Walter would have disregarded the ad under 'Rentals, Misc.' in last Sunday's edition (April 27, 2014) of the *Portland Oregonian*:

SECLUDED CABIN,
furnished—1 BR, fireplace,
carport. $500/mo. utilities
incl. No short-term rentals.
Responsible persons only.
(541)-555-2968.

However, lacking any forewarning, he had decided to give it a try.

Today, some 160 days before the Great Confrontation, a brief cell phone call had led him to Malin, Oregon (pop. 637), some 30 miles southeast of Klamath Falls, to the Malin Country Diner where he now awaited the arrival of his prospective landlord. "Ted" was the only name he had; his cordial self-introduction, "I'm Walter Baker," had not been reciprocated. He had arrived early to do a little reconnaissance, a habit ingrained by thirteen years as an Air Force pilot followed by a decade more with Alaska Airlines. A window seat with a good view of the main street seemed an ideal spot to follow all the comings-and-goings. Slowly eating his sandwich, he strained to pick up tidbits of conversation among the local farmers gathered there, but gained no information that seemed significant, in large part because he simply didn't know what he was getting himself into.

Just before 1:00 PM an old Ford pickup, showing more rust than white, slowly approached from the North and parked in front of the hardware store across the street. Its driver got out and carefully surveyed the surroundings, as if wary of outlaws or Indians waiting in ambush. His gaze stopped momentarily on Walter's blue Chevy pickup bearing California plates and continued until he had noted every vehicle and every pedestrian in sight. Only then did he cross over to the diner. As he stepped inside, Walter stood up and smiled. "Hi, I'm Walter Baker," he said, extending his hand. The response was almost a grunt—"Ted"—along with a cursory handshake. *He still hasn't told me his full name*, Walter thought, but he let it pass, asking, "Can I buy you a cup of coffee?" Still unsmiling, Ted nodded a "yes," and sat down quickly, his body language indicating he wanted to be inconspicuous.

The waitress approached, Walter ordered "Two coffees, please," and she left them to study each other across the table for three minutes that seemed more like thirty. Ted was of average height and build, with searching blue eyes, semi-concealed by the brim of his black cowboy hat. A two-day growth of black beard made it difficult to guess his age, but Walter tentatively put it at early-to-mid-fifties, five-to-ten years older than himself. Dressed in work shirt, jeans, denim jacket, and work boots, all well-worn but clean, Ted apparently wanted to project the image of a backwoodsman, but it wasn't authentic: Walter's gut told him that Ted had been transplanted into this place and time, and that he wasn't a local, much as he wished to pass for one.

"Let me tell you about the cabin," Ted began, speaking softly as if imparting a secret. "It's probably fifty years old, but I've fixed it up—about 800 square feet, with one bedroom, a bathroom—shower, not tub—and the rest open space, all on one level. In the kitchen area there's a two-burner hot plate, a toaster-oven, and a medium-sized refrigerator—all about three years old—but no dishwasher. Heating is by a good-quality wood stove that can also be used for cooking if the electricity goes out. Over the past couple years I've installed insulation, dual-pane windows with screens, and a decent hot water heater."

The coffee arrived. Ted paused to add cream and sugar, then continued. "The main drawback is that there are no laundry facilities. You'd have to hand-wash your things in the sink or go to a laundromat in one of the towns around here." Walter nodded. "There's a small front porch where you can sit and drink beer and watch the world go by, and there's a covered carport and storage shed. The cabin is furnished—well, sort of—with stuff left over from when I lived there, plus some odds and ends from yard sales, including kitchen utensils and linens. If you're fussy about things like that, you would probably want to add a few items of your own. The mattress on the bed is almost new—good quality and very comfortable." Ted paused before delivering the clincher that he hoped would make the sale. "The whole place is in move-in condition. It should work just fine for one or two persons." Then he stopped to sip some coffee.

"Where is it located?" Walter asked.

"In the middle of a forty-acre plot, mostly rolling hills and thin woods, a few miles from here." Walter recalled seeing low wooded hills to the North as he had driven toward Malin. "Access is by paved county road to the edge of the property, then a half-mile gravel driveway through the trees. You shouldn't have any problem getting in or out unless we get more than a foot of snow. My house is a hundred yards away, through the woods, and shares the same well as the cabin. There are no other neighbors for a mile in any direction, and my wife and I have no kids." A short pause and another clincher: "It's real quiet."

"I believe your ad said the rent is $500 per month."

"That's right, but let me give you the fine print. This is the first time we've rented it out—I've been fixing it up in my spare time over the past couple years— so we're sort of feeling our way along. The main thing is we don't want a lot of turnover in tenants. We also want a security deposit—let's say $300—that will be refunded when you leave if you don't trash the place. The rent includes electricity because both houses are on the same meter. If we find the tenant is running up our bill, we'll have to dicker about it. There's no telephone—we assume you'll use a cell phone like we do, but the signal is awfully weak at times, as you found out when you called me yesterday. And there's no TV, but if you want you could sign up for satellite service at your own expense—we've got it at our house. There might even be a way to get Internet access through the TV."

"The Internet isn't important to me right now," Walter replied. "If I need it, I'll go to the library. What about postal service?"

"We rent a box at the post office in town. If you don't want to do that, you can have your mail sent to General Delivery and just stop by to pick it up now and then."

He stopped. Several seconds passed as Walter mulled over all he'd learned. Ted seemed to be impatient for his reaction, so he said, "It sounds like what I had in mind. What information do you need about me?"

Ted's eyes narrowed to slits, like he was turning on some kind of X-ray vision. "Well, let's start with you telling me a little about yourself: who you are, where you come from, and why you're here."

Walter took a couple sips of coffee, buying time to decide what to say and what to leave out. "I'm almost forty-five years old, born and raised near Mendocino. I'm recently divorced; my ex-wife and two kids are living in the East Bay area. I graduated from the Air Force Academy in 1991 and got trained as a pilot. Ten years ago, I resigned my commission and joined Alaska Airlines, where I worked my way up to Captain. After all the recent acquisitions and mergers, I was far enough down on the seniority ladder that I had to choose between dropping back to First Officer status or accepting the severance package. Given the divorce and the fact that my kids don't even want to talk to me now, I decided to take the severance. My plan is to hang out in the woods for a while, do a little fishing, and sort out where I want to go from here. I figure I can get by for a year or two on the cash from the severance. If you like, I can get you a copy of a recent bank statement as evidence that I will be financially responsible."

Ted had switched off his X-ray scan after Walter mentioned the Air Force. "No need to do that, but since you're in the process of pulling up roots and all that, I would like to get a background check on you. There are some weirdo groups in this area I'd rather not get mixed up with."

Walter flashed a smile. "Whatever you wish. I can assure you I've never done drugs nor had any run-ins with the law beyond a couple traffic tickets. I wouldn't have been able to keep my airline job if I'd had any problems like that."

Ted's eyes narrowed down again. "All the same, I'd like you to write your full name, date and place of birth, and Social Security number on this piece of paper—if you don't mind." He pulled a pen and a small square of paper from his shirt pocket and slid them across the table. A yellow caution light flashed in Walter's mind. *He hasn't told me his full name or where the cabin is or anything else about himself, but now he wants me to disclose the basic information needed for identity theft. Why should I trust him?* For a few seconds Walter considered demanding the same information from Ted so he could get his own background check, but his gut warned him it would be a deal-breaker. Further consultation with his gut told him he was not likely to quickly find another domicile that met his needs so he decided to take the risk. He wrote down the information and handed the paper and pen back. Ted read, nodded approvingly, and said, "OK. It will take a couple days, maybe even a week, to run the check. How can I get in touch with you?"

Walter retrieved the piece of paper long enough to write his cell phone number on it, then asked, "Do you have any recommendations on how I might pass the time for a week?"

Ted's eyes softened, and he seemed to warm a little. "There's lots to do around here if you want a change from big city life. It's not hunting season, but the trout fishing is excellent. There's hiking and rock climbing and horseback riding and bird watching. You can go take in the scenery over at Crater Lake—or you can drive back up to Chiloquin and piss away your money at the casino." He seemed on the verge of smiling. "There's at least a dozen so-called resorts hereabouts that would gladly help you lighten your wallet. I suggest you go to the tourist information center in Klamath Falls. They can advise you on the options and help you with reservations."

"I know the place. It sounds like a good way for me to start."

Ted stood up. "I'm sorry that this might take longer than you expected. As I said, this is my first shot at renting the cabin, so I need to go slow and careful. But I give you my word I won't rent it to anybody else before getting back to you."

"That's fair enough," Walter agreed. He paid the bill and followed Ted out the door. They shook hands, exchanged short 'Thank you's, and Ted crossed the street to go into the hardware store.

As he drove back to Klamath Falls, Walter reviewed the meeting in his mind. *He sure is cautious. It was clear he didn't want me to know the precise location of the cabin until he had checked me out. Not that I wouldn't do the same if I were in his situation. Then there was his cryptic comment about "some weirdo groups in this area." What weirdo groups? Do I need to do some further investigating to see what I might be getting myself into? If so, where do I start?* The Klamath Welcome Center was the obvious answer. Walter checked his watch. *I should have plenty of time to get there before they close today.* Nevertheless, he pressed down a little more on the accelerator in his eagerness. Besides, he had noticed that drivers in southern Oregon seem to have a low regard for speed limits.

2.

It was just shy of three o'clock when Walter stepped through the doors of the one-story tan brick building that housed the Welcome Center, along with the Klamath Falls Chamber of Commerce. The slender, late-twenty-something woman standing behind the counter smiled as he approached; her name badge read "Susan." A second, closer look added a decade to her age, but Walter still found her very attractive, perhaps because it put her near his age or because he was newly divorced and rather horny. Trying not to leer, he explained that he was new in town and he needed to kill some time, perhaps as much as a week, while he waited to see how a pending business deal would work out. Did she have any suggestions?

"Lots of people come here for the fishing," she offered. "I don't suppose you have any gear with you."

"Nope," he replied.

"Not a problem," she said. "Odell Lake Resort, about ninety miles north of here, can provide equipment and a guide for a modest amount of money. The cabins are rustic but comfortable, the restaurant is good, and Odell Lake has some of the best fishing in the state. Let me see if I can find some info for you."

While she searched, Walter discreetly attempted to discern whether there was a ring on her left hand. When she turned back to the counter to hand him a brochure, he got his answer: there wasn't! "Have a look at this, and if you like what you see, I can call to inquire about availability and rates." She gestured toward a sofa across the room. "You can have a seat over there."

He sat down and scanned the brochure. The Lodge looked antiquated but inviting, and lake trout, kokanee salmon, and rainbow trout were claimed to be plentiful at that time of year. *Even if I don't catch anything, it's situated in a beautiful, peaceful surrounding where I could get started on detoxing my life. Let's see how much it costs.*

Susan was now busy helping some other visitors, so he watched her while he waited, hoping he wasn't making her uncomfortable. She was efficient in her demeanor, with little wasted energy, but she wasn't cold. *Awake and attentive,* he thought. *Although I wouldn't rate her as a raving beauty, she is definitely good looking, at least according to my standards: long auburn hair, tied up in a ponytail; big, dark*

7

eyes; small well-shaped nose and elegant cheekbones; good body (insofar as the packaging allows me to judge), slightly athletic but not muscular. At least a '7' or '8' on a scale of 10—maybe even better. The other visitors left. "Thanks for waiting," she called to him. *She noticed I've been noticing. Don't screw this up by coming on too strong, too fast,* he told himself.

He walked back to the counter. "Please do call the Resort for me," he said. "I have a room at the Comfort Inn tonight, but I'd like you to see what's available starting tomorrow."

"Will this be for you and your family or just you?" she asked. Her eyes flickered downward, seeking his ring finger. *Ah, ha! Now she's checking me out,* he thought. He couldn't suppress a small smile. She knew she'd been caught and there was no place to hide. She blushed and her well-organized comportment briefly disintegrated.

"Just me," he replied, adding "I'm all alone in the world now" to confirm that he was indeed available, and then mentally kicking himself for sounding like a flake.

"Excuse me a moment," she said as she turned and walked to a telephone at the end of the counter. He took advantage of the opportunity to have a better look at her legs and tush. *Not bad, not bad at all.* For the next two minutes he entertained fantasies of further exploring this enticing new territory, until she turned back to face him with telephone in hand. "They've got a vacancy. You can have a single room in the Lodge for sixty-five dollars a night or a small cabin for ninety. There's a ten percent discount on either one if you stay for a week. They can't give me a price quote on the gear and guide, but they assured me they can work something out for you after you arrive and it will be 'reasonable'—whatever that means." She put her hand over the phone and added, "The busy season doesn't really begin until next month, so you can negotiate."

He hesitated. Sensing his indecision, she added, "The Lodge rooms are rather small—too cramped if you're planning to spend much time in your room. On the other hand, if you're inclined to cook some of your own meals, you can save the price difference with a cabin."

That helped. "I'll take the cabin, for a week, starting tomorrow night."

She turned back to the phone, engaged in a brief conversation, and then looked up at him. "They need some credit card information to hold the room. Please come over here and talk to them." They almost touched as she handed him the phone, and he could have sworn her ponytail brushed his cheek as she turned to go back to her chair. He felt a tingling deep down in a place they don't talk about at parties, and it was an effort for him to focus on the telephone conversation. He managed to complete the transaction, hung up the phone, and returned to front-and-center at the counter.

"Is there anything else I can do for you, Mister...?" she inquired warmly.

" Baker..." he stammered. "... Walter Baker ... or you can just call me Walt."

"I'm Susan. Susan Farnsworth." She extended her hand. "But please don't call me Susie."

"No, you don't look like the 'Susie' type," he replied, taking her hand in both of his. "I'm very pleased to meet you, Susan."

She hesitated, trying to figure out what he meant by the "Susie type" remark, but she didn't blush, nor did she withdraw her hand. Instead she looked him squarely in the eye and said, "I'm pleased to meet you too, Walter." It told him she didn't want him to leave just yet.

"There is something else," he babbled as he tried to think of something—*anything*—to keep the conversation going. After a few seconds of embarrassed searching, he came up with it. "I was talking with a business associate earlier today and he mentioned something about 'weirdos' living in this area. He said it in passing, so I didn't get an opportunity to ask him what he meant, but it troubled me when I thought about it later. Do you have any idea what he could have been talking about?"

Her smile faded and some sort of protective filter went up in front of her eyes. "Well, there have been some 'incidents,' but that happens in every community." She spoke slowly, as if choosing her words carefully then looked down. "I don't think I should say more. It's not the sort of information you pass out at a public center like this."

He too proceeded cautiously. "I can understand something like that.... All the same, I need to know what I might be getting into before I make a decision about moving into this area."

The maneuver worked. He sensed that she didn't like the idea that he could walk out the door and she might never see him again. He could almost hear her brain spinning now as she scrambled to prolong the encounter. At last she said, "I definitely don't want to talk about it here"—she glanced around as if somebody might be eavesdropping—"but I could meet you somewhere over a cup of coffee."

Bingo! That's a safe way for us to get better acquainted—and, feeling a little guilt over his ploy, *I can get answers to my questions at the same time.* "OK," he said, trying not to appear too anxious. "Tell me where and when."

She took a tourist map of the downtown area from a pile at the end of the counter and began to mark on it with a felt-tip pen. "We are right here, and this is South Sixth Street, and your hotel is here near the Washburn Way intersection. If you go a block-and-a-half north on Washburn, you'll find a big Fred Meyer store at the intersection with Shasta Way." She marked a big red "X" on the map. "Inside the store there's a Peet's Coffee & Tea shop where we can meet. I get off work here at five o'clock, so I'll be there at 5:15."

Walter thanked her and left. He could feel her eyes following him as he walked to his car—*or was it only his imagination?* He went back to his motel with the intention of taking a nap until 5:00. He set the alarm and sprawled out on the bed, but he was too fired up by the day's events to sleep. For a while his mind focused on Susan: not so much fantasies as questions about who she was, where she had come from, and where she was going in her life. That led to speculation about how their futures, hers and his, might become intertwined, and that led back to Ted and what their connection might lead to, even if it were nothing more than a landlord-tenant relationship.

He remembered Ted would be initiating some kind of background check on him. Not that Walter had anything to worry about—his record was clean as a whistle, as it had to be for any airline pilot—but he wondered *how* Ted would investigate him. *Is he going to hire a private detective to make some inquiries? Not likely, considering the expense of that as compared with the amount of rent I might pay him. Does he have contacts in law enforcement he could ask for 'a favor?' A remote possibility, based upon appearances. However, Ted had been very guarded in disclosing much of anything about himself, so there really wasn't very much in the way of 'appearances.' For all I know, he could be a former head of the FBI, or the CIA, or another one of those spooky government agencies. On the other hand, his reasons for privacy could be more sinister. Is he concerned about 'weirdo groups' because he was once a member of one? Is he still involved in one?*

Mercifully, fatigue set in at that point; Walter's mind went numb, and he dozed, sleeping quite soundly until he was startled by the alarm. He jumped up and splashed some water on his face. The friction of the towel told him he should have shaved, but there wasn't time. *Besides, this isn't like an actual date, so why should I get all gussied up? Why start out by building an impression that isn't really me? No, she will have to take me as I am, and if that doesn't work out, it's probably for the better.... Hmm, maybe I did learn a few things in my fifteen years with Angela after all. Maybe my marriage wasn't completely 'unsuccessful.'* He snapped out of his reverie, realizing that time was short. He had to walk two long blocks to the Fred Meyer store.

3.

Meanwhile, Susan was running late. Some visitors had arrived at the Welcome Center just as she was about to close up. Being the always-gracious person she aspired to be, she didn't try to hurry them along. Consequently, it was almost 5:15 when she got in her trusty Toyota Corolla and headed north on Riverside Drive. She had to wait at the 'STOP' sign at Main Street and traffic was slow on Klamath Avenue as it usually is, even when the evening 'rush minutes' aren't in full sway. By the time she reached the Washburn Way intersection, the Corolla's dashboard clock was edging past 5:20. The Fred Meyer parking lot was always crowded and congested, but she lucked out and quickly found a space near the building.

As she walked to the entrance—actually it was more like a trot—she tried to smooth her hair. It was only five minutes—well, maybe six or seven—but being late made her uneasy. *Why am I getting worked up over this?* she asked herself. *I hardly know this guy, and we're just getting together to chat. It's not like it's a serious date, so why does it seem so ... so important?*

Her unease eased somewhat when she spotted Walter standing just beyond the shopping carts inside the door at Fred Meyer, trying to look casual but sophisticated in his brown leather aviator jacket, khaki Dockers, and penny loafers. There were a few awkward milliseconds as both of them pondered whether to shake hands—*it's so stiff and formal*—or hug—*no, it's too soon for that!* Almost simultaneously they chose *neither* and simply walked together to the Peet's counter. They ordered—she a mocha, he a cappuccino—each making a mental note of the other's tastes in hopes of remembering that on future occasions. As they waited for their drinks, he mumbled something like "Thanks for coming" and she babbled an apology for being late, both trying to fill in the pregnant pause before conversation could begin in earnest.

All the tables were in a large, wide-open space, so there was no possibility of seclusion or intimacy, but Walter let her lead the way, hoping to demonstrate that he wasn't an 'alpha male' type and thereby to neutralize any bad impressions he might have made by coming on too strong at the Welcome Center. Susan accepted his deference with feigned reluctance, so as not to put him off with her independent nature. She selected what promised to be a quiet table in the farthest corner, and he almost spilled his cappuccino in trying to maneuver around her to hold her chair. She, unaccustomed to such chivalry, had started to reach for it and had to pull her hand back awkwardly to avoid a tug-of-war. Both sat down with a sense of relief and stared at their drinks momentarily while they regained their composure. Only then did both look up into the other's eyes, 'the windows of the heart' as the Bible says, to see what might be revealed there.

He looks intelligent, she thought, *gentle ... kind ... sensitive*. She tried not to let hopes cloud her discernment. It had been a long time since she had even had coffee with a man who appeared to be genuinely available, much less one who was handsome (which he surely was) and seemed to be the 'right age' for her (an ambiguity she hoped to resolve in the next few minutes). Then doubt overtook her: she wondered if she was setting herself up for disappointment—to be taken advantage of, hurt, and eventually abandoned. *Was I too quick in suggesting we meet like this? Am I being too eager now? Steady, girl, don't get carried away!*

Walter, too, was momentarily lost in his own thoughts, trying to figure out how best to start the conversation. He quickly decided the best approach was simplicity, directness, and honesty. In the calmest voice he could muster, he began, "I think I should explain why I asked you about 'weirdos.' I'm exploring moving to this area, at least for a few months. When I was talking with a prospective landlord, he expressed concern that his renter not 'be associated with any of the weirdo groups around here,' as he put it. This came as a bit of a shock to me, since I have no knowledge of anything like that in this area—and because I don't want to get mixed up with 'weirdo groups' either." He paused until she nodded her understanding. "So what can you tell me about that? What should I know before deciding whether to move here?"

Susan opened her purse, pulled out a sheet of paper, unfolded it, and handed it to him. "Before I left the office I did a little searching on the Internet. It made no sense to use 'weirdo groups' as the search key, so I tried 'militias.' Here is one of the items I found. It's extracted from an ongoing study by the Southern Poverty Law Center entitled *Active 'Patriot' Groups in the United States in 2010*. I printed out the page on Oregon. As you can see, it lists some groups like the John Birch Society that are well known and have existed in the US for quite some time. To the best of my knowledge, none of those is particularly noteworthy. However, it also lists half-a-dozen that are apparently based in Oregon: one of them right here in Klamath Falls; another in Merrill, which is about 15 miles southeast of here; another in Cave Junction, which is closer to the coast, about 30 miles southwest of Grants Pass; and three more up north, near Portland. Two of the groups, including the one in Merrill, are flagged with an asterisk, meaning that they are regarded as 'militias.'" She pointed to the line that said 'Jefferson State Militia.'

Walter scanned the sheet slowly, then asked, "Do you have any idea what these groups are all about—what motivates them, what their agendas are, what they really do?"

Susan thought several seconds before answering. "I've never had any direct personal experience with any of them in the seventeen years I've lived here. They keep a low profile most of the time. Not that they are secretive, but they tend to focus on their own circles of like-minded folk. They seek public attention only to attract additional members or when situations arise that they feel deserve public outcry—i.e., opposition or at least indignation. I don't know of any instances where this has escalated into actual violence or unlawfulness, but the term 'militia' certainly suggests some of them are prepared to go there when and if they think action is warranted."

She stopped to let this sink in, then continued. "As for what motivates them, what led to their formation in the first place, I think"—she paused and repeated, "I *think*" for emphasis—"in the case of these local groups it is the age-old conflict between the farmers/ranchers/loggers/miners and the environmentalists. Mostly it's about water: who gets to use it and how much of it and what they are allowed to dump into it. That's nothing new. Furthermore, the farmers and ranchers don't always agree with the loggers and/or miners, and sometimes the farmers disagree with the ranchers. While there are inevitably some extremist members of all of those groups, I wouldn't call any of them 'weirdos.'"

Walter nodded in agreement. *This is a woman who thinks,* he told himself. *That's another reason I'm attracted to her.* Almost as if she had overheard his thoughts, Susan added, "There is another issue that pervades most, if not all, of the so-called 'patriot' groups, both now and throughout history: individual freedom versus government control. As you probably know, this region has been occupied by Native American tribes for some 10,000 years, but the first white settlers came only in the last 160 years. It stands to reason that the settlers were an independent, self-reliant lot, so there is a tradition hereabouts of self-governance, which sometimes gets expressed as open resistance to 'government meddling' regardless of where it comes from—local, state, or federal.

"That has been amplified in recent years because there are now *six* National Wildlife Refuges in the Klamath Basin. They owe their very existence to the power of the federal government and to the influence of national and even international environmentalist groups—that is, 'outsiders' whose interests and priorities don't align very well with those of the white settlers and their descendants—although they may line up just fine with the values of the Native American tribes. In any event, the US government has a say in almost everything around here, and sometimes the bureaucrats can be heavy-handed—or at least it seems that way. Consequently, the Bureau of Land Management is a dirty word in the minds of a sizable segment of the local community, but probably not a majority. On the other hand, a good portion of the Klamath County economy is based on tourist travel and outdoor recreation—such as you signed up for earlier today—and therefore dependent upon maintaining a pristine environment."

Walter was impressed with her analysis. "Tourists don't come here to visit the farms or the logging areas."

"Right you are." She smiled. "You catch on real fast."

"I'm not as dumb as I look—not quite, anyhow."

"If I thought you were, I wouldn't be sitting here with you now," she countered, still smiling. "Not that I think you look dumb, of course," she added as she patted his hand. A little blip of electricity jumped between them. Both felt it send them spinning into a small space of semi-stunned silence. Susan recovered first. "If you want to dig deeper into this, I suggest you go to the local library and do an Internet search on any of the groups listed on this sheet, or on the Bureau of Land Management, which is part of the US Department of the Interior. You could also log into the website of the local newspaper, the *Herald and News*, and see what's there. I think they maintain an archival database, but I don't know how far back it goes."

"Yeah, I might try that," he replied, "but not tonight." Seizing the opportunity, he changed the subject. "I'd rather interest you in joining me for dinner."

"I'd like that, but I can't do it tonight. I have a class beginning in about an hour." His raised eyebrows and almost inaudible "Oh," requested an explanation: *What kind of class? Where?* In response she elaborated, "I'm taking a course in developmental psychology at the community college. I expect to get my Associate of Applied Science degree in June."

"Well, then, allow me to be among the first to extend my congratulations," he said with mock seriousness. "In what area of study?"

"Educational Services. The AAS degree will enable me to transfer into a Bachelor's degree program in applied psychology at OIT, the Oregon Institute of Technology here in town, or maybe at one of the other state universities. My ultimate goal is to become a social worker or a school counselor. It's something I've been working toward for a long time."

Walter paused to think about what she had said. *She just told me something important about herself—a first step in opening up to me. Whatever you do, don't respond insensitively.* "You want to help others," he said. It was as much a question as a statement.

"Yes, I guess it's part of my mothering instinct. And since I turned my daughter loose in the world three years ago, I've been pursuing it more intensely."

Another revelation, he thought. *Keep it going.* "Where is your daughter now?" he asked.

"She's in the Army, but I don't know where in the world she is. She's an interpreter. She speaks Arabic and Farsi and maybe some other central Asian dialects, so most of her work is rather secretive."

"Is she planning to make the Army her career?"

"Yes, that's what she hopes to do. She has a natural talent for languages, and the Army offered her both a first-rate training program and extraordinary opportunities to gain experience. So she signed up right out of high school."

"I did much the same thing about twenty-six years ago, except I chose the Air Force."

It was Susan's turn. *Ah-ha*, she thought. *That explains the aviator jacket he's wearing.* "In retrospect, I wish I had done something like that," she said, "although I don't have the linguistic talent Lucy has—that's my daughter's name. I didn't have much career guidance either, so I did the obvious thing: I got married about two months after graduation."

"Was that here in Klamath Falls?"

"No, over in Medford. That's where I was born and raised. My parents both died when I was very young, so I grew up in foster homes. When I turned eighteen, I was 'released' from the program, so I hitched up with my high school sweetheart. We both took entry-level jobs: he worked in construction, I waited table in a diner—that is, until Lucy came along two years later."

"Where is your husband now?" he probed, and then hastily added, "I hope you don't mind my questions."

"No, it's OK.... He was killed in a motorcycle accident—riding without a helmet—when Lucy was about three. So there I was, a twenty-three-year-old single mom with minimal education and no kinfolk to help me. I decided to make a clean break with my past and move to Klamath Falls to raise my daughter. She became the center of my life for the next fifteen years—although as she got older, my own career aspirations began to take shape, so I started taking classes at Klamath Community College." She paused. "I guess you could say I'm a late bloomer."

It was his turn to pat her on the hand. Another spark, but no surprise this time. "Well, in my opinion you're blooming very nicely—but, of course, that's based on less than two hours of observation." He grinned to make sure she took it as a joke.

She glanced at her watch and realized there was no time for repartee—or much of anything else. "Oh! I've got to go.... I'm very sorry, because we were just getting started, and I still haven't heard your story. Can we continue this when you come back next week?"

"Of course," he said. "We can do it over dinner. How can I get in touch with you once I know my schedule? May I have your phone number?"

She stood up and started pulling on her jacket. "Just track me down through the Welcome Center. If I'm not there, the director, Virginia Cox, will know where to find me. She's sort of been my big sister since I started working there several years ago."

As she spoke, he opened his wallet and extracted a somewhat dog-eared business card. He scribbled a number on the back and handed it to her. "Here's my cell phone number, in case you want to call me. Ignore what it says on the other side of the card. Except for my name, that's all history."

She turned the card over. Beneath the Alaska Airlines logo it read, "WALTER P. BAKER, Captain," and gave a San Francisco address. Susan had another *Ah-ha!* moment. She could discern in Walter traces of the calm cockiness that pervades the stereotypical image of pilots, but there was something different about him. The image was imperfect—scarred, as if he had suffered an injury that had not yet healed completely. She tucked the card into her purse, then checked her watch again. "I really gotta run. Thanks for the mocha ... and for listening. See you in a week."

He reached down to clear the dishes from the table, then immediately regretted doing so because it pre-empted a farewell touch, a handshake or maybe even a hug. All he could do was mumble a weak "See you" and smile at her back as she breezed toward the exit. He dumped the dishes as fast as he could and tried to follow her without running to catch up. Once outside, he tracked her visually until she disappeared into a row of cars in the parking lot. Seconds later he saw what he presumed was her green Toyota pull onto Washburn Way, heading south. He strained to catch the number on the license plate, but without success.

4.

It was after 8:30 when Walter awoke the next morning—a big departure from his early wake-up regimen of the past twenty-plus years. He hadn't set the alarm—there was no need to—although he had stayed up past 11:30 the night before watching a stupid movie. He had slept well, which amazed him, considering the somewhat momentous encounters of the previous day. The movie had finally drowned out the fugue his mind was wandering through after his meeting with Susan: *she said ... I said ... I should have said ... maybe she meant ... I felt....* But it didn't pitch him down a rabbit hole of mental exhaustion like the trials of the past half-year had repeatedly done. Instead he felt a kind of calm reassurance that this time he wasn't heading for another crash. It wasn't quite elation, but it felt good.

His mood even improved as he sailed through his morning routine, his Four '*SH*' Drill, as he liked to call it: *SH*ampoo, *SH*ave, *SH*it, and *SH*ower—not necessarily in that order. He smiled to himself as he recalled it had been a Five '*SH*' Drill in his six-AM-wake-up days, but *SH*ine had been dropped in recent months when he no longer needed to wear a uniform. He mused he might soon have the freedom to forsake a daily *SH*ampoo, *SH*ave, and *SH*ower as well, then realized that wouldn't work if he expected to develop a relationship with Susan. *It would be awesome to have to make that choice,* he concluded as he headed out the door. *There are some things worth giving up freedom for.* He stopped in the lobby to buy a newspaper, the *Klamath Falls Herald and News*, not the vacuous *USA Today* distributed by most hotels nowadays, and studied the entire paper—headlines, local calendar, sports, advertisements, and even the classifieds—over a leisurely breakfast and several cups of coffee. Not that the newspaper was terribly enlightening—it wasn't—but he was trying to get a more intimate sense of the city and the surrounding area. The signals he had picked up thus far were, he had to admit, somewhat mixed, but they hadn't diminished his resolve to step out of his old life and hang out in the wilderness until he could figure out a new one.

Post-breakfast, he resisted the urge to surprise Susan by dropping by the Welcome Center before he left town. Instead, he went to the motel's 'business center' and logged onto the Internet. He googled on 'Jefferson State Militia' and found a couple news stories indicating there had been some near-confrontations between the militia and law enforcement officials in recent years. Another article, by a person billing himself as an officer in the Militia, said the organization had originally been formed in 1993 "to assist local law enforcement if overall anarchy occurred locally, similar to the riots that broke out in South Central Los Angeles after the Rodney King riots...."The thought that southern Oregon towns such as Merrill (pop. 844), Klamath Falls (pop. 20,000), or even Medford (pop. 72,000) would be susceptible to anarchy like South Central Los Angeles amused Walter. On the other hand, he was sobered by the allegations, farther along in the same article, that the offered 'assistance' was not only unwanted, but "considered a threat to the 'power' of local law enforcement" and that "local law enforcement entities were their own 'Organized Crime' entities" in the area, thus creating a more-or-less permanent adversarial relationship between said local law enforcement and the Jefferson State Militia.

The *pièce de résistance* came at the end of the article: some maxims to guide anyone who wants to form "a viable citizen militia group...."

Do everything you can to avoid being infiltrated by law enforcement or anybody who doesn't share the aims of your group. Never hold open meetings, and train your members to never discuss militia matters where they might be overheard or monitored: telephone, Internet, radio, fax, etc. Protect the identities of all persons involved in the group.

Privately approach like-minded individuals to join your group. Despite the inherent risks, carefully recruit banking and government employees/officials, so you can follow the money. On the other hand, never recruit anybody who expresses racist or anti-Semitic views, and if you discover such persons in your group, "set them aside" from knowing anything more about your group and any training exercises you conduct.

If anyone, including your own mother, asks to join, hold them at "arms length." Obtain their intelligence, but never allow them access to what your group is doing or who is involved.

Although none of these were unreasonable, Walter sensed an undercurrent of paranoia. More disconcerting, however, was that this reminded him of Ted. *Is he mixed up in this group?* Walter wondered. After a moment of anxiety, he decided to put it out of his mind for the time being.

He packed his bag, checked out of the hotel, and found his way onto US 97 northbound. *Now for something really different,* he told himself. He was looking forward to a few days of not caring about much of anything. His mind began to wander as he drove alongside the broad expanse of Upper Klamath Lake, at 141 square miles one of the largest in the state. *I wonder why Susan didn't book me into a local resort next to this lake,* he thought. *Why did she send me way to hell and gone, ninety miles to the North?* A half-hour later, he passed the *Kla-Mo-Ya Casino,*

"OPEN 24/7" in the incorporated town of Chiloquin (population 716—of which 52% are Native American, Walter read in a tourist brochure). Breakfast was only an hour ago and he was all coffeed out, so he decided not to stop. *I'll check it out on the way back—maybe even piss away a little money like Ted said.*

Another 45 minutes of driving through a high plateau of evergreens, with long straight stretches of two-lane road showing few signs of human habitation other than occasional signs warning dimwitted motorists, "DO NOT PASS SNOW PLOWS ON THE RIGHT," brought him to Chemult, an unincorporated community whose main claim to fame was as the Amtrak stop for Crater Lake National Park, some 20 miles southwest. The town was not much more than a wide place in the road, but there were a few motels and eateries. Walter chose the Crater Lake Café & Art Gallery, in a yellow concrete-block building in the middle of town. The café's 'art' seemed to exist more in the owner's imagination than in anything Walter would call a 'gallery,' but the food was cheap and good.

About eight miles out of Chemult, he turned left onto Highway 58, toward Eugene. This was the somewhat famous Willamette Highway, opened July 30, 1940, to expedite traffic between US 97 on the east side of the Cascades and US 99 on the West, and still one of only four major routes through the Cascades in Oregon. After nearly ten miles straight through the junipers of the Deschutes National Forest the road began a gentle winding climb to Crescent Lake Junction, the only commercial center of any significance in the next fifty miles. Two miles beyond, he turned left at the brown-and-yellow National Forest sign announcing "ODELL LAKE LODGE & RESORT." Almost instantly, he was in another world: a grove of Ponderosa pine, the lake just off to the North, with picnic and camping areas alongside, the one-and-a-half-lane blacktop road narrowing for a one-lane bridge and ending abruptly in the gravel-and-dust parking lot of Odell Lake Resort.

The Lodge itself, a rustic log structure dating back to World War II, loomed above. Walter parked, jogged up the stairs and across the deck, and opened the heavy wooden door. The dimly lit lobby was tiny, barely more than a vestibule, with a large lounge room on the right and a long, narrow restaurant area straight ahead. He turned left toward the reception desk and announced himself to the clerk, a slender young blonde dressed in blue jeans and T-shirt, with a couple tattoos peeking out through the gap between. *Attractive,* Walter thought, *but way too young for me.* As she searched for his reservation card, he surveyed the array of fishing lures and other magical devices displayed on the wall to his left and the stock of beer, wine, and glucose-laden beverages in the cooler to his right.

The registration ritual was slow, computerless, and probably unchanged since the Lodge opened. It concluded with the clerk handing Walter an archaic key and giving him directions Cabin 2. "Is there anything else I can do for you?" she asked.

"Yes, there is," he replied. "When I made the reservation, I was told I could contract with a guide to take me fishing and provide a boat and fishing gear. How do I go about doing that?"

"You talk to Mac, that's all. He's our fishing guide, one of the very best in these parts. He's been guiding fishermen on this lake for nearly twenty years, and you wouldn't believe some of the monster mackinaw and kokanee he has helped them find and catch—and some super rainbows, too." She gestured toward a distant wall where there were photos of smiling men and women, all of them proudly holding humongous fish, then paused to see if Walter had begun to salivate in anticipation of landing a champion-sized catch himself.

"I'm a relative novice," he said, "and I haven't fished since I was a teenager, so it's not important whether what I catch is record-setting." Sensing the clerk's disappointment, he added, "But I would like to catch *something*, and if I get to work with a topnotch guide, maybe it will rekindle my interest in serious fishing." She brightened a little. "Where to I find this ... this Mr. Mac?"

"Mac McCarter," the clerk corrected. "He's out with another group right now, but he should be back around dinner time. I'll have him call your cabin when he returns."

Walter drove his truck very slowly up the bumpy, dusty dirt road to his cabin, situated in a grove of trees on the hill behind the Lodge, parked in the lone space, and took out two of his bags. The lock on the cabin door was worn, requiring him to fiddle with the key to open it, and as he stepped inside he couldn't help but notice the contrast between the almost sterile ambience of the franchise motel where he had stayed in Klamath Falls and his present surroundings. Sandwiched along one side of the main room was a half-size refrigerator, a microwave sitting on top, a somewhat worn four-burner gas cook stove, a sink and a work counter. On the other side was a gas heater in the front corner, followed by a small table and four chairs, then an ominous black leatherette sofa in the back corner. The teensy bathroom cowered opposite the sofa and the 8-by-12 bedroom huddled at the rear. *It certainly lives up to the first half of its advance billing of 'rustic and comfortable,'* he thought. *Now we'll see about 'comfortable' part.* He opened his bags and sorted most of their contents into the drawers of the venerable dresser, then plopped himself down onto the inviting bed. It was soft, but not saggy, with a firmness underneath. The thought of a nap slithered into his mind. *Two nap days in a row! I'm going soft!* He soon slipped into insouciant slumber.

It took two rings of the phone to wake him up—*Where am I? What day is this? What time is it?*—another one to help him locate it on the wall outside the bathroom—*Why did they put the damned thing way over there?*—and a fourth before he could stumble out of the bedroom to answer. "Hullo?" he mumbled, still not ready for takeoff.

"Mr. Baker?" a tinny voice inquired.

"Yes, this is Walter Baker." He was almost sentient now.

"This is Mac McCarter. The desk clerk said you wanted to talk with me."

Walter glanced at his watch. It was 5:38. "Are you here in the Resort? Or shall we talk by phone?"

"I'm down in the lounge, opposite the front desk. Why don't you come down here so you can see how ugly I am and I can see how many heads you have?"

Quaint, Walter thought. "I'll be there in a minute." He started to hang up, then added, "Thank you." He checked the mirror and searched for his comb. *Gotta make sure all my heads are beauteous.* Stuffing the cabin key in his pocket, he tromped out the door and down the path to the Lodge.

The man standing in the lounge was wiry, just short of six feet tall, with close-cropped, salt-and-pepper graying hair and weathered skin suggesting six decades of wear and tear. But his eyes were bright and his grip was strong as he shook Walter's extended hand. "I'm Mac."

"I'm Walter ... and I have only one head with me today. I hope you're not disappointed."

That brought a chuckle and an extra squeeze before Mac let go of his hand. "Well, you never can tell what you're going to meet up with, my daddy always said. What can I do for you?"

Walter gave him the five-second briefing: "I came here to kill some time for a week, forget about the rest of the world, and see if the fishing is as good as it's cracked up to be."

"You're off to a good start," Mac confirmed.

"But I'm not an expert fisherman. It's been almost thirty years since I had a rod in my hand," Walter demurred.

"Not a problem. We all gotta start somewhere. When I began, I couldn't tell a 'Royal Coachman' from a monkey wrench. But let me ask you this, 'What is your intention?'" That took Walter aback. Seeing the bewilderment, Mac explained, "Do you want to come away with a monumental fish to mount above your fireplace? Or a great entree for your dinner party next week? Or do you just want to sit on a boat out in the middle of the lake and drown some worms?"

"I don't have a house, much less a fireplace, and trophies have never been my style. And I don't have a family or a gaggle of friends to party with either. Sitting in the middle of the lake is appealing, but it would be better to say I had caught something besides a cold. Catch-and-release is OK, though."

Mac nodded. "I get the picture. I'll take you out and set you up with a spinning rig that will let you use a variety of lures and baits. A half-day should be more than enough for you to get the feel of it, and if you want more, we can book some time on another day." He quoted a price that Walter found surprisingly reasonable, considering that it included the boat, all the equipment, snacks and drinks, and Mac's time and expert assistance. "You don't need to pay up front. You can put it on your hotel bill, or you can pay me in cash—in small, unmarked bills." He grinned and winked. "One thing, though—if you want, you can bring a six-pack of beer, but nothing more than that. I don't care to spend my time babysitting drunks."

"I'd rather skip alcohol altogether until I get to the dinner table. Some bottled water and a thermos of black coffee will be just fine. When do we do this?" Walter asked.

"I'm booked up tomorrow, and besides it's likely to rain. How about the day after? In the morning?" Mac proposed.

"OK with me," Walter concurred. "What time do we start?"

"Odell Lake is notoriously windy in midday, so we should get out there as early as possible, while it's still calm. I'd like to start at 7:00 AM, if that's OK with you. The Lodge doesn't open until 8:00, so I'll meet you down at the dock."

"Sounds like a plan," Walter said.

Mac turned as if to leave, then stopped. "There's one other matter: you need to get an Oregon Angling License and for that you should to go to the Sportsman Center down in Crescent Lake Junction. If you smile real nice and the gods at the Oregon Department of Fish and Wildlife are magnanimous, the Center can get the license while you wait."

"Wonderful," Walter said. "Thank you very much." They shook hands and Walter ambled off to the restaurant for a delicious, soul-satisfying dinner.

5.

Just as Mac had predicted, it was raining when Walter awoke the next morning. He listened to the soft, steady drizzle a good ten minutes before his insistent bladder rousted him out of bed. He had decided the night before to stop shaving during his Odell Lake sojourn, a prerogative he had not been allowed since his teens, when nobody could tell whether he had shaved or not. Because he wasn't going anywhere or meeting anyone that day, he elected to dispense with the *SH*ampoo and *SH*ower elements of his Four '*SH*' Drill as well. Attired in grungy moccasins, an old sweatshirt, and cargo pants, he ambled into the restaurant and sat next to the row of windows overlooking the patio and the lake beyond, slurping the strong hot coffee and gazing out through a thin screen of evergreens at the raindrops peppering the water, creating an undulating *pointillé* on the surface. In due course, he ordered a bagel and cream cheese and a small glass of orange juice, in the cause of semi-fasting throughout what promised to be a day of inactivity.

After breakfast, Walter drove to the Odell Sportsman Center. While the clerk was making intercession on his behalf with the Oregon Department of Fish and Wildlife (ODFW), he shopped for groceries: sandwich makings for lunch, yogurt and cereal for breakfast, and—almost as an afterthought—some munchy snacks and a six-pack of beer. To assuage a brief tinge of guilt over the beer, he skipped the ice cream and dessert sweets. By the time he finished shopping, his fishing license was ready. The ODFW gods had cooperated, but not without a price: the fee for out-of-state residents was $106.25. He dismissed it with the rationalization that the license was good for a year, and he expected to do a good bit of fishing in the coming months.

Back at the Resort, he stashed his groceries in the cabin and walked over to the Lodge to see what was there to help him pass the time. Not much, was the answer. The lounge offered a TV set—the only one in the Resort, as far as he could tell—plus a motley collection of tired books and a few recent issues of fishing magazines. Mixed in with the magazines he found some Technical Bulletins printed out from the websites of local suppliers of fishing gear, boats, and such. He read them all, two or three times, finding the jargon somewhat impenetrable and the enthusiasm over trophy fish cloying. With his spirits thus subdued he opted to not brave the rain for an outside stroll and instead returned to his cabin. The previous night he had resolved to shun the TV and even the newspapers, to make his stay there a genuine *retreat*, something he had never done before but which seemed to be calling him now with increasing persistence.

Briefly yielding to that call in Portland the week before, Walter had gone to Powell's Books, billed as "the largest independent used and new bookstore in the world," and browsed for a book on meditation. Bewildered by the huge number and variety of candidates, he had eventually sought assistance at one of the information desks. The clerk, a scruffy, bewhiskered septuagenarian, who could well have been a former archeologist or perhaps a fashion designer, had slowly scrutinized him from top to bottom, almost sniffing him like a dog—*first the nose, then the asshole*—before delivering his pronouncement, "Something by Joel Goldsmith." Peering downward through his half-eye spectacles, the clerk had pecked furiously on the computer keyboard with his two index fingers, scanned the screen, and exclaimed joyously, "Yes, we have it! Please come with me." Ricocheting through a maze of towering bookcases with Walter following dutifully, the clerk had homed in on a *particular* shelf in a *particular* bookcase where there were some two dozen books, all showing Joel Goldsmith as the author. He had traced the collection left-to-right with his finger, snatched a *particular* book, and presented it triumphantly to Walter, "*Voila!*"

Somewhat intimidated, Walter had chosen not to challenge the clerk's discernment by leafing through the book immediately. Instead, he had merely glanced at the title—*The Art of Meditation*—and the endorsements on the back cover—effusive praise from four people he had never heard of—and declared, "This will be excellent. Thank you very much"—*like a dog with a new bone*, he recalled.

Now he retrieved the book from his bag and sat down in the easy chair. Starting with where he had left off, the back cover, he read:

Joel Goldsmith, one of the great American Christian mystics of the twentieth century, spent his life educating others on "The Infinite Way," his personally developed principles of spirituality. The Art of Meditation is a fascinating introduction to a regular program of daily meditation that creates a oneness with God and an understanding of each person's place in the world. Goldsmith is not concerned with theory or theology, but with the need for prayer. Beginning with the universal conviction of humanity that we are not alone—that there must be some higher force—Goldsmith's practical guide will help readers to be truly free from the day-to-day trappings of the world.

I certainly like the part about not being concerned with theory or theology, Walter thought, *but I'm not so sure that prayer is what I need.* He read the next paragraph:

The art of listening for the inner voice is the advanced form of prayer
practiced by mystics down through the ages, regardless of their religious tradition.
Practicing the simple procedures outlined in The Art of Meditation will connect
readers seeking spiritual wisdom with God and open their consciousness to the
knowledge of who they really are.

The words "advanced form of prayer" caught his attention. *Maybe my problem
is I've been taught the wrong things about prayer—what I've believed about prayer is
erroneous—the "prayer" I've tried to do isn't "the right stuff."* Farther on, the phrase
"simple procedures" also sounded inviting, and the prospect of "connecting with
God" and especially "opening [his] consciousness to the knowledge of who [he]
really [is]" was more than enough to spur him onward. He opened the book and
started reading.

"Some books are to be tasted, others to be swallowed, and some few to be
chewed and digested," wrote Francis Bacon some four hundred years ago. For the
next four hours, Walter chewed and chewed on *The Art of Meditation.* Digestion,
however, was elusive: the 'food' was new and strange to his 'mental digestive system.'
Not that it tasted bad—indeed, it was far more palatable than any other religious
or spiritual teaching he had ever come across—but it was also very different from
any other religious or spiritual teaching he had ever known. *How could I have lived
this long and never come across something like this?* he marveled repeatedly.

He read ... reread ... and re-reread chapters, pages, paragraphs, sentences,
phrases, trying to get his head around it, until he was exhausted and almost in
tears. At last he put down the book and stretched. His watch told him it was well
past lunchtime, but he really wasn't hungry. The rain appeared to have subsided
temporarily, so he put on his most water-repellant jacket and hat and went outside.
The cool fresh air tried to clear his muddled brain, but he was in no hurry for that,
sensing he was better off to remain in a state of confusion. Some distant words
of Winston Churchill came to mind: "Men occasionally stumble over the truth,
but most of them pick themselves up and hurry off as if nothing ever happened."
Thus self-chastened, he walked, slowly, so he did not have to attend to where he
was going, immersing his body in the cool dampness, inducing his mind to admit
new ideas and insights—in a word, *digestion.*

Some thirty minutes later he found himself back at the Lodge entrance,
his mind considerably clearer and calmer, and his other digestive system now
calling for attention. He went to the restaurant, inhaled a bowl of soup, and
returned to his cabin. Haphazardly following what he recalled of his book's
instructions, he sat in the easy chair, closed his eyes, and attempted to meditate.
A barrage of distractions pummeled his consciousness: thoughts of Ted, itches

and tingles in various parts of his body, thoughts of Susan, birds cheeping in the trees beyond the window, random vignettes from his fifteen years of marriage, assorted creaks and groans from the building—anything but stillness. After ten minutes he gave up, not so much in despair of failing as in resignation to the fact that learning to meditate would not be quick and easy. *Not a very auspicious beginning for a relaxing, detoxing retreat,* he thought.

6.

Walter had set his alarm for 6:00 AM, but he awakened a few minutes *before* it went off. He bounced out of bed, washed his face—it was a one-*SH* day—made coffee, and assembled his breakfast: two slices of toast, and cereal with yogurt. As he sat down to sip some coffee, he wished he had had the forethought to buy some sausage and eggs for a more substantial breakfast. *Got to think ahead more, especially if I'm going to live out in the boonies.* Dressed warmly against the morning chill, he left the cabin at 6:50 AM and slowly walked down to the dock, sniffing the morning air, the lake smooth as glass, glistening under the breaking dawn, quietly awaiting the day's activities. He looked around for Mac, but saw nobody until he began checking the boats at the dock, one by one. There, in the third one, was a figure seated cross-legged like a Buddha, in the bow well: it was Mac, eyes closed, apparently deep in meditation. Walter stood silent and motionless, attempting to meld into the mood of the moment, until Mac's eyes blinked and a big smile lit up his face. "Good morning," he said softly.

"Sorry to disturb you," Walter replied. "Have you been waiting long?"

Mac glanced at his watch. "Oh, maybe twenty minutes or so. I like to get here early so I can calibrate my senses and settle into the situation."

"Were you really meditating?" Walter asked.

"Yes, that's part of my routine. It helps me put aside irrelevant concerns and worries that might distract from the activity at hand—which is *fishing!*"

"Ah, yes," agreed Walter. He walked onto the dock and scrutinized the boat: an 18-foot Alumaweld 'Stryker,' with a 135-horsepower Honda four-stroke outboard motor, plus the popular Honda 9.9 trolling motor at the side. "Good boat," he said.

"Thanks," Mac replied. "I buy a new one every other year. Not that the old ones need to be replaced, but the public seems to expect a new boat, as if it vouches for my credibility and trustworthiness. The fish, on the other hand, don't seem to mind one way or the other."

Walter cautiously stepped into the stern well and sat down on a cushioned seat at the side. Mac climbed around the canopy, reached inside and picked up two life vests, giving one to Walter and donning the other himself. As Walter cinched up his vest, Mac handed him a seven-foot fishing rod. "Have you ever used a spinning rig?"

"Yes, but it was a long time ago. I'm sure I'll need some practice to get the hang of casting again."

"For now, that won't be necessary," said Mac. "We'll start out with some trolling, so all you'll have to do is dangle your line over the side and keep it from getting tangled up in the propeller. You familiarize yourself with the feel of the rod and the workings of the reel while I get us going." He unwound the line holding the boat against the dock and stowed it, started the larger outboard motor, and maneuvered the boat away from the dock, out into the lake. About a half-mile out, Mac turned toward the shore and cut the motor. As the boat drifted to a stop, he explained his strategy for the day. "This lake is known for its big mackinaw and kokanee, but since you're just getting back into fishing, you don't want to have a twenty-pound lunker on the end of your line yet—a good three-or-four-pounder will give you enough of a challenge. What is not widely known is that there is a good supply of rainbow trout in this lake, and they will strike just about anything—flies, lures, and even night crawlers. They like to hang out under rocks and ledges near the shore, so the best way to attract their attention is to cast from a boat toward the shore and slowly reel it back. The downside is, because you're out of practice, you'll probably have trouble putting the bait where you want it and you may get your line tangled up if you fling it too far."

He paused to give Walter a chance to ask questions but Walter only nodded his head as if he understood, so Mac continued. "Consequently, we're going to try the next-best thing, which is trolling parallel to the shore in areas that are relatively shallow. We'll start out with night crawlers, and if that doesn't work, I have a few lures I've had good success with in the past. Later on, we can try casting when you think you're ready for that, and when you decide you're ready for the big stuff, we'll go out in the middle of the lake where the mackinaw hang out."

"I doubt if I'll get to that today," Walter said. "I'll be happy with a couple decent rainbows."

"OK, then. Grab your pole and I'll put a big juicy worm on the line. You flip it off to the side toward the shore—sort of a half-cast or whatever you can do to get it out about fifteen feet—and just hold it there while I steer the boat." He moved back the stern to start the smaller trolling motor. Almost imperceptibly, at barely one mile per hour, the boat began moving again. Walter swished his rod tentatively and managed to get the bait into the water a few feet beyond the tip. He looked up at Mac as though to ask if he should try again. "That's good enough," Mac said. Walter sat down, holding the rod level, focusing his attention on the tension of the line against his index finger, hoping to detect the slightest nibble.

Nothing happened—and it continued not happening for the next ten minutes. Walter reeled in the line to see if the bait was still there—it was—and made another flip-cast, this time sending the bait out about twenty feet. After another ten minutes, he began to be overtaken by doubt. *Maybe it's time to try lures instead of night crawlers. Is there some other part of the lake we should explore?* Seeking suggestions, he surreptitiously glanced at Mac, but Mac sat calm and motionless, eyes fixed on the shore. Noting his own impatience, Walter scolded himself. *Why should I expect instant results? What the hell did I come here for? It certainly wasn't to see how many fish I can catch, or to get a trophy to hang above my fireplace. I already told Mac that much. So what is my real objective, other than killing time until Ted gets his shit together?* His brain shifted gears, chipping a few teeth in the process. *Why do I want to learn to meditate? Why do I want to get out of California—the rat race—and hole up in a secluded cabin in the middle of nowhere?*

Just as his mind was about to plunge deeply into the pool of introspection, there was a tug on his line, then another much stronger. Instinctively he lifted his rod and a flash of silver shot a foot out of the water, turned a half-somersault, and splashed into the lake again about fifteen feet away. "Bingo!" shouted Mac, heading the boat toward deeper water. "Looks like a rainbow. Don't give him any line. He'll want to head back into hiding and try to shake the hook or snare the line. Work your rod side to side and let the flex wear him out, but avoid letting him pull directly against you until he's spent some of that energy." For the next few minutes, Walter maneuvered his quarry this way and that, shortening the line whenever the tension lessened, until there was only a few feet separating the fish from the tip of his rod. Mac took out a dip net and, as Walter swung his rod toward the end of the boat, expertly scooped up the trout. Holding up the net, he pronounced, "It's a beauty, and good-sized, too. Maybe even six pounds. Do you want to keep him?"

"Naw," Walter replied, "that's too much for dinner for just me. So unless you want him for your dinner, let's toss him back—that is, if you think he will survive after all the strenuous exercise."

"That's OK with me," said Mac, "but let's get a picture first." He lowered the dip net, reached in to grasp the trout, carefully removed the hook from its mouth with needle-nose pliers, and handed the fish to Walter. Then he pulled out a small digital camera, stepped back, and snapped three shots: first a somber Walter, next Walter smiling, and finally Walter with a shit-eating grin—the trout stolidly endured the indignity of it all throughout. Mac put the camera back in his vest pocket, took the wriggling fish from Walter, lowered it gently into the water, and released it, with the night crawler in its belly but a scant reward for its ordeal.

Walter was elated. He wanted to do it again, if only to prove to himself it wasn't entirely beginner's luck—but first, a belt of hot coffee was most appropriate. He stowed his rod while Mac fetched the Thermos and poured two cups. They took seats on opposite sides of the stern well, relaxing in silence, swigging slowly, savoring the warmth against the morning chill. After the coffee had time to take effect, Walter spoke up. "I gather you have some expertise in meditation."

Mac chuckled. "Well, I've been doing it for a few dozen years, but I'm not sure that qualifies me as an expert, if that's what you mean."

Walter searched for words. "I've just begun in my attempt to learn to meditate. The book I'm reading says to start with brief periods of time—only a few minutes, or even less than a minute, but frequently throughout the day or night—and then build up to longer duration. I spent most of yesterday afternoon trying to get into it, but I didn't make much progress. Not that I expected everything to fall into place right away, but I couldn't seem to get any kind of handle on it."

"What's the book you're using?" asked Mac.

"*The Art of Meditation* by Joel Goldsmith. It was recommended by a clerk at Powell's Books in Portland."

Mac raised an eyebrow at the mention of Goldsmith. "I sure can't fault your choice of author. That was an exceptional recommendation."

"You know of Goldsmith?" Walter asked.

"Yes, although I haven't seen that particular book. Goldsmith wrote more than thirty books in his lifetime, and they all sort of fit together like pieces of a gigantic jigsaw puzzle." Mac paused, then inquired pointedly. "Why do you want to learn to meditate?"

Walter edited his thoughts before answering. *I've only known this guy a couple hours—and besides we came out here to fish—so I should spare the details.* "I'm trying to turn my life around: recent divorce, downsized out of my job, general disenchantment with the world as I've experienced it in the past thirty years." He shrugged.

"In other words, a typical mid-life transition, if you don't mind my saying so," Mac responded. "You'd be surprised how often I hear those things out here in the boat. I'd guess that at least two-thirds of the men I guide have the same issues and wind up unloading them on me. The other third probably have them too, but keep them bottled up. Sometimes I think I ought to come right out and tell them I'm a mental health counselor, but that would probably scare them all away."

Walter blanched a little. "Sorry. I didn't intend to dump on you when I signed on for this. We can go back to fishing now."

"It's not a problem for me," Mac reassured. "I've come to regard it as an integral part of this job. Truth is, I do some counseling of sorts when I'm not guiding fishing, especially in the winter months, but that's another story for another time." He picked up Walter's rod and began detaching the leader connecting the hook and bait to the line. "Now the agenda is your casting skills, and for that we'll switch to a lure." He attached a Panther Martin to Walter's line and handed the rod back to him. For the next hour, Walter played cast-and-retrieve, trying to place the lure where Mac directed. From time to time Mac would move the boat up the shoreline to present new casting challenges or fishing opportunities. In that time Walter caught three more fish, all rainbows somewhat smaller than the first, but good-sized, feisty three-or-four-pounders nonetheless. He released two of them, keeping one at Mac's suggestion that he ask the chef to prepare it for his dinner that evening.

As nine o-clock came, so also did the wind. The choppy water and gently rocking boat didn't bother Walter—he had endured far worse air turbulence in his years as a pilot—but it interfered with the slow, almost contemplative style of fishing Mac had instituted. At length, Mac turned to Walter and said, "I don't think we're going to get any more rainbows to bite in this breeze. Do you want to head out to the middle of the lake and go after some bigger stuff?"

Walter considered that prospect a moment and decided against it. "No, I think I've had enough for one day. However, I would like to try that at some later time—maybe next week, if it fits your schedule."

"We'll figure that out when we get back," Mac said as he stowed Walter's rod. He stepped under the canopy, started the bigger motor, and circled the boat toward the center of the lake.

Walter took the other seat. "OK, Mister Mental Health Counselor, what do you say to all the men who come to you on the pretext of fishing but really to get

30

your help with their mid-life traumas. Is there some pixie dust you sprinkle on them to make all their troubles go away?"

Mac laughed. "No, there's no pixie dust. I don't have anything like that, and neither does anybody else. If somebody tells you he or she has the magic that will cure your every pain, you should run away as fast as you can. That applies not only to so-called counselors but also to hucksters of all kinds, especially ministers and politicians. Notwithstanding that, I already gave you the most important piece of information—call it wisdom, if you like—you need in dealing with your own life, which is that just about everybody goes through essentially the same things you are going through. And I'll now give you the second most important piece, which is that whatever works for other persons probably won't work for you. Some of it may help—*maybe*—but there's no guarantee it will. Nobody else's answer is an exact fit for you. You've got to find your own—and kiss a lot of toads along the way."

Mac stopped to see if that was getting through and, if so, whether Walter would accept it or come back with the all-too-frequent "Yes, but ..." reply. Walter said nothing, which Mac took as indication of his tentative acceptance. "What I *can* do," Mac continued, "is help you with the process, and it's kinda like what I do as a fishing guide. I can advise you on what tackle and bait or lures to use and how to use them, and I can haul you to some better-than-average spots to start looking—for fish or for solutions to your problems. If you get your line snagged or a hook stuck in your finger, I can kiss it to make it well—although that service doesn't necessarily extend to other parts of your anatomy—and if you come away empty-handed, I can have a beer with you and commiserate. That's as close as I come to a comprehensive guarantee of satisfaction."

"That's fair," said Walter. "I think I can work with that." He stood in silence the rest of the way back to the Resort, trying to fully enjoy the beautiful lake and the lovely day. At the dock, Mac tied up the boat and began tidying up for his next customer. "Do you want to schedule some time next week to go after kokanee?" he asked.

"Yes, I would," Walter replied enthusiastically. "I plan to leave Wednesday, so Monday or Tuesday would be good."

Mac consulted a small appointment book. "Tuesday would be better for me—say, in the morning, like today?"

"OK—and there's one thing more. If there's a time we could get together for a beer this weekend, I'd like to do that too—that is, if you were serious about providing commiseration counseling."

Mac grinned. "Yes, I was serious, and if you hadn't asked, I would have suggested it before you got away today. My wife will be coming up from Klamath Falls tonight and I've got a group of six booked for fishing tomorrow, but we could meet after she heads back late Sunday afternoon."

"Works for me," Walter said. "Would you like to join me here for dinner?"

"Thanks for the offer," Mac replied, "but I'd rather eat with her. I don't see much of her at this time of year because she's busy teaching. She comes up to our cabin most weekends before school is out, and then we spend ten weeks together here in the summer. Come September, we go back to the commuter marriage routine until the lake shuts down on November 1. Then I close up the cabin and move back to our home in KFalls until the following spring. It's sorta crazy, but we like it. We've been doing it that way for years."

"Actually, it doesn't sound crazy at all. It strikes me as very sensible," Walter said. "So you'll come over here Sunday evening?"

"Yup. Let's say six o-clock. I'll call you from the lobby when I get here." They shook hands, and Walter strolled back to his cabin with a little spring in his step and optimism in his outlook. It wasn't much, but it was a definite improvement over what he had been feeling only a week before.

7.

Walter had just finished breakfast the next morning when his cell phone rang. Surprised and curious, he answered. "Hello, this is Ted," said the voice.

"Good morning, Ted," Walter said cheerily. "You're coming through loud and clear. Did you get a new cell phone?"

Ted wasn't amused. "No, I'm just calling from town, where the reception is better. Your background check came through OK late yesterday. I'll show you the cabin whenever you've got time."

Walter did some quick triage on his schedule. *Sunday is out, because I'm meeting Mac. Ditto next Tuesday. So it's either today or next Monday. Monday is better.* "I'm up at Odell Lake, kinda tied up all weekend, but I could come down there on Monday if it suits you"

"That's good," said Ted. "It will be a little closer for you if we meet in Bonanza instead of Malin. Coming down from Odell Lake on US 97, turn east onto

Highway 422, on the north side of Chiloquin, and go to the middle of town. There's a Shell gas station at what seems like the main intersection, and you make a left just beyond it, onto Sprague River Road. Follow that about 35 miles, all the way to the end, where it will drop you onto Highway 140 five miles west of Beatty. Turn right on 140 and go eight or nine miles to Bly Mountain Cutoff, on the left. Take that road another eight miles into the town of Bonanza. At the main intersection, there's a town park on the southeast corner. I'll be sitting in my truck somewhere next to the park. Is eleven o'clock OK?"

Walter's head spun from the rapid-fire directions, but he didn't ask for a rerun so he could take notes. "Eleven is fine with me. See you there." He switched off the phone, took his laptop out of the drawer, and headed for the lounge where there was wi-fi service. Spending two hours in on-line exploration, mostly with MapQuest and Google Earth, he discovered that Bonanza (pop. 415) was about 14 miles due north of Malin, where he had met Ted a week earlier. The change in meeting place led him to speculate that Ted's cabin was somewhere between the two towns, probably off Harpold Road. *Why else would Ted change their next meeting to Bonanza—unless he was deliberately attempting to obscure the cabin's location? If so, what else was he trying to hide?* Troubled by these questions, Walter's attempts at meditation that afternoon were not very successful.

8.

The next day Walter awoke thinking about his imminent meeting with Mac, who was turning out to be something of an enigma, definitely not the good-ol' country boy Walter had expected in a fishing guide. There was an aura of self-discipline about him that reminded Walter of instructors he had met in the Air Force. *OK, so maybe he's retired military, which isn't inconsistent with serious fishing in later life or even doing a little counseling and mentoring on the side, but where did meditation figure into all that?*

In any event, Walter felt he'd better have his shit together for the 'counseling session,' so he spent the day preparing, making a list of salient points about his life thus far, what had gone well and what had not, and another list of questions and issues facing him now, not the least of which was the decision he would have to make after Ted—*another enigma, that's for sure*—showed him the cabin. He concluded that the cabin matter is where he should start, and if various aspects of his life history were relevant, he could fill them in as they came up.

Thus primed, he made two more attempts at meditating, before and after his now-customary afternoon nap. To his satisfaction, he found his mind had calmed somewhat from its usual blitz of worries, suspicions, and half-baked thoughts. No, it wasn't silent or empty, but the stream of impressions flowed more gently over and through the boulders of fear and opinion that served as the foundation for his ego. *Just watch, don't judge*, he told himself.

Six o'clock found him relaxed and centered, looking forward to his meeting without nervousness or misgivings. The phone rang at 6:03, and within minutes Walter was facing Mac over beers in the restaurant. Mac didn't waste any time in getting down to the nitty-gritty. After the initial exchange of pleasantries, he said, "You've told me a little about your past, all I need to know to get started. What I'd like to hear from you now is your *intention*—why are you here? what do you plan to do here? where do you expect to go afterward—things like that."

Even with his forethought and preparation, Walter was caught off-guard by Mac's directness. He struggled to find words until he realized that Mac's questions led straight into the second of the two lists he had made, thus enabling him to begin exactly where he had planned: the cabin. "I came to this area in response to a newspaper ad about a 'secluded cabin' for rent. I'm hoping to hole up for a while to sort out my life and figure out where to go from here. I met with the cabin owner last week, at a diner in Malin"—Mac rolled his eyes at the mention of Malin—"and came away with more questions than answers. He seemed rather secretive in that he simply gave his name as 'Ted,' but declined to give me his full name. Not that I flat-out asked him about his last name, but he did it twice—both times after I had given him *my* full name. He told me about the cabin—general stuff about size and furnishings—but he didn't tell me where it was. He said he wanted to run a background check on me before he took me to see it. His excuse was that this was his first shot at renting it, so he needed to go slow. He also said he needed the background check because there are some 'weirdos' around here he didn't want to get mixed up with."

"How did you get all the way up here from Malin?" Mac inquired.

"Ted said he needed up to a week for the background check, and he suggested I go to the Welcome Center in Klamath Falls to find some ways to pass the time. The lovely lady at the Center recommended this place and helped me make reservations." At the mention of 'the lovely lady' Mac reacted ever so slightly, as if he might know her. Walter continued, "Anyhow, Ted called yesterday morning to say I had passed the background check, so I'm meeting him tomorrow to have a look at the cabin. Then I'll have to make a decision about whether to take it or look elsewhere."

Mac leaned back in his chair and stared out the window, as if considering where to go next in the conversation. Turning back to face Walter, he said, "First of all, I don't find anything very unusual in what you've told me. You'll find quite a few people around here who are rather eccentric, some of them even more buttoned-up than this guy Ted, and for all sorts of reasons. I can't give you much help there."

"What about the weirdos?"

Mac smiled. "As I just said, there are all kinds of eccentric folk hereabouts, probably more than you will find in the 'civilized' parts of the state, like Portland or even Medford and Ashland. But don't let yourself get caught up in Ted's fears—or anybody else's, for that matter." He paused to let that penetrate, then continued. "I'm pretty sure you can handle individual weirdos just fine, as long as it's just one-on-one, but if you come up against a bunch of 'em, it could be dicey. When people with multiple fears and fantasies come together in groups, they tend to feed off one another and the hysteria builds, sometimes to the point where they all go bat-shit crazy. Oftentimes, there's a religious component, with some power-hungry self-anointed preacher fanning the flames in order to inflate his own ego and probably line his own pockets in the process—or if not that, a patriotic message or some other wackiness. If you examine it closely and impartially, it's about one percent 'truth' and ninety-nine percent idolatry."

It was Walter's turn to lean back and reach for a little more perspective. "Yeah, I've seen a good bit of wackiness in my life, and heard about a lot more, but I've never actually gone toe-to-toe with anything approaching a mob, nor do I want to."

"There's been a history of fringe political movements in this part of the country, just as there has been in other parts of the wild, wild West. You may have heard of a movement, just before World War II, to create a new State of Jefferson from parts of northern California and southern Oregon, with Yreka as the interim capital. The issue was lack of roads and bridges to support mining and timber business in the area, and the decision-makers in Sacramento and Salem weren't giving that enough priority. Some rather prominent public officials got out in front of the campaign, and it was scheduled to hit the national news on December 8, 1941. However, the Japanese bombed Pearl Harbor the day before, and the great 'State of Jefferson rebellion' collapsed like a three-dollar tent in a hurricane."

"I remember that," said Walter. "I grew up in Mendocino, and my grandfather told me stories about it."

"More recently," Mac continued, "a couple local groups have gained a few minutes of fame for their activities in and around Klamath Falls. The Jefferson State Militia is a so-called 'patriot' group with its own ideas about how local law enforcement should be carried out, and Freedom Bound International is all worked up over how the country is being run. Both have received support from other groups of a similar bent, mostly libertarian, in other parts of the country, especially when conflicts have arisen between local farmers and ranchers and the environmentalists. The latter usually have backing from national and even international tree-huggers and such, as well as the federal government, so the local guys feel it's an unfair fight. To some extent they're right, but they get all screwed up by their own fear and fanaticism."

Walter nodded. "I read a little about the Jefferson State Militia in some on-line newspaper archives last week. The Militia seems to be docile as long as nobody pushes their buttons."

"What worries me," Mac said, "is the possibility that one of these groups *will* push the buttons of another group to the point of provoking a small civil war. They're all armed to the teeth, so they could probably overwhelm local law enforcement, and if they called in their sympathizers from around the country, it could escalate into a really nasty situation. And lest you think that is too far-fetched, you should know there was an attempt to set up a training camp for Muslim terrorists on a ranch near Bly—that's about forty miles east of KFalls— back in 1999. A couple people were eventually arrested and convicted on charges of providing material support to *al-Qaeda* and the *Taliban*. So you never know what you're going to find in some of the more isolated areas hereabouts. Maybe your friend Ted has good reason to be fearful."

9.

Nine o'clock Monday morning found Walter on the road again, following the directions Ted had rattled off and he had later reconstructed through MapQuest. After driving lazily along some fifty miles of secondary roads, skirting Klamath Falls on the northeast, he entered the incorporated burg of Bonanza. A quarter-mile into town he came to a broad intersection with a sign at the southeast corner, "Welcome to BIG SPRINGS PARK" in large red letters. Ted's grungy white pickup was parked in the shade along the western edge, with Ted at the wheel, attentively watching all the action at what was obviously the busiest point in town. Walter pulled over opposite Ted, facing in the opposite direction on the side street, but leaving the engine idling. Ted leaned out his window and called, "Make a U-turn and follow me!" He started his truck and turned left at the intersection, heading west, with Walter following in unhurried procession.

At the edge of town, Ted did *not* turn south on Harpold Road, as Walter's MapQuest research had led him to expect. Instead they continued northwest about two miles on Highway 70, a.k.a. Dairy-Bonanza Highway, past several dairy farms, and then *north*—to Walter's surprise—on Haskins Road. After another two miles, Ted slowed and turned onto a narrow gravel lane heading slightly uphill into the trees. Walter noted there was no mailbox and the lane was unmarked except for a small round red reflector on a two-foot aluminum rod stuck in the ground next to the main road. *My hunch was right*, Walter thought. *Ted deliberately chose Malin for our initial meeting to make sure I couldn't figure out where the cabin is. There's no way I could have found my way here on my own.*

Over the next half-mile the trees grew denser and taller: more Ponderosa pines, less juniper. Another driveway branched off to the left and about fifty yards beyond the gravel lane ended in a small grassy clearing with a cabin at the far side, about fifteen feet from the denser forest behind. A one-story building, more-or-less square, about 28 feet on a side, it appeared to be conventional log construction, with an over-layer of cedar board-and-batten siding, unfinished and dark with age. There was a low open porch about eight feet deep along the front, a detached carport, more than big enough for Walter's pickup, alongside, and a small storage shed at the rear.

They both got out of their trucks and walked to the front door. Ted selected a key from the ring hanging on his belt, unlocked the door, and pushed it open. Walter stepped to the middle of the room, taking it all in. It was mostly as Ted had described in their first meeting: the furnishings were not new, but they were in good condition; the colors and patterns sometimes clashed, but the whole place was spotlessly clean. After a quick walk-thru to get an overall impression, Walter returned to the central living-dining-kitchen space, sniffing and listening. *Martha Stewart doesn't live here*, he thought, *but it doesn't matter. It feels good!*

Next he switched on the other side of his brain and began the equivalent of a preflight inspection of a plane he was about to fly. First he went into the bedroom and tested the bed: firm, but no back-twisting sag. Then he checked out the bathroom: good quality faucets, towel racks, and shower head; new shower curtain and toilet seat; everything all squeaky clean, smelling faintly of Lysol. He flushed the toilet—it worked fine—and turned on the hot water tap at the sink—there was good water pressure, and the water came hot within ten seconds. Moving to the kitchen area, he poked at the hot plate, opened and closed the toaster-oven and refrigerator doors, and turned the water off and on at the sink. He flipped every light switch up and down, noting where each was located and what it controlled, checking for burned-out bulbs; he fingered the towels, sheets, and blankets in the linen closet; he sat on the sofa; he peeked inside the wood stove and examined the flue—everything checked out.

Finally, he sprawled in the easy chair and propped up his legs on the ottoman. Taking in a large bubble of air and letting it out slowly, he sifted through his mind for anything he hadn't checked. Finding nothing, he got up and walked outside, around the house, and through the carport: once to get the overall picture, and again to inspect the details. Ted watched it all with concealed amusement, and when Walter seemed to have finished, he pointed to an almost-overgrown path leading into the trees beyond the clearing. "My wife and I live over there, about a hundred yards down the driveway you saw a little ways back. Most of the time you'll hardly know we're there, but you can get to us fairly quick in an emergency."

"Do I need to be wary of wild animals?" Walter asked.

"Just use a little common sense. There are deer, elk, and antelope in this county, and, of course, some critters that like to feed off 'em: bears, cougars, bobcats, and coyotes. This was *their* territory before humans moved in, but they've retreated to the less populated areas to the East. We've never had any problems in the three years we've been here, but you should get yourself a can of pepper spray, just in case anything comes snooping around, and take it along whenever you walk in the woods. However, you don't need a firearm. I've got a couple guns if we ever need them."

Yeah, Walter thought, *but how the hell do I get word to you to break out the artillery?* Then he recalled Mac's advice about not getting caught up in 'fears and fantasies' and put aside his concerns about being devoured by rabid grizzlies. "I think this will work just fine for me," he said.

"I'm glad to hear that." Ted sounded as if he truly meant it. "Since we're about one-fourth of the way through the month, let's make it $375 in rent for the rest of May. Oh, and there is one thing I forgot to mention...." *Uh-oh. Here it comes,* Walter thought. "If it's not too much trouble, I'd like the rent and the deposit to be paid in cash. I can give you written receipts for everything, and I will draw up a simple rental agreement we can both sign, but beyond that I'd like to keep a very low profile on all of this."

Walter's imagination and quick wit got the better of him. "Do you want the payment in small, unmarked bills?" he asked, then quickly regretted his impertinence. He flashed a big smile as if to pass it off as a joke.

Ted winced as if he had been slapped. A flicker of anger surfaced in his face but quickly disappeared as he forced a smile of his own, replying softly and deliberately, "No, that won't be necessary." He paused, looking intently into Walter's eyes to gain and hold his full attention. "But I will say this: there are some very good reasons why my wife and I are living in virtual anonymity way out here in the sticks. So we will insist that you respect and honor that—which includes your exercise of extreme discretion in what you say to people about where you live, what you're doing here, and most of all, who your neighbors are. I'm not at liberty to explain the reasons to you, but I give you my word we are not involved in any way in anything that is illegal, immoral, or improper..." Breaking into a grin, he added, "... or even fattening."

A breakthrough! thought Walter. *It wasn't much, but he opened up a little. Maybe we might even develop a friendship.* He extended his hand and Ted shook it. "I'm scheduled to check out at Odell Lake on Wednesday, and I should stay in town that night so I can get the money from the bank. Is it OK if I move in Thursday?"

"That will be fine."

"I'll be back Thursday morning—say, around 11:00 AM."

"Do you think you can find your way back here again?" Ted asked. "If you want, I can draw you a map or write out directions right now. Or I can meet you someplace closer to so-called civilization and lead you here one more time."

He's getting downright hospitable, Walter thought. *I wonder how long it will take for him to invite me over for a beer.* "I think I can find it, provided I don't get lost getting out of here. If I have any problems, I can always contact you by cell phone."

"Good luck with that," said Ted.

Walter walked to his truck, picked up the GPS unit, and recorded his present position, labeling it "CABIN."

10.

It was almost noon, and Walter's stomach was reminding him he had denied it the customary donut when he stopped for coffee in Chiloquin. He decided to go back to Bonanza and see what it had to offer. Although he drove slowly so he could rubberneck, it took him only ten minutes to reach the west end of town, and he found the Library right in the middle: a new building behind the older, smaller Community Center. The sign out front said it was open four days per week, but today (Monday) wasn't one of them. The Community Center wasn't operating either, so Walter drove on to the east end of North Street where, he remembered, there was a real estate office just across the street from the Big Springs Park. He parked his truck in the shade where Ted had been waiting earlier and walked to the ancient one-story stone building that may have once been a bank but now served as the humble home of Ranch & Rural Real Estate.

The aging real estate agent was rather humble as well—uncharacteristically so for his profession—but he willingly supplied answers to Walter's questions with scarcely a pause for breath: the town was incorporated in 1901—the population was almost 500, median age 31—about 160 households, 35 percent of them with kids under 18—40 percent single, 1 lesbian household, no gays, 1 registered sex offender (that he knew of)—most residents were white, of German-Irish-English-Swedish-Scottish ancestry, but about 50 were Latino—most folk worked on nearby farms or in KFalls 25 miles to the west—unemployment was above average, but crime was well below average—not much interest in religion, but what there was was pretty conservative—two-to-one Republican, like the rest of the county—the cost-of-living index was low: "in the 80s"—the town was 4,116 feet above sea level—average annual rainfall 13 inches, snowfall 27—average July high 83, January low 22—214 days of sunshine per year—was he (Walter) interested in buying or renting? Had it not been for years of accurately decoding the rapid-fire chatter of control tower personnel at LAX, SJC, SFO, PDX, SEA, etc., Walter's head would have been spinning. Here he just took it all in and filed it away before politely-but-non-committally answering the question. "I've got a rental for the time being, and if that goes well, I might be interested in buying something in a year or so, after I've explored the area more thoroughly."

"Well, be sure to come back to see me when you want to proceed with that," was the equally perfunctory reply as the agent handed Walter his card. "Once again, your name is...?"

"Baker. Walter Baker. You'll probably see me around town in the coming months when I come in to check my mail."

The agent warmed visibly at the prospect that Walter might indeed return, instead of disappearing forever like most 'customers' who come through his door. Extending his hand, he smiled and said, "I'm Henry Parsons. Drop in any time, even if it's just to chat."

"Thanks. I'll do that." Walter gently closed the door behind him. Turning left, he walked along the south side of the main street, skeptically surveying the slightly scruffy gas-station-*cum*-grocery-store that seemed to have a monopoly on those market segments in Bonanza. A little farther on was a clean white one-story concrete building bearing a large "LAUNDRYMAT" sign. That was good news, and so was the smaller sign below it that said, "Country Clips." Not that Walter had yet made any decisions about the future of his beard, presently at the week-old pre-shaggy stage, having passed successfully through the earlier itchy phase at which many men give up on the endeavor. That and the matter of haircuts would depend greatly upon Susan's reaction to his appearance, which was connected to his yet-to-be-determined relationship with her.

He snapped out of his reverie to cross the street, having seen nothing more of interest on the south side. To the West was the Community Center and Library. Immediately in front of him was the Bonanza General Store, which appeared to be exactly what it said it was, no more, no less. He decided not to explore it further now, but it was good to know that something akin to a full-fledged hardware store was close at hand. Next door, to the East, was The Branding Iron Café whose red neon 'OPEN' sign in the window was all the enticement Walter needed. He entered, took a seat at the counter, and ordered a ham-and-cheese sandwich.

His daydream from the other side of the street resumed. It had been almost a week since he had had any contact with Susan and much longer since he had had a protracted conversation of any depth with any woman. Now, as the issue of 'Security and Survival'—in particular, lodging—was getting resolved, the matter of 'Esteem and Affection' was coming to the fore. He was hopeful that he could build and maintain a friendship with Mac despite the logistical problems presented by who lived where, and maybe he could eventually penetrate Ted's defenses to have some semblance of friendship, but that still left unanswered the question of female companionship. Not that he wanted to jump back into the whole dating scene, much less consider the possibility of another marriage, but neither did he want the self-imposed retreat he was about to enter upon to be one of complete asceticism. How was he going to balance the demands of disciplined isolation and contemplation with at least a minimal social life? He ate his sandwich and followed it with a piece of cherry pie—*thank you, stomach, for not making a big fuss over your donut deprivation*—then paid his tab and continued his walking tour of Beautiful Downtown Bonanza.

Looming in the distance two blocks behind the Library was a large brick structure, the Bonanza School, grades K-12. Walking in the opposite direction on the back street he passed the Bonanza Town Hall, a small doublewide he would have mistaken for a lower-middle-class home had it not been for the blacktop parking lot and the prominent flagpole out front. There was no mistaking the next building, however: a church that took up almost a whole city block, with the traditional white clapboard chapel in front and a huge gymnasium behind. Further walking revealed two other churches nearby, which Walter duly noted and filed away for the possibility that he would eventually explore what some of these churches could offer to aid and comfort him in his quest.

The back street ended at Bly Mountain Cutoff Road as it was turning northward out of town. Immediately east of the intersection was the US Post Office, so Walter went in and inquired about renting a PO box. Yes, there were 'Size 1' (3x5.5 inches) boxes available at $20.00 for six months. 'Line 4, Address' on the application form presented a problem, so he just wrote, "Haskins Road, Bonanza, OR" and explained to the clerk that he was moving in from California and there were no mailboxes along Haskins Road for the cabin he was renting. All that seemed acceptable to the clerk, especially after Walter presented a current California driver's license and a valid US passport, which he had luckily thought to bring along, as if a little voice inside his head had told him he was going to need it. Five minutes later Walter was all set up with his new mailing address: PO Box 279, Bonanza, OR 97623. He almost danced out of the Post Office and back across Market Street to what seemed to be the only stretch of sidewalk in town, extending one block southwest to the main intersection. On his right was a long one-story building, the best looking one in town based upon design and condition, housing the Longhorn Restaurant and Saloon. It looked like a friendly place, maybe even somewhat upscale as suggested by a sign in the window indicating that the Bonanza Lion's Club met there. *I could bring Susan here for a romantic dinner sometime*, he thought. Diagonally across the main intersection from the Longhorn was his starting point: the Big Springs Park, where he had parked his truck.

An hour later he pulled into the parking lot at the Klamath Falls Welcome Center, jumped out, and trotted to the entrance. He expected to find Susan standing behind the service counter, but instead there was an older woman wearing a nametag identifying her as 'Virginia.' Walter recalled that Susan had mentioned somebody by that name: the director of the Center, whom she had characterized as 'sort of a big sister.' "Hello. Could I speak with Susan, please?" he said, putting on his 'friendly' face as best he could behind the beard.

"Susan is off today. Can I assist you with something?" was the cordial-but-cautious reply.

Feeling a tinge of regret about the beard, Walter turned up the 'friendly' a notch. "I'm Walter Baker. When I stopped by last week, Susan helped me with a reservation at Odell Lake. I had some business here in town earlier today, and I was hoping I might connect with her over dinner tonight—that is, if she doesn't have a class." He avoided any mention of their meeting at Peet's so as not to get Susan in trouble in case she had bent any rules governing fraternization with clients, but he added the allusion to her class to indicate that their relationship had surpassed the initial host-client stage. "She didn't give me her phone number, but she did say I could track her down here through Virginia Cox, who I presume is you."

The woman's protective reserve melted a little at the mention of her full name, which was not given on her badge or anywhere else in sight. "Yes, I'm Virginia Cox, and yes, I can pass a message to Susan for you." She glanced at her watch. "However, I doubt I can get it to her in time to set up a dinner engagement for this evening."

"I understand. I apologize for trying to arrange this on short notice." Walter deliberately allowed a dollop of disappointment to smudge his otherwise friendly countenance. "Let's try it another way. I'll be staying at the Odell Lake Resort tonight and tomorrow night, returning to Klamath Falls on Wednesday. If Susan would like to join me for dinner Wednesday evening—or if not then, later in the week—have her call me at the Resort." Again, discretion told him not to reveal that he had given Susan his cell phone number, so as not to arouse Virginia's protective 'big sister' instincts.

"OK," she replied as she reached for pencil and paper. "Give me your name again."

"Walter Baker. I don't remember the phone number of the Resort, but I'm sure you have it here, because Susan called to make my reservation there last Tuesday."

Virginia wrote down his name. "I'll look up the number and give it to Susan along with your message when she comes in tomorrow afternoon. That will still leave plenty of lead time for a Wednesday dinner."

"You might also ask her to think of where she would like to go for dinner. I'm new in town, so I don't know my way around. Besides, since she works here, she should have all kinds of recommendations."

Virginia smiled—*at last*, Walter thought. "I'll do that."

Walter retreated to his truck. On his way back to Odell Lake he stopped for dinner at the casino in Chiloquin, partly to check out another piece of the territory that now seemed destined to become his new stomping ground, partly to distract himself from the loneliness that had suddenly sprung up deep inside him.

11.

Walter didn't sleep well that night—it was probably a combination of excitement over his imminent move into the cabin and disappointment over not connecting with Susan—so he was anything but bright-eyed and bushy-tailed when he met Mac the next morning. Nevertheless, he wanted to talk more with Mac, and he didn't want to default on the fishing he had contracted for. Mac immediately sensed that Walter was not running on all cylinders and asked if he was OK. Walter's tepid "yeah" didn't convince him, but he took it as indication Walter wasn't ready to talk about it and directed the conversation to fishing as they walked to the boat dock. Yes, Walter still wanted to go fishing. Yes, he wanted to try his hand at fishing for kokanee. No, he had never done anything like that before. No, he couldn't recall ever actually seeing, or eating, a kokanee. But all the same, he was here, now, at Odell Lake, which is famous for great kokanee fishing, so....

Mac started up the boat and headed off in a different direction from where they had fished previously. Still making small talk, he asked, "You realize, don't you, we don't do catch-and-release with kokanee?"

"No, I didn't know that. Why?"

"Kokanee have 'soft' mouths, so the hooks tend to do more damage than with other fish. A fish with a busted mouth may have trouble surviving," Mac explained.

"Oh. Can I give whatever I catch to you or someone else: the Resort chef, perhaps? I won't be set up with a refrigerator or freezer until later this week."

"The health regulations don't allow Frank to use it for sale in the restaurant, but he knows of people who can use it: one of the homeless shelters up in Bend, or something like that. He donates surplus food to them rather than let it go bad in the restaurant freezer or storeroom."

Mac shut down the motor when they neared the midpoint along the north shore. As the boat drifted to a stop, he began hooking up a contraption he called a 'downrigger.' Walter had never seen, nor even heard of, such a device before, so Mac explained its function: to position the lure or bait being trolled at a depth where the fish are likely to be. It took him several minutes to get it set up and to connect the line from Walter's rod to a 'flasher,' next through a lure slightly more than a foot beyond, then to a series of hooks with a kernel of White Shoe Peg Corn placed at the bend of each. Finally he inserted Walter's line into a gizmo he called 'a stacker release' on the downrigger, put the whole shebang into the water, and lowered a weighted ball to the depth he had selected, all the while explaining that when a kokanee bites on the lure, the stacker release will free the line so Walter can fight and land the fish without the encumbrance of the downrigger. If he could feel the fish bite and immediately jerked the tip of the rod upward, Walter could also trigger the release, setting the hook in the fish's mouth at the same time.

Tutorial completed, Mac started the trolling motor and turned his attention to an electronic fish finder as they slowly headed away from the morning sun. After trolling thirty minutes with no bites, he stopped the boat, retrieved the downrigger, and changed the lure. Then they trolled back in the opposite direction. His fish finder told him kokanee were down there, but for some reason they weren't interested in what was being offered. After two more runs and lure changes, Walter got a strike. Mac quickly pulled the downrigger out of the water so Walter's line wouldn't get tangled in it as the kokanee swam rapidly from side to side. With Mac's coaching, Walter patiently worked the fish back and forth until fatigue overcame its fight, then reeled it into Mac's waiting net. Over the next hour, this scenario was repeated four more times, with similar results. Walter's mood and energy improved with each catch, and as nine o'clock approached he was positively beaming over his accomplishment. However, fatigue from his sleepless night was threatening to encroach on the fun, so he decided to call it a day.

As they cruised back to the dock, Mac decided to follow up on the lead Walter had given him earlier. "You said you would have a refrigerator later this week. Does that mean that you've rented the cabin in Malin?"

Walter nodded. "In fact, the cabin is closer to Bonanza. I think Ted originally met me in Malin to obscure its location until he had checked up on me. In any event, I move in Thursday. I decided to give it a go—that is, trust that my landlord is the honest, upstanding citizen he claims to be—although I almost got spooked when he said he wanted payment in cash."

"You're lucky he didn't ask for it in gold bullion," said Mac. "A lot of folk around here won't take checks or credit cards—anything that leaves a record somebody else might be able to investigate. It usually isn't clear who that 'somebody else' might be, but the Federal government seems to be at the top of the list."

"Well, he said rather emphatically he and his wife weren't doing anything the least bit illegal, immoral, or improper, but that was after he also insisted on rather strict confidentiality regarding the whole situation: where the place is, what I'm doing there, and most of all, who he is."

Mac considered this a minute before responding. "He must have his reasons, and I guess you'll have to assume they're legitimate if you're going to move in next door. Did he say whether you could have firearms?"

"I asked about that, and he said I wouldn't need them for protection from wild animals, but he had a couple guns just in case. He didn't say I *couldn't* bring my own AK-47"—Walter grinned—"if I had one."

Mac grinned back. "You don't strike me as the AK-47 type—nine-millimeter pistol maybe."

"Yeah, they gave the airline cockpit crews handguns after '9/11,' and I spent a little time on the firing range getting acquainted with one, but I didn't cherish the idea of trying to fly the plane with one hand and fending off *al-Qaeda* with the other."

"I gather you now have cause for optimism in your living situation," Mac observed, "but you didn't give that impression when I first saw you this morning."

Walter's smile faded. "Well, after I reached agreement on the cabin, I tried to contact a woman I met in KFalls so I could invite her out to dinner tomorrow night. But she had the day off, and I couldn't find her."

"A woman! I might have known." Mac was laughing.

"There's no logical reason why it upset me. I should be able to track her down at work later this week if she doesn't respond to the message I left for her. Besides, I've only talked with her twice—rather briefly both times—but there did seem to be some mutual attraction there."

"Hoo, boy!" chortled Mac. "You say you've just come through a divorce and you're trying to regain some equilibrium, but here you are, already chasing some skirt!"

Walter scowled. "No, I'm not just chasing skirt. It's not like that. Not that she's hard to look at—she's really quite attractive—but there seems to be a mental affinity I never experienced in my marriage, at least not in recent years."

"Do you mean to tell me you're more interested in what's between her ears than what's between her legs?"

"Well, ... maybe both ... eventually ... but for the time being, I'll settle for some nice congenial conversation."

"Whaddya know?" said Mac. "You really are into a mid-life transition. We'll have to stay in touch. I'm curious to see how all this turns out: the cabin thing, the woman thing, and even the meditation thing."

"Yes, I'd like to stay in touch with you, too. You're one of only three people I know in this area, and I need to have somebody I can turn too in an emergency, somebody local. I don't want to be a burden to you or anybody else, but I do need to make some new friends."

"That's fine with me." Mac reached in his vest pocket, pulled out a business card, turned it over, wrote down a phone number, and handed it to Walter. "Here's how you can reach me. The number on the front is my cell phone. The number on the back is my house in KFalls. When I'm not there, my wife Mary will know where to find me. You can call any time."

Walter found a scrap of notepaper from the Resort in his shirt pocket. He scribbled his name and phone number and gave it to Mac. "Here's my cell phone number. The reception isn't very good at the cabin, but there's a voice mail feature that works well. When I get myself organized better, I'll give you an email address, and I'll come back for more fishing after I see what kind of refrigerator is at the cabin."

"Since you'll be living near Bonanza, we could do some fishing in that vicinity. The Lost River, which runs just outside of Bonanza and down through the Poe Valley to Klamath Falls, isn't the greatest, but the Sprague River is a great trout stream, especially for fly fishing."

"I've never done any fly fishing, but I'm game to give it a try. It looks like it would be very different from what we've done today."

"Yes, indeed. You could even say it's meditative—which is why I prefer it—but a lot of people dislike it for the same reason." Mac cut the motor and let the boat drift to the dock. As they shook hands, Mac said, "I was serious when I said I hope you'll stay in touch. Give me a call when you get settled in at your cabin, and we'll meet up somewhere when I'm down in KFalls again. Don't worry about the money because the meter isn't running when I'm fly fishing."

When Walter got back to his cabin, he saw that the message light on the phone was flashing. He called the front desk, and the clerk read the message. "You had a call from Susan. She said 'yes' to dinner tomorrow night and left this number where you can reach her after class tonight: (541)-555-9365. She will get home between 9:45 and 10:00 PM."

Walter literally jumped for joy. "Thank you *very* much," he said to the desk clerk. "And thank you, God," he said under his breath as he hung up the phone. He shook his head and thought, *Where did that come from?*

After lunch, Walter was too excited to take a nap, so he drove to the RV camp at Crescent Lake Junction to do some laundry. By the time the dryer had finished its cycle, fatigue from his previous night's insomnia, compounded by his fishing exertions, had returned with a vengeance. He hurriedly folded his clean clothes, drove back to his cabin, set the alarm for 6:00 PM as a precaution, and stretched out on the bed. In less than two minutes, he was sound asleep.

He didn't simply doze, he dreamt. He was a fish, a Fish Named Walter that had been put into a strange, new lake where he had encountered a Fish Named Ted, a Fish Named Susan, and a Fish Named Mac. Then he, the Fish Named Walter, was magically transmogrified into a Fisherman, and his primary task was to catch these three other fish—Ted, Susan, and Mac—not to eat them, but to *bond* with them in a kind of *symbiosis*, a network of mutual support and affection. Thus, he was led to consider what kind of bait he should use, and what kind of tackle. Rather than the boat equipped with outboard motors, electronic fish finder, downrigger, and all the rest of the *stuff* the Fisherman Named Walter had used that very morning, he was drawn to the opposite end of the spectrum, something akin to fly fishing, even *dry* fly fishing. His knowledge of it was very limited, coming primarily from an enchanting movie, *A River Runs Through It*, he had seen some years before. Haunted by the movie's opening, "In our family, there was no clear line between religion and fly fishing," the Fisherman Named Walter was struggling to attain that knowledge when the alarm went off.

Jolted awake but still disoriented, he shut off the alarm and collapsed back onto the bed to review the dream and ponder its meaning. Another hour passed, a collage of dozing, thinking, and maybe a little meditation. Finally he got up and made himself a sandwich, ate it, and washed the dishes. With more than an hour to wait before calling Susan, he resumed reading Joel Goldsmith's book, persisting in his struggle with understanding the subtle nuances of what was being said. He became quickly absorbed, so it didn't seem long until both hands on his watch reached a conjunction at 9:49 PM. Walter picked up his cell phone and entered Susan's number. After three rings, Susan answered, sounding out of breath, as if she had been hurrying.

"Hi. This is Walter."

"Hi, Walter. It's good to hear from you. How's it going?"

"It's been a good week, maybe not exactly what I expected, but then I really didn't know what to expect. Anyhow, I'm coming back to KFalls tomorrow, and I'll be moving into a cabin about twenty miles east of town on Thursday morning. I'll tell you more about it when I see you. Speaking of which, are you available to have dinner with me tomorrow night?"

"Yes, I'd like that. Where will you be staying?"

"I don't know yet. Probably at the Comfort Inn over on the South Sixth Street strip like before. Is there a particular restaurant where you'd like to eat?"

"There are so many choices I thought we'd decide that when you get here. I'm sure we can find something good without making advance reservations. I suggest you come to the Welcome Center just before we close at five. We can go through the menus on file there and see what looks inviting."

"Sounds like a plan. However, I should also warn you I haven't shaved since I saw you last, so you'll have to put up with my scruffy beard."

She laughed. "I wasn't expecting you to show up in coat and tie, but the beard will make things interesting. You'll pass for a local, so we could even go to a truck stop."

"Well, I had something a little classier in mind, someplace without a sign that says, 'No Shirt, No Shoes, No Service.'"

Susan laughed. "We'll figure it out—*after* you've passed my inspection."

"OK. See you tomorrow."

"Good night, Walter." She said it so sweetly it was almost seductive, but he restrained himself from indulging in that fantasy. *Take it slow and easy*, he whispered to himself.

12.

Wednesday morning Walter slept in. He hadn't set the alarm because there was ample time for all the things he needed to do that day and he was trying to adopt a more 'natural' pace of living, as Goldsmith advocated. *Don't hurry up and then wait.* By 11:00 AM he had SHowered and SHampooed, breakfasted, tidied up the cooking area, took out the garbage, packed his stuff, loaded the truck, and paid his bill, and by 2:30 he had checked in at the Comfort Inn in KFalls, visited the bank to get ten crisp new $100 bills, purchased an Oregon map book at the bookstore in the shopping center across the street, and had his truck washed and vacuumed at the nearby Texaco station. Having completed all the items on his 'to do' list, he settled in for a nap at the motel, but his mind kept digging up things he needed to set up housekeeping in his new abode. Irritated with his failure to make a shopping list when he was at the cabin two days before, he resigned himself to making another trip to town for shopping later in the week—*and maybe see Susan again?*

At 4:30 he set out for the Welcome Center. His excitement grew as he neared 205 Riverside Drive, but he stopped to calm himself before he entered the building. Susan was standing behind the service counter along the back wall, her long auburn hair draped down over her shoulders in contrast to her previous ponytail, thereby making her even more attractive than he had remembered. Because of his beard, it took her an extra second to recognize him, but she broke into a broad smile as all pretense of nonchalance left him and he fairly danced across the room. They awkwardly mumbled greetings and shook hands over the counter, blushing with embarrassment all the while. Virginia Cox observed the interaction from her office door at the side of the room, then walked over to stand protectively at Susan's side. Playing the 'big sister' role to the hilt, she sternly scrutinized Walter's 6'2" frame from head to toe as Susan made introductions, but she broke into a broad grin when she could no longer hold character.

Susan placed a large loose-leaf binder on the countertop and opened it to show Walter several restaurant menus. They quickly settled on Italian, choosing a moderately priced local favorite on Main Street. It wasn't quite five o'clock yet, but Virginia shooed them out the door in her finest maternal manner. Walter did his gallant best at opening and holding all the doors from Center to pickup and pickup to restaurant, and Susan followed his lead with grace and poise, but a critical observer would have noticed that both of them were out of practice in the dances of courtship. Nevertheless, they were soon seated in a comfortable booth, ignoring the menus in favor of again looking at one another in childlike wonder. Susan spoke first, "How was Odell Lake?"

Walter was effusive. "It was wonderful—quiet and peaceful—natural beauty—mountains, water, trees. The cabin was rustic but comfortable—well-maintained—good restaurant—friendly people—great fishing—not too expensive. What more can I say?"

Susan paused to let the energy level subside. "Most everybody says that. That's why I recommended the place. But I'm not wearing my Welcome Center hat now." Her voice softened. "What I meant to ask was, how did your stay at Odell Lake affect *you*?"

That put the conversation on a whole different level, and it temporarily brought Walter to a standstill. "Well," he replied after a moment, "the reconnection with nature lured me into a much more relaxed pace of living than what I've been preoccupied with for the past twenty-some years. I completely avoided the TV and the newspapers, and I spent only a small amount of time on the cell phone and the Internet. I ate sensibly, walked a good bit, took naps every afternoon, read a little, and tried to meditate. I stopped worrying about where I've been and what might happen, and put my attention on observing where I am now and thinking about where I want to go."

Susan considered his answer, then revealed a little more of herself. "When you first came into the Welcome Center, I sensed there was something different about you and why you were there—that you were searching but you didn't know what for, and you were open to accepting answers, or suggestions, or approaches that are new and foreign to you."

"Wow! Do you do that for all your clients at the Welcome Center?"

She laughed. "No. I never did that before—for anyone—but it is what gave me the idea of sending you to Odell Lake."

Understanding was beginning to dawn in Walter. "So something happened when I came to the Welcome Center?"

"... and when we had coffee later at Peet's, and it's still happening now." She looked intensely into his eyes.

The mood was shattered by the waitress who seemed to come out of nowhere to stand by the table. "Are you ready to order?"

"Gracious, no!" Walter exclaimed. "We've been too busy talking to even look at the menu. Let me start with the wine list." He looked at Susan. "Do you enjoy wine?"

"Of course. All kinds, but I prefer red over white."

"Great. So do I." He turned back to the wine list and selected a moderately priced Tuscan blend. The waitress glided off while Susan and Walter energetically dissected the menu options, choosing typical pasta dishes with robust sauces. Right on cue, the waitress returned with the wine, two glasses, and a basket of warm garlic bread. Next came the almost trite ritual of uncorking the wine, splashing a sample into Walter's glass, scrutinizing-swirling-sniffing-tasting the sample, nodding approval, and finally pouring generous portions into both glasses. Walter gave the waitress their food order, and she left them to lift their glasses in a toast. "To what's happening," said Walter.

"Yes! To what's happening!" cheered Susan.

They sipped and swallowed, then rested their glasses on the table as the wine's magnanimity flowed through them. Walter toyed with his glass and said, "You know, this may be the last wine—the last alcoholic beverage of any kind—I'll have for a while."

A look of puzzlement washed across Susan's face. "Why is that? Do you have a drinking problem?"

Walter laughed. "No, nothing like that, although I've always had to be careful about when and how much I drank when I was flying airplanes—'At least 24 hours between cocktail and cockpit,' as the old saying goes. Starting tomorrow I intend to follow a rather austere regimen of exercise, eating, sleeping, meditating, and so forth. I haven't worked out all the details, but certainly there will be no booze, no drugs—I've never done drugs —..." He paused to consider what he was about to say, then plunged ahead, "... no sex ...." He smiled faintly and waited to see what her reaction would be.

Is he serious?! she thought. *Is he propositioning me?* Her mind raced from incredulity to outrage to hilarity and settled there. She countered with feigned mockery, her voice up an octave, "No sex?! You're the only man I've gone out with in nearly twenty years, and the first thing you tell me is you're swearing off sex!"

It was the perfect response. It took him completely by surprise, and all he could do was melt in a puddle of laughter. Susan sighed with relief, then joined in. With the tension thus dissipated, he continued in a humble tone. "I've come through a rather traumatic year in which my marriage came apart, my kids rejected me, and my job was eliminated. Consequently, I decided to go all the way back to basics, to strip everything away except the barest essentials, to live in solitude and sort myself out, to determine out what I want to do with the rest of my life..." She started on another sigh, but cut it short when he said, "... and then *you* happened."

Fortuitously, the waitress chose that moment to deliver the appetizer, giving Susan time to gather her thoughts and compose an appropriate reply. Memory came to her rescue. "When we talked on the phone yesterday, you said something about moving into a cabin twenty miles east of town."

He nodded. "The first time I stopped in at the Welcome Center, I had just come from meeting with a man who had put an ad in the Portland paper: 'Secluded cabin, completely furnished, $500 per month, all utilities included.' It sounded exactly like what I was looking for, but the owner—Ted is his name—turned out to be a strange bird, cautious in the extreme. He insisted on getting some kind of background check on me before he would show me the place or even tell me where it is. That's why I had to kill time for a week."

Between bites of food, he told her the rest, sparing the details to maintain the secrecy Ted was demanding. Susan seemed to understand, as if she might have had some experiences of a similar nature. When he had finished, she knew that as of tomorrow he would be living in a cabin somewhere near Bonanza, where he would receive mail at Box 279 in the local Post Office. Although he would be only a half hour's drive away, cell phone service was uncertain, and he planned to put up the Internet periscope only once a week. *So I guess we'll have to communicate intuitively*, she told herself. *Could be interesting*. She began probing in a slightly different direction. "How did you come up with the idea of living in solitude? Have you ever done anything like that before?"

"Yes and no," was the answer. "The United States Air Force requires its pilots and navigators to complete training in *SERE*—Survival, Evasion, Resistance and Escape—through a series of increasingly rigorous and demanding courses taught in the wilds of eastern Washington, near Spokane. I got the training as a Cadet at the U.S Air Force Academy in Colorado Springs. I experienced what it's like to live on my own, with virtually no support, in the middle of nowhere, and I learned how that affects one's psyche: you either grow into a new level of self-awareness and self-reliance, a consciousness most people don't even know exists, or you crack up and flunk out. Compared to SERE, living in a fully-furnished cabin with all utilities provided—except that I won't have TV, the Internet, or laundry facilities—is a piece of cake, at least on the physical level. The psychological level, however, may turn out to be quite different, but I'm confident I can handle it."

Susan's appraisal of the man across the table from her went up several notches. She was only vaguely aware of these facets of military training, although she was not surprised to learn of their existence. She had, however, done some *zazen*, including intensive retreats lasting up to thirty days, so she had an inkling of what was involved psychologically. "OK, I have two questions for you. When will I see you again after tonight? And how long do you think your beard will be?"

"I don't think it will be necessary for me to do this like a marathon. I plan to take one day per week, sort of like a sabbatical in reverse, to tend to 'earthly' matters—you know, things like grocery shopping, doing laundry, checking my mail, maybe even getting a haircut—and I would like—very much—to meet up with you then, to do whatever you want, if you're available and willing." He discreetly skipped any further mention of booze and sex.

She reached across the table and touched his hand. "I'm willing, and I'll do what I can to be available—as long as it continues to support and nurture both of us."

There was a glisten in her eyes. For a few seconds Walter thought he was going to lose his composure, but he fought off the tears—*there will be other times and places for that*—and gently laid his other hand on hers. "Thank you," he said, and he really, *really* meant it. They both allowed the moment to 'fade to black' and resumed eating in silence. A few bites and a swig of wine later, Walter initiated a switch in roles. "Enough about me. How is school going for you? Have you graduated yet?"

"Commencement is sometime in early June," she said, "but I don't remember the exact date. I think it's usually on a Friday. Would you like to come and heckle?"

"Possibly, if I wouldn't be an embarrassment. That's almost a month away, so let's see what kind of shape I'm in by then. Won't you have your own support contingent there to applaud for you?"

"Just Virginia Cox—if she can find somebody to fill in for both of us at work. My daughter will be serving Uncle Sam in some 'undisclosed location' far, far away, and the rest of my support team will be seated in the faculty section. You and Virginia could sit together and stomp and cheer when they hand me my diploma."

"That settles it. I'll take a special 'sabbatical day' just for the occasion. But I still don't know about shaving, though. Whaddya think? You never did say precisely how you feel about my beard."

"Well, it certainly changes your aura. The first time I saw you, you were the quintessential professional pilot—maybe not in full uniform, but the demeanor was there. Now you seem to have more of a sled-dog ambience. With another month of growth, you should be downright shaggy—you know, like that big bushy uncontrollable sheepdog in the movie...."

"*Beethoven*," he said. "He was actually a Saint Bernard, but I get the idea. I'll have to work on my canine mannerisms."

"Or you could do 'Sasquatch,' if that suits you better."

"How about a Wookiee—like 'Chewbacca' in *Star Wars*?"

"Wasn't he a pilot, too? That would be perfect."

"He was the co-pilot, but that's close enough. If I ever go back to flying, I'll probably be the co-pilot—which we now euphemistically call the First Officer—because I won't have enough seniority to be Captain—that is, the pilot. That's how I came to lose my job in the airline merger last year—but it's another unhappy story you don't want to hear and I want even less to repeat. And then there was my divorce...." He rolled his eyes.

"Spare me," she grimaced.

By then their plates were empty and the waitress had come to clear the table. "How about some dessert?" she asked.

"I'm kinda full," said Susan, holding her stomach.

"But I'm not ready to leave yet," said Walter. "How about we share a dessert—say, something like *cannoli*. Have you ever had *cannoli*?"

"Not that I'm aware of."

"Well, then, we must have *cannoli*." He turned to the waitress, who nodded. "And some espresso." He turned back to Susan. "Is espresso OK?"

"You're corrupting me," she protested mildly, "but I like it. Sure, let's have some espresso."

The waitress left. Walter looked into Susan's eyes and said, "And you're corrupting me, too. I haven't even started my retreat yet, and you've already seduced me into taking an extra 'sabbatical day' so I can attend your graduation."

"'Seduce' is the wrong word," she countered. "It was too quick and easy." A *risqué* comeback popped up from the nether corners of his mind, but he swatted it down and said nothing. *Don't rush things*, he admonished himself. *Neither of us is ready to jump into bed yet.* Susan must have read his thoughts. *Thank you*, she said to herself, directing her consciousness toward what Taoists call 'nurturing the occasion.'

The waitress returned bearing a tray with the *cannoli*, two demitasse cups, a small pot of espresso, cream, sugar, and assorted silverware. As she arranged all this on the table between them and poured the espresso, Walter gave a brief discourse—*something he apparently revels in doing*, Susan thought—on *cannoli*: "tube-shaped shells of fried pastry dough, filled with a sweet, creamy filling usually containing ricotta cheese and other scrumptious ingredients according to the whims of the chef." Susan picked up a fork and started dissecting one of the *cannoli*. "Mmmm, this is good, maybe even addicting. Are you going to allow yourself *cannoli* in your new ascetic regimen?"

"Only on special occasions, like this—with special people, like you—and likewise for other things of a similar nature: *baklava*, cream puffs, fruit cake, banana splits, and.... Don't get me going on that. It might lead me to change my mind about the whole retreat thing." They both laughed and he continued. "There is one indulgence—sort of—I intend to allow myself: fly fishing." Susan raised her eyebrows in mock astonishment. "I tried a couple versions of fishing up at Odell Lake, under the supervision of an experienced fishing guide. I'll skip the details and just say we worked from a boat and used the motion of a lure in the water to attract the fish. It required a little experimentation with the type and positioning of the lure, but we were ultimately successful. I got several nice rainbows, one of which I had for dinner, and several kokanee, which I donated to a local shelter kitchen. In the process of doing all that, I developed a rapport with the guide, 'Mac' McCarter, and I told him a good bit about my past and what I intend to do here. He took on the 'big brother' role, which he seems to be good at, and gave me some advice, which I certainly can use. We agreed to stay in touch in the coming weeks and months and to occasionally get together to do some fly fishing, so I'm counting him in my small circle of new friends: you, him, and maybe my landlord Ted."

Susan's eyes revealed a flicker of recognition at the mention of Mac's name, but she said nothing. When Walter finished, she replied, "Sounds like your relationship with this Mac person may develop into the kind of thing I've got going with Virginia. It's good to have at least one friend like that in your life—a mentor you can trust. Everybody needs it, but a lot of folk don't seem to know how to get it started or keep it going."

"Yes, that may be Ted's situation. He seems to have a good bit of ambivalence. Maybe in due time he'll crawl out from the rock he's hiding under. I'll keep you apprised of how it's going—that is, to the extent he seems comfortable with having me share anything about him with you." Another blip darted in and out of Susan's eyes, as if Walter had touched a spot that was still sensitive from some unpleasant episode in her past.

The waitress reappeared, having seen that the *cannoli* plate had been scoured clean of every last morsel and the espresso cups were empty. Walter requested the bill and paid with one of the new $100s from the bank, trying not to be ostentatious. He was going to be on a strict budget, and he didn't want to give Susan the impression he had money to burn. Not that she seemed to be the gold-digger type; she dressed modestly, without heavy makeup or gobs of flashy jewelry, and her apparent lack of familiarity with *cannoli* suggested she hadn't done much high living, even by KFalls standards.

As they walked to Walter's pickup, he asked whether she wanted to go to a movie or someplace where there was music, but Susan declined, saying they could save that for the next time. They drove in silence back to her car at the Welcome Center. He turned off his truck engine and opened a discussion of when their next date would be. Together they settled on a plan, subject to future modification: Wednesdays or Thursdays would be his 'sabbatical day,' when they would meet. Walter would call her at home after 9:00 on Sunday evenings, at which point she would know her schedule for the week, and they could decide which day, what time, what to do, and where.

With that resolved, Susan disconnected her seat belt and picked up her purse. Walter hurried around to hold the door and assist her down from the high step. As they walked across the parking lot, she reached for his hand, and when they got to her car, she turned to face him. Without hesitation, as if she had carefully planned it in advance, she embraced him in a full-body hug, positioning herself so it wasn't seductive, but it definitely wasn't a Baptist A-frame-style hug either. Nor did she shy in the least from his beard. With their cheeks touching to the extent his shrubbery would allow, she whispered in his ear: "Thanks for a lovely evening, Walter. I'm really looking forward to seeing you again next week and learning how your wilderness retreat is working out." With a final soft "Good night," she turned to her car, unlocked the door, and got in.

Walter stood, savoring the faint whiff of her perfume and the delectable feel of her body against his. Almost transfixed, he watched her drive away, and only after she was out of sight did he turn and stroll slowly back to his pickup. He wasn't yet ready to make a Declaration of Love, but what he was feeling was sure a lot closer to love than anything else he had felt in several years.

13.

Walter woke at 7:00 the next morning without need of an alarm clock. Taking advantage of the hotel's relatively elegant bathroom and ample supply of hot water, he had a long *SH*ower, painstakingly soaping-scrubbing-rinsing every nook and cranny of his body, followed by an equally thorough *SH*ampoo of his hair and beard. Thus cleansed, he ate an ample breakfast, not a truck-stop-style gut-buster, but as much as the hotel's complimentary buffet would allow short of outright gluttony. Stopping at the hotel's Business Center, he checked his email, finding little of significance, and composed a message:

> Effective immediately my mailing address is PO Box 279, Bonanza, OR 97623. My cell phone number is unchanged, although the signal strength is poor at my residence. I expect to check email only once per week. Good luck if you need to contact me in a hurry.
>
> Best,
>
> Walter

He sent it to his lawyer, his accountant, his stockbroker, and his ex-wife.

He checked out of the hotel, making sure to take the unused soap and shampoo from the hotel room, and drove to the Fred Meyer store. Shopping slowly and deliberately, trying to anticipate his needs without being extravagant, he bought only grocery items, except for one box of Kleenex, a roll of paper towels, and three rolls of toilet paper, deferring purchase of cleaning supplies and equipment until he could determine precisely what he needed. It was not yet 10:00 AM when he set sail for Bonanza, so he had plenty of time to explore an alternate route suggested by his newly acquired map book: North Poe Valley Road from Stevenson Park to Harpold Road, then directly into Bonanza. Even though he drove at slow-to-moderate speeds, it was only 10:30 when he pulled into town, leaving another fifteen minutes to drive all around, surveying the houses and lots, driveways and vehicles, streets and sidewalks, trees and shrubs, dogs and cats.

At 10:45 he headed west on Highway 70, and at 10:55 he pulled up in front of his new home. Ted was sitting in a shabby folding armchair on the front porch. He stood up as Walter approached. "Good to see you. You're right on time." He motioned toward the front door. "After you left the other day, I realized I had forgotten to put up the screen door. I got it out and there it is. I also found an old electric fan in my barn that might come in handy when the summer weather comes. I stashed it in your bedroom closet. And I assume you saw the woodpile behind the storage shed when you made your inspection the other day. There should be enough wood to hold you until summer arrives. After that, we can figure out how to restock it for next fall and winter. We'll need to get to that no later than August, because you can expect frost as early as Labor Day."

"Many thanks," said Walter, reaching for his billfold. He counted out six $100 bills and four twenties and gave them to Ted. "If you haven't got change now, you can give it to me later." Ted led the way inside, picked up two sheets of paper from the small dining table, and handed one to Walter to read. It was a simple and straightforward lease agreement, giving either party the right to terminate the rental with thirty days written notice. Walter signed both copies and Ted did likewise, giving one back to Walter, who scanned it to learn Ted's full name. "Ted Wilson, eh? Have I heard of you somewhere before?"

Ted managed a weak smile. "I sure hope not. I'd rather that neither of us turn up on milk cartons." *He's beginning to loosen up*, Walter thought. *That's real progress.* Ted reached in his pocket, pulled out two keys, and handed them to Walter. "I made two duplicates for you. They open both the front and back doors, and the locks are set up so you can't lock yourself out of the house unless you try real hard." Reaching into another pocket with his other hand, he produced another key. "This is for the padlock on the storage shed. You'll find the garbage can in there, along with some tools and things that might come in handy. I recommend that you keep the garbage locked up, so animals can't get to it and spread it all over the property. I make a run to the transfer station in KFalls every two or three weeks, and I can take your trash when I go. Any questions?"

"Not that I can think of, but I'm sure something will come up. How do I find you when they do?"

"Come with me. I'll show you where I live." Ted strode out the door and over to the north side of the clearing, where there was a thin trail leading back through the trees. Walter tagged along, noting that the power line to the cabin was strung overhead. The trail was straight and level, but partially overgrown from lack of use. It ended at a clearing several times larger than the one where his cabin stood. Ted paused there, and Walter began scanning the surroundings. The nearest building was a two-story house, almost new—about 2,500 square feet, three bedrooms, Walter guesstimated. The design was plain but tasteful, suggesting that a first-rate architect had been involved. Walter noticed that the southward-facing portion of the roof was covered with solar panels, probably enough to produce nearly five kilowatts of electricity. On the far side of the house was a two-car attached garage, with a late-model Toyota Camry sedan peeking out of one space and Ted's crusty pickup parked in front of the other.

Before he could look further, Ted interrupted. "I'll apologize now. I won't be inviting you to come into the house—not now, and maybe not ever. My wife, Lottie, has an extreme fear of strangers, resulting from some rather terrible things that happened to her a few years ago. That's one of the reasons we live here in such seclusion. I drive her into town for psychological counseling once a week, but other than that she stays hidden in the house. It's only in the past six months that she's been able to come out and walk in the woods occasionally." Walter nodded, more in acquiescence than understanding. "If you'll wait here, I'll go write out your receipt and get your five bucks." Without waiting for a reply, Ted shuffled over to the garage and went inside. Walter thought he could see the face of a woman peeking through the window curtains on the near side of the house, so he deliberately looked away to minimize his intrusion.

The driveway entered the clearing from his left, aiming almost straight into the garage. Beyond the house was a barn/storage building slightly larger than his cabin, and behind it, set back some distance, was a windmill generator of moderate size. *Looks like Ted might be able to generate about half of his total power needs. That's great for emergencies, but with my cabin drawing power at the same time, the margin would be pretty thin.* His electrical engineering analysis ended when Ted emerged from the garage, followed by a white duck, the Pekin variety that is most popular in the US. Ted handed him a receipt and a five-dollar bill, but Walter's attention was on the duck. It had stopped about ten feet away and appeared to be inspecting him, as if trying to decide if he were friend or foe. Ted picked up on Walter's interest and grinned. "That's Abigail. She's sort of our watchdog. I got her at the feed store in Dairy when she was just a little thing. I thought she might cheer up Lottie like some kind of pet—you know, divert her mind to something besides her fears." From the tone of his voice, Walter inferred Abigail hadn't been much of a success in that department.

Walter turned to go back to his cabin, but Ted stopped him with some final instructions. "If ever you do need to talk with me, come to the front door and ring the doorbell. Or drive your truck over here and blow the horn six or eight times. And I may mosey over to your place once a week, just to see how you're getting along. Matter of fact, I'll come by about five this evening to see if everything is OK." Walter thanked him and ambled back to his truck to unload the groceries. While storing them in the kitchen/pantry area, he discovered that the coffee he had bought was the wrong grind for the automatic coffee maker. He resolved to make do—*if that's the biggest problem I run into, I'll be in Fat City,* he told himself—but he immediately fetched a small notepad from his pickup and began making a list of things to get on his next trip into town.

For lunch, he made himself a sandwich, a good ol' PB&J, garnished with his favorite veggie chips—a not-too-sinful indulgence he had decided to allow himself—and some fruit salad from the Fred Meyer deli. He washed it down with a glass of water from the tap, happily finding it tasted quite good—no iron or hard minerals—at least good enough that he wouldn't have to squander any money on bottled water. After lunch he went out to the front porch to sit a spell, but the chair Ted had provided was marginal: about to collapse under his weight and anything but comfortable. He decided to buy a better chair and went back inside to put that on his list, writing a large '2' on the same line in the hope Susan would visit him there someday. The time for his now-habitual nap was approaching, so he deferred moving the rest of his stuff from the truck to the cabin. Indecision ambushed him when he got to the bedroom—*do I set the alarm or not?*—but he ultimately decided to turn it on, lest Ted find him in slovenly slumber when he came back later. The bed was quite comfortable and he slept soundly, luxuriating in his new digs.

By the time Ted arrived, Walter had awakened and returned to teetering on the rickety porch chair, attempting to look relaxed as Ted approached, so as not to embarrass him about the chair's sorry condition. Ted sat down on the porch floor and leaned back against one of the four-by-fours supporting the roof. "Everything OK?" he asked.

"Just fine so far," Walter said. "I'm making a list of things I hadn't thought about, but since I'd rather not go to KFalls more than once a week, I'll try to find them in Bonanza. My problem is that the Bonanza Library is closed on Friday and open on Saturday, but it's the reverse for the Post Office. I signed up for a PO Box in Bonanza, by the way."

"Sounds like you've been doing your homework. I'd bet you'll settle on going to Bonanza on Tuesday, Wednesday, or Thursday. That's what I do."

"For me the primary determinant will probably be the schedule of a certain lady I had dinner with last night in KFalls."

Walter couldn't help breaking into a wide grin, and Ted almost matched it. "I'd say you've *really* been doing your homework!"

"Well, it's not as serious as I may have let on—at least not yet. I don't want to get involved in anything more than a nice Platonic friendship for a good long time." Ted nodded 'I understand.' "All the same, how do you want to deal with the possibility I might invite my lady friend out to the cabin? No hanky-panky, but just sit here on the porch with me and maybe share a meal."

Ted frowned. "I don't know. Once I got the impression you were taking a vow of asceticism, I gave no thought to how to deal with your houseguests. My initial reaction is to ask that you go slow, but if it looks like you'll be having your lady friend out for a visit, give me her name at least a week in advance. I don't think I'll want to get a full background check on her like I did you, but ... well, I just don't know right now. In the meantime, however, please use discretion in what you tell her, as we discussed earlier."

By damn! He really did get a full background check on me, Walter thought. "No problem with that," he assured Ted. "I'm sort of treating this like classified information, which I dealt with in the Air Force. The only solid info I'm giving out is my PO Box address, my cell phone number, and my e-mail address. The basic principle I'm following is 'need-to-know.'"

"I can't ask for better than that," said Ted, standing up. "Thanks for being so accommodating." He walked slowly to the path and disappeared into the trees, leaving Walter to wonder what was behind Ted's strong need for people *not-to-know.* Then the idea hit him: *maybe what the Universe—God, whatever—was trying to teach him was that he, Walter, should adopt a similar policy and practice of discretion. Ted doesn't seem irrational,* he mused, *and I've learned from sources I consider reliable that there are indeed plenty of weirdos in this county. Maybe I need to be more wary, for my own safety as well as Ted's.* Nevertheless, Walter didn't lock the cabin doors before going to bed that night. He considered it and decided that he had learned of no reason to be *that* protective, at least not yet.

PART TWO

Wilderness

One does not discover new lands
without consenting to lose sight of the shore
for a very long time
— André Gide (1869-1951)

14.

'Day One' of Walter's wilderness retreat began at 6:15 AM, Thursday, May 8, 2014. He turned off the alarm and sat up on the edge of the bed, trying to get his bearings. *Wha...? Oh, yes, I'm in the cabin. The bathroom is that-away.* The floor was cool on his feet, but not rough. *I don't need slippers, not until winter.* He peed, splashed some cold water on his face, toweled off, and took a sip of water. Then, according to the routine he was making up as he went along, he sat down in the middle of the sofa with his legs folded beneath him, but not attempting the 'lotus' position—he knew he couldn't do it, and he really saw no need to try. He just sat there, eyes closed, body relaxed, trying to empty his mind—or better, trying to allow his mind to empty itself. His mind, alas, had other ideas—zillions of them—and they filed across his consciousness in disorderly procession. He tried to not focus on them, to not judge them, just to let them go, as Goldsmith's book on meditation had advised. Gradually, the procession thinned, and by the time he got to the end of his planned half-hour 'sit,' the main thing on his mind was the mounting pain in his legs. He had learned from extended periods of sitting at the controls of an airplane how to keep his body alert and flexible, and he put that knowledge to good use now. He put his feet down on the floor, wiggling his toes to restore circulation, then stood up slowly and shuffled over to the kitchen area to ladle some wrong-grind coffee into the coffee maker, making a mental note to buy more filters on his next trip into town. As he waited for the coffee to drizzle into the pot, he decided to amend his wake-up routine to start the coffee maker *before* he sat down to meditate—but that was *tomorrow*, and today was *today*.

He opened the front door and stepped onto the porch. The air was crisp—about 50 degrees, he estimated, making another mental note to buy a cheap thermometer. He traipsed back to the kitchen to transfer both of the day's mental notes to paper, as the coffee maker chugged and wheezed to the end of its brewing cycle. Pouring himself a cup, he pondered whether to buy himself a bathrobe so he could drink his coffee on the porch even on chilly mornings, then remembered he had a perfectly good bathrobe and slippers in storage in California. *Guess I'll have to go down there, empty out the storage locker, and haul it all back up here.* Next his attention shifted to his coffee cup—functional, perfectly adequate, except it wasn't *his* cup—and decided to buy a *special* coffee mug just for his personal use. *Should I get one for Susan, too? No, I'll buy one for me, but wait to let Susan pick out her own cup, when the time comes.*

Thus began Walter's retreat, and thus was the level of his mentation that morning and most mornings to follow: nothing profound, pressing, or earthshaking—just nice and easy. After the second cup of coffee, he made his breakfast—whole-wheat toast and yogurt with a half-cup of granola mixed in—then headed back to the bathroom. His plan called for an alternating Three 'SH'/One 'SH' schedule, SHowering and SHampooing only every other day, except when his dates with Susan demanded more frequent cleansing. *Much of the world makes do with one bath per week, if that,* he rationalized, *so why do Americans waste so much water with obsessive bathing and washing? Because they can!* he concluded.

Dressed in what he expected to be his standard cabin attire—jeans, sweatshirt, and Dockers—he went outside to see what treasures the storage shed might hold. He found the garbage can, the fire extinguisher, a broom and dustpan, a mop and bucket, a bow saw and sawbuck, an axe, a rake, a shovel, and a garden hose—all of them well-used but in good condition, neatly hung on the side wall and/or stored in a corner—plus a plastic tool tray with an assortment of hand tools, and a modest supply of wood scraps apparently left over from remodeling the cabin, stacked in a bin in the other corner. *Ted obviously likes to keep everything clean and neat. He must be a Virgo.* Recalling that he also had work clothes, shoes, and gloves in his California cache, Walter escalated the priority on his planned trip. Behind the shed he found a stack of firewood he hadn't noticed previously, now estimating it to be about a cord.

Continuing his inventory of equipment and supplies, Walter returned to the cabin and checked under the kitchen and bathroom sinks. Like the storage shed, they were well stocked with cleaning tools, liquids, and powders, all thoughtfully positioned where they were most likely to be needed. *Maybe Martha Stewart has been here after all,* he chuckled to himself. Going through all the cupboards, drawers, and closets, thoroughly examining each and every item, he determined that the only 'missing' things were laundry detergent and clothespins. He added those items to his shopping list, along with extra clothes hangers and rope for a clothesline.

Having satisfied his own obsessive-compulsive tendencies for at least one day, Walter went back to the front porch and sat down gingerly in the spavined chair. The porch faced west, so there was no morning sun to warm him. After a few chilling minutes, he went back inside to slip on a light windbreaker over his sweatshirt and donned an old baseball cap that was to become an indispensable part of his daily attire, especially on bad-hair, One 'SH' days. *That's better*, he thought, as he returned to his precarious perch on the porch, but he didn't remain perched very long—or on the porch either. As he leaned back to relax into another spell of semi-meditation, one of the rear legs on the chair collapsed, pitching him over backwards onto the grass. A flash of anger rushed through him, but left quickly as he realized he wasn't hurt and he should have known such a catastrophe was imminent. Besides, the whole thing would have been hilarious if anyone had been there to watch.

However, the pratfall did have one immediate consequence: Walter decided immediately to go into KFalls and shop for new chairs, plus the several other items he had added to his list that morning. *No sense screwing around*, he told himself. *I'm better off going back now than spinning my wheels here all day.* He went inside, picked up his cell phone, and called Ted. The signal quality was weak, but the call went through. When Ted answered, Walter said he had an item to return and he would bring it over right away.

Ted was standing in the clearing in front of his house when Walter got there, and he burst into laughter when he saw the busted chair. "I hope you didn't hurt yourself trying to sit in that thing," he remarked.

Walter grinned, "Well, I did go ass-end-over-apple-cart off the front porch, but the only thing that got bruised was my dignity. If this chair was a family heirloom or had some other sentimental value, I'll reimburse you for it. Otherwise, I'll just buy a replacement."

Ted laughed some more, "I think it belonged to my great-grandfather, so I may go out behind the barn and have a good cry—but seriously, I can buy another chair for you."

"No, don't worry about it. I'm heading into town pretty soon. See you later." He turned and walked back to the cabin, changed out of his grungy clothes, and took off for KFalls. Two hours later, he was back again with two new porch chairs and a small plastic table. He poured himself a glass of lemonade and returned to the porch to arrange his new furniture. The new chairs were sturdy and comfortable, so Walter was pleased with how the day had gone. Before going to bed that evening, he made the first entry in his Journal:

Day One: Still getting the cabin organized. Another trip to town for porch chairs. Itching to really get started with what I came here for. Tomorrow, I hope.

15.

Friday, 'Day Two,' began like the previous one, except that Walter *SH*owered and *SH*ampooed *after* breakfast. He drank from the new coffee mug he had bought the day before, attempting to feel some aesthetic pleasure from its shape and heft, but this initial foray into Intentional Simplicity didn't inspire him at all. Settling into one of his new porch chairs, he told himself *it's time to get down to serious business. I've put it off as long as I can, fussing around with the cabin.*

His first task, Walter decided, was to assess where he had been: what he had done in his life, what had worked out well for him, and what had not. He began with his youth in Mendocino and quickly concluded there was nothing particularly noteworthy there, one way or the other. He had been the only child of working-class parents, a 'B+' student through middle school, improving to 'A-' as he set his sights on becoming a pilot. He played on the high school basketball team and ran middle-distance events on the track team. Not that he was all that good, but his parents and teachers had convinced him that the athletic participation would be helpful in getting admitted to the college of his choice.

In the end, it had worked out even better than anyone had expected: he was appointed to the United States Air Force Academy in Colorado Springs. The competition was considerably stiffer there, but he had worked hard at his studies and graduated in the top third of his class. Luck was also with him in subsequent Air Force training assignments, which took him through fighter planes and into larger, but less glamorous, multiengine aircraft. He had made it to Major on the fast track, thanks to winning an assignment as Flight Instructor for his unit.

It was about then that some cracks began to appear in the facade of his marriage. He had worked hard for that last promotion, putting in a great deal of extra time, which meant less time with his wife and infant daughter Katie. When Angela got pregnant again, even the additional pay as a Major didn't seem adequate: they needed a bigger house and a new car, just as they were about to have another mouth to feed. That's when he abandoned the Air Force career to take advantage of the strong demand for commercial airline pilots. Adding to his personal financial crisis, the advent of the Iraq War had put him in line to be away from home much of the time, flying into combat zones. The 'pretty pictures'—the dreams he and Angela had shared, the basis for their marriage—faded, eroding his and Angela's tolerance for each other's petty foibles.

Had it not been for the imminent birth of their son Ryan, the marriage might well have ended then, but they had both decided to tough it out, albeit for different reasons. A marriage counselor might have been able to save the day by helping them acknowledge and accept those differences, but neither of them had anything in their upbringing to suggest that approach. Angela gritted her teeth and buried herself in raising the two kids, while Walter flung himself into his new job at Alaska Airlines. With less of Angela's attention at home and more exposure to young, attractive female flight attendants staying overnight in the same hotels with cockpit crews, it seemed inevitable that Walter's affections would wander. But the fact now hitting him between the eyes was that *it hadn't been inevitable at all.* There were choices that could have been made differently—*his* choices—regardless of what Angela had said or done. His mind raced through incident after incident, scenario upon scenario that could have turned out otherwise, if ... *if*....

"*QUACK!*" The noise caught him completely by surprise, jolting him out of his concentration, jerking his attention toward the trail to Ted's house. There at the edge of the clearing was Abigail, looking right at him as if she expected a welcoming response to her greeting. At first Walter was a little irked at the interruption, but amusement overcame his irritation. Saying nothing, he slowly climbed down from his chair to sit on the edge of the porch. She watched and waited, as if reevaluating her freeze/fight/flight options, then took a few halting steps toward him. Walter smiled, hummed a little tune, and tried to emit warm friendly feelings. After a few more steps, Abigail stopped in a sunlit area and sat down. For the next ten minutes, they both just sat there, motionless, gaping at one another, waiting for the other to make the next move. Walter's patience crumbled first: he slowly rose to his feet, and as soon as he did, Abigail stood up, on full alert. He turned slowly, stepped back onto the porch, and sat down in his chair. She watched all this, appeared to consider it momentarily, then turned around to waddle slowly back to the edge of the clearing and disappear down the trail. Walter tried to regain his thoughts and return to his contemplation, but Abigail's image remained lodged front and center in his mind. After five minutes, he gave up and went inside for his afternoon nap.

16.

For Walter, Saturday, 'Day Three,' was something of a rerun of 'Day Two': wake up, make coffee, meditate while the coffee brews, drink two cups, eat breakfast, 'SH' Drill (Variation One), get dressed, and sit on the front porch. Just like the day before, Abigail showed up about twenty minutes into his 'sit,' but this time she walked directly to her spot in the sun and sat down. Walter noted her arrival and continued his life review, beginning where he had left off. *Why wasn't I aware of where things were heading? Why didn't I see I had other options? Or if I did see them, why did I make the choices I did?* As he sorted through all this in his mind, it gradually dawned on him that he had consistently put his own needs and wants first and foremost and he had rarely given much consideration to those of his wife. She had probably done the same thing, but it was impossible to discern who started it—and it really didn't matter. What did matter is they had become locked in an increasingly vicious game of tit-for-tat and neither of them had been able to break out of it—or had even wanted to—when they finally became aware of what was happening.

'What was happening'—that phrase brought back memories of his dinner with Susan just three days earlier. The contrast between that 'happening' and what had transpired in the waning days of his marriage gripped his attention. He explored it for a few minutes, eventually coming to the idea that the key to achieving such different outcomes was *awareness*—that is, observing oneself and others objectively. That did not imply emotions were to be avoided or suppressed: they too were to be observed with some level of detachment and allowed to drift away like clouds on a windy day. "*Quack!*" No sooner had the thought crossed Walter's mind than Abigail let forth a vigorous cry, almost like an exclamation point or an "Amen" shouted in church. As before, her yelp interrupted Walter's contemplation, but this time his reaction was different. *She did it again. Is she trying to tell me something? Or am I just imagining things?* He tentatively decided it was only the latter, but resolved to pay attention to it in the future—to carefully observe 'what was happening,' even with the duck!

Sunday was another rerun, with only minor variations from Saturday. Walter noticed he was settling into a routine—and so was Abigail: she appeared right on schedule and sat patiently while Walter contemplated his life. Today, however, Walter's attention was less on his former marriage and more on his relationship with Susan, whom he planned to call that evening. As he focused on what he might say to her and suggest they do when they met later in the week, the answer came quickly: "*Listen!*" In reviewing their dinner conversation, he saw that his needs, his situation, had tended to dominate—which, if not controlled, could eventually sour the relationship. He decided to draw her out about how she would spend the time if he were *not* in the picture, to get a better handle on *her* wants and needs, and explore with her how he *could* fit into that picture. This led him to resolve to be flexible in the scheduling, so as to not monopolize her time, and to make allowances for other things that might be going on in her life, that had been going on before he entered the scene. He considered the possibility they might not even meet at all—say, if something urgent came up for her, or maybe if she just wanted to do something that didn't include him.

"*Quack.*" Walter wasn't surprised by Abigail's interjection, although he couldn't have predicted when it would occur. As before, her timing was superb. *Is that just a coincidence? Or is there some kind of communication taking place here?* He'd have to give it more thought if the occurrence persisted—but not now, not today. His thoughts returned to Susan and how they might learn more about one another, preferably without spending too much money. Abigail sat quietly, and after about another half hour, she got up and waddled off—*without further comment,* Walter noted.

At 8:30 PM he got in his pickup and drove out to the main road to see what kind of cell phone signal he could get there. It was a little stronger than at the cabin, but he wanted to do better. He drove to the Haskins Road/Highway 70 intersection and checked again—it *was* better—and then on into downtown Bonanza where he parked next to the Library—still better. The air was cool and the sun had set, so most folk had gone inside. With little else to attract his attention, Walter's consciousness merged with the darkening dusk, and a sense of peace and freedom slowly took over. By nine o'clock he was quite serene, a perfect mood for calling Susan. She answered right away. "Hello. Walter?"

"Hi, Susan. How are you doing?"

"I'm doing fine, as usual. How are *you* doing? Have you become one with everything?"

Laughing, "I haven't gotten that far yet, but I'm feeling pretty mellow, sitting here in my truck in the middle of Beautiful Downtown Bonanza."

"You're not at your cabin?"

"No, I wanted to be sure I'd get a good signal on my cell phone. I'm still experimenting with what works at the cabin. I was able to call Ted the other day, but I don't think the signal is reliable. Maybe we should conduct a series of tests whereby I call you from various locations, or you call me."

"Yes, let's work out a plan when we get together. Speaking of which, I'm off all day Wednesday this week. What's on your schedule then?"

"I need to do some laundry, either in Bonanza or in KFalls, and I have a little shopping to do. That's about it." He paused, then shifted into his planned tactics. "What would you like to do?"

"The weather is supposed to be good, so I was thinking a picnic would be enjoyable—and maybe we could go for a long walk afterward."

"Sounds good. Where and when?"

"There's a park, Stevenson Park, alongside Highway 140 about midway between KFalls and Dairy. Let's meet there for lunch. I'll make some sandwiches."

"OK. Can I contribute anything?"

"Nope, this is my treat. I can't promise *cannoli* or anything like that, but I'll try to make it interesting."

"I have no doubt you can do that."

"Afterward we can walk on the OC&E Woods Line State Trail. It's an old logging railroad right-of-way that begins in Klamath Falls and ends up on the other side of Bly after winding around through the county for some 100 miles. We won't go anywhere near that far, but it won't be like a stroll through an urban park either. Although the Trail is relatively level, most of it is paved in gravel, so wear some sturdy shoes."

"I'm rarin' to go. I haven't had much exercise lately, and I need to do something about it."

"Well, there are scads of places to go and things to do in this area. The summer season is beginning, so we can both get into tiptop shape."

I don't see anything wrong with your shape just the way it is now, Walter thought, biting his tongue. "You can be my guide and teacher."

Susan ignored the suggestion. "Let's meet at 11:30. It should give you enough time to get your laundry done first. And if you like, I can join you in shopping afterward."

So she wants to spend most of the day with me! Walter caught the implication and would have jumped for joy, had he not been sitting in his truck. "You can advise me on my diet, too," he suggested.

"Well, let's see how you like what I bring for lunch."

That much wasn't too maternal for her to accept. "OK, see you Wednesday."

"Good night, Walter," she said softly. The thought of her warm, naked body lying next to his flooded his imagination. *She did it again,* he thought. *It must be intentional. I wonder if she has any idea of the effect it has on me.* He sat there basking in the glow for nearly ten minutes, then started his truck and drove slowly, almost tenderly, back to the cabin, to write it all down in his journal.

17.

Walter's Monday morning routine was the same as in the previous week, but his attitude was different. The warmth from his phone conversation the night before was still there, and he sort of floated about the cabin, his feet barely touching the floor. Nevertheless, he forced himself to 'get down to business' in his morning contemplation on the porch, again examining his former marriage, starting with his decision to forsake a career in the Air Force, a sharp change of direction that precipitated the separation and divorce. The stage had been set some years before when he failed to fully adjust to the roles and responsibilities of being a husband and, subsequently, a father. He had tried to go on living his life as he had done in his twenties, *as if it were all about him.*

"*Quack.*" He hadn't noticed Abigail's arrival, but her statement was timely—if indeed it was a statement. Walter noticed his reaction and realized that he was coming to expect and even welcome her input to his introspection. Mentally, he sent a 'thank you' in her direction before continuing. He could identify similar marital 'failings' in his former wife, especially as the relationship evolved from courtship to domestic responsibilities. Uncertainty, naiveté, and—most of all—*guilt* muddied and thereby prolonged the process of ending. Now that process was nearly complete, or so he thought. He very much wanted it to be over soon, so he could get on with the rest of his life, envisioning the 'new Walter Baker' and then growing into that image. However, there were some loose ends to be tied up: most notably, his relationships with his two children. The present impasse and the hardened positions of the parties involved couldn't be resolved quickly, but he didn't want to let it just bumble along. It then occurred to him the kids were only in their early teens and their development over the next few years would change things considerably. *He just needed to be patient.* He anticipated another utterance from Abigail at that point, but she remained silent, sitting in her usual spot in the sun. *Apparently, I get only one "quack" a day.*

On Tuesday morning Walter awoke full of anticipation, even impatience, because of his scheduled outing with Susan. In contrast with Monday, he found it difficult to concentrate on anything related to his former marriage. Instead, his thoughts kept drifting back to Susan and what kind of relationship they might have together. *I really don't know what kind of relationship she wants, and I ought to find out before I go charging off, trying to impose my ideas on her. That can't be hurried either, and attempting to do so would be counterproductive at best. Nice 'N' Easy,* he told himself, repeating it over and over like a *mantra.*

Frank Sinatra's rendition of *Nice 'N' Easy* started spinning through his mind. Although it had been written and recorded nearly a decade before Walter was born, it had always been one of his favorites, and it seemed an appropriate theme for his life now, especially as it involved Susan. He began humming the tune, mischievously trying to lure Abigail into joining in, but she just sat there. *Apparently, ducks don't swing,* he mused as the thought morphed into an image of a big band composed entirely of ducks, honking away on *anseriform* jazz favorites like *Fly Me to the Moon, Lullaby of Birdland,* and (of course) *What'll (Waddle) I Do*—which effectively scotched any hopes he had of further contemplation or meditation that morning.

In the afternoon, Walter busied himself with getting his laundry together, making out his shopping list, and taking a 45-minute walk, a warm-up for what he expected to do with Susan the next day. The sun was warm, the temperature in the mid-70s, with a light breeze, and the terrain was almost level, with only a slight uphill on the driveway return. Nevertheless he worked up a good sweat. *Darn, I'm getting soft. I should have started 'training' yesterday.*

18.

The next day being a Sabbatical Day, Walter had not turned on his alarm clock, but he awoke only a few minutes after his 'regular' 6:15 time. As on 'regular' days, he sat in silence on the sofa for 30 minutes, while the coffee brewed. He tried to pace himself through his breakfast and Three 'SH' Drill, but he was full of anticipation for his picnic with Susan. *Just like a little kid,* he thought. He was about to toss his clothes in the pickup and take off to do the laundry in Bonanza when he remembered Abigail. *What's she going to do if she comes down here and I'm not home?* He felt a small twinge of guilt, then scolded himself for being sentimental about a duck. He sat down in one of the porch chairs, intending to stay as long as half an hour to see if she showed up.

Sure enough, she waddled into the clearing about fifteen minutes later. Walter waited until she sat down in her favorite spot, then got up and moved slowly to a sitting position on the edge of the porch. She watched intently but didn't budge. He leaned forward, stretched out one hand, and called to her softly. With that, she stood up. He stood up too, took two cautious steps forward, and got down on his knees, continuing to call to her. She hesitated, then also took two steps forward. The dance continued—two 'steps' on his knees by Walter, two ducky-size steps by Abigail—until they were about four feet apart. He reached out his hand toward her, but she took two rather clumsy steps backward. He crawled forward two more steps and reached out again; she backed up again, keeping at least two feet distance between herself and his outstretched hand. Walter dropped his hands into his lap and just waited. Still standing, she regarded him with what he imagined to be puzzlement for a few minutes, then turned around, and waddled back to the path. Walter made no effort to stop her. He just watched in amusement tinged with disappointment, wondering what was going on in her mind. When she was well out of sight down the path, he got up, plodded to his truck, and drove off.

It was still early, barely past eight o'clock, and Walter was concerned the Big Springs Laundromat in Bonanza would not be open yet. When he pulled up in front of the building, he found his concern was unfounded: the business hours were 6:00 AM to 8:30 PM daily. He gathered up his clothes, taking care not to drop a few socks in the parking lot. *Got to buy myself a laundry basket,* he thought. By 9:30 he was all done. He plopped the stack of neatly folded clothes on the seat of his pickup and strolled across the street to The Branding Iron Café. Sitting at the counter, nursing a cup of coffee, he watched a few customers come and go as he tuned in on the waitress' local gossip. The discussion seemed to center on (a) the approaching summer weather and (b) events scheduled for the coming Memorial Day weekend: a parade and a picnic jointly sponsored by the local churches. *Nothing exciting,* he thought, *but maybe Susan and I could go to the picnic and hobnob with the local folk.*

Back at his cabin again, he still had time to kill before departing for Stevenson Park. He picked up his book on meditation, read a paragraph, and put it down.

It really wasn't the sort of book he wanted now. *I should get a couple more books today, maybe ask Susan to recommend something.* Next he got out his map book and studied the pages showing the park, the OC&E Trail, and the surrounding territory. That took only ten minutes. *Screw it!* he thought. *I'll just be early.* As he locked up the cabin, an idea hit him. On the way to Stevenson Park, he could stop at the feed store in Dairy and buy something for Abigail. Not that he wanted to lure her away from Ted and Lottie, but it shouldn't do any harm to give her a handful of grain occasionally, and maybe it would entice her to let him pet her. That thought gave him a further idea: he should make a comfortable place for her to sit next to him on the porch.

Ten minutes later he parked in front of *Rice Feed & Supply* and walked in. Scarcely more than a large Quonset building at the intersection of Highways 70 and 140, the store and O'Connor's Irish Pub & Diner next door were the two principal businesses in Dairy, which seemed even smaller than its alleged population of 290. A skinny young man in dusty overalls appeared from the semidarkness at the rear of the building. "Can I help you?"

Walter stammered, unsure of how to express his needs. "There's this duck ... a white Pekin duck ... that keeps wandering into my yard. It's my neighbor's, but I'd like to feed it a little. Do you have some special kind of feed for ducks?"

The man looked at Walter as if he were daft, but since Walter wasn't convulsing erratically or drooling uncontrollably, he allowed as how the question was serious. "Well, some folks use chicken mash or cracked corn, but neither of them are what ducks really need. We have a non-medicated mash—medicated is not recommended—that provides the right kind of protein for ducks. You might try it."

"OK," said Walter. "Can I buy just five or ten pounds? Or is that too little for you to bother with? I really don't need very much."

The man seemed to stifle a sneer at the mention of 'five or ten pounds,' but he smiled and replied, "Sure. I'll get it for you." He walked back into the depths of the building and returned a few minutes later with a clear plastic bag filled with mash.

"How much?" Walter asked.

"Oh, let's say five bucks."

Walter paid, stashed the bag behind the driver's seat in his pickup, and drove off toward KFalls on Highway 140. Three miles later he found Stevenson Park, a couple acres with a few deciduous trees and some picnic tables between the highway and the stream, situated at the northwest corner of the Poe Valley, a triangular alluvial plain extending to the Southeast. Walter pulled into the bare dirt parking area. There was nobody else around, so he rolled down the windows, turned off the ignition, and waited. At about 11:25, he saw Susan's green Corolla come through 'The Gap' a half-mile southwest on Highway 140. She parked next to his truck and got out—"Hi, Walter!"—welcoming him with a warm hug, not quite as passionate as the one that concluded their dinner date a week earlier, but definitely confirming the message she delivered orally: "It's good to see you again."

"It's good to see you, too," he said enthusiastically, looking directly into her hazel eyes. They held the pose for half a minute, as if waiting for a photographer to snap off three or four shots, until Susan dropped her arms and stepped back.

"Are you hungry?" she asked.

"Well, yes—although there's no reason I should be. I haven't done much of anything this past week except eat, sleep, and sit on my front porch. I didn't even walk much until yesterday, when it finally dawned on me I was getting fat and lazy—old, too."

She took another step backward and ostentatiously scanned him from head to toe and back to head again. "I dunno. You look good to me."

He laughed. "Flattery will get you anywhere, anywhere you want to go."

"I'll be careful what I wish for," she retorted as she began withdrawing a picnic basket from the rear seat of her car. She led the way to one of the tables partially shaded by a large tree, Walter following with the basket, three paces behind, captivated by the sway of her hips. Spreading a blue-and-white checkered tablecloth on the table, Susan set two places, side by side, facing the stream, with real china plates, glass goblets, stainless steel flatware, and red cotton napkins. Then she put out a platter of sandwiches, two serving dishes with pasta salad and cranberry salad, a jar of pickles, and a bag of potato chips. After making some minute adjustments to the arrangement, she turned to Walter, gestured toward the table, and said, "*Voila!*"

"Wow! If I had known this was going to be such a formal occasion, I'd have rented a tux. All that's missing is a candelabrum and some strolling violinists."

"The violinists are late," she shot back, "but they should be along in a few minutes."

"I could whistle until they get here," he offered.

"Nah. You'd just dribble your food down the front of your shirt."

They suspended the wordplay and sat down. She reached into the picnic basket to pull out a large bottle of lemonade, wrapped in a small towel to keep it cool, unscrewed the top, and poured into both goblets. "I was going to bring a bottle of Gewürztraminer until I remembered your vow of temperance. This food would be much better with wine, but I guess we'll have to wait until you decide to moderate your religious views."

"Get thee behind me, Satan," he replied in mock piety.

They giggled some more as she served the food, explaining that the cranberry salad could be added to the sandwiches—'organic, free-range' sliced turkey with lettuce and a dab of chipotle mayo on eight-grain bread—"if you want to be messy and lick your fingers." In keeping with the formality of the table setting, Walter declined the finger licking option, but the food was certainly 'finger-licking good,' as delicious as it was elegant. The conversation waned as they satisfied their hunger and gazed out at the Lost River, now flowing due south, having made a sharp 135-degree turn from its northwestward course through the Poe Valley farmlands. *Mac was right,* Walter thought, *it doesn't look like a very good trout stream. It's too slow.* His mind bounced from 'trout' to 'fly fishing' to 'religion,' two short hops in his scheme of things.

"Speaking of religion," he said as he finished his second half-sandwich, "you haven't told me much about your views in that area."

"Nor have you," she replied.

"I asked you first," he grinned.

She took another bite and chewed unhurriedly while considering where to start. "From the standpoint of organized religion, I guess you'd say I'm not very religious at all. I don't belong to any church and I never have, except for a couple years in my teens when my foster parents hauled me off to a Unity church. On the other hand, I regard myself as very *spiritual*, which is to say that I believe in some kind of God, but not necessarily the kind defined by any particular religion, at least not any kind of religion I've run into so far. Over the past twenty years, especially in the last four or five, I've read far and wide, attended lectures, and joined various study groups in an attempt to learn more about religion and to sort out where I stand, but I wouldn't say I've come up with anything I'd want to die for or go to war over. I've also done several meditation retreats in recent years, but I'm still searching. Sometimes I think that's the way it's *intended* to be, that we aren't supposed to find any solid answers, at least not in this life." She turned to look at him. "What about you?"

"Some of what you said about yourself describes where I'm at," he said. "I'm searching now, and I expect to intensify that in the coming weeks and months, but it has started only recently. My parents weren't religious at all, so I had very little contact with churches when I was growing up—maybe a funeral or wedding now and then. I didn't even learn The Lord's Prayer until I got to the Air Force Academy, where we were required to attend various kinds of religious activities to a limited extent. There were all sorts of options available, even Buddhist and Muslim, but there was also strong pressure to follow the conservative Protestant crowd unless you had arrived already firmly committed to some other path. I went along with the preferred option, but I didn't like all the preaching about what you had to do, to believe, to think, and the hell and damnation that would beset you if you didn't. I got enough power-and-control in the everyday military discipline, and I didn't want more of it from the so-called spiritual angle as well. And the last thing you said really makes sense to me, the part about never ever finding any solid answers. Mac, my fishing friend from Odell Lake, said if you find somebody claiming to have definite answers and wanting to foist them on you, you should run in the opposite direction. 'Hucksters,' he called them, and he included politicians and counselors along with the ministers."

"Yeah, he would say something like that," she agreed, "and he's probably right."

"Do you know him?" Walter asked. "Every time his name has come up, you've reacted like you do."

"I know *of* him," Susan replied, "but I wouldn't say I know him well. Our paths have crossed a few times—for example, in some of the lectures and study groups I just mentioned."

"You also mentioned meditation retreats. I'm just getting started with meditation, and it's not going very well. Of course, I really shouldn't expect it to, because all I've done is bought a book on meditation and read it—or tried to read it. However, Mac seemed to think it's a very good book, that the author is one of the best, and he also seemed willing to give me a little hand-holding on meditation in the days ahead—that and fly fishing, which is probably a form of meditation, too."

"Mac should be a great help to you," she agreed. "Everything I've learned says it's very hard to get into meditation all by yourself. You need a live teacher to guide and support you. It might also be helpful for you to sign up for a formal meditation retreat somewhere. There are a number of meditation centers in Oregon and northern California where you could do a ten-day introductory course that you could subsequently build on in your personal retreat here. If you like, I can get you some information on them."

"Yes, I would like," he said enthusiastically. He paused, then continued as if slightly embarrassed. "I did consider going to church in Bonanza last Sunday, just to see what was going one there. From all appearances, it's the same old evangelical version of Protestantism, but I keep coming back to it—maybe because it's the only thing I know and because it's so prevalent in our culture."

"Insanity has been defined as 'doing the same thing over and over, while expecting different results,'" she joked. "But seriously, I don't see any harm in going to have a look-see. Just be sure there's no exchange of bodily fluids." As he doubled up in laughter, Walter thought, *I sure like her sense of humor and the episodes of repartee we jump into from time to time. It's as good as sex, maybe even better.* Then, surprised at himself, *What the hell am I thinking? The 'old Walter' would never have entertained a notion like that!* Susan began to cover the uneaten food and return it to the picnic basket. As she stowed the dirty plates and utensils in plastic bags, she proposed, "Let's hold off on dessert until after our walk."

"OK with me," he said. "But first I want to thank you for a wonderful lunch. Everything was delicious, and beautiful too. You obviously like to have nice things in your life."

"Thank you. I'm glad you enjoyed the lunch. And yes, I do like 'nice things,' as you call them—things that are beautiful in themselves and a little out of the ordinary in the kind of attention that has gone into their making. I've never had much money to spend on fancy, expensive things, so I go out of my way to find beauty in unexpected places." She gestured toward the Lost River a few yards away. "Like this stream, for example—I enjoy walking alongside it, sampling its changing moods, and I keep coming back to it at different times of the year to see what has changed and what has remained the same."

"In the stream, or in yourself?" he asked.

His penetrating query surprised her, but it was obvious he had scored some points. She didn't try to run or hide: with the gentle directness that seemed to be her preferred style, she replied, "I guess that's why I suggested we come to this place, and why I fixed a special lunch with all the linens, and dishes, and such: to invite you to join me in that ... that..."

"Exploration?" he offered. "Adventure?"

"Yes, all that—and more—wherever it leads, as long as it goes."

"Invitation accepted, gladly and with gratitude." Acting strictly on instinct, he stepped forward and kissed her gently on the lips. It wasn't a long kiss, and it wasn't loaded with passion, but he felt her accept the energy and return it without hesitation.

Now that Walter had slipped inside her personal facade, Susan was ready, even eager, to reveal more. "It was tough when my husband was killed eighteen years ago. I had nobody else to turn to, so I threw myself into raising my daughter. The money was really tight. The jobs, the rental apartments came and went, but I maintained a positive attitude, for myself as much as for Lucy. I found that when I was grateful for what we had, no matter how meager it was, we always had enough and more soon followed. As I look back now, I can see that things got better over the years, although it was hard to notice as it was happening. I took delight in Lucy's growth and development, and it eventually dawned on me I was growing and developing too, which led me into enrolling at the community college. When Lucy left home for a career in the Army, I threw myself into the studying all the more, and that is now about to pay off with my graduation in a couple weeks."

"I plan to be there to help you celebrate," Walter interjected.

"More of my energy has gone into taking care of me in the past few years, but that only goes so far in my sense of personal satisfaction or giving meaning to my life. Consequently, I want to become some kind of counselor or social worker, and I should be ready to move into that in another three or four years. On the other hand, I really don't want to be an old maid either. The self-sacrificing spinster who tries to be 'Mother to All the World' is not the image I aspire to." She looked him squarely in the eye. "I really do want companionship. More than that, I want a loving, trusting, mutually supporting relationship with a man who is open to sharing life's adventures with joy and gratitude. Do you know of somebody like that? If you do, send him my way."

Walter scrambled for a suitable response and came up with "How do I apply for the position?"

This time Susan stepped forward. "You already have." She kissed him, a little longer and more fervently than before. As they lingered in the embrace, the thought of advancing into the next stages of foreplay crossed Walter's mind—Susan's, too—but they both realized there and now was neither the place nor the time. Somewhat awkwardly they separated and returned to the task of putting all the luncheon items back into the picnic basket.

19.

With lunch completed, Susan explained her plan for the next part of the day's activities. They would drive both their vehicles to the Klamath Community College and leave hers in the parking lot there. (Being currently enrolled at KCC, she had the requisite parking sticker.) Next they would drive in Walter's truck back to Olene, where Highway 140, the Lost River, and the OC&E Woods Line State Trail all passed through 'The Gap' between Klamath Falls and points east, and they would walk the four miles back to KCC on the State Trail. As he followed her down Highway 140 to KCC, Walter observed her driving with his pilot's critical eye. She was confident, but not aggressive, keeping her speed within a few miles-per-hour of the limit, but also anticipating cross traffic and other disruptions to traffic flow so she didn't have to jam on her brakes at the last moment. *I'd fly with her,* he thought. *She could even have the left seat if she wanted it.* She parked her Corolla in the middle of the large parking lot that seemed to be the main feature of the young but spare KCC campus and climbed into his pickup. They drove east to a point where the highway and the State Trail crossed, and started their hike.

For a while they walked slowly, hand-in-hand, as if they wanted to prolong the moments of intimacy and tenderness they had just shared. Gradually, their attention shifted to their surroundings, and they made occasional comments about the birds, flowers, river, mountains, exchanging stories of similar experiences from their childhood, stories that were unimportant in point of fact but significant in revealing who they really were, how they got to be that way, and most of all, how much in common was accumulated in their separate histories. It took them nearly two hours to cover the four miles, but the time evaporated in the warm spring sun. When they got to her car at KCC, Susan opted to drive to Nibbley's Café on Washburn Way for 'serious desserts' (her term) and she cautioned in advance that *she* was going to pick up the check—*no argument allowed!*

Seated in Nibbley's, order given to the waitress, they rested their tired feet and returned to their rambling conversation. "You haven't told me how it's going with your retreat," Susan probed. "I know you are prohibited from telling me where your cabin is, but what's it like?" Walter described the cabin and its setting, intentionally skipping details about Ted's house and its proximity as well as any mention of Abigail. He mentioned his need to find some books to support his soul-searching without distracting from it, but not too heavy—some kind of fiction, perhaps. Susan responded by suggesting Tolstoy, whose writing she had come to appreciate in the liberal-arts courses she had taken at KCC. He also told her of his developing plan to drive back to the Bay Area to retrieve the belongings he had left in storage there. That prompted Susan to disclose, "I wish I could go with you to California. I haven't seen much of San Francisco or Portland or any other major city. The plain truth is I haven't traveled much at all. Maybe you can help rectify that—be my guide and teacher—although it's too soon for that." It was the closest thing to sadness he had yet seen her express.

"It's not too soon to dream," he said, hoping to cheer her. "And in the meantime, we can revel in the various Memorial Day celebrations in the Greater Klamath Falls Metroplex."

Her smile returned. "And in a couple hours I can introduce you to another of the local wonders—but don't you have some shopping to do first?"

He reviewed his shopping list and told her he wanted to stroll through the Goodwill store, just to see if they had some odds and ends he might need at the cabin. Then he wanted to get some groceries and other household items. "And after that, how about pizza for dinner?" Susan readily agreed, and off they went. When the shopping was finished, Susan announced it was time to have another rendezvous with nature, but she refused Walter's request to tell him what or where. She drove south on Washburn Way to the part of Highway 140 known locally as the Southside Bypass, then zigzagged south-southeast again through a strip of cattle and vegetable farms. After some five miles, Walter realized they were approaching the town of Merrill and asked again, "Where are you taking us? California?"

She smiled and said, "Well, yes—but just barely." With that, she turned right across the Union Pacific tracks to head due south. After a few more miles of cattle farms, the road ended in a T-intersection where the signs said, 'State Line Road' and 'California Highway 161,' and she announced, "Here we are: California!" A broad vista stretched out before them. To the North were pastures with beef cattle and low hills beyond; to the South and West the land was low and flat, soon melding into a vast marsh. Susan drove four miles west and pulled off into a paved parking area overlooking the swamp, now a lake. "Welcome to the Lower Klamath National Wildlife Refuge," she said as she got out of the car. "Have you ever done any bird watching?" She reached into the back seat and retrieved some binoculars.

They walked over to the low wall separating the parking lot from Lower Klamath Lake, which seemed to go on forever, as if San Rafael and San Pablo were on the south shore. As the enormity of the place engulfed him, Susan briefly assumed her Welcome Center persona. "This was the first waterfowl refuge in the United States, established by President Theodore Roosevelt in 1908. It has a total area of about fifty-thousand acres. It is one of six national wildlife refuges in the Klamath Basin: three lying entirely in Oregon, two in California, and this one, which straddles the line. Together they comprise only about twenty percent of the original wetlands, the rest having been taken over by farming and development. Each year the Refuges serve as a migratory stopover for about three-quarters of the Pacific Flyway waterfowl, with peak fall populations of over one million birds. From December through February, the Klamath Basin hosts the largest concentration of bald eagles in the contiguous United States, with more than 1,000 birds, mostly in this and the Tule Lake Refuge." She gave a little end-of-speech bow, and Walter applauded. "I hope you don't mind the commercial message," she added. "I've given that *spiel* so many times it's almost spontaneous with me, like a reflex. This is one of my favorite places. It's also one of the top tourist attractions in this area and a major item of contention in local land management and, consequently, local politics."

"I doubt that you brought me here for further instruction in local politics," Walter said. "Let's go back to the part about it being one of your favorite places." He sidled up next to her, putting his arm around her waist. She leaned her head against his shoulder, and they both savored how well their bodies fitted together. They stood like that for quite a while, occasionally pointing out this or that bird among the hundreds—nay, thousands—that swam, splashed, and nestled only a few yards away. "Although I've spent a good portion of my life guiding man-made birds through the sky, I never paid much attention to real birds, and I certainly never did any serious bird watching. But now that I've landed here in a bird watching Mecca, I guess I should expand my consciousness in that direction. Do you consider yourself master birder?" he asked.

"I'm not a fanatic like many of the people who come here, but I do enjoy it. I got into it because (a) it was readily available and (b) it was cheap—especially the latter. When Lucy was growing up, I used to take her to nearby spots where we could just sit and watch the birds, the water, the mountains, and the changing light and seasons. It taught her—and me, too—that there is much more to life than watching TV or piddling around on the Internet. It's not that I'm opposed to technology, but I do take issue with the extent to which it seems to dominate our culture. It keeps us off balance."

"Ah, balance," he pounced. "You can't fly an airplane that's more than a little out of balance. That's one of the first things they teach you. They also teach that you can make the plane do all sorts of interesting things by shifting the balance— *if* you don't exceed certain limits and lose control—that is, the ability to regain the balance. In the twenty-some years I've been flying I've seen huge changes in the amount and kinds of technology that have been invented to help deal with that, but they still haven't figured out a way to completely eliminate humans. At times they've tried to force humans into weird situations and behaviors in order to adjust to the technology, but it usually hasn't worked. Then they have to go back to the drawing board and redo the technology to accommodate to the humans. So there's also a balancing act between humans and technology, too—and I agree with you that our culture tends to overload the technology side."

"Well, you seem to be stepping back from technology in a big way these days. I don't know how primitive your cabin is, but if there's no TV and no Internet, that must be quite a change for you."

"And no telephone service and no laundry," he added. "But it really hasn't been difficult for me, at least not yet. The lousy cell phone service is the biggest inconvenience. Speaking of which, I'd like to engage you in helping me figure out just how bad it is when you take me back to my truck tonight." This reminder of tasks remaining to be done, plus incipient hunger as the clock approached 7:00 PM, brought them back to practicality. They stood a few minutes longer, watching the sun sink below the horizon, then got in the car and drove back to a franchise pizza shop on the road to Olene where Walter's truck was parked. Once again they engaged in the 'Discovery Game,' learning each other's likes and dislikes: *'no'* to anchovies and Hawaiian style pizza; *'yes'* to mushrooms, green peppers, onions, black olives, pepperoni, and sausage; *'maybe a little'* to jalapeños and other 'hot' items.

The conversation returned to flying, with Susan asking what had attracted Walter to a career as a pilot. It was hard for him to put into words, but the phrase 'free as a bird' kind of said it all. "I've never been up in a plane," Susan confessed after Walter had attempted to wax poetic about the experience of flight. "I've never had the discretionary money nor the pressing need go somewhere that would cause me to make the financial sacrifice to fly. Flying is on my 'like-to list' though, and what you've just told me has moved it up several notches in priority. Do you think you'll go back to piloting someday?"

"I haven't thought much about it," Walter replied. "With the training and experience I have, I'm quite confident I could find work as a pilot just about anywhere at any time, so being away from the profession doesn't worry me. But for now and the immediate future, I don't see any need to fly, either financially or spiritually." He grinned. "On the other hand, if you were to tell me you simply *must* have the experience of flight, I'd probably find a way to get my hands on a plane and take you up."

"You know, don't you, that Kingsley Field, KFalls' airport, is home to the 173rd Fighter Wing of the Oregon Air National Guard and is a major training center for F-15 pilots," she asked.

"I didn't know all that was happening at Kingsley, although I was aware the airport is handling considerably more than a few daily commuter flights to San Francisco and Portland. In any event, I probably wouldn't fit into the program as a flight instructor because (a) I'm getting old and (b) I moved beyond fighters to larger multiengine planes a long time ago. Nevertheless, there might be some opportunities for me in a peripheral capacity—you know, a desk job."

"Uh-huh. There might also be desk job opportunities in the Air Force flight surgeon training school at Kingsley."

That got Walter's attention. "I didn't know about that activity. I guess I should look into it when I'm ready to reenter mainstream society—maybe in a few months, or a year. I might also explore opportunities with the United commuter service that flies out of Kingsley or go back to my former Alaska connections to see what's happening at Medford and Bend."

"I think there are some seven or eight-hundred people employed in aviation-related businesses at or near Kingsley, so there are probably all kinds of things for you to explore."

Walter leaned back. "It sure is great to date somebody from the local Welcome Center. I get free advice and guidance on everything from outdoor recreation—fishing and bird watching—to employment and career counseling."

"Don't forget spirituality and meditation," she countered, "and don't assume that it all will be free."

"Ah, but that may be the best part, so I'm going to keep barreling ahead—with your permission and cooperation, of course."

She gave a mock sigh. "And I have to put up with all that just to get a plane ride." For the *Nth* time that day—neither of them was keeping a count—their conversation dissolved into a cloud of giggles, followed by an interminable period of silently gazing into each other's eyes.

Walter paid the bill, and they climbed into Susan's car. Again he observed her demeanor behind the wheel: not aggressive, but not timid either—attentive and competent. *Maybe I should find a way to give her flying lessons*, he thought. At Olene they transferred his purchases to his truck, and he explained how he wanted to test his cell phone service: he would make a series of calls to her answering machine from several locations, and she would listen to the messages to assess the signal quality send him an email message with her evaluations. That understood and agreed, it was time to say 'good night.' There was no question whether a kiss would be involved, and no hesitation either. It wasn't a long, wet, passionate kiss that signaled imminent sexual engagement, but it sure wasn't perfunctory either. When it ended, both were satisfied, but both wanted more—somewhere else, some other time—soon.

20.

Before Walter went out to meditate on his front porch the next morning, he put the small plastic tub he had bought at Goodwill on the ground next to the corner of the house and filled it with fresh water. Next he folded the old beach towel from the Goodwill grab bag into an eighteen-inch square and positioned it on the porch corner behind his chair. Finally, he took a handful of duck mash from the bag he had bought in Dairy and made a thin trail of mash from the porch steps to the middle of the clearing in front of his cabin.

Sometime later, after he had begun his daily contemplation, Abigail arrived. He didn't see her coming, but suddenly there she was, snuffling the mash he had left near her 'favorite spot.' She followed his trail, cautiously, eating as she went, until she got to the porch step. There she stopped and looked around as if to say, "Now what do I do?" Walter leaned down from his chair and tried to coax her up onto the porch, to no avail. After a brief standoff, she just sat down, right where she was. Very slowly, Walter got up from his chair, went into the cabin, and returned with another handful of mash. Abigail watched him attentively but showed no sign of fright as he reached down and deposited a pinch of mash on the porch step in front of her and another on the porch above it. He used the rest of the mash to make a trail over to the folded towel. Then he sat down and waited.

Abigail eyed the porch step for a minute, stood up, walked closer, and ate the mash on the step. She looked at the next bit of mash on the porch, over at Walter, and back at the mash. The synapses in her brain seemed to connect *andante* leading to a *sforzando* wherein she flapped her wings twice and leaped onto the porch. "Bravo!" Walter whispered. "That wasn't so hard, was it?" She looked back at Walter again, to make sure he wasn't about to pounce, and followed the trail of mash to the folded towel, stopping occasionally to eat some. At that point, she was behind Walter, a little to the side, so he couldn't follow her actions without shifting his body and risk scaring her. He sat still for a couple minutes. Having heard no further movement from her, he turned his head very, very slowly. *It had worked!* Abigail was sitting on the towel as if it were her throne, admiring the view from the porch. "Good girl," Walter whispered, then returned to his contemplation as if she were not there at all.

His thoughts that morning were on flying, prompted by yesterday's discussion with Susan. *Would he ever fly again—that is, as a pilot? What difference would it make if he didn't? Would it matter?* Certainly, leaving the Air Force marked the end of a long-held dream, but he had quickly become so preoccupied with settling into his new job at Alaska Airlines he had felt no sense of loss, no remorse. Now he was giving up on the Act Two dream of being a senior captain at Alaska, but this time he had let go of the trapeze before the next one had come into view. Although yesterday's conversation with Susan had given him some hints of where the next trapeze would appear and what it might look like, he had set himself on a course of not knowing—and not even caring.

As the thought crossed Walter's mind, Abigail gave an emphatic "*Quack!*" He'd forgotten about her, so it startled him, but when he reconsidered what he had been thinking, her timing didn't surprise him at all. *She's telling me not to sweat it. This is the wilderness period—between trapezes. I'm lost between the ending of one phase of my life and the beginning of another. I've got to let it happen and not force things.* Walter paused. He'd imagined Abigail talking to him by interjecting exclamation points and question marks. *Was she was able to read his thoughts? Whoa! That's far out! Am I losing it? Or have I lost it already?* He looked over at Abigail for some kind of reinforcement—but she just sat, unmoved. *What should I expect?* he berated himself. *She's just a goddamn duck!* At that Abigail stood up, as if she had heard him. She waddled over to the porch step and jumped to the ground, wings flapping to break her fall, and continued across the clearing and down the path, not bothering to stop and eat any of the remaining mash. Walter watched her with growing wonder and amusement.

His concentration had been broken, so he didn't want to return to his meditation/contemplation. He was at a loss how pass the time, something that had happened repeatedly in the preceding week. But rather than wander aimlessly around the cabin, he recalled Susan had given him pointers to more constructive activity—namely, reading and walking. He filled his water bottle, put on his hat, and got into his truck. It took him only ten minutes to get to Bonanza. He parked in front of the Library and went in. The librarian—a buxom, graying, slightly-past-middle-age woman seated at the desk—greeted him.

"Hello. My name is Walter Baker. I recently moved into this area. I'd like to get a library card."

As she entered his name and personal information into a computer, he was relieved to learn that his P.O. box number was all the address was all she needed. "You'll receive your library card in the mail within a few days. If you'd like to check out a book or two in the meantime, I can handle it for you," she offered.

"What do you have by Tolstoy?" he asked. She masked her surprise; it was obvious she didn't get many requests of that kind. She tapped a few seconds on her computer keyboard and squinted through her bifocals at the screen. "We have several copies of his best-known work, *War and Peace*, but none of them are at this branch. The same is true for his other major novel, *Anna Karenina*. I can have either or both of them here by Saturday morning, however. We are open from 11:00 AM to 5:00 PM on Saturdays."

"Which book do you recommend? I've never read anything by Tolstoy, but a friend of mine likes his writing."

"In that case, you might want to start with an anthology containing selections from his writings." She glanced at her computer screen. "We have one called *The Portable Tolstoy*, and I can have it here by Saturday."

"Let's go with that. And while I'm here, I'd like to use one of your computers."

The librarian led Walter to one of the two tables with computers and showed him how to log in. "My name is Miriam Tucker, by the way. I apologize for not introducing myself earlier."

"Pleased to meet you, Miriam. You can expect to see me here at least once a week from now on, most likely on Tuesdays or Thursdays. I'll be in to check my email and get a book or two." He turned to the computer and logged into his email account. There were three acknowledgements of his most recent message regarding his new snail-mail address—albeit nothing from his ex-wife—and a message from Susan! *She sure didn't waste any time responding to my cell phone tests*, he thought. Susan's message indicated his phone calls from Olene,

Stevenson Park, and the Highway 70-Haskins Road intersection showed good signal strength, but the test call from his cabin was barely intelligible, with heavy static. He sent her a quick acknowledgement:

Got it. Thank you for your help and for a wonderful day yesterday. Will call you at 9:00 Sunday evening, as per our arrangement.
Love,
Walter

He hesitated momentarily before typing the salutation, but decided 'Love' is common enough and ambiguous enough that he wasn't pushing the river.

He thanked the librarian, got in his truck, and drove to the Post Office. There were two items in his box: a monthly Statement of Account from his stockbroker and a note from the postmaster to 'Call at Window' for a package too large to fit into the box. He stepped to the service window and handed the note to the clerk. The package was a large padded envelope, stuffed with a month's accumulation of mail that had been sent to his old house in California. Included was a terse handwritten note from his ex-wife:

PLEASE NOTIFY THESE IDIOTS OF YOUR CHANGE OF ADDRESS.
Angela

Noting she hadn't written 'Love' above her signature, Walter was chuckling to himself as he left the Post Office.

21.

The next day Walter put out a little more mash for Abigail. *I hope she's not still miffed at me from yesterday*, he thought. Realizing how much he was projecting his fantasies onto the duck, he laughed. *I guess I might as well have a fantasy to keep myself entertained. It's better than most TV shows nowadays.* Abigail appeared right on schedule, waddled straight to the porch, and leaped up with two flaps of her wings and a mighty push from her legs. She stopped to eat most of the mash before going to the towel and settling herself.

Satisfied that everything was copacetic with the duck, Walter settled in, too. His thoughts drifted to what Susan had said about her religious beliefs. She believed in God, but not necessarily the kind of God defined by any particular religion she had yet come across. In reviewing his own religious training, or lack thereof, Walter found himself in a similar situation. Digging deeper, he realized

89

he really hadn't explored much, because religion simply hadn't been a concern in his life. He had gone along with what had been presented to him, and that was all. It hadn't grabbed him. When the presentation stopped—when the evangelists went away—he forgot about it.

Susan, on the other hand, had apparently become more infected with the religious itch, and when the scratching of one church/doctrine/faith had failed to soothe it, she had looked elsewhere. He now found that idea appealing, so he began to identify his options. One, he could try one of the churches in Bonanza. Most likely, they would reprise the indoctrination he got at the Air Force Academy, but he wanted to make sure. *Who knows? What I'm looking for might be sitting right in front of me, and I'm just too blockheaded to realize it.* He decided to attend services at a local church later in the month. Two, when the subject of meditation had come up, both Susan and Mac had acknowledged some experience there and had offered guidance. He could follow up on that with both of them, ask them to recommend a meditation course or center or group where he might speed up his progress. *So much for my retreat into isolation and contemplation,* he thought. *If I do all that, I'll be a regular social butterfly, flitting all over the place but really going nowhere. On the other hand, if I don't explore many possibilities, if I just latch onto the first one that comes along and seems 'good enough,' it won't work out in the long run.* He lapsed into a momentary funk—confused, frustrated, even feeling a little sorry for himself.

He looked around to Abigail, as if expecting her to provide some guidance. The duck's response was to get up, flutter off the deck, and waddle out of the clearing. *Humph! A lot of help she is,* he grumbled. Then, out of the corner of his eye he noticed something on the folded towel where she had sat. He turned, looked, and *there it was: a beautiful white egg,* right in the middle of the towel. *Of course!* he thought. *I gave her a nest, and she responded just as nature told her to. But what the hell am I going to do with it?* He pondered the situation briefly, then picked up the egg—it was still warm—and, cradling it in his hands like a newborn baby, walked down the path to Ted's house. Ted was nowhere to be seen, so he went to the front door and rang the bell. He heard the sound of hurried footsteps from somewhere inside, which he surmised was Lottie running for cover, then a woman's voice, followed by heavier footsteps approaching. The door opened, and Ted said, "Hi. What's up?"

Walter handed Ted the egg. "I brought you this."

"What is it?"

"An egg."

"I can see that," said Ted. "Where did you get it?"

"Abigail laid it for me." Ted looked confused, so Walter added. "On my front porch." Ted looked more confused. "She's been coming down to my cabin every morning for the past week or so. She just sits there while I meditate." Walter wisely chose not to mention his courting of her with a little food, much less her timely comments on his ruminations. "I put an old towel down for her to sit on, and she laid an egg."

"Congratulations! You're a father, sort of," Ted said, grinning. "Why are you giving it to me?"

"She's your duck."

"Yes, but she laid the egg on the nest *you* provided for her. She obviously wanted *you* to have it."

"But she's *your* duck, and it's even *your* cabin, so it should be *your* egg."

"Well, that's *your* logic. But according to *her* logic, she lays eggs for us *here* when she wants *us* to have them. We find them in various places where she likes to nest, and Lottie uses them in her cooking."

"I understand that. But I don't want to use this egg in my cooking."

"I didn't know you're a vegetarian."

"I'm not. I just don't want to eat this egg. If I want an egg, I'll eat one I buy at the store—but not Abigail's eggs."

"Well, that's very considerate of you, but it still doesn't square with the fact that Abigail laid the egg—*this* egg—for *you*."

Walter sighed. "I accept that, and believe me, I'm grateful. But she doesn't have to know I gave it to you." He looked around nervously. "I don't think she saw me bring it down here."

Ted was beginning to have trouble keeping his mirth under control. "No, I don't think so—and I won't tell her."

"Good. Thank you for understanding."

"And thank you for the egg."

"Don't thank me. Thank Abigail," Walter said.

"If I did that, she would know."

Walter was now completely flummoxed. He backed away from the door, turned, and trudged back to his cabin, from where he was unable to hear the prolonged laughter inside Ted's house minutes later. Further contemplation was out of the question for him at that point. Without a library book to read, staying in the cabin was also intolerable. He got in his truck and drove north on Haskins Road for the first time, to see if it connected with Highway 140 as his map book said it would. It did, two miles later. Reversing his path to explore other routes, he eventually arrived at the Dairy trailhead for the OC&E State Trail. He stopped to examine the Trail surface; it was hard gravel, not paved like the part of the Trail he and Susan had walked a few days earlier, but it was satisfactory for mountain bikes as well as hiking. He wondered if Susan owned a bicycle. *No time like the present to find out*, he told himself as he got back into his truck and headed off toward the Welcome Center in KFalls. Susan was surprised to see him. "What are you doing here?" she asked as he marched up to the service counter. "Is something wrong?"

"Yes, but it's not serious," he answered, "just cabin fever, which was probably inevitable, although I didn't expect it to hit this soon, or this hard. Anyhow, I decided to explore some of the local territory and wound up at the OC&E Trail at Dairy, which gave me the idea of riding it on a bike. Do you have a bicycle, a mountain bike?"

"Yes, I do. I've ridden it on the Trail many times."

"Great! What do you say to the idea of you and me going riding on the Trail next week, whichever day we get together?"

"I'd like that."

"I thought you would. I'm going to buy myself a mountain bike—today, right now—nothing fancy, just cheap but serviceable. Any suggestions on where to shop?"

"If you're not persnickety about what you ride, you should check at the Goodwill store. If you don't find anything you like there, go across the street to Wal-Mart."

"OK. I'll tell you what I bought when we talk by phone Sunday night. We can plan our bike hike then. See ya later."

Walter started to leave, but she called him back. "Wait! Here's a brochure on the State Trail. Study it and see what appeals to you." Standing up to hand him the brochure brought her face-to-face with him, only inches away. A kiss seemed compulsory, even if not an intense one. She leaned forward; Walter picked up the signal and responded. Virginia Cox watched the whole scenario, chuckling softly as Walter bounded out the door. Susan noticed they had been observed and couldn't help blushing as she sat down and tried to appear busily involved in her work.

Walter drove first to his bank to get some cash, then to the Goodwill store about a mile to the South. Their selection was very thin, except for children's bikes, so he went across Washburn Way to Wal-Mart, where he found nearly a dozen models ranging in price from $80 to $500. Like the trained pilot he was, he inspected all of them thoroughly, undaunted by the variety and complexity of the features: suspension, gears and shifting, brakes, etc. After a half hour, he chose the 21-speed Mongoose bike with dual suspension. Then, shopping impulsively at a much quicker pace, he added some bike shorts (on sale), riding gloves (ditto), and a moderately priced helmet to his basket, but managed to restrain himself on the riding jersey, socks, shoes, and other accessories. Leaving the store as excited as a ten-year-old, wallet some $200 lighter, he could hardly wait to get back to the cabin and complete the 'Assembly Required.' However, a tinge of guilt over how much he had spent dimmed his exuberance as he drove toward Bonanza. *I didn't really have to get the shorts and gloves. I came out here into the boonies to get away from the consumer culture, so I shouldn't buy anything else until I'm sure I need it.*

22.

Saturday morning Walter breezed through his routine in high spirits, anticipating a bike ride into Bonanza to pick up the library book he had requested. Indeed, he couldn't get his mind off the bicycle as he began his daily contemplation on the front porch, and consequently he forgot to put out any mash for Abigail. She made her entrance right on time, flapped onto the porch, and marched straight over to her nest on the towel without stopping to look for food. Realizing his oversight, Walter speculated briefly about *how to apologize to a duck* but soon went back to thinking about cycling, bringing him to realize he had no way to carry the library book on the bicycle: no rack over the rear tire and no handlebar bag. In his excitement over his new purchase the day before, he hadn't thought things through to consider his possible need to transport various items such as food, books, and water, or—it occurred to him now—to ride at night or in the rain. That failure was not like him—*it was most UN-pilot-like*—nor, for that matter, was his neglect of Abigail. He corrected himself: *to be more precise, it was not like the person he had been for the past 25+ years, but he had already made the conscious decision to* stop *being that person—or persons: pilot, husband, father. Well, not* father—*he hadn't wanted to stop being a father to his two children, but that's the way it had worked out. He needed to do something about that, but first he needed to think about it—a lot—and probably talk it through with somebody: Susan? Mac? Ted? Abigail?!*

93

For Chrissake, I'm really fucked up! he scolded himself. *Here I am, not even two weeks into 'reinventing my life,' as I so grandiosely envisioned it, and I'm more confused than when I started.* He was tempted to feel sorry for himself again—*that's been happening a lot lately*—but wouldn't allow it. *I'm certainly not going to cry on Susan's shoulder. What would she think of me then?* Mac, on the other hand, had used those very words when he gave Walter his phone number and told him to stay in touch. *What did I do with that business card?* Before Walter could get up to search for the card, Abigail put in her two cents worth: a soft '*Quack*' from her nest behind his chair. He twisted in his seat and reached down to pat her. She gave a small, apprehensive shudder, but didn't move to avoid his touch. "Thank you, Abigail," he said gently.

He went into the cabin and found Mac's card among other papers from his Odell Lake stay, stuck it in his shirt pocket, and gathered up his billfold and cell phone for a trip into town. He made a detour to grab some mash for Abigail, but she was gone when he returned to the porch. Although he was sorry she hadn't stayed, he was relieved to find she hadn't laid another egg. He put the mash on the porch floor next to her nest, locked the front door, and got into his truck. *I'll take the bicycle next time.* Arriving at the Library in Bonanza, he stayed in his parked truck long enough to call the number on Mac's business card. As expected, he got Mac's answering machine. "Hello, Mac. This is Walter Baker. I hope you remember me from two weeks ago at Odell Lake. As you suggested, I'm calling to stay in touch, and if there is time in your schedule for us to meet up somewhere in the not-too-distant future, I'd like to do that. The cell phone signal is poor where I live, but if you leave a voice mail message telling me where and when I can call you, that will probably work. I'll check for messages daily. Here's the number...."

He went inside to get his library book. En route, he scanned the bulletin board for community news, noting that there was to be a Sunday afternoon community picnic at Big Springs Park and a parade at 11:00 AM on Memorial Day. *I hope Susan will be off work at least one of those days,* he thought. Before heading home, he drove around town looking for churches he might attend, quickly narrowing his choice to two. He flipped a coin to make the final selection and drove back to read the sign in front: "Sunday Worship 10:00 AM." His agenda for the rest of the day was set: he had a book to read, *The Portable Tolstoy*—some 900 pages!—and a new bicycle to ride. He alternated between the two, with time out for food and a nap. *The cabin fever was gone!*

23.

Although the next day was Sunday, Walter decided to forego church in favor of Tolstoy. After scanning the 'Editor's Introduction' in *The Portable Tolstoy*, he chose to start with 'A Confession,' which the editor said was "written 'with the left hand of Tolstoy,' the hand of the preacher and dogmatic exponent of his own form of religion." That, and the fact that Tolstoy was into 'the second half of life'—his early fifties—when he wrote it, caught Walter's interest. However, when he plunged into the essay, he found it was not easy going: the prose was 'thick'—torrents of words conveying complex, finely reasoned arguments and deep introspection—and it didn't 'read like a novel'—because it *wasn't* a novel, but a heart-rending, tear-jerking *confession*, revealing Tolstoy's thoughts of suicide and torturous climb out of despair. Yes, he chose to go on living, but at a different level, in a different world—like 'a parallel universe.' Walter could relate to the emotions, if not the details of Tolstoy's situation in late nineteenth-century Russia, but what stuck in his mind, playing over and over like a music box, was Tolstoy's statement: "One can live magnificently in this world if one knows how to work and how to love." Walter resolved to remember it and to live by it.

Sometime during the morning, Abigail came back to her nest on his porch, but Walter had become so absorbed in reading he didn't notice her arrival. When he finally emerged from his sixty-six-page séance, she got up and walked around to the other side of his chair, as if preparing to leave, then stopped and just stood there looking at him. *She seems to be waiting for something*, he thought, *like food*. He looked back at the folded towel to see if she had eaten the mash he had left there. Sure enough, it was gone, and in the middle of the towel was—*ta-dah!*—another egg! *She's training me well*, he laughed as he went inside to fetch more mash. He put it on the porch floor in front of her, and she ate it all, every last morsel, albeit at a rather relaxed pace, savoring (he imagined) the treat. Then she hopped off the porch and waddled down the path to Ted's house. Walter waited until she had been gone ten minutes lest she catch him in the act of rejecting her gift. As before, he rang Ted's doorbell and allowed Lottie time to hide before Ted opened the door. "She did it again," he said, handing Ted the egg.

95

"I guess she likes you," Ted said, smiling. "She's becoming rather prolific these days. As I said before, we really don't mind sharing this abundance with you if you decide to make an omelet out of what she sends your way."

"Oh, no, I couldn't do that," Walter protested. "It would be like devouring one of her young. I guess I might eat something that *contains* one of her eggs in unidentifiable form—like cake or muffins—but my cooking skills haven't advanced to that level. So I'll just keep bringing *my* eggs—which I still regard as really *your* eggs—over to you—that is, if I'm not disturbing your privacy."

"No problem. The other egg you brought captured Lottie's interest, so perhaps the continuing saga will give her something to think about, something positive instead of all her fantasies and phobias."

"I'll be happy to contribute to that," Walter said. "See you later." This time, instead of trudging dejectedly back to his cabin, there was a bounce in his step, and he whistled a little tune as he strode down the path.

Sunday evening was the time for his weekly call to Susan to schedule their weekly get-together. He had intended to ride his bike down to Highway 70 where the cell phone signal was better, but it began raining late afternoon, so he drove to Stevenson Park instead. He was more than a half-hour early, partly in anticipation and partly because he just wanted to watch the sunset. When he turned on his cell phone, he found he had a voice message from Mac: he was indeed happy to hear from Walter and looked forward to talking with him and doing a little fly fishing as well, suggesting they meet Tuesday morning. Walter called the cell phone number in the message and got an immediate answer. They agreed to meet at 8:00 AM in a small parking area at the southwest corner of Route 140 and Hildebrand Road, near the Dairy trailhead. All Walter needed to do was show up in pants and shoes suitable for wading in water up to his knees.

That settled, it was still ten minutes before his scheduled time to call Susan, but Walter called anyhow. Susan seemed out of breath when she answered, saying she had been working outside. Yes, she again had Wednesday off, but she asked to put off bicycling for at least a week. "When I got out my bike to clean it up, I discovered the gear shifter wasn't working properly. I took it to the bike shop, but they couldn't promise it would be repaired by Wednesday because they had to order some parts." Walter suggested they meet for lunch at Nibbley's—it was his turn to buy—and then take a walk somewhere. He also asked her about joining him at the Memorial Day festivities in Bonanza. "I'd like that. I'll check with Virginia tomorrow and let you know Wednesday."

She seemed distracted and distant. Walter wondered if something was troubling her but decided not to pry. Rather than prolong the conversation with small talk, he said, "You sound very tired. I should let you go so you can get some rest."

"Yes, I am bushed," she admitted. "I spent most of the day at a volunteer cleanup project at a local community park, and I'm all dirty, sore, and bug-bitten. I'm probably not fit company to be around this evening." She paused, then shifted into a softer, warmer tone of voice. "What I'd really like more than anything else right now is to be sitting in a lovely hot tub with a tall glass of iced lemonade, and you beside me to massage away my aches and pains."

"... and kiss it all to make it well," he finished the sentence for her. She giggled and gave out that special little purr he had noticed after each time they kissed. "If you tell me where you live, I'll be right over," he offered.

"Oh, no, no, no! There's no hot tub here, and besides the place is a total mess. I'm not ready for that yet." Now there was a hint of panic in her voice, feeding Walter's growing perplexity, but his intuition told him to let it pass.

"Well, then, good night, Susan, and sweet dreams," he said softly.

"Good night, Walter. See you Wednesday."

24.

Walter's meditation the next morning was troubled. Although his phone call to Susan the night before had ended on a romantic note, he had a nagging feeling that she had not leveled with him. He tried to look at it from her point of view, but the only thing he could come up with was that telling him what was bothering her was more uncomfortable for her than *not* sharing it, and she was probably unhappy over that as well, further compounding her misery. Having created this confusing little knot in his own imagination, Walter was not about to let it spawn a funk all of his own. *Susan is a mature adult,* he reasoned, *and she is quite capable of dealing with life's ups and downs all by herself, just as she has done for many years. Besides, we've only known each other for 2-1/2 weeks, so I can't expect her to tell me everything and to trust me completely.*

Putting himself under the microscope, he wondered what things about himself he was still unwilling to share with her. Sex was still off-limits—more his doing than hers. He also hadn't shared much about his financial situation, although he had told her enough to make some reasonable inferences. She, on the other hand, had been fairly candid about how limited her resources were, and she had told him a good bit about her daughter, whereas he had revealed next to nothing about his kids and his relationship with them. *Sex, money, and kids*—the three principal issues in marriage, a counselor had once told him—*and we haven't gone past square one on any of them! The prospects for a long and happy relationship don't look so good. I guess I'd better get to work on myself.*

"*Quack.*" Abigail added her endorsement to his last sentiment. He looked around at her and reached back to give her a loving pat on the back, but he didn't rush off to get her some mash. *If I do that, she'll think I want her to lay another egg for me. Better that I don't give her any more food until she's gotten off the nest, provided she hasn't laid an egg anyhow.* Walter began to consider how complex even his relationship with the duck had become, shaking his head in mild disgust with himself as he concluded he wasn't managing that relationship very well either. *Ted, on the other hand, seems to be loosening up and warming up,* he mused. *The whole thing with Abigail's eggs has revealed his sense of humor and general sensitivity. His wife obviously has serious emotional problems, and he seems committed to looking out for her welfare. That easily explains his protective, somewhat secretive, behavior,* he concluded.

Then there's Mac, another strange bird. In a way, he's every bit as secretive about himself as Ted, but he's warmer, much more trusting of other people, even near-strangers like me, so he comes across as being very 'open.' Because he readily trusts other people, they are quickly drawn into trusting him, too—at least it appears that way. It's possible he's really a totally corrupt, scheming con man, but I don't think so. Walter went on to sorting out his agenda for Tuesday's meeting with Mac. *I want to ask him to point me at a meditation course somewhere. Then I may want to talk with him about my relationships with Susan and/or Ted—but I sure as hell don't want to mention anything about Abigail. That's an awful lot to jam into a few hours of fishing, especially fly fishing, which is supposed to be a spiritual experience. All that talk could even counteract the benefits of fishing altogether.*

After thrashing around in the thicket of these multiple issues and options for half an hour, Walter concluded that his imminent discussion with Mac should focus on what drove him to make the telephone call two days ago: (a) his wilderness retreat was not going as planned; (b) clarity about his past, present, and future life had not dawned on him like the morning sun; (c) his attempts at meditation were often as chaotic as what was going on in his mind right now; and

(d) if anything, he was more confused than ever. Somewhat dejectedly, Walter got up from his chair and went into the cabin to read further in *The Portable Tolstoy*, ignoring the loyal Abigail dutifully seated on her nest. When he didn't return with a handful of mash after a few minutes, she got up, jumped off the porch, and waddled away through the thick drizzle. She left no egg.

25.

Walter's Tuesday morning schedule was a little tight, with scarcely more than hour from the alarm chirp until he had to meet Mac. He put the coffee on to brew while he did his daily meditation on the sofa, but he skipped building a fire in the wood stove. It would make for a chilly exit from the shower half-an-hour later, but he had endured worse in the military. Although he was a few minutes early pulling into the parking area at Dairy, Mac was already there, sipping coffee in the cab of a three-year-old Ford Ranger 4x4, SuperCab 2DR, bright red. Walter rolled down his window and hollered, "Do you want me to drive?"

"Nah. I've got all the stuff loaded into the back of this truck. Just park, and we can roll."

Walter got in Mac's truck and buckled up. Mac handed him a paper cup of hot coffee. "I couldn't remember whether you used cream and sugar, so I played it safe and left it out."

"This is fine. Hot, black, and strong."

Mac swung onto Highway 140, heading east. "We're going to my favorite fishing spot in all the world—well, at least in all of Klamath County. It's the Sprague River, just outside of Bly. Ever been to Bly?" he asked.

"Nope, but I sort of know where it is."

"It's got an interesting history in a couple respects." Mac was primed to give a tutorial, but not on fishing. "On May 5, 1945, a minister from the Christian and Missionary Alliance Church in Bly took his pregnant wife and five Sunday school children on a picnic and fishing trip. The logging road they followed was blocked, so they stopped next to Leonard Creek, eight miles east of town, near Gearhart Mountain. While the minister was unloading the food, he heard one of the children say, 'Look what I found!' His wife and the children ran to see what it was, and there was an explosion, killing all six of them instantly. The children had found the unexploded remains of a Japanese 'balloon-bomb,' one of approximately 9,000 launched from Japan between November 1944 and April 1945. Each consisted of a hydrogen-filled balloon about 33 feet in diameter and five explosive devices: four incendiaries and one high-explosive antipersonnel type."

Mac went on to explain that the balloons drifted across the Pacific to North America via the jet stream in about three days. As many as 1,000 balloons may have reached the US and Canada, but the Royal Canadian Air Force sent up fighters to shoot most of them down over the ocean. "There were only 285 confirmed balloon-bomb sightings on the West Coast, although a few were found at various points all over the Midwest and South, as far as Michigan and Texas. Except for the six deaths at Bly they caused only minor damage and no injuries. Despite that, the bombs had a potential psychological effect on the American people, so the Office of Censorship, an emergency wartime agency set up right after the Pearl Harbor attack, asked newspapers and radio stations not to mention balloon-bomb incidents. Perhaps as a result, the Japanese learned of only one bomb's landing in Wyoming and failing to explode, and they stopped the launches after less than six months, thinking they were useless. In 1950 the Weyerhaeuser Corporation, which owned the land where the bomb was found, erected a monument with a bronze plaque bearing the names and ages of the explosion victims. The minister and his wife were Archie and Elsie Mitchell, so it's called the Mitchell Monument."

"Wow, that's quite a history lesson. Thank you," said Walter.

"Don't mention it," Mac replied. "There's more where that came from. I'm just warming up." Walter began to wonder if he should be taking notes. "My second history lesson begins more recently, in 1999. James Ujaama, a Muslim convert who was born in Denver, came down from Seattle with a Lebanese buddy named Osman and tried to set up a *jihad* training center on the Frisco Ranch, a 158-acre sheep ranch just outside Bly, where the terrain reminded them of Afghanistan, so they said. Ujaama convinced Abu Hamza al-Masri, a major terrorist leader living in London, to send over a couple of his henchmen to check it out, but they were very disappointed. They didn't find a big bunch of eager recruits waiting to be trained in combat techniques and how to make bombs and poisons—just Ujaama, a mentally impaired 18-year-old, and a couple women who were more interested in raising and canning vegetables than in terrorism. When the guys from London asked for guns, they were given one pistol and a .22-caliber rifle. Nevertheless, they ran some training sessions for a few Muslims who came down from Seattle, and when that didn't arouse much enthusiasm, they went up to Seattle to train Muslims who didn't want to move to Bly. That didn't work out either, so they eventually packed their bags and went home."

"I never heard anything about that," Walter protested mildly.

"No, Muslim terrorism wasn't on the radar screen of most Americans in those days," Mac explained, "but the September 11 incident changed all that. US law enforcement officials became interested in what had gone on at Frisco Ranch and obtained indictments against Ujaama, Osman, Abu Hamza, and the two trainers, Kassir and Aswat. Ujaama was arrested in 2002 and convicted in 2007, but he got off easy by agreeing to testify against the others, especially the alleged kingpin, Abu Hamza. Kassir was convicted in 2009 and is now serving a life sentence, and Osman did time on a state weapons charge. The other two are still fighting extradition to the US, but they've been in and out of prisons in England and Sweden in the meantime."

"That's bizarre!" exclaimed Walter.

"Yes, and what makes it almost comical is that the whole thing was started as a 'hustle' by Ujaama. In his courtroom testimony, he repeatedly admitted to having lied to his Muslim brothers to elicit their participation in his venture, figuring if he got Abu Hamza's endorsement, people would come running to Bly for *jihad* training."

"So that's the end of it? Everything has returned to peace and love in Bly?" Walter asked.

"It seems that way, but we can't be sure. People around here are kinda close-mouthed about everything. I'm certainly not aware of any terrorist training activity. If I were and I told you about it, I'd have to kill you." He laughed and Walter joined in, albeit nervously.

As he thought more about what he'd just heard, Walter's grin faded. *Why hadn't Susan mentioned anything about all this? Yes, the 'balloon-bomb' thing was before her time and was irrelevant to current world affairs, but the Muslim training camp was certainly something she would have known about and been concerned about. The 'weirdo' epithet definitely applied! Why hadn't she told him? Was she hiding something, something more sinister than she had let on in Sunday night's phone conversation?* Walter's planned agenda for discussion with Mac was now completely trashed. His head was spinning, propelled mostly by an insidious sense of having been betrayed by Susan. A clot of anger boiled up briefly, and he fought to put it down, to calm his mind, to find a charitable explanation for her conduct. In a few brief moments of clarity, he realized how much he wanted to trust her and, yes, to love her—and to have her trust and love him in return. He knew all too well such hopes could sabotage his judgment, but hope was the main thing that had kept him going throughout the past six months.

He was roused out of his funk when Mac turned off Highway 140 onto a small gravel road some six miles west of Bly and drove through about fifty yards of scrub and sagebrush to a small parking area. There, right in front of them, was the OC&E State Trail and just beyond it, the Sprague River. "Here we are," Mac announced as he opened his door and stepped down. He lifted the tonneau cover over the truck bed and pulled out two fishing rods, a dip net, and a tackle box. Handing the net and one rod to Walter, he closed the cover and strode off toward the river with Walter tagging along behind, like the little brother he seemed to have become. At the riverbank, Mac laid his rod and tackle box on the grass and sat down next to them, nodding his head to indicate that Walter should do likewise.

Yet another tutorial? Walter thought. *Why is Mac telling me all this? What does it have to do with me?* He was relieved to learn that the topic was now fishing, which is one of the reasons why he had requested this time with Mac.

Mac, however, was on a roll, and nothing Walter could have said would have stopped him from launching into Tutorial Number Three. "The fishing we did at Odell Lake involved lots of technology: boat and motor, sonar fish finder and downrigger, rods and reels, and lines, leaders, and lures." Walter smiled at the alliteration. *At least, he's trying to make it entertaining.* "The whole idea is for the fisherman to get a fish on every cast. Believe me, some of the big-city executive types, even politicians from Salem and doctors from Bend *expect* to get a fish, a good-sized fish, on every cast, and they become indignant if they fail to do so. If I didn't enjoy fishing and being out on the lake so much, I wouldn't put up the abuse I get. However, it gives me a chance to observe bare naked humanity without the thousand-dollar suits, designer neckties, Gucci shoes, and impressive job titles on their business cards." He leaned over toward Walter as if disclosing a deep, dark secret. "The most egotistical of them never fail to give me their business card, first thing." Walter remembered that the business card Mac had given him said simply, "Mac McCarter, Fishing Guide," and he thanked the stars it hadn't occurred to him to give Mac his Alaska Airlines card.

"In fly fishing, on the other hand," Mac continued, "the object is not so much to catch fish as to *commune* with them, to visit them in their native habitat, and to play a game of hide-and-seek with them. Just being there is enough reward for the fisherman, and that's the paradox: although you're not really 'trying' to catch fish, you will of course catch them if you abide by the rules of the game. Standing at the edge of a river or in the middle of it, you simply listen to the sounds of the wind and the water, which requires you to develop a heightened sensitivity, to drop your internal dialogue in order to be more in tune with things 'just as they are.' That's also the object of Zen, and that's why fly fishing has been likened to Zen, and *vice versa*. Both of them help us to understand two fundamental truths we otherwise might not see: the *interdependence* of all things, and the *impermanence* of all things. Those are at the heart of the Buddha's teaching and also the teachings of numerous saints of all religions."

As Mac paused, Walter seized the opportunity to bring up one of the items on *his* agenda. "I'm glad you mentioned Zen. It reminded me I'd like you to recommend a teacher, a course, a place where I can go for a week or two to study meditation. It doesn't have to be Zen *per se*, but it does have to be geared toward the novice, because I'm most definitely a beginner. And if it's not too far away and not too expensive, so much the better."

"I can do that, and gladly," Mac responded. "When I get home today, I'll rummage around on the Internet and gather information on two or three situations that should work for you. Be sure to give me your email address so I can send it to you." He stopped to recollect his thoughts. "Where was I? Oh, yes— Zen. We could just as well be meditating in a temple somewhere, with our butts getting sore and our legs aching from sitting a long time in an unnatural position, but today we're going to use fly fishing. All you have to do is apply whatever you've already learned about meditation. Focus your attention on the water and your line and leader, and whenever other thoughts come up—as they most assuredly will— let them drop away like you do in sitting meditation. Eventually, with practice, fly fishing will become a *spiritual* experience, and you won't give a damn about how many fish you catch or how big they are."

Great! Let's do it! thought Walter, but alas, Mac still wasn't finished. "Nevertheless, to maintain the pretense we are here to catch fish, let me tell you a little about the tools and techniques. In the fly fishing game, we tempt the fish with a hook—barbless, for catch-and-release—that has been disguised to resemble something a fish would naturally eat: namely, an insect. If the fish is really hungry, it will strike at just about anything, and you could probably get away with baiting the hook with bubble gum, but most times, the fish is more discerning. That's where the *art* comes in, that's what makes this a sport—because the odds are balanced, or even tilted toward the fish, as compared with what we did with all that technology at Odell Lake."

Walter's interest stirred a little. It seemed that Mac was nearing the end of his harangue. "In general, the bigger fish like to hang out near the bottom, especially in relatively quiet pools like we're looking at here, so our approach is to insinuate the bait—the lure, the fly—into their awareness as unobtrusively as possible. Therefore, we don't cast directly at them, because it would frighten them away, or at least warn them we're present and thus invoke their 'freeze' response. Instead, we cast in such a way that the fly will gradually drift toward them, and we fiddle with the line in such a way it causes the fly to resemble the action of a real live insect, but *not* in such a way that the line itself tips off the fish to the deception taking place. Now I doubt that you know 'diddly-squat' about insect behavior—I sure as hell don't—so you have to make it up as you go along. The main point is if the fish isn't really hungry or isn't sure it's confronted with a good scrumptious insect, it won't charge at the fly and go 'kerchomp,' it will just softly nibble at it. You've got to be sensitive enough to detect that and jerk your rod at just the right time so as to lodge the hook in the fish's mouth. That's where the Zen awareness and focus come in. It was there in the fishing we did at Odell Lake too, but nowhere near as subtle." At that point, Mac opened the tackle box, selected a fly and leader, attached them to Walter's line, and did the same for his own line. "Any questions?" he asked.

Walter was afraid to ask anything for fear that it would send Mac into another ten minutes of 'instruction.' He shook his head and said, "Nope."

"Then let's do it," Mac said with gusto. He stood up, walked over to the edge of the Sprague River, and made his cast, while Walter followed to a spot about twenty feet farther upstream and followed suit. The next hour was uneventful: cast, let it drift, reel it in a little, let it drift some more, reel it in all the way, cast again, etc. *Like watching paint dry*, Walter thought, but he worked on maintaining his concentration on himself, the rod, the line, the fly, and the water. Gradually, the chitchat of other thoughts receded and his awareness seemed to expand to include more of the surroundings: the riverbanks, the scrub trees and sagebrush, the sky, passing clouds, the sun. From time to time, Mac would change the fly on his or Walter's line—a different shape, a different color—but neither of them got any bites or even a nibble they could discern.

Finally Mac suggested they move to another spot farther downstream, where the river was shallower and the water was running faster. Another hour passed without success, at least in terms of catching fish, although Walter was enjoying the sound of the tumbling water. They moved again, another hundred yards to a place where the river began to twist and turn like a wounded dragon as it cascaded over larger rocks. After some minutes there, they *saw* a fish—a rainbow, Mac said—leap twice as it threaded its way upstream. They cast their lines in what they hoped would be its path, and both felt what they thought were nibbles, enough to cause them to jerk their rods upward to engage the hooks—but they caught nothing. After another twenty minutes, Mac reeled in his line and said, "I think that's all the excitement we're going to get this morning."

They stowed their gear in the back of the pickup and headed eastward to Bly. Mac drove slowly all the way through town so Walter could see the sights: the Ranger Station, the Post Office, the Chevron station and convenience store, a couple antique shops, a bar, a Senior Center (apparently defunct). "Not much to write home about," was Walter's comment as they reached the eastern edge of town.

"About what you'd expect for a town of 500 in a sparsely populated area like this," Mac concurred. He turned around and drove back to the best looking eatery, The Coyote Café, just past the Ranger Station, on the west side of Bly. As they walked through the split-rail-fenced picnic area in front of the Café, Mac stopped to scan the half-dozen vehicles in the parking lot, all well-worn pickups of a not-too-recent vintage. "This is a very different scene from a trout stream, but I suggest you dial up your awareness all the same," he said quietly. Inside, Mac guided Walter to a rear table where they could both see all the activity. The table talk had come to an abrupt halt as they entered, and all eyes had followed them until they sat down. Without looking at a menu, Mac ordered "a plate of 'Coyote Howlers' and two beers" in a slightly-louder-than-necessary voice, hoping to establish his credentials as 'a local' even though nobody knew his name. It worked. The collective mood in the room seemed to relax and conversations slowly resumed. Walter settled into his chair and surveyed the patrons: all men, probably WASPs, at least his age, their attire suggesting they were sheep ranchers.

The beer and 'Howlers'—stuffed jalapeños—arrived quickly. Without being obvious about it as they slowly sipped their drinks and picked at the appetizers, Mac and Walter strained to listen. The chatter meandered from the weather to fishing to community events planned for the approaching holiday weekend—all of it detached and 'safe' for the ears of strangers. Having nursed their appetizers as long as they could, Mac and Walter ordered hamburger platters and another round of beer, and then returned to their surveillance. Ever so gradually, they began to catch things revealing personal attitudes, feelings, and activities: first the state of the local and national economy, next crime and war, and finally politics. Governmental incompetence and corruption were common themes;

individualism, libertarianism, and even insurrection were the consensus remedies; but everybody stopped short of openly advocating any kind of collective action.

Between bites of food, Mac occasionally exchanged brief comments with two men at an adjacent table, and after they had warmed to the point of initiating exchanges with him, he dared to ask a dangerous question: "What ever became of those Muslim guys that lived out at Frisco Ranch about fifteen years ago?" Walter tensed in anticipation of a hostile reaction throughout the Café, but nobody beyond the next table seemed to have heard—or if they did, they didn't care. The initial reply told Mac nothing he didn't already know. Indeed, he had shared it with Walter earlier that morning, but Mac pretended like it was 'new news' to him, nodding appreciatively. Then he asked an even more dangerous question: "I gather all the Muslims have gone back to Afghanistan, and there's nothing but peace and quiet at the Ranch these days?" The two men at the next table looked at each other as if to ask how much they should reveal, but again no alarm bells went off. One turned back to Mac and said something to the effect that the inference about 'peace and quiet' was not correct. The other man chimed in, adding that a few 'furriners' had been seen in and around Bly in the past year and they appeared to be living at the Ranch. Now the first man was drawn in, eager to outdo his colleague in providing juicy tidbits: Yes, Bly residents had occasionally heard gunfire—some said automatic weapon fire—coming from the Ranch, and a couple folk had claimed to hear explosions. His partner provided the *pièce de résistance:* local and federal law enforcement officials seemed to be oblivious to all this, but—never fear!—the Jefferson State Militia had been alerted and was prepared to mobilize if the situation became threatening.

Mac acknowledged these nuggets of information with a look and statement of gratitude, "That's good to know." He leaned back in his chair, signaling he had no need to pry further. The two men seemed pleased with Mac's adulation and got up to leave. Mac gave them one more smile and 'thank you' while Walter paid the bill. Once out of earshot in the pickup Walter exclaimed. "I had no idea we were going to do *that* kind of fishing today! We may not have caught anything in the Sprague River, but what we got in the Coyote Café sure made the trip worthwhile."

Mac grinned. "Don't write off your Sprague River experience as a total loss either. This was only the first lesson in fly fishing, and it will take several more for me to teach you everything you should know before you go out on your own. Although we didn't catch any fish today, you did seem to settle into the spirit of the occasion quite well. Do you think it will help your meditation practice at all?"

"Oh, yes. I'll know better how much it helped once I sit at my cabin again, but I'm sure it will make a difference." He put on his own look of gratitude. "Thank you very much."

"Don't mention it." Changing the subject, Mac said, "When you called the other night, you sounded like you had some other things on your mind that you wanted to talk over."

"That's right." Walter paused to consider where to begin. "My first week of wilderness retreat—or whatever you want to call it—went mostly according to plan. I was able to settle into a routine in the cabin and discipline myself to sitting for an hour, two or three times a day, either thinking about where I am in life and where I want to go, or trying to empty my mind entirely. It went fairly well, although I realize I have a lot to work through and it will take weeks or months. As the second week began, however, everything seemed to come unglued. I couldn't concentrate. I was unable to put aside distracting thoughts and activities. I ran around doing errands and other things that could just as well have waited until my planned one-day-per-week 'sabbatical.' The more I allowed myself to be distracted, the more additional distractions arose and the more distracted I got. So that's when I made the 'Mayday' call to you."

Mac laughed. "I've got some 'good news' and some 'bad news,' and they are both the same thing: what's happening with you is typical, and it will keep on happening for a while. There's no magic pill or ritual I can give you to make it go away. You've just got to slog through it as best you can. Of course, you can get some help from your friends—me, your lady friend, maybe some other folk you've run into—mostly in the form of listening and empathy. And just when you think you've gotten past it, it will probably happen some more."

"Oh, great," Walter said dejectedly, "that's what I thought you'd say."

"That's to your credit. The only advice I have to offer is (a) keep on keeping on, and (b) don't be too hard on yourself. For what it's worth, the Klamath County Mental Health Department is sponsoring some lectures that may give you some insights into what you're going through. They'll be held in various communities throughout the county, beginning next month. Keep checking the bulletin boards at the Library and the Community Center for notice of dates, times, and places."

"OK." Walter lapsed into silence.

After a couple minutes, Mac asked, "That's it? There's nothing else on your mind? Everything is going swimmingly with your lady friend?"

"Susan and I have had some wonderful moments together in the last two weeks. I can't ask for better. There may be a couple clouds looming on the horizon, but I'll work through it. It's probably only my imagination, and I really don't want to talk about it now."

"OK. That's your choice."

Now it was Walter's turn to change the subject. "I'm planning on going down to California next week to get my stuff out of storage and bring it up here. I'll try to contact my kids while I'm there, but I'm not optimistic I'll get a good reception. I'm kinda dreading the rejection, but I know I've got to keep trying."

"Yes, it's important to keep showing that you want to maintain some kind of relationship with them, for your benefit as well as theirs. They will come around eventually if you persist—but not too hard. 'Time heals all wounds,' as they say."

"... and wounds all heels," Walter joked.

They rode in silence the rest of the way back to where Walter's truck was parked. Pulling up alongside it, Mac said, "Let's plan on another fly fishing lesson after you get back from California. In the meantime, I'll send you an email about meditation opportunities, and if you have questions about any of that, give me a call."

"OK. Thanks for spending the time with me and for all the helpful advice."

"No problem. It's what I do." He reached over and shook Walter's hand. "Be sure to eat right and get out into nature every day. Be gentle with yourself and all God's creatures."

"Even the ducks," Walter quipped.

"*Especially* the ducks," Mac shot back.

Ducks, specifically Abigail, were on Walter's mind as he returned to his cabin. He sat in his porch chair and surveyed the scene: no sign of Abigail, no indication she had been there. *Not surprising,* he thought, *considering my absence. I wonder what she does when she comes here and finds me missing. Where does she go, what does she do, when she's not here with me?* None of these considerations were important in the grander scheme of things, he knew, but they served to center him, to help bring his mind back to the agenda for the rest of the day. The morning with Mac had been very good because it had strengthened their friendship. What he had learned about Bly, past and present, had been a little disturbing, but useful information nevertheless. What he had learned about fly fishing was what he had hoped for: (a) it reinforced his efforts to establish a meditation practice; (b) it took him out into nature; and (c) most important, he enjoyed it regardless of whether he caught any fish.

All that should have given Walter a feeling of well-being, but that was not what he felt. He knew what the problem was. He was *not* looking forward to his day with Susan; he seemed to be actually *dreading* it. He also knew why. He felt a looming confrontation with her over *openness* and *honesty*. She seemed to be hiding something in not disclosing to him where she lived, and she hadn't told him anything about the Muslims in Bly, although she surely had at least some knowledge of it.

Walter could feel the emotion bubbling up inside himself. Then he realized that Abigail was standing right in front of him and that his emotions had made him oblivious to her approach. It was like a whack upside his head. *If he hadn't been able to notice Abigail, how the hell could he look objectively at his emotions?* Mentally, he took another step back and looked at himself. *Is this Major Walter Baker, the ace jet jockey with ice water in his veins and a sure hand on the controls as his aircraft streaks along at twice the speed of sound? Most certainly not! What has become of him?*

Abigail turned around, jumped off the porch, and started walking away. Walter called to her, but she ignored him, not that she had ever responded to his words. *I think she's telling me I'm not fit company right now. I'd better get my poop in a group before tomorrow if I don't want to screw things up with Susan.* He got out his bicycle and rode down to Haskins Road, then north to Wu Road, west and south to Highway 140, east to Haskins again, and north to home—about a five mile loop. The exertion sweated the emotion out of him: he was tired but calm when he got back. *Time for an afternoon nap.*

26.

Walter's mood hadn't improved by the time he awoke the next morning. He still had a nagging feeling that there was a lot Susan wasn't telling him. Ted's secrecy was difficult enough to deal with, *but why Susan?* Mac seemed to be the only person he knew who was completely open and honest—and yet when Walter gave it some critical thought, he had to admit that even Mac hadn't shared everything about his past. So whom could Walter trust? The answer came slowly, grudgingly: *himself.* Put another way, if he couldn't trust himself—his head *and* his heart—he was really in deep tapioca. *'As soon as you trust yourself, you will know how to live'*—that aphorism was on a poster Walter had seen somewhere a long time ago. It didn't matter where or when or who said it, the memory had come to him now, when he needed it.

He went through his morning routine in a dull gray mood—*battleship gray*, he would have said. There was a chip on his shoulder, a small chip, but he saw no reason to take it off. Maybe it was there to warn him against becoming too deeply involved, too quickly. Abigail was a no-show, as if she too were expressing caution or even disapproval. For a few unpleasant moments, Walter entertained the idea of calling Susan and canceling out on the day's get-together, but he reasoned it would simply make matters worse: it wouldn't cure his funk and it might alienate Susan. Almost reluctantly, he got in his truck and drove into KFalls. He found Susan standing in the customer-waiting area in Nibbley's, and rather than kiss her, he dodged around some other patrons to signal the hostess he and Susan were a party of two. The hostess responded as Walter would have programmed it: she immediately led them to a booth—not a table, so Walter didn't have to hold Susan's chair—and lingered to take their beverage order. When she left, Walter buried his attention in the menu. When he finally looked up, he could see the hurt in Susan's eyes.

"Hello," she said timidly. "Are you OK?"

He didn't want to start things off by soiling her with his bad mood, but he knew he couldn't hide. "I'm sorry," he said. "I seem to be having a bad day. I shouldn't take it out on you."

"It's all right. I was having a bad day when you called Sunday night, and you lifted me out of it. It's my turn to return the favor. Or am I the problem? Did I say something wrong?"

Whoosh! She can sure go right to the heart of things. It's not what she said as much as what she didn't *say.* "No, it's not you," he said, looking back down at the menu.

She sensed it was a lie, but a *white* lie. *Whatever it is, he doesn't want to discuss it here and now. Let's drop it.* "Tell me about your fly fishing expedition with Mac," she said, seeking a 'safe' spot where they might connect.

Walter felt a little relief, allowing him to smile, albeit weakly. "We didn't catch anything, but I would say it was successful nevertheless in that I enjoyed it very much. Mac gave me an initial fly fishing lesson, but I will need several more in the coming months. And there were some mini-lectures on Zen and on local history. I'm sure I'll get more of that from him, too."

"Tell me about the lectures," she probed, hoping to coax him into opening up.

"Well, from what you've told me about yourself and your past, I would guess you already know quite a bit about Zen and lots of local history too, so none of what he said would be new to you." Walter edited Mac's account of a Muslim training center from his mind. "Since we were fishing in the Sprague River near Bly, he told me about the balloon-bomb incident there during World War II. It was fascinating: I had no knowledge of the Japanese balloon-bombs, much less that any Americans had been killed on the US mainland during the war."

"We'll have to have a picnic at the Mitchell Monument later this summer. I haven't been there in—let's see—fifteen years. I wonder what the town of Bly is like these days."

"In my opinion, it doesn't measure up to Bonanza. There's a US Forest Service Ranger Station and half-a-dozen businesses, but not much else. We had a good lunch at The Coyote Café, though—lots of local color." The waitress arrived with their drinks, then stood waiting, pen poised above pad, to take their food order. They hurriedly consulted the menus, picking the first things that suited—'satisficing,' as Herbert Simon called it. Walter went on to explain that he had asked Mac for recommendations on meditation centers where he could take a course in the next few months, prompting Susan to tell about some of her experiences in the meditation 'sits' she had done, confirming the transformative effects of the self-knowledge and understanding gained in meditation retreats.

The food came—large portions and delicious, for which Nibbley's is duly famous. As they ate, Susan outlined her plans for Friday, June 6, when she would receive her degree from Klamath Community College. The commencement ceremonies would be held in 'the Commons' at KCC, beginning at 2:00 PM. She expected Virginia Cox and her husband to be there, and she hoped Walter would come too. After the ceremony, she would host a small party at her house, with drinks and snacks, followed by a modest buffet dinner. Some neighbors and other friends might drop by, which would give Walter a chance to meet some of her circle. Walter took all of this as an encouraging sign that Susan was opening the book of her life to him, and he enthusiastically stated his intention to be there.

Deferring coffee and perhaps dessert until later in the day, they decided to take in the Klamath County Museum in the interest of advancing Walter's knowledge of local history. In the course of looking for a parking space, they passed a bicycle store, reminding Walter he needed to get some accessories for his new bike: a rear rack in which to haul groceries, head and tail lights, and perhaps a handlebar bag. Ignoring an ill-concealed reluctance in Susan, he insisted on going to the bike store first, and once in the shop, he suggested they check on the status of repairs to Susan's bike. She immediately balked, a strange look coming over her face. "The bike isn't at this store," she said.

"It's at some other store?" he asked. "Maybe we should go there."

"No, it's at home." She hesitated, then blurted, "It wasn't broken at all. I made it up, because I knew the logical thing would be for you to come to my house to pick me up, and I wasn't ready for that yet." She had the look of a little girl caught snitching cookies.

Walter stopped in his tracks and glared at her, feeling his face getting red. Struggling to keep his anger under control, he silently started counting to ten, but at 'six' he stopped and ordered, "Let's go!" He turned and stomped out of the store, Susan following and trying to utter apologies and explanations he wasn't about to allow himself to hear. The odd procession continued half a block to his truck. He unlocked it with his remote control and got in without opening and holding the door for her. When she had climbed onto the seat, he said, "Buckle up," started the engine, and pulled into traffic. Maintaining enough self-control to not drive aggressively or recklessly—twenty years of flying had taught him that much—he drove directly and efficiently to Nibbley's, spotted Susan's car in the parking lot, and pulled up alongside it.

Susan had ridden in silence, sensing the futility of trying to explain her actions. Now she made one more attempt at reconciliation. "I'm sorry. I should have told you the truth, but I was afraid...." As she spoke he turned his head to look away from her. His message was unmistakable. Tears began to flood her eyes, tears she didn't want him to see. Walter made no effort to stop her as she got out of the truck and into her car. He glanced in her direction long enough to keep from running over her as he backed out of the parking space, then turned away to avoid witnessing her weeping. Yanking the shifter into 'Drive,' he drove off with his teeth clenched and his jaw frozen in 'full brace' position. Heading south on Washburn Way, he calmed down enough to realize his proximity to Wal-Mart and stopped there to shop for the bicycle accessories and a few groceries. Motoring back to his cabin about twenty minutes later, he got a call on his cell phone—the 'Caller ID' indicated it was Susan. Without answering, he switched the phone to 'Off.'

To say Walter subsequently had a rough afternoon would be a gross understatement, and the rocky ride lasted all evening and through the night as well. Only after a few hours of fitful sleep and forty minutes of half-assed meditation the next morning did things begin to smooth out. Sipping his coffee, Walter retraced the previous day's interaction with Susan in an attempt to discover where and how the wheels had come off. His memory was jumbled by the lingering discombobulation in his stomach and the reoccurring voice in his head: *you really screwed the pooch this time.* He poured himself a second cup and went out on the porch despite the lingering overnight chill, barely settling into his chair before Abigail appeared. He hustled into the cabin for a smidgen of mash which he let her eat from his hand as she ensconced herself on the folded towel. *Bless you, little ducky,* he thought as her bill tickled his hand, delicately searching for the last few grains.

Returning to his chair, he went over it again—*she said, I said*—peering underneath the words in hope of learning how they might have been intended *versus* how they had been taken. It was obvious that Susan had tried to make amends; she had 'fessed up immediately and had tried to explain and apologize. It was also obvious—painfully so—that he hadn't given her a fair chance; his emotions had taken over, resulting in his temporary deafness, topped off with a touch of insanity. Further consideration told him that 'insanity' was too harsh a judgment, but 'stupidity' and 'hardheadedness' were probably apt. As if on cue, Abigail concurred. Her emphatic '*Quack!*' didn't surprise him; it actually amused and energized him. *Another whack upside the head.*

The question now was how to patch things up. He had already blown one opportunity for that by refusing to take her call. Would he get a second chance? He decided to call her ASAP, but he didn't want to jeopardize such an important conversation with the awful cell phone signal at the cabin. He thanked Abigail and gave her a little pat, then went inside and ate a halfhearted breakfast. It was still early enough that Susan wouldn't be at work yet, but he felt it was impolitic to call her at home, since she seemed so sensitive about how much access he had to her sanctuary. Choosing to ride his bicycle toward Bonanza and make the call from there, he quickly attached the new handlebar bag and put his cell phone in it. By the time he got to where Haskins Road meets Highway 70, he remembered the cell phone was still 'Off' and he hadn't listened to Susan's message—if she had left one. He stopped, retrieved his phone, and powered it up. Yes, there was a message: "Hello, Walter. This is Susan. I'm so very, very sorry about what has happened. Please, please, let's get together and talk this out. I don't want our relationship to end, especially not like this. Call me at home this evening." She sounded like she was still crying, nearly an hour after his explosion in the bike store.

Now it was Walter's turn to puddle up. He searched his pockets for a tissue or a handkerchief. Finding none, he was forced to use his shirtsleeve. He briefly considered returning to the cabin to make himself presentable, but it was already 10:00 AM and Susan should be at work by now. He rode on towards Bonanza to give himself time to digest her message. It was spot on. She said all the 'right' things—echoing what he was thinking and feeling, too—and it opened the door for reconciliation. A growing panic over having failed to respond to Susan the night before, as she had requested, precipitated another small shower of tears, forcing Walter to pull over and mop up with his other shirtsleeve. He wondered how much he might have to undress to clean himself up by the time he got to Bonanza. Twenty minutes more pedaling brought him to the edge of town and a large shade tree where he could cool off while he made his call. Fortunately, the Welcome Center's number was still stored in his cell phone's memory.

"Hello. Klamath Falls Welcome Center, Virginia speaking. May I help you?"

"Hello, Virginia. This is Walter Baker. May I speak with Susan please?"

"She's not here. She called in sick this morning. She seemed upset, but she wouldn't tell me why. Do you know what's going on?"

"I've got a pretty good idea: we had a disagreement. I'm trying to contact her to fix it."

"I suggest you try her at home." Virginia's voice assumed a motherly tone.

"I'll do that. Thank you very much, Virginia." He ended the call, then entered Susan's home number and hit 'Send.' There was no answer, and after ten rings, apparently no answering machine either. *I'm going to have to stew in my own juices for a while,* he reflected. *Not that I don't deserve it.* He got back on his bike and rode a few blocks farther to The Branding Iron Café for coffee and a Danish, his tear-soaked shirtsleeves prompting an incredulous look from the waitress. On his way back to the cabin, he called Susan's home again—still no answer—and at intervals throughout the day he made four more calls—all to no avail. For the last one, he biked to Stevenson Park, hoping to make contact with some of the magic he and Susan had shared there. As he rounded the last turn before the park, he saw what he thought was her green Toyota Corolla pulling onto Highway 140. He waved and shouted, but the car was too far away for its driver to notice.

27.

The next day Walter hopped into his truck at 8:00 AM and drove to Haskins Road to call Susan at home. There was still no answer. Waves of panic, driven mostly by his fantasies, washed over him. All he could do was wait until the

Welcome Center opened at 10:00 AM and try to reach her there. At 10:01 he made the call, and Virginia answered again. "Susan is off this morning because she has to take the final exam for her course at KCC. She's supposed to come in afterward and work the rest of the day, until we close at 7:00 PM. I expect she'll get here after lunch." Walter thanked her and promised to call back. Learning that Susan was taking an exam in the midst of all this emotional upset made him feel even worse about his behavior. *If I've sabotaged her graduation, she'll never forgive me,* he fretted.

Time dragged throughout the morning, but there was nothing Walter could do to improve his outlook. Shortly after 1:00 PM he drove to Highway 70 and called the Welcome Center again, and again Virginia answered. "No, Susan isn't here. She came in just before noon, and she was a total mess. She tried to do her work, but after twenty minutes I sent her home." Walter thought he detected a note of irritation in her voice, but she patiently answered his questions. "She said she had done all right on the exam, but not as well as she would have liked. She was sure she will pass the course, but she may get a 'B' instead of an 'A.'" Walter found a little consolation in the last statement, but he was still worried. He thanked Virginia for her understanding of the situation, especially for looking out for Susan's welfare. "I hope you get things straightened out between you and Susan," she responded. "I've never seen her this emotionally distraught in all the years I've known her." Walter ended the call feeling like a 'class-A heel.' He put in another call to Susan's home but there was still no answer. His 'class-A heel' feeling intensified to 'class-AAA.'

On Saturday Walter gave up on trying to reach Susan by phone. After breakfast he drove into KFalls and was sitting in his truck in the parking lot when the Welcome Center opened. There was no sign of Susan, so he went inside and found Virginia at the reception desk. "Why am I not surprised to see you here?" was her greeting. Walter apologized to Virginia for coming to the Center, saying he hadn't been able to leave a message on Susan's home phone. "She doesn't have an answering machine, but she does have 'Caller ID.' She's very concerned about her privacy," Virginia explained. *You can say that again,* Walter thought as Virginia continued, "She called in late afternoon yesterday, and I told her not to come in today either. She insisted on making up the time, so we agreed she would work tomorrow and Monday. Earlier this week she had been planning to be off Memorial Day—to go somewhere with you, I think — but yesterday she seemed to think that those arrangements had been canceled."

Walter let out a big sigh. "I guess I really hurt her," he said.

"*You hit her?!*" Virginia screeched.

"Oh, no, nothing like that! I just summarily ended our day together after we had a disagreement, a *small* disagreement. In retrospect, I admit I was overreacting, but Susan has taken this to a whole new level. I must have pushed some very sensitive button in her to trigger such a strong reaction."

"I think you're right on, there. As I told you yesterday, I'm surprised and perplexed by how upset she is. Whatever you said or did touched something in her I'm not aware of, and I'm probably her closest friend in the world. Ever since you called yesterday I've been racking my brain to figure out what it might be. I know she's got a fierce independent streak, and getting involved with any man is bound to contest that, especially after she has endured twenty years as a single mom. I've been pleased to see her opening up to you and how happy it has made her to do that, but you must have stumbled into some territory she doesn't want you to see."

All that made good sense to Walter, and his intuition told him the best thing he could do in the situation was give Susan time and space to work it out. Of course, he wanted to help her do that, but if he forced himself on her, it might make things worse. All he could do is wait and be ready when she finally got back in touch—*if....* He expressed that to Virginia, and she concurred.

He was sure Virginia knew where Susan lived, but he felt it was unwise to ask her to divulge that to him unless there was an outright emergency—which there wasn't—yet—they hoped. Susan's reluctance to share that information with Walter was exactly what had started the whole fracas, so he had to dance around it. However, noting that Susan had 'Caller ID' on her home phone, it occurred to him that she might be intentionally not answering when he called. *After all, that's what I did when she tried to call me on Wednesday afternoon.* He asked Virginia to call Susan—later, after he had left the Center—to tell her that he would try to contact her at their usual time on Sunday evening. Maybe with a little more time to calm down and some advance warning, Susan would be in a more receptive mood. Virginia agreed to his plan and even gave him a consoling hug before he left the Center.

What to do next? Walter thought about riding out to the Lower Klamath National Wildlife Refuge where he and Susan had watched the sun go down a week earlier. She had said it was one of her favorite spots. On second thought, he decided to give himself a little distance from the situation for an hour or two. He went to the Klamath County Library, the main branch on South 3rd Street, to check his email. As expected, there was a message from Mac giving pointers to three centers in northern California where Walter could do meditation retreats under the guidance of experienced teachers. One by one, he looked at their websites, finding that their introductory courses were quite similar: ten days of *vipassana* or 'insight' meditation in a secluded setting, vegetarian meals, dormitory housing, strict segregation of men and women, etc. He studied their course schedules, selected a course in early August that seemed to suit his needs, filled out the online application, and sent it off.

From the Library Walter went to Peet's Coffee & Tea in the Fred Meyer store, another place with sentimental value for him because of its role in building the relationship that was now teetering on the edge. He ordered a coffee and Danish in lieu of lunch and sat for an hour, scrutinizing all the passersby in hopes of catching a glimpse of Susan. He had a sense that Susan's house was not far from there, perhaps in the residential neighborhood to the Northwest, so he got in his pickup and drove back and forth, up and down the maze of streets. He recognized the futility of it, given the slim odds of seeing Susan's car parked in a driveway or along the street, but it made him feel he was doing something constructive toward reconnecting with her.

Finally, he gave up and headed for the Wildlife Refuge parking overlook to sit in his truck, watching the birds in the marsh. He found it fascinating and soothing all at the same time. Susan had introduced him to this entire domain that he had been unaware of, and he wanted to thank her for that—*if only she were here.* He alternated between wonder and melancholy until mid-afternoon, then went back home. Along the way, he buzzed through the KCC parking lot and slowed as he passed Stevenson Park, but there was no sign of Susan's car. Having skipped lunch and his afternoon nap, Walter was tired, hungry, and sleepy when he got back to the cabin. He soon snoozed off, and when he awoke it was almost dark. He opened a can of noodle soup and heated it. Plain and humble though it was, it both satisfied his hunger and took the edge off the evening chill. He read about thirty pages in the library book of Tolstoy's writings, which were anything but cheering, and then went back to bed, searching in vain for the sound sleep that had eluded him three nights in a row.

28.

On Sunday Walter did his Three 'SH' Drill and the rest of his early morning routine, then headed off to the Bonanza Bible Church hoping to find some comfort there. However, the first thing he felt as he entered the church was *dis*comfort. He had dressed casually in slacks and sport shirt because he expected to go to the community picnic after church, but when an usher dressed in suit and tie greeted him coolly, shoving a printed bulletin into Walter's outstretched hand rather than shaking it, he became concerned that his informal attire and scruffy beard marked him as a heathen. He decided to tough it out nevertheless, taking a rear pew seat where he could remain inconspicuous, but from which he could see everybody who came and went.

One woman in particular caught his attention. Seeking an empty pew, she had looked over at him as she entered the sanctuary, and their glances had locked in for a few milliseconds as she passed him. Now she was seated on the other side of the center aisle, a few rows closer to the front, a position that gave Walter a more comprehensive perspective than a direct frontal, side, or rear view. Fifty-ish, with long raven hair, large eyes, small nose, full lips, bright teeth, and an ellipsoidal jaw line—all that was tantalizing enough, but what really got Walter's immediate and enduring attention was that she was built like the proverbial brick outhouse. Moreover, the dress she was wearing, made of a flimsy floral print, presented the merchandise in its best possible aspect, causing Walter to recall the old Groucho Marx line, "Her dress was like a barbed-wire fence: it was enough for protection, but it didn't spoil the view." Out of respect for the religious setting in which they were sitting, Walter tried to limit his scrutiny of the woman to occasional glimpses in her general direction, but on a couple occasions he thought that she had turned to look back at him, as if she sensed his attention. Alas—or perhaps fortuitously—he had looked away before their eyes met again, but the cat-and-mouse exchange persisted through at least three iterations.

Accordingly, Walter was somewhat oblivious to the organ prelude and the robed choir filing into place until everybody suddenly stood up and launched into the opening hymn, *God of Our Fathers*. He had to scramble through the first stanza—looking up the hymn number in his bulletin, lifting a hymnal from the

rack on the pew ahead of him, and thumbing through to the appropriate page—
to be ready for the second one, not that his faltering baritone added much to the
euphony. Inevitably, his gaze again drifted over to the aforementioned damsel,
now standing, and the vista immediately captured what little breath he could
spare for singing. The clinging fabric of her dress made it appear there were no
undergarments within—no bra, no thong, no nothing—only some cologne and
body lotion.

Walter's attention was yanked back to ostensible worship when the music
stopped and everybody sat down—everybody, that is, but the minister, the
Reverend Raymond Q. Morris, who had magically materialized to stand front-
and-center before the altar, facing the congregation—a meticulously contrived
figure in a black gown and multicolored stole, portly and not too tall, a mane of
white hair combed straight back, mutton-chops beard outlining his pink round
face, beaming in a beatific smile that had paid off an orthodontist's college loans.
"Good morning!" he boomed.

"Good morning," the congregation acquiesced.

Closing his eyes and lifting his countenance skyward as if receiving a vision
from God Himself, 'The Rev,' as he was affectionately known to his parishioners,
intoned, "Ah, I can see Jesus looking down on us from his golden heavenly throne
at the right hand of God. He is smiling, smiling in delight that we have come here
to worship him today—to praise him—to follow him—to serve him—to love
him." A few of the more devout congregants interjected 'Amen's after 'today,' and
the number and fervor grew in response to each succeeding phrase. Walter half-
expected that The Rev would next lead the faithful into something like a college
cheer: "Gimme a 'J'—"J!"—Gimme an 'E'—"E!"—and so on, and he was relieved
when it didn't happen. Instead, The Rev lowered his head, eyes still closed, and
posed with hands clasped prayerfully beneath his large pectoral cross, while the
choir chimed in with a chorus of the Bill and Gloria Gaither gospel classic, *There's
Something About That Name*:
Jesus, Jesus, Jesus —
There's just something about that name.
Master, Savior, Jesus—

...

Kings and kingdoms shall all pass away
But there's something about that name.

It was beautiful music—it had made the Gaithers deservedly rich and
famous—and the choir sang it well, creating an extraordinary interval of peace
and love, drawing the congregation in and enticing them to become available to

God in the worship service to follow. It also made Walter slightly queasy. Cloaked inside the saccharin sweetness, he intuited, was an infection of idolatry, not readily apparent to the undiscerning observer. It was like the sword lurking beneath a matador's mesmerizing mantle, and Walter wondered when it would be exposed at some point later in the service.

He didn't have to wait long. Excerpts from *Psalm 18*, printed in the bulletin, were read responsively:

²The Lord is my rock, and my fortress, and my deliverer; my God, my strength, in whom I trust; my buckler, and the horn of my salvation, and my high tower.
³I will call upon the Lord, who is worthy to be praised; so shall I be saved from mine enemies.
⁶In my distress I called upon the Lord, and cried unto my God; he heard my voice out of his temple, and my cry came before him, even into his ears.
⁷Then the earth shook and trembled; the foundations also of the hills moved and were shaken, because he was wroth.
¹³The Lord also thundered in the heavens, and the Highest gave his voice: hailstones and coals of fire.
¹⁴Yea, he sent out his arrows, and scattered them; and he shot out lightnings, and discomfited them.

On and on it went, hopscotching through the rest of the psalm, landing on the bellicose verses, skipping over the rest.

Walter could see where this was heading. The fact that this was Memorial Day weekend gave him a pretty obvious clue, and if there was any doubt, successive Scripture Lessons drove the message home. These were all read by 'deacons'—non-ordained members of the congregation who might have received special training for the privilege of assisting the minister—but the concluding Gospel Lesson was declaimed by The Rev himself, as if lay persons are not worthy of such an auspicious assignment. Thus, when the Lesson was ended, the minister was already positioned in the pulpit—the others had been humbly stationed at the lectern—ready to let 'er rip.

And rip it he did, a real stem-winder worthy of his other nickname, 'Thunder Ray.' His previously cherubic countenance transmogrified into a Charlton Heston-esque visage exuding a panoply of formidable emotions. He began with the 1979 occupation of the United States Embassy in Tehran by Iranian Muslim militants and the subsequent capture of American diplomats who were held hostage 444 days. Then he progressed through the continuing deterioration of American-Muslim relations: the first Gulf War in 1990 and 1991, the World Trade Center and Pentagon attacks on September 11, 2001, and the ensuing wars in Iraq and Afghanistan. "America, 'the land of the free and the home of the brave,' has been increasingly under attack by its enemies around the world, forsaken by former allies it helped defend in World Wars I and II, and weakened from within by halfhearted immigration policies, gutless diplomacy, and economic pandemonium. Our once-proud nation has fallen into a pit of moral depravity, condoning such abominations as homosexuality and abortion. [*Pause for effect.*] Why is God allowing this to happen to us?"

The Rev held up a Bible, waving it back and forth to focus attention on it. "It has happened before—it's all right here in the Holy Bible." Citing and repeating the relevant Scripture Lesson passages from *Jeremiah*, he told the story of how God allowed Israel to be taken captive by the Babylonians and sent into exile. "God himself fought against Israel, siding with her enemies," he said, "in order to punish the Israelites—*his chosen people!*—for their disobedience." Sensing the blast that was imminent, Walter slouched down in his seat. "It happened before—and it's happening again. God punished America—in the words of former President George W. Bush: '[a nation] chosen by God and commissioned by history to be a model for the world'—and God will again punish America for its sins: for turning away from God's commandments." A few 'Amen's drifted up from the congregation, and Thunder Ray adroitly shifted into a hushed tone, as if imparting a deep, dark secret.

Reading verbatim the text of the Reverend Jerry Falwell's post-9/11 appearance on 'The 700 Club,' a nationwide television show hosted by the Reverend Pat Robertson, he laid the blame on "the pagans, and the abortionists, and the feminists, and the gays and the lesbians who are actively trying to make that an alternative lifestyle, the ACLU, People for the American Way, all of them who have tried to secularize America," ending with a quote from the press release Robertson issued later that same day: 'We have insulted God at the highest level of our government. Then, we say, "Why does this happen?" It is happening because God Almighty is lifting His protection from us.'

The Rev paused again, and a few more 'Amen's were heard, more embarrassed than enthusiastic. Walter's queasiness, however, began to swell into outright nausea. "We all know that Pat Robertson and Jerry Falwell were widely ridiculed in the liberal media for their remarks, but we also know that prophets have always been ridiculed ... and persecuted ... and even crucified." He held up the Bible again. "It's all right here in God's holy book." Reverting to his former fire, he shouted, "But there is *hope*, brothers and sisters, there is *salvation!*" Scattered calls of 'Hallelujah!' and 'Praise God!' cropped up. Switching to *Isaiah*, Ray went dancing through the text, citing the passages that supported his argument. Now the 'Hallelujahs' came in number and in earnest, and the 'Praise Gods' came even more so—and yea, Walter's nausea came in earnest as well.

"Then what happened?" The Rev asked, more rhetorically than not. "Jesus came, but did we welcome him? No!!! As Isaiah had prophesied, his own people, the Jews, did not accept him—instead they crucified him—and even after he rose from the dead, they didn't get the message. To this very day, they still don't get the message, and God has punished them because of that, caused them to be persecuted again and again. Do you think the Holocaust was just a fluke? No, no, no!!!

"And God sent another prophet—at least, he claimed to be God's prophet—a former camel driver named Muhammad, who tried to get the Jews, the Christians, and a whole bunch of pagans on the same page, worshiping *one* God, the *same* God, a God he called '*Allah.*' But Muhammad messed up too, by denying that Jesus was the Son of God, by contradicting what Jesus himself said: 'The Father and I are one.' It's right there in *John*, chapter 10, verse 30. Yes, the Muslims accepted Jesus as a prophet—they still claim to do that—but it was second-class status, behind Muhammad, whom they exalt as the last and the greatest of the prophets. Islam flourished for several centuries until God sent reformers like Martin Luther and John Calvin and several others to rebuild His church in Western Europe. Like Jesus, they too struggled to gain acceptance and to be allowed preach their message. So the Protestants came to America and founded a new nation, *a Christian nation*, where they would be free to worship God in their own way." A crescendo of 'Praise God's' rang out, joined by the former 'Hallelujahs' who had been outdone in the previous outcry.

The matador's sword was in full view now, and Thunder Ray was brandishing it ferociously. "But once again, history is repeating itself as America is straying from the straight-and-narrow of God's path, just like the Reverend Jerry Falwell said. And God is using Islam to enforce His will. The 'bad news' is that America probably isn't going to make it. It has served its purpose in God's scenario of salvation and is now destined for oblivion.

Then The Rev again lowered his voice so he could make another crescendo in his closer. "It's all summed up in *1 Thessalonians*, chapter 4, verses 16 & 17—and I want you to carry this with you in your hearts and minds as you go forth today:
For the Lord himself shall descend from heaven with a shout, with the voice of the archangel, and with the trump of God: and the dead in Christ shall rise first: Then we which are alive, and remain shall be caught up together with them in the clouds, to meet the Lord in the air: and so shall we ever be with the Lord.'

And so we shall ever be with the Lord!" He paused to signal all present to join with him in a final resounding *"Amen,"* then strode triumphantly to his throne-like seat.

The choir rose to sing an anthem, the time-honored Fred Waring arrangement of *The Battle Hymn of the Republic.* Again, it performed superbly: eight women and four men, all well-trained and well-rehearsed by a leader whose billowy robe, slender build, and long gray hair obscured his/her gender. As the sermon's spleen faded into the soothing music, Walter's biliousness abated, and he congratulated himself for having been able to keep his breakfast down. Nevertheless, Ray's thunder had showered him with sweat because he had been caught up in the expertly engineered tornado of emotion—so much so he had forgotten all about the winsome wench seated a few yards away. Now he turned his eyes in her direction just in time to catch her swiveling her head back to the front. *I wonder what her game is,* he thought, as a 'rapture' very different from Thunder Ray's slithered into his awareness—but not for long. The choir's 'terrible swift sword' lopped it off as they climbed to their final chord, and Walter shifted his attention back to the front of the church, where The Rev was now standing at the lectern.

In stark contrast to his previous inspiring persona, he matter-of-factly read several announcements and reminders of coming events, including the community picnic to be held in Big Springs Park that afternoon. Meanwhile, the ushers began methodically circulating through the congregation to collect the morning offering. When they had completed their rounds, they marched in formation down the center aisle to present the morning's take to the waiting Rev. With that as their signal, the congregation stood and bowed their heads for the ensuing prayer. Still somewhat dazed by the apocalyptic vision Thunder Ray had conjured up in his sermon, Walter's brain went walkabout into a fantasy of being ground down in a bed by the voluptuous woman a few pews away.

Immediately following the 'Amen,' The Rev intoned, "The Peace of the Lord be with you," and the congregation dutifully droned, "And also with you." Then The Rev exhorted, "Let us share His Peace," whereupon all the faithful embraced others nearby in a veritable *allemande left* of hand-shaking, back-slapping, and even a little chaste hugging. Walter was initially caught up in exchanging greetings with a couple seated to his right, but when he turned back to his left, *there she was!*—the buxom beauty had come over from several pews distant to stand before him, and *en route* she had given a couple discrete downward tugs at the waist of her dress so as to further deepen its plunging neckline. Walter's jaw plummeted in empathy, limiting his articulation to a longer-than-average grunt: "*Uhhhhh.*" She grabbed his hand and held it warmly in hers as his gaze reluctantly ascended from the provocative panorama below to melt into her clear, dark eyes. "Hello," she purred. "My name is Nancy and I'd like to share a piece with you." (Actually, she probably said "I'd like to share my peace with you," but that's not what Walter heard.)

His mind reflexively retrieved his sagging jaw long enough for him to mumble, "Hi, I'm Walter."

"Nice to meet you, Walter. I haven't seen you before. You must be new around here."

His faculty of speech gradually returning, he stuttered, "I moved into this area about three weeks ago."

"Welcome to Bonanza," she meowed. "I hope you'll be coming to the picnic today."

"I was thinking about it."

"Well, please do come—and look for me in the food service area." The Rev was now pleading with the congregation to come back to order. "Gotta go. See ya later," she said, and undulated off to her seat, Walter's enchanted eyes tracking her licentiously.

The Rev pronounced a benediction and announced the closing hymn: *Onward, Christian Soldiers.* The organist, the choir, the congregation—everybody let it all hang out, singing with gusto and conviction—that is, everybody but Walter. His attention was still focused on Nancy—in particular her *zaftig* tush which she was wiggling ever-so-slightly in time with the music. When the hymn ended, Thunder Ray strode down the center aisle and stood at the church entrance to meet and greet worshipers as they left. Walter got caught up in the mass exodus and lost sight of Nancy. After shaking hands and exchanging pleasantries with The Rev, he took a few steps toward the street and then turned for another glimpse of her, but she was gone, having slipped out a side door to hurry off to the picnic area.

29.

Officially the picnic was to begin at noon, but it was a good ten minutes past twelve when Thunder Ray and four other ministers stepped onto the makeshift stage in Big Springs Park. The Rev took the lead, welcoming everybody and introducing one of his colleagues, who gave a short prayer. Then Ray introduced a matronly woman about the size of an NFL linebacker gone to seed, who did her best imitation of Kate Smith leading the assembled throng in singing *God Bless America*. Without further ado, the singer and ministers left the platform, and everybody began lining up for food.

Walter observed it all from the edge of the park, well away from the stage, and he lagged back from the food line, engaged in his people-watching pastime. Standing on tiptoes, he spotted Nancy busily serving food, positioned where it was impossible to avoid her if he wanted something to eat. In the brief lull between church and picnic, he had suffered some misgivings about his earlier interactions with her and had considered skipping the picnic altogether. *Am I attracted to Nancy because of my tiff with Susan? Or is Nancy's appearance in my life an indication that I need to widen my horizon beyond Susan—or, for that matter, any one woman—at least for a while? What would Mac advise? What would Abigail say?* The absurd idea of seeking lonely-heart advice from a duck shook him out of his soul-searching and reinserted him into the present situation, wherein recollection of Nancy's bountiful boobs a-bobbing at him, as if trying to completely escape the confinement of her low-cut dress, pushed him across the line.

It wasn't until he was almost directly across from the serving table from her that she saw him. She was wearing a large white cook's apron that covered her *décolletage*, but her come-hither smile and body language offered considerable consolation. "Would you like some fried chicken?" she asked.

"Yes, thank you," he replied, consciously choosing his words so as not to request 'a piece.'

He held out his paper plate and she plunked *some* chicken on it, saying, "Here's a nice big breast. You *do* like breasts, don't you?"

Outmaneuvered again, he groused, his libido prompting him to answer, "Of course."

Before he could move on, she leaned across the serving table and said in a stage whisper, "I'll be tied up here until one-thirty or maybe two o'clock. I'll wait for you over near the portable toilets"—she motioned toward the southeast corner of the park—"so you can find me when you come by to water your lizard." She flashed a big grin and glanced lecherously at his crotch.

Walter winced and moved on to the veggie station as fast as decorum would allow. Once his plate was loaded, he looked around to find an empty seat at one of the picnic tables. Most of the places were taken, but he spied a space opposite one of the very few people he knew in Bonanza: Henry Parsons, the real estate agent. "Hello, Henry. Do you remember me? I'm Walter Baker. May I join you?"

"Certainly. Have a seat," Henry answered. Between bites of food, he and Walter swapped small talk until the others at the table finished their meal and left. Taking the last bite from his own plate, Henry bumped the conversation into a more comradely groove: "I saw you chatting with Nancy Norwood as you came through the food line."

"Oh, is that her name?" Walter replied. "All I knew was 'Nancy.' I met her at the Bible Church this morning. She seemed friendly."

Henry rolled his eyes. "That's an understatement, if there ever was one. I'd be careful there if I were you—that is, unless you want your 'johnson' swathed in Johnson & Johnson, if you get my drift. She's probably tried to screw every single man in town, and quite a few who aren't single. Apparently you are her latest conquest."

"Yeah, she was even coming on to me in church. She was oblivious to the fact that most churches don't approve of aggressive promiscuity during their services."

"She seems to be using the church as her hunting ground," Henry speculated. "I guess she thinks she will find a better quality of mate there than in a honky-tonk bar."

"Stands to reason," Walter agreed. "Is she really looking for a mate—a husband—or is she just a latent nymphomaniac?"

"It's hard to tell, judging by her behavior, but based upon what I know of her past, I'd say that she really wants a husband—a man that's rugged and raunchy, to be sure, but a husband all the same. She arrived here about ten years ago with a man like that. They came up from Texas, where she grew up, and they wanted to leverage the name of the town by opening an old-time saloon, something like you see in the old Western movies, with card tables, a piano player, a big standup bar, and Mae West-type hostesses. The local churches all presumed that the saloon would include a whorehouse upstairs and immediately applied their political muscle to block the necessary permits. As the whole thing was coming to a head, her husband upped and died of a heart attack. Some folks said it was brought on by the stress from the saloon conflict, others said Nancy had fucked him to death. In any event, she dropped the saloon venture, took a job as a waitress, and joined the very church that had led the opposition, almost like an 'in your face' gesture." Just as he had done when Walter had come into his office two weeks earlier, Henry rushed to 'the bottom line' without pausing for breath, "So are ya gonna take her for a roll in the hay?"

Walter briefly considered his reply, then asked, "What would you recommend?"

Henry was unnerved by how quickly the ball came back into his own court, but he covered it well. "I've never had the pleasure of Nancy's intimate company, and I think it's because she knows I've got a pretty good marriage, or maybe it's because I'm not *macho* enough for her tastes. In any case, I doubt I'll ever be another notch in her bedpost. You, however, seem to have passed her preliminary screening."

Walter replied, "So it seems—but I don't know yet what I'm going to do. I guess it depends on what she says and does when I see her next"—he glanced at his watch—"which should be within the next hour. In the meantime, I think I'll take a walk to mull it over."

"That's a good idea," Henry agreed. "I'd definitely recommend that."

"Thanks for the information. It's most helpful."

"Nice talkin' to ya. Stop by the office any time you wanna chat some more. And good luck!" Henry winked the exclamation point.

Walter pitched his paper plate and cup and plastic utensils into one of the garbage cans and walked to the southwest corner of the park, then west on Union Street, taking his time, so he didn't have to be concerned about where he was putting his feet and could concentrate instead on where he might be putting other parts of his body later that day. The first thing that came to his mind was STD, Sexually Transmitted Disease, which Henry had hinted at. If Nancy had been sleeping around as much as he implied, disease could be a significant risk. On the other hand, she seemed to be intelligent enough to know what precautions to take, and taking them—*religiously?*—would be consistent with her hopes of re-marriage— if Henry's assessment was on target. Furthermore, he, Walter, had certainly danced through the STD minefield in his sexual meanderings during the last few years of his recent marriage and had done so without any problems or even much concern.

Next, his introspection returned to his relationship with Susan. Would he have regrets about a one-night stand with Nancy if he and Susan were able to patch things up and keep going in the direction they had seemed to be heading? Although they had had no explicit discussion of 'the rules of the game,' there certainly was an implied assumption of monogamy they both seemed to share. Therefore, any deviation from that, even at this early stage of courtship, wouldn't augur well for Walter's ability to return to a proper marriage. *Better to curtail the wandering urge now*, he thought, *than to wait until later when retreat may be more difficult. Furthermore, if my relationship with Susan does go ka-foop, I can always seek out Nancy again. If she's no longer interested in me, there are other fish in the ocean—or the lake—or the Sprague River. That does it! My mind is made up. I'll just go back to the cabin, and Nancy will get the message when I don't show up.* However, as he looped back to the park, a complication arose: he had to pee. All the way down North Street, Walter looked for a business with a public restroom, but all the likely candidates were closed for the afternoon. As he neared Big Springs Park, he began to steel himself for the unpleasant task of delivering the news to Nancy face-to-face.

He needed no acting to put on an air of urgency as he strode toward the toilets. When saw Nancy standing near the edge of the trees about ten yards off to the right, he gave her a quick glance that said, "I'll be back in a minute," and she nodded with an understanding smile. He relieved himself and dabbed his hands in the disposable sanitary wipes provided on a nearby table, then began walking, more slowly now, in her general direction. She came forward to meet him, now smiling lasciviously, with her hand extended. "Let me shake the hand that just 'shook Ike.' If you'll come by my place, I'll be happy to 'shake Ike' too." Walter took her hand, finding therein a small piece of paper, which he palmed and stuck into his pants pocket—not too obviously, he hoped. "That's my address," she said. "My house is about two minutes walk from here. I'm going there now to take a bath and get prettied up. By three o'clock I'll be waiting for you—with nothing on but the radio." Before he could say a word, she pirouetted and glided off.

Walter headed toward the Bonanza Bible Church parking lot where he had left his truck, walking at a slower, time-killing pace. He discreetly retrieved the slip of paper from his pocket and read the address, then turned and went to the Ranch & Rural Real Estate office. Poking his head inside the door, Walter found Henry reading a copy of *Ranch & Rural Living Magazine*. "I just want you to know Nancy is expecting me at her house in about 45 minutes. However, I plan to be several miles out of town by then, so if you go over there at about three-fifteen, she might let you take my place. Now's your big chance." Henry gave out a loud "Ha!" and buried his face deeper in the magazine. Walter backed out the door and strode briskly to his truck. Driving home, he kept to back streets until he was well beyond—he hoped—any place where Nancy might see him.

30.

Back at the cabin, Walter found himself exhausted by the double-whammy Nancy and The Rev had tag-teamed to inflict on him, so he spread-eagled on his bed and quickly fell asleep. It was getting on toward 6:30 PM when he awoke, but he really wasn't very hungry. He dumped some nuts and veggie chips into a bowl and took it out to the porch to munch and think. The day's earlier events were too recent to be processed, so he pushed them into his brain's root cellar, there to ferment until he was ready to deal with them. They had eclipsed his worry about Susan and the future of their relationship—*which was probably for the better,* he thought. *Otherwise I would have stewed and fretted to the point where I'd be a nervous wreck by now. If I made it through Thunder Ray's sermon without puking or screaming, I should be able to maintain some kind of equilibrium until 9:00 PM.*

As he chomped the last chip, he decided to have a go at meditating, hoping to empty his mind to make room for whatever God/the Universe/whatever wanted to tell him. He wished Abigail were there to help steady him and perhaps bestow an exclamation point to assure that he didn't miss an important idea, but it was her bedtime. Keeping a firm grip on his emotions, he tried to recall just how the whole squabble with Susan began and how it had escalated into a full-scale blowup. *I started it when I got bent out of shape over Susan not telling me where she lives. No, she started it when she declined to tell me that. No, before that I plainly told her I couldn't reveal where my cabin is, so I started it.* That was enough to convince him there was more than enough blame for them both to share. Next he looked at the escalation. *There's no doubt I 'lost it' in the bike shop, and then compounded matters when I went on to scuttle the rest of the day with her, and then compounded things twice over when I refused to take her call and turned off my cell phone. But her going incommunicado Thursday, Friday, and Saturday indicates she 'lost it' too, or was trying to keep from losing it. Yes, she apparently did keep herself together enough to take and pass her final exam on Friday morning, but Virginia's account of her actions after that indicate something deep inside was eating at her. So what does all that recommend for this evening's phone call?* he wondered. *First, don't overreact again. Better yet, don't react at all, just listen, and think twice, or more, before saying anything. Most of all, forgive, no matter what happens, or what she says.* He couldn't think of anything else, so he just sat there another hour, rehearsing it in his mind.

By then it was dark and starting to get chilly. In his few weeks of living at this altitude, above 4,000 feet, he had learned that things cool off very quickly when the sun goes down. He went inside to heat some water for tea. He really didn't feel like cooking, so he grabbed another handful of nuts from the jar. *Not much of a supper*, he thought as he sat at the table, sipping the tea and drumming his fingers nervously. He considered going into Bonanza for a sandwich, but rejected that lest he bump into Nancy somewhere. Finally, he decided to go in the opposite direction, to Stevenson Park, to call Susan. He hoped the diner in Dairy might still be open, but that wasn't likely this late on a Sunday evening, even in summer. He gulped down the last of his tea, went out to his pickup, and climbed into the saddle. Ten minutes later, he pulled into Stevenson Park, parked, and watched the moonlight tickle the river. Despite his anxious impatience, nine-o'clock came soon enough.

Susan answered on the second ring, indicating that she too had been waiting. "Hello? Walter?"

"Hi, Susan," he said softly. "It's good to hear your voice."

"Yes, I'm glad to hear yours, too. It's been a rough couple of days."

"I'm so very, very sorry," he said. "I behaved very badly, and I want to take it all back. I do apologize."

"Don't blame yourself," she replied. "You had no way of knowing you were hitting a nerve, that what was happening between us was causing me to bring up some old hurts I thought I had resolved many years ago. I hung on by my fingernails at first, just to get past my exam, but once that was out of the way, I really came unglued. I was stunned by what I was feeling, and I had to go off by myself to sort it out."

"I wish we could have sorted it out together."

"Yes, I do too—but that's hindsight. For now, I just want to get back together with you, so we can talk it out and keep going from there."

"Do you want me to come into KFalls now? I could be there in fifteen minutes. I'm already at Stevenson Park."

Susan didn't answer immediately. Her five seconds of 'think time' seemed like five years. "I've got to go to work in the morning, so I can't stay out with you all night, even though it's what I'd like to do. But yes, I would like to see you now, in the flesh and all the rest. I could drive out to the park if you like."

Walter tried to follow Susan's example by engaging his brain a few seconds before he opened his mouth. "I'd rather meet somewhere in town. I haven't had much supper, and my stomach just started reminding me of that. Is there a fast food restaurant you can tolerate?"

"I try to avoid them, but these are what I consider 'extenuating circumstances.'" She giggled a special little gurgle she used to indicate she's joking, as Walter had learned on their first coffee date. "There's a McDonald's at the Wal-Mart on Washburn Way. Let's meet there."

"I'm on my way. See you in fifteen minutes, maybe ten."

"Drive carefully," she cautioned. "I don't want to come bail you out if you get a speeding ticket."

"I'll try, but if I'm not there by nine-thirty, start checking the county jail and the police station."

"And the dog pound. See you." *Click.* Walter almost jumped for joy inside his truck. *She's got her old sense of humor back. We're going to make it.*

Eleven miles and thirteen minutes later, Walter pulled into the McDonald's parking area. Susan was already there, standing next to her car. He parked, jumped out, and ran over to her. It was the classic love scene, straight out of Hollywood movies the Boomer Generation watched in their youth: big full-body hug with his face buried in her ponytail, her face soaking his shoulder with tears; next a slight pullback to look at each other, her tears prompting him to puddle up as well; then the kiss.... It was the best one yet, not that anybody was keeping score. Eventually breaking the clinch in order to breathe, they walked hand-in-hand into McD's. Rather than order immediately, they went to a remote corner and wordlessly held hands across the table, gazing into each other's tear-drenched eyes, both of them relieved that the crisis was past. Susan finally broke the spell by reaching into her jacket pocket for two tissues, giving one to Walter. "Thank you for coming into town. Thank you for hanging in there with me these last few days when I wasn't taking or returning your calls. Virginia told me how concerned you were, and how understanding."

Walter considered a classic John Wayne "Shucks, ma'am" reply, but felt the wounds were still too fresh for that kind of humor. Instead he explained, "When I saw that Virginia was keeping up with where you were and what you were doing, that she was able to contact you, and that she wasn't hitting the panic button, it told me you were going to be OK, that you were working through some things in your own process and didn't want or need my involvement at that point. So I backed off to stay out of your way and used Virginia to pass along reassuring signals. I must say she was wonderful. I don't know what I would have done if she hadn't been there."

"I don't know what I would have done without her either, although I did get some further help from another friend when I really felt overwhelmed on Saturday. That was when I hit absolute bottom."

"It's good to have a few good friends, people you can really trust. I hope I can become one of those people for you and you can be a trusted friend for me. I thought that's where we were headed until things turned to runny doo-doo last Wednesday. The shock and the disappointment really hit me hard, too."

"Yes, that's what I want to do now: start rebuilding the trust we had going between us and take it to a new level. Let's begin with this coming week. I'll be working every day through Thursday and a half-day on Friday as well. After I get off work at two, I'd like you to meet me at my house so we can go ride our bicycles together. After that, we can go back to my place for dinner—pick up some carryout food along the way, since I won't have time to cook us a decent meal—not this time, but soon." She reached out to turn one of his hands palm-up on the table, and with her other hand she fished a slip of paper out of her jacket pocket and placed it on his palm. "Here's my address. My house is not far from the Fred Meyer store, but on the other side of Washburn Way. I'll give you more explicit directions if you need them."

Walter looked at the neat script on the paper. He had probably driven right past her house when he was frantically looking for her on Saturday! A sixth sense had told him he was in the right neighborhood, but he had ignored it. "If that's your plan, I should move up my trip to California by leaving tomorrow morning. That way I can be back Wednesday night, or Thursday worst case, and we won't have to worry about me getting to your house by Friday afternoon—or being too pooped to pedal."

"You expect to be away two nights?" she asked.

"Yes, it's about four hundred miles in each direction, so I'll drive down the first day, get my stuff the second, see my kids if possible, and come back the third. If I leave tomorrow, I'll have Thursday as a cushion in case I hit any snags."

"Do you think your ex-wife might send the sheriff after you?" she joked.

"No," he smiled, "I'm not worried about it but just in case, I don't intend to call her until I'm all packed up and ready to leave instantly. I certainly won't tell her where I'm staying—which is, for the record, in a cheap motel in Livermore. I don't have the address or phone number with me now, but I can call you when I get there."

"Yes, please do. In fact, I'd like you to call me *every* night, and not just when you're on the road, but when you're here in Klamath County, too."

That took Walter by surprise, albeit a very pleasant one, especially after having spent several consecutive days not knowing where Susan was or whether she was OK. "I'll gladly do that, although it does raise a minor problem: the poor cell phone signal at my cabin. I'd rather not have to drive down to Dairy every night to call you, so while I'm in the Bay Area on Tuesday, I'll go to an electronics store and get a signal booster for the cell phone. That way, you'll also be able to get calls through to me when I'm at the cabin."

"Good. I've been wanting to do that. I thought about trying smoke signals, or tin cans and a string—a very long string—or, as I suggested to you once before, some kind of psychic communication. Maybe we could try it while you're in California. I know California and Oregon laws prohibit talking on cell phones while you're driving, but I doubt that ESP is illegal."

"Not yet, at least, but with the way things seem to be advancing in electronic eavesdropping, it may be only a matter of time," Walter conjectured facetiously. "Anyhow, I promise that, starting tonight, I'll call you *every* night at nine o'clock, come hell or high water. But what will be my reward for such conscientiousness? Or my punishment if I fail to call, or am late?"

"My religion, such as it is, tells me that sin is its own punishment and doing good is its own reward," she responded, "so that's all you're going to get. If we can't adjust our attitudes to be grateful for each other's company, we might as well call the whole thing off right now."

Walter did a double-take to make sure she was kidding, but on second thought he had to admit he liked what she had just said. It was a far cry from the God-as-cranky-old-judgmental-curmudgeon belief that Thunder Ray had pitched and that had definitely turned Walter's stomach. His stomach now turned to food and the fact that it had been promised some when he set out for McD's. Picking up on Susan's latest utterance, he said, "I too am grateful you agreed to meet me tonight and to meet me *here*, so I can devour some junk food, an act you will agree is *sinful* in that consuming it will constitute its own punishment."

Susan giggled. "I see that you understood my statement about sin and you are already embracing the principle. In light of that, how could I possibly object? What's your poison: a Big Mac or a Quarter Pounder?"

"I'm going with the Big Mac attack. And you?"

"The Garden Salad," she said.

"How virtuous! I'll bet you're already feeling grateful, just by having made the choice."

"Nah. I'd really like a dessert item, but none of the things available here are sinful enough. If I'm going to pig out on something sweet, I want it to be really obscene—like *cannoli*, remember?"

Walter went to buy the food. When he returned, Susan asked about the Memorial Day picnic in Bonanza. Walter hung out the yellow caution flag in his brain to make sure his answer didn't reveal anything about his encounter with Nancy. "Oh, it was OK as picnics go. The fried chicken was good, and I had an entertaining chat with the local real estate agent, an interesting fellow who seems to know all and see all, but tells only forty percent. I didn't stick around past two-thirty, though. I had gone to the Bonanza Bible Church this morning, just to check it out, and the sermon made me ill. I'll tell you more about it some other time, when we're not eating."

It was getting late, well past Walter's customary bedtime and probably Susan's too. Out in the parking lot again, they reprised the earlier movie scene with only slightly less passion and no tears. Just before Susan closed her car door, she reminded him, "Be sure to call me at nine tomorrow night, or earlier if you want. And turn on your ESP along with your GPS." Then her signature farewell: "Good night, Walter."

"Good night, Susan." He almost added, 'I love you,' but caught himself. *I'm ready to say it, and she's probably ready to hear it, but I want it to be at a more romantic time and place than 10:15 PM in a McDonald's parking lot.*

31.

Walter slept in the next morning. After a long and emotionally draining day with church, Nancy, and Susan, he had deliberately switched off his alarm, rewarding himself for having made it through with no major *faux-pas*. *Besides, today is a national holiday,* he thought to himself as he opened his eyes to a long-since-risen morning sun. Coffee, his morning ablutions, thirty minutes' meditation, and breakfast took him to 9:30. He tossed some clothes and his toilet kit into an overnight bag, put his laptop and some maps and papers in his battered briefcase, and stowed it all behind the passenger seat in his truck. On the way out the door, Abigail's folded-towel roost caught his eye. He decided to leave it in place, but part way down the driveway he made a sharp right turn onto the narrow lane leading to Ted's house. Parking in front of the garage, he beeped the horn three times and got out as Ted came through the garage to meet him. "I just want you to know I'll be away for the next few days. I'm going down to California to get my things out of storage. I expect to be back by late evening Wednesday, but it might be Thursday if I get sidetracked. You may want to check my front porch while I'm gone. There's a folded towel on the corner where Abigail likes to sit, and she might lay an egg there. I wouldn't want it to go bad from neglect."

"Why don't you remove the towel until you come back? Maybe she'll understand that she should hold her fire," Ted suggested.

"That's a thought," Walter conceded. "I could do that, but maybe you should check the porch all the same. Where does she lay her eggs over here?"

"All over, but always in places resembling a nest. We never thought of trying to coerce her into doing it at a particular spot. It seemed counter to our idea of 'free range.'"

"Well, I may have corrupted her. Now that she's become conditioned to sit on the towel on my porch, she'll really be confused if I'm gone for three days."

" 'Seduced and abandoned,' eh? You're nothing but a hardhearted gigolo," Ted teased.

Walter laughed. "I'd like to believe that my gigolo days are over. At least, I'm making a sincere effort in that direction." He chose not to reveal more about his relationship with Susan, but the reminder that it was back on track again put a smile on his face as he got back into his pickup.

"Have a good trip," Ted said.

Walter held up his cell phone. "You can always call me in case the Indians attack."

"It's not the Indians I'm worried about," came the reply.

Walter drove slowly down the gravel driveway, accelerated to 40 on Haskins Road, and kicked it on up to 60 once he got to Highway 70. It was a bright, clear morning and the truck seemed to be saying, "Let's go." Once on US 97, the old north-south highway, now christened the Volcanic Legacy Scenic Byway, was two-lane blacktop, although there was a surprising amount of eighteen-wheeler traffic, cruising along at fifty-five-plus. Crossing into California about twenty miles south, he slowed for the town of Dorris and again after Macdoel as the road climbed a thousand feet inside of seven miles to Mount Hebron Summit at 5,202 feet, then down the other side and back up again to Grass Lake Summit (5,101 feet) eleven miles later. He played peek-a-boo with perennially snowcapped Mount Shasta, more than 14,000 feet high, all the way, eventually skirting around the northwest base and descending into Weed where he stopped at a diner to drain off some coffee and top up again.

Again in the truck, Walter's mind drifted back to the emotional roller-coaster of the day before. Yesterday had certainly ended on a high note, and a whiff of the euphoria returned to him as he recalled his *tête-à-tête* with Susan. In retrospect, it seemed as if a miracle had occurred, at least in comparison with where things had been in the preceding four days. Walter didn't believe in miracles—not yet, at least—so the analytical side of his brain went to work dissecting the *she-said-I-said* that resulted in the even-better-than-hoped-for outcome. Twenty minutes later, well past Dunsmuir, the closest he could come to *causality* was *intention*—which is to say both he and Susan had made up their minds, *independently*, to do and say whatever was necessary to restore their relationship. Once they had entered that spirit, or allowed that spirit to enter them, all they had to do was *go with the flow* and the miracle occurred! He searched for another word, but no luck—*miracle* would have to suffice for now.

Next he remembered Susan's admonition about ESP. He didn't know exactly what she meant by it, but the term had the same alien aroma as *miracle*, making him equally uneasy. His left brain cut in again with the definition: ESP, ExtraSensory Perception, 'the faculty of perceiving things by means other than the known senses, e.g., by telepathy or clairvoyance.' He ran this backward and forward a few times to sift out the essence, ending with *telepathy. OK, I'm supposed to clear my mind and let her thoughts flutter through the seventh dimension and alight somewhere in my brain. Fat chance! I've never done anything like that in my life.*

Then a different thought swooped down and perched smack dab in the middle of his consciousness, flapping its wings to gain his full attention: *What the hell do you think has been going on between you and Susan ever since you met, at least when you haven't been letting your fears and fantasies take over?* And another: *What do you think was happening between you and Nancy yesterday when you weren't preoccupied with Thunder Ray's harangue?* Those thoughts were sent screeching away like a flock of frightened crows as Walter found himself doing 70 in a turn flagged at 45. *Damn!* he fumed. *I gotta pay attention to my driving.* He expertly brought the truck under control, only to have another thought dive-bomb him. This time it was a white duck. *And what do you think we've been doing on the front porch these past few weeks, numb-nuts?* Abigail's image dissolved as Walter took note of a caution sign announcing another tight turn. He navigated through it easily and decided to defer further consideration of ESP until he could learn more about it—from Susan perhaps, or maybe Mac.

Backspacing his memory tape further, he began reflecting on his aborted tryst with Nancy. *What was that all about? Was I just plain horny or was I hedging my bets in case reconciliation with Susan didn't work out?* Neither option seemed particularly palatable because both revealed character flaws in him. Maybe they were only minor, maybe not. Minor flaws he could accept, but he concluded that the whole experience should serve as a warning lest they fester into major transgressions. Pursuing that thread further, he wondered how his phone call with Susan would have turned out if he *had* gone to Nancy's house as per her almost insistent invitation. He let the fantasy play in his imagination to discover possible outcomes that might have resulted. *I might have become so enthralled with Nancy's charms I would have taken a hard line with Susan, just like I did at the bike store.* His mind briefly flashed a clip in which he was frenetically screwing Nancy while talking on the phone with Susan. *Hell, I might not have called Susan at all—not then, not ever.*

Walter broke into a cold sweat, shaking as if afflicted with a high fever, painfully aware of how close he had come to disaster. He had experienced such episodes before, with the few near-miss incidents that had occurred in his flying career. Each time, he had wondered afterward whether something or someone, somewhere, was looking out for him. It certainly seemed that way, but he hadn't really delved into it. Again the twists and turns of Interstate 5 demanded his full attention, so Walter put his introspection on hold and focused on the road, the terrain, the weather, and the truck while he breezed past Redding.

After lunch at Red Bluff the driving wasn't very interesting, one hundred miles of nearly straight road, threading through the agricultural heartland of California's Central Valley, which afforded Walter another opportunity to reevaluate the previous day's events, this time the Bonanza Bible Church. Except for Nancy, nothing he had seen or heard there had surprised him, although much of it—the sermon especially—had made him uncomfortable. That in itself wasn't so bad—*after all, many ministers regard it their calling to comfort the afflicted and afflict the comfortable*—but the manner in which the affliction was delivered, the words used and the sentiments expressed, had troubled him deeply.

He had heard hell-and-damnation sermons before, during his sojourn at the United States Air Force Academy. Some of more rabidly radical reverends had certainly put it on the line that God was watching every last move you made, every word you uttered, and every thought you harbored, and they did their utmost to erase any doubt that if you strayed the least bit off the straight-and-narrow path, God would become a mean, vindictive *sonofabitch*. They seemed to hope you wouldn't notice—*maybe they didn't notice either*—that this was *completely contrary* to the picture they painted of Jesus, God's second-in-command and chief, if not sole, representative here on earth, as the embodiment of love, compassion, and forgiveness. Jesus' own words as recounted in the Bible, especially in the 'Sermon on the Mount,' affirmed and supported this appraisal of him and his mission.

Yes, Thunder Ray may have matched or even slightly surpassed the put-on passion and oxymoronic unctuousness of the Colorado Bible-thumpers, but what was new and different in The Rev's rendition was the hate-mongering directed at Muslims. Walter had little doubt that fundamentalist—and perhaps some not-so-fundamentalist—preachers all over the country were spewing the same vitriol, but he hadn't encountered it in person until yesterday. It seemed to him the hate, the fear, the intolerance, and the elevation of ignorance over reason have metastasized since '9/11,' and Jesus' message has been folded, stapled, and mutilated beyond all recognition. Fanatical fundamentalist Muslims have added fuel to the fire, he acknowledged, because it serves their violent visions of *jihad*.

Walter wondered if the symmetry between Christianity and Islam extends to the subordination of a more peaceful and loving interpretation of Muhammad's life and teaching, but he didn't know enough about Islam to form more than a worthless opinion. He resolved to study up on the Koran and other Islamic doctrines, so he could make his own reasonably well-informed judgment. *Perhaps I can find an Islamic center, or some kind of interfaith center, in the Livermore area, where I can buy some books*, he speculated. Having thus arrived at a plan to improve his understanding of religion beyond the narrow confines of Joe Sixpack's America, Walter suspended his critique of the Bonanza Bible Church for the time being. He wasn't accustomed to spending much time and energy on things like God, faith, and spirituality, and he was already getting a stronger-than-usual dose of all that from his books by Joel Goldsmith and Tolstoy. It seemed like he was destined to plunge into the deeper end of the pool, but he wasn't confident of his ability to swim—or even tread water.

More than an hour later he was gunning southward on I-680 past the affluent 'burbs of Alamo and Danville, and at Dublin he was into his old stomping ground, where he knew every exit, short cut, and traffic hazard. Choosing his lane changes expertly, he navigated onto eastbound I-580 and promptly got swallowed up in the multilane commuter traffic. Keeping his cool and laughing at the antics of some wannabe race-car drivers intent on getting to their destinations a few seconds sooner, he left the freeway and drove up to the entrance of an economy motel. He hadn't phoned ahead for reservations, but it was "No problem, sir," and by 4:30 he was in his room, pulling down the bedspread for a belated afternoon nap.

He didn't sleep long. Whether it was excitement over being back in his old turf or just his subconscious alarm clock, it didn't matter—he was up-and-at-'em again within an hour. The first item of business was to call his old phone number to check up on his kids and, he hoped, arrange to spend a little time with them. Considering his last communication with them and their mother, he wasn't very optimistic it would happen, but it was worth a try—if only to keep up appearances. As it turned out his assessment was correct. "No, the kids aren't available tonight," Angela scolded, "because they're spending the holiday with schoolmates. And they won't be available tomorrow night either because tomorrow and Wednesday are school days. It's the end of the school year, and they've got exams. Maybe if you had given me a little warning we could have worked something out, but if you just pop into town whenever the impulse hits you, you can't expect us to rearrange our lives for your convenience." *Yada, yada, yada....*

Walter took the ritual browbeating in good humor, replying in appropriate tones of humility and contrition. "Do you suppose I could spend some time with them later in the summer if I contact you a month in advance to work out the arrangements? My living situation in Oregon really isn't conducive to having them visit me there, but I could come down here and rent a vacation home for a week."

Angela backed off a little from her aggression. "Yes, we could probably do something like that." She sounded disappointed that his conciliatory tone had spoiled the opportunity for a good argument—*just like old times*, he thought—but she recovered nicely by imposing some limitations of her own making. "The kids will be spending the summer at a camp in Maine. I'll be financing it all by working there as a counselor, but I'll be in a different part of the camp, so they'll have a little independence. We'll come back sometime in the first week of August, which will leave a two-or-three-week window before school starts. It might help me for you to take them for a week, to give me time to prepare for the next school year." Angela had gone back to teaching once both kids were in school, which proved to be fortuitous for Walter in negotiating the financial terms of the divorce.

Seizing the opportunity for a little one-upmanship to get even for her aggression, he asked solicitously, "How's the teaching going? Are you still enjoying it?"

She was taken aback slightly—*score three points for Walter.* "Er—yes—it's going well, and I'm still enjoying it. I plan to start back to school next year to complete my master's degree, but it will take a few years." Then, almost as an afterthought, "And you? How are you doing?" *Score another point for Walter.*

"I'm doing well. You probably wouldn't recognize me. I've lost about ten pounds and I've grown a beard."

That elicited a small laugh from Angela—*and another point for Walter.* "No, I might not recognize you"—*although I'm sure you're the same old self-centered bastard underneath,* she thought. "I'll have to warn the kids before you come to see them."

Walter wisely chose to quit while he was ahead. "Well, that's all that's on my mind today. Send me an email when you nail down your schedule for August, and when you get an address and phone number for the camp in Maine, send me that too—just in case. Maybe I'll send the kids a postcard or something."

"Birthday cards would be appropriate, even small gifts"—*Angela got in three points of her own before Walter could escape with a clean victory.* "Thanks for calling." *She reached for another point.*

"Any time"—*he matched it.*

Walter hung up and rummaged around in the nightstand for a phone directory. Looking up 'Interfaith Centers' In the *Yellow Pages,* he was delighted to find more than a hundred listed for the East Bay area. Christian churches constituted the largest number, with Muslims close behind, but there were also Jewish, Buddhist, Hindu, and Jain groups, plus a few others Walter couldn't decode. He went through the list carefully to pick out three or four he might seek out on Tuesday.

After dinner he called Susan. She answered right away, her cheerful voice telling him she was in good spirits. The conversation meandered through tidbits of small talk: his trip, the weather, her day at the Welcome Center, and so forth. Susan inquired whether he had remembered to turn on his ESP. "Yes, I did—or at least I tried. I was confused about what I'm supposed to do, or what you had in mind. I think you'll have to explain more about that, maybe give me some personal lessons."

"I've been giving you lessons ever since we met," she replied, "only you didn't realize it. Did you have any unusual or unexpected thoughts or insights as you were driving today? Did your intuition tell you anything?"

"Well, ... yes. I felt that what happened last night was the result of our *shared intention*—we had both thought through what happened last week and we had both concluded we wanted, more than anything else, to put our relationship back on track. Does that make any sense to you?"

"Bingo! You're right on target. That's the message I was sending to you all morning. You get three gold stars."

Gold stars! he thought. *That's a different game than I was playing with Angela—not competitive, but 'win-win' instead of 'win-lose.'* Somewhere in the back of his mind a memory stirred. A philosophy teacher had written a book about 'finite games' in which the object is to *win* by outscoring the opponent, and 'infinite games' in which the object is merely *to continue the game.* His marriage with Angela had degenerated into a finite game which both of them eventually found to be not worth sustaining, whereas his relationship with Susan seemed to be flowering into an infinite game. He was instantly delighted with that insight but decided to defer expounding on it to Susan until a time and place where he could hold her hand and bathe in her eyes as he did so.

"I also thought a bit about the sermon I heard yesterday morning. I'll spare you the gory details, but the upshot is that I've decided to study up on Islam and the whole issue of religious tolerance in general. After I got here today, I checked in the local phone directory to find some interfaith centers where I might get some books or further guidance while I'm here. I'll share all that with you when I get back. It's probably much too intellectual and complex to send via ESP."

"Yes, I agree. We'll keep it simple and not too intellectual on the ESP side, but I look forward to hearing what you learn in your exploring. There are some things coming up in the interfaith arena here in KFalls that I think will also interest you, and you might be surprised who else in town is interested in all that."

Her cryptic comment pushed him into mild irritation. *Why doesn't she just come out and tell me? Why does she have to make it a game?* he chafed. Then it dawned on him Susan was making it an infinite game! *New game, new rules,* he told himself. *Forget the old rules and the old strategies. They don't work here. They're actually counter-productive.* The conversation lapsed back into comforting comments to reassure one another. Neither of them needed to keep talking. They could hang up and let the nonverbal communication—*the ESP?*—keep going all night.

32.

For the second day in a row Walter did not turn on the alarm. He did, however, take time to meditate thirty minutes. After breakfast he went directly to the rental storage facility where he had put some of his belongings when he moved out of the house where Angela and the kids still lived. Now he could barely remember what he had stored and what he had donated to various charities. *This is going to be like Christmas morning,* he thought. *I might as well make it seem like fun, rather than a chore.*

His first impression upon opening the door to his storage unit was one of relief: the combined volume of boxes and other items appeared small enough it would all fit in the bed of his pickup and still allow him to close the tonneau cover. Thus, he could simply load it now and leave the task of sorting through it until he got back to the cabin, which would give him more time for the other items on the day's 'to-do' list. Almost joyfully, he began hoisting boxes into the truck, concerned only with arranging them for good weight balance and positioning them so they wouldn't shift as he drove along—things pilots are always wary of. He left the odd items—golf clubs, tennis and squash rackets, a backpack, and a couple tool boxes—until last, wedging them into remaining nooks and crannies in the load. Walter locked the tonneau cover, closed the storage unit, and checked out at the office.

Before driving away, he called the customer service number for his cell phone and inquired about devices to improve the signal in remote areas. Armed with the names and model numbers of recommended boosters, he set sail for an 'electronics supermarket' store in Fremont. Within an hour, he had found the store, talked at length with a salesman about the relative merits of the half-dozen units on display, and made his selection, trying not to skimp on features and quality while keeping the cost within reason.

Now only one thing remained to do. Consulting the list of interfaith centers he had compiled the night before, he saw that one of them, an Islamic Center, was close to the route back to Livermore. Fifteen minutes later he was at the Center, in a beautifully landscaped courtyard with an elaborate water fountain in the middle. Off to the right, next to a doorway, was a sign: Reception & Book Store. As he entered, he was greeted by a tall, dark-skinned, thirty-ish man dressed in loose-fitting white pants and tunic of a style Walter associated with parts of India and Africa.

Walter said he was looking for some introductory material on Islam. The man, who gave his name as Hussein, inquired about his purpose, and Walter explained he had been prompted to learn more about the faith because he had been put off by the hate-ridden rants of so-called Christians who were blind to their own ignorance and intolerance. Hussein smiled and nodded knowingly. He started to lead the way to some tables and shelves displaying books but stopped short as the sound of musical chanting issued from loudspeakers in the courtyard. "It is time for noonday prayer," he said. "Would you like to observe? It will last about thirty minutes."

Surprised by the unexpected invitation, Walter hesitated, then said, "Yes, if it's not too much trouble."

"Not at all," came the reply. "Please follow me." Hussein led Walter out the door and around the edge of the courtyard to a large pair of doors in the back wall. Several pairs of shoes were lined up along the wall. Hussein went to the end of one line and kicked off his shoes, and Walter did likewise. Crossing the threshold into a large high-ceilinged room, Hussein turned to follow the wall to a corner area where there were two rows of straight chairs. "Sit here," he said. "You don't have to say anything or do anything, just watch and listen. I'll come back when the prayers are done."

Hussein walked back to a community sink just beyond the entrance, washed his hands, mouth, face, and feet, and stepped onto the large carpet covering most of the room's floor. Reverently, he proceeded to a place in a row of kneeling men, others following, quickly filling most of the carpeted space. The 'Call to Prayer' from the loudspeaker stopped and an elderly man in a black robe walked slowly to the front of the room and took his place. Almost as one, the entire group went through a succession of bows and prostrations, sometimes standing, sometimes kneeling, all the while reciting prayers in what Walter presumed was Arabic. Unable to understand a word or gesture, he looked around the room. Unlike the Christian churches he had visited, there were no statues, no paintings, no ornamentation of any kind except for some inscriptions, apparently also in Arabic, on the frieze around the room. There was also a semicircular niche set into the middle of the front wall, which Walter guessed—correctly, he later learned—indicated the direction to Mecca, toward which Muslims face when they pray. The prayers continued at an even pace but stopped abruptly. One moment everybody had been kneeling and praying, the next they were all standing and milling about, greeting and talking quietly with friends. After a minute, Hussein emerged from the multitude and came over to where Walter was sitting, still mesmerized, lulled into an altered state of consciousness by the quiet rumble of the Arabic. "Did we put you to sleep?" he asked, smiling.

Walter shook himself fully awake. "No, but you definitely tranquilized me."

Hussein's smile split into a broad grin. "That's good. Our prayers are meant to put us at peace, not to excite us. The closing petition, in fact, asks for peace, mercy, and the blessing of God."

They returned to the book store, where Hussein selected a book from one of the tables and handed it to Walter. "This is a good introductory book on Islam: clear and concise. It's by a professor I studied under at Berkeley some years ago. He was born and raised in China where his parents were Methodist missionaries."

Walter glanced at the front cover, turned the book over, and began reading the back cover:

> Huston Smith is internationally known and revered as the premier teacher of world religions and for his bestselling books The World's Religions and Why Religion Matters. He was the focus of a five-part PBS television series with Bill Moyers, and has taught at Washington University, the Massachusetts Institute of Technology, Syracuse University, and the University of California, Berkeley.

"This looks like a winner," he said. "Anything else?"

"Most of these other books are rather specialized, written by scholars *for* scholars," Hussein replied. "I wouldn't recommend them to anyone just beginning to study Islam. There is, however, another book I might suggest, although we don't have it here because it is somewhat controversial, at least among religious scholars. It's Deepak Chopra's fictionalized biography of Muhammad. It reads like a novel—because it *is* a kind of novel—so it's a good way to get the *feel* of Islam without getting bogged down in a morass of history and dogma." He added in a half-whisper, "You can find it at any of the big bookstores in town."

"OK, I'll look for it this afternoon." Walter glanced around to see if was anything else might be of interest. His gaze landed on a small display of CDs. "Do you have any recordings of the 'Call to Prayer' that came over the sound system?"

Hussein frowned. "Most recordings like that are part of highly specialized scholarly studies, for hard-core Muslims, so to speak"—he scratched his head—"but there is something that might satisfy your need: its a CD by *'Yusuf,'* formerly known as 'Cat Stevens.' He was a big pop star who converted to Islam at the peak of his fame in 1977. He changed his name to 'Yusuf Islam,' auctioned away all his guitars for charity, and left his music career to devote himself to educational and philanthropic causes in the Muslim community. After being given several awards for his work in promoting peace in the world, he returned to pop music in 2006, using the professional name *Yusuf.*" He picked up a CD from the display. "We don't usually stock any pop music here, but we got this one because it consists of songs he recorded during the twenty-some years he immersed himself in Islam. The last track is the *'Adhan,'* the Islamic Call to Prayer."

Walter didn't need a longer sales pitch. "Sold," he said, accepting the CD from Hussein. "I think that will be enough for today."

From his decade of residing in that area, Walter knew where the Barnes & Noble bookstore was, so he made that his next stop, except for a short detour for lunch at McDonald's. *That's two Big Macs in less than a week,* he rebuked himself. *Gotta watch my diet.* At the bookstore, he discovered that Chopra's *Muhammad: A Story of the Last Prophet* was available not only in book form but also as an unabridged seven-CD audiobook narrated by the author himself. *I can listen to that in the truck on the way home,* he thought, *and maybe play it for Abigail when I get back,* his impish mind added. Before checking out, he browsed through the store's expansive display of magazines, not looking for anything in particular, but just to see if anything jumped out at him. Something did, a thin 5-by-8 magazine, *Science of Mind: A Guide for Spiritual Living.* Leafing through it, he found 'Daily Guides' for the upcoming month and some articles that promised an interesting perspective.

It was now early afternoon and Walter had finished his 'to-do' list, so he went back to the motel for a nap. It was well past check-out time and he had already paid for the second night's stay; otherwise he would have hit the road for home immediately. He awoke from his nap just after 4:00. Rather than spend the evening alone watching idiotic TV fare in his room, he decided to call one of his former flying buddies, Tom Ketchum, in hopes of rekindling an old friendship. Luck was with him; Tom answered on the third ring. "Hello, Tomcat. This is Walt Baker. Remember me?"

"Walt! You old good-for-nothing! How the hell are you?"

"I am well, thank you. I'm back in town for a day to collect all the stuff I had in storage and move it back to my new digs. I was wondering if we might get together this evening and drink a few beers."

"Sure," was the answer. "I don't go back to work until Friday, so we can stay out all night if you want."

"No, nothing like that. I want to be on the road back to Oregon early tomorrow morning."

"Oregon?! That's a helluva place to go. What the bleep are you doing up there?"

"I'll tell you about it tonight. What time do you want to meet up?"

"How about six-thirty, so we can get a burger, too? At Harry's, like old times?"

"Great! See you there."

Walter checked his watch. He had more than an hour to kill before Susan would be home. He picked up Huston Smith's book on Islam and started reading. In his 'Introduction,' the author attempted to dispel three stereotypes about Islam: violence, the place of women, and fundamentalism. He claimed that the Koran contains over ten times more references to Allah's forbearance and mercy than to his judgment and wrath, and that the Bible contains at least as many violent injunctions as the Koran. *Is Thunder Ray aware of that?* Walter wondered. *He sure doesn't act like it.* The Islamic concept of *jihad*—which literally means 'effort, exertion, or struggle'—has been perverted to mean 'Holy War,' but even that is "virtually identical with the 'Just War' doctrine in Christian canon law, right down to the notion that martyrs in both [Islam and Christianity] are assured of entry into heaven," according to Smith.

Walter skimmed past the author's comments about Islamic treatment of women, except to note it is 'cultural baggage' carried over from patriarchal societies that have embraced Islam, but it is not inherent to Islamic teaching itself. As for Islamic fundamentalism, Smith said it is much the same thing: a desire to maintain a traditional outlook and way of life in the face of the relentless change inherent in Western modernity. This stems in part from the Islamic mindset that fuses religious and civil power into a single all-pervading authority. Smith lamented, "it is virtually impossible for us to understand [such] a world" and "no part of the world is more hopelessly, systematically, and stubbornly misunderstood by us." *That pretty much sums up Thunder Ray and his ilk,* Walter concluded, inferring it would be a waste of time and effort to try to convince The Rev to change his tune. *I guess I won't be going back to the Bonanza Bible Church again. The 'good news' is I'll be that much less likely to bump into Nancy again.*

As the time passed 5:30, Walter decided to call Susan, hoping she wouldn't be out running errands. Yes, he could call her later from Harry's, but it wouldn't be very conducive to an extended conversation. He was lucky again; Susan had come straight home from work—her intuition had told her to put off her shopping until tomorrow, she said. Walter wondered if this was ESP or just a coincidence, but said nothing.

They reviewed the day's events and nonevents for each other. Susan was interested in his impressions of the noonday prayers at the Islamic center and said she wanted to listen to the *Yusuf* CD with Walter after dinner at her house when he returned. Walter told her he was going to the pub with Tom that evening, but he wouldn't be out late. "I thought you were giving up alcohol," she reminded him.

"I'll drink non-alcoholic beer," Walter replied. "It doesn't taste as good as the real stuff, but I don't want to even come close to getting drunk. I'll have to drive from the pub back to the motel tonight, and I want to get an early start tomorrow morning."

"I didn't mean to sound like a nagging wife," Susan said defensively. "I'm sorry."

"You weren't nagging. You were just expressing your concern for my welfare," Walter corrected, "and I deeply appreciate it."

"Thank you," said Susan. "I appreciate your attitude, too—deeply." The ensuing joint giggle signaled that the verbal portion of their conversation was over. They said 'good night,' Susan in her usual seductive tone, and hung up.

Walter checked his watch again. If there were no snafus on the freeway, he would have just enough time to get to Harry's by 6:30. His streak of good luck continued; he parked in front of Harry's at 6:29 sharp, spotting Tom's shiny black Porsche Carrera, with 'TOMCAT' vanity plates, two spaces over. Tom was already seated at a table, as far away from the blaring TV as he could get—he had come to talk, and he knew Walter had too. He did a double-take when he saw Walter's beard. "Is it really you, Walter Baker, under all that shrubbery, or is it Sasquatch?"

"It's Chewbacca," Walter joked. "You always knew he was my secret hero, didn't you." They ordered food and drinks. Tom put on another show of surprise when Walter ordered non-alcoholic beer, but Walter played it down, saying, "I gotta drive later." Tom's face took on a look that said, "That never stopped you before," but he held his tongue.

Tom and Walter had been drinking buddies when they both worked for the airline and often paired on the same flights. Before that they had flown together in the Air Force, where Tom, the elder by three years, had become a big-brother role model for Walter. It was Tom who had jumped ship first, giving up a military career for a less-regimented, higher-paying job with the airline, and it was he who had recruited Walter to follow in his footsteps. It was also Tom who, by example, led Walter to stray outside his marriage into a series of torrid one-night stands with readily available members of the cabin crews, and it was he who had provided moral support and barroom legal counsel as

Walter slogged through a divorce. However, the downsizing resulting from the airline merger had forced a parting of their ways. Tom had enough seniority to command a good position in the merged airline, whereas Walter did not. Consequently, Tom was still flying and partying and womanizing, and Walter had dropped out of the East Bay social scene.

As the beers arrived, Tom turned to Walter and dived into the important business of the evening. "So you're moving to Oregon, eh? Becoming an '*Oregano*?'"

"It's '*Oregonian*,'" Walter corrected, even though he knew it was a joke. "I actually moved three weeks ago. I just came down to get the last of my things." He went on to briefly describe his living arrangement, and Tom's incredulity grew with every sentence.

When Walter paused for breath, Tom could no longer contain himself. "Let me get this straight," he interrupted. "You've taken vows of poverty, chastity, and God-only-knows-what-other-strictures, and you've sentenced yourself to living like a hermit in Bumfuck, Oregon. Why?! What for?"

"Don't make it sound so bad," Walter protested. "It's not like I've given up on life, liberty, and the pursuit of happiness. If anything, it's the exact opposite. For the first time in my life I'm really examining who I am and who I want to be, where I've come from and where I want to go. I've got minimal restrictions, minimal responsibilities, minimal obligations, so I'm free to go anywhere and do most anything as long as it doesn't require huge sums of money."

"OK, I can accept that," Tom backed down a little, "but there are other ways, easier ways, to go about that. For instance, you could stay right here in the Bay Area and party and screw 'til your balls glow in the dark and your dick turns to silly putty—just like we used to do, only more and better." The look on Walter's face told Tom that option had already been considered and rejected. "Or I could introduce you to a friend of mine: Samantha. She's a little older than you, smart, gorgeous, and unbelievably rich—she's either widowed or divorced, but either way but she's got a shitload of money. You could move in with her and minister to her sexual needs—which I dare say would also surpass your wildest fantasies, unless you've got a demon inside you that you haven't told me about—and you could have an incredible car, a fabulous house, fantastic clothes, maybe even your own plane. Hell, you could make like you're her private pilot, and you two could go jetting off to all sorts of exotic places."

"She sounds like any man's dream," Walter admitted, "but if she's all that, why aren't you already diddling her?"

"Ah, Walter, don't you remember? I'm into younger women, preferably in their mid-to-late-twenties. They can indulge their father fetishes with me, and they look so cool with me on the dance floor or beside me in the Porsche. Every other man we pass has his eyes bulging and his tongue hanging out, but I know she's going home with *me*, into *my* bed. When the novelty wears off, or the conversation lags—that usually occurs first because I have an affinity for air-heads—I can pat her on the butt and send her out the door. There's always another one, an even better one, just around the corner."

"Well, we always did have different tastes in women," Walter conceded. "I guess that's why we got along so well—we never competed with each other."

"Right, m'boy. We were a great team, and we can do it again. Just say the word and I'll dial it into my magic lamp, wake up the Genie, and—*poof!*—you'll be in heaven."

Walter frowned. "Somehow I don't think that's what heaven is like, or all about. I don't subscribe to this seventy-two virgin, overflowing-milk-and-honey fairy tale that seems to motivate Muslim terrorists. The imams and ayatollahs who put out that garbage are nothing but a clique of dirty old men, lying through their teeth in order to advance their own personal power."

"Whoa! Take it easy. I didn't mean to make this a religious issue, but I do believe God wants us to play, to lighten up, to not take things so seriously. As Benjamin Franklin said, 'Beer is proof God loves us and wants us to be happy.'" He lifted his mug, Walter did likewise, they clanked the mugs together and drained them, chug-a-lug.

As they plunked the mugs down on the table, the waitress delivered their food—finally!—and Walter signaled for another round of beers. Tom bit voraciously into his hamburger, while Walter picked at his fries and tried to move the conversation back to less flamboyant matters. "If truth be told, there *is* a new woman in my life. I met her the first day I was in Klamath Falls. She's about my age or a little younger, a single mom whose daughter has left the nest. She's attractive and intelligent and, most of all, she's interested in a serious, long-term relationship. We haven't jumped into the sack together yet, but that will happen in due time. Right now we just talk, finish each other's sentences, and laugh a lot."

"Keeping at least three feet between you and both feet on the floor at all times," Tom kidded.

Walter joined in his laughter. "No, it's not puritanical. She kisses really good, and if I may be allowed to extrapolate from that, she'll be great in bed too when we finally get there."

"In the meantime, you play lots of pocket polo." Tom was incurable; sex was always uppermost on his mind, except—thank God—when he was flying.

Walter continued, trying to wrap up the description of his relationship with Susan. "We haven't even begun to discuss marriage—we've only known each other for three weeks, for Chrissake—but we could very well end up there in a year or so. I expect we'll shack up first and then take it from there." Walter was surprised and shocked by his own words. *Am I really saying this?* he asked himself.

"How do you expect to support the two of you in the style to which you have become accustomed?" Tom asked.

"The style may not be what I had these past few years in the Bay Area. She's got a job in the local tourist bureau that has enabled her to support herself and her kid, and she's now back in college, about halfway to a bachelor's degree in social work. I haven't begun exploring career opportunities in the area, but I'm reasonably sure I could hire on with any of the commuter airlines serving southern Oregon. There's also an Air Force National Guard training center at the local airport, so I might find something there."

"I suggest you look into corporate air businesses, if there are any around there," Tom advised. "It's usually a flexible, low-stress environment, and it pays well. They like to hire guys like you: experienced, mature, stable."

"That's a good idea. I'll put out some feelers when I get back. I've been preoccupied with getting my living situation set up to my liking and with getting to know Susan."

"It's good to know you've got your feelers functioning. For a minute, I was afraid you'd gone monastic on me."

Last Sunday's preliminary foreplay with Nancy popped into Walter's mind. "No, the feelers are still functioning, but mostly at 'standby' level for now. I'm confident they will be up to the challenge when the time comes."

"May your feelers never falter," Tom pronounced his blessing as he raised his mug in another toast, "and your swash never buckle."

"Amen! And the same to you," Walter concurred as he reached for his beer.

33.

Up at seven, on the road by eight, Walter was eager to get home. Rather than mix it up with the heavy commuter traffic heading west into the Bay Area on Interstate 580 at that hour, he went twenty miles east on 580 and 205 and north on Interstate 5. By the time he got to Sacramento 90 minutes later, traffic had lightened up considerably, as much as it ever does in that part of central California. At Williams, a scant hour beyond Sacramento, he swung off the Interstate to visit Granzella's Restaurant and Bakery, one of his favorite coffee stops in the whole world. He grooved on the feast of aromas as he walked in the front door and back along the polished wood plank floor: coffee, bread and rolls, and an indescribable mélange from the deli. He selected a not-too-gluttonous Danish to go with his dark roast coffee and devoured it shamelessly at one of the tables. Then he wandered through the display of condiments and picked out some stuffed olives and spicy mustard to take back to Susan.

Back on the interstate, he resumed listening to the audiobook on Muhammad he had started when he cleared the congestion around Sacramento. Deepak Chopra's deep, slightly accented voice transported Walter from the bright cleanliness of Granzella's to the dark, stinking pollution of Mecca, a barbaric Arabian trade center 1400 years ago. It was easy for him to understand why many religious scholars were unsympathetic to Chopra's vivid fictionalized account, but something Chopra had said in the 'Prelude' caught Walter's attention:

... Islam has been branded with barbarity in a unique way, in part because, in its zeal to maintain the Prophet's world as well as his word, the customs of antiquity have been preserved with modern times.

This not only more-than-adequately justified the author's literary license, but it also explained the past and present clashes between conservative Islamic culture and modern Western civilization.

After Disk One of the audiobook ended somewhere between Williams and Red Bluff, Walter elected to drive in silence for the next hour, continuing with Disk Two after lunch in Redding. That lasted him to a few miles beyond Weed, where the two-lane mountain road demanded his full attention, and once past Macdoel, he broke out the *Yusuf* CD to serenade him through the unexciting terrain extending to KFalls. Consequently, his mind was somewhere in the Middle East when his body arrived at the Welcome Center, shortly before four o'clock, although the sight of Susan at her usual duty station quickly brought his awareness back to the here-and-now. *Decorum be damned!* He stepped around the end of the counter to give her a proper kiss, albeit of moderate duration and passion as compared with what had transpired in McDonald's parking lot three days before. Whatever disapproval this might have engendered in Susan's boss was overwhelmed by her joy to see Susan and Walter exhilarating in each other's company once again, and his gift jar of Granzella's garlic stuffed olives added to her delight. Saying that he wasn't staying but a minute, Walter set his other gift items on the counter in front of Susan and asked her for a piece of paper so he could write down her full name, date and place of birth, and Social Security number. As she revealed that her maiden name, which she now used as her middle name, was Tierney, and that she was born on October 2, 1972, he explained that Ted would want to do a background check on visitors that he, Walter, might invite to the cabin.

"You're planning to show me your digs too? Just what do you have in mind?" Susan asked.

"I have a birthday in about two weeks, June 12 to be exact," Walter answered. "I'd like to take you to dinner in Bonanza to celebrate, and I thought you might like to see where I live while you're in the vicinity." Susan wrinkled her nose as if she were thinking, '*That's all? I expected something more erotic than that,*' but she said nothing as he tucked the paper into his shirt pocket. He promised to call her later in the evening, after he had unloaded his truck.

That task proved to be more time-consuming than anticipated, however, because of the limited storage space in his cabin. He wound up stacking several boxes in the middle of his living room and stashing his golf-clubs in the storage shed so he could spend the evening reading the installation/instruction manual for the new cell phone booster, with 'time out' for a bike ride to call Susan.

Their phone conversation celebrated a new feature of their daily routines, with Walter explaining they could readily contact one another 'like normal people do' after he got the phone booster working. Susan was more interested in Walter's outing with 'Tomcat' and whether Walter had remained true to his no-alcohol pledge. He happily reassured her that he had, wisely skipping the discussions of past and prospective womanizing. Walter was amazed that he didn't feel 'nagged' in doing this. He found her interest comforting, because it signaled an element of *stability* in the midst of all the changes he had been going through.

34.

Although he had slept in past his usual 6:15 rising time the past three mornings, Walter was rarin' to go when the alarm went off the next day. He did his usual half-hour meditation while the coffee brewed, then went outside, coffee mug in one hand and cell phone in the other, to scout out the best location for the booster's external antenna. Barefoot and in pajamas, he walked around the house three times before making his choice and going back inside to write down a list of needed items. He decided to see if Ted had any of them, but not knowing how early Ted got up, deferred it until later.

To fill the time he busied himself with opening the boxes in his living room. Two of them contained winter clothing, which went right back into the boxes to be stored until needed—*but where?*—and another had work clothes he could put to use immediately. A fourth held two suits, a blazer, some slacks, and dress-up accessories he would rather have put back, but he reluctantly allocated some of his limited closet space to them because Susan's graduation was approaching and he might be expected to wear coat-and-tie to the ceremony. *I could show up in blue jeans and nobody would probably bat an eye*, he thought. A final smaller carton presented a few almost-forgotten treasures: a multi-band radio, some hiking/camping items, and in the bottom, carefully wrapped in a towel, his Italian-made 9mm *Beretta* pistol. He caressed it for a moment, as if getting reacquainted with an old friend, then placed it in the back of his nightstand drawer.

It was now past 8:00 AM, so the Bonanza General Store should be open and Ted should be awake. Stuffing his shopping list in his pocket, he got in his truck and drove to Ted's house. There was a light on in what he thought was the kitchen, so he gave a couple 'beep-beeps' with the horn. Ted came out through the garage, coffee mug in hand. "Welcome back," he said. "How was the trip?"

"It was good. I got everything accomplished I went for, maybe even a little more. I didn't get to see my kids, but it looks like I'll be able to spend a week with them when I go back down in August." Walter chose his words carefully so as not to panic Ted with the possibility of having children compromise his privacy. "I bought a cell phone booster in an electronics store. It was suggested by my cell phone company as a way to improve the signal strength out here in the sticks. The installation instructions recommend using a metal pole to position the antenna at least ten feet away from a metal roof like on the cabin and storage shed. You wouldn't happen to have a pole lying around unused, would you?"

"Well, I just might," Ted replied. "Wait here a sec." He trudged off toward one of the outbuildings and soon returned with a piece of two-inch pipe about fifteen feet long. "I think this will work. Where do you plan to put it?"

"Behind the shed, but not too close to the trees if I can do that and still maintain the ten-foot separation from the house. I've got fifty feet of cable to work with."

"You're probably going to need a post-hole digger and maybe some kind of ladder. I can provide those, too. Why don't you schlep the pipe over now and come back for the rest when you figure out exactly what you need? I'll be going into town right after lunch, returning about four, but otherwise I'll be here."

"OK," Walter said, picking up the pipe and starting down the trail to his cabin. Five minutes later he returned to find the post-hole digger leaning against the side of his truck. He tossed it into the back and drove off to Bonanza. Now the uppermost thought in his mind was avoiding Nancy. He hoped she wasn't an early riser.

The General Store didn't have ammunition for his *Beretta*, but the clerk told him where he could buy it in KFalls. He shopped for the other items on his list and then went to the Post Office to pick up his mail: a credit card statement, a few items of junk mail, and a letter from the meditation center where he had applied for admission. He ripped open the letter and read: yes, his application had been accepted, and he was tentatively enrolled in a ten-day Insight Meditation Course beginning August 1!

Walter was delighted. His first thought was to call Mac to share the good news, which reminded him that Mac had said something about a forthcoming lecture he should attend. *I hope there isn't a scheduling conflict with the meditation course*, he thought. The Library wasn't open yet, so he went to the Community Center next door to scan the bulletin board. Sure enough, there was a single sheet announcing 'the first in a series of educational lectures sponsored by the Klamath County Mental Health Department.' It would take place at OIT in the evening of Thursday, June 19. *That's four weeks from tonight*, Walter reckoned. The topic would be 'Transitions: The Contributions of William Bridges,' and the speaker would be 'Dr. Delbert McCarter (Lt. Col., USAF, retired), local psychiatrist and Adjunct Professor of Applied Psychology at the Oregon Institute of Technology.' Walter was bowled over. He had been regarding his Mac as a Fishing Guide who sometimes masquerades as a mental health counselor, whereas in reality Mac was a Mental Health Counselor—a rather accomplished one with strong professional credentials—who sometimes masquerades as a fishing guide! So his 'friend' had been giving him professional counseling, almost free of charge! Walter thought of the somewhat cryptic comments Susan had made whenever Mac's name had come up. *Now that she's graduating from KCC, she will soon be taking courses from Mac at OIT. Maybe she has been getting counseling from him as well.*

He called Mac, who answered right away. Walter told him of the good news from the meditation center and then blurted out his surprise about Mac's forthcoming lecture. Mac just laughed and said something about never claiming he *wasn't* a mental health counselor and if there had been any misrepresentation, it was about his credentials as a fishing guide. It was Walter's turn to laugh and reply, "Well, I'm going to continue acting as if you *are* a competent fishing guide, regardless of whether we catch anything. When can we get together for another go at fly fishing?"

"Next Tuesday? Meet at the same time and place as before?"

"That works for me." Walter chose to not test his hypotheses about Mac's relationship with Susan at that point. He wanted to bounce them off Susan first, to see what her answers were. That would be tomorrow.

Back at the cabin, he spent the rest of the morning setting up the pole and completing the cell phone booster installation, then made a final trek down the path to Ted's to return the post-hole digger and borrowed ladder. While he was there, he gave Ted the piece of paper with Susan's birth information on it. "I'll have a birthday in two weeks, and I'm planning to take my lady friend out to dinner in Bonanza. We may stop by the cabin briefly before or after, so here's her vital statistics in case you want to get a background check on her." Ted scanned the paper and grunted his assent. Walter turned and started to leave, then stopped as he remembered some 'old business.' "I forgot to ask you how Abigail fared in my absence these past three days. I haven't seen her since I got back."

"She didn't seem disturbed by the change in her routine," Ted replied. "I saw her head down the path to your place on Monday morning, but she came back within ten minutes. I figured that wasn't enough time for her to squeeze out an egg, so I didn't check your front porch. And as far as I could tell, she hung around here all day Tuesday and Wednesday, and all morning today as well."

"I wonder if she's given up on me," Walter speculated.

"Why don't you ask her? She's right behind you."

Walter turned around, knelt, and extended his hand. She stepped forward to nuzzle it, looking for food. "Sorry, old girl," Walter said softly. "If you want a snack from me, you'll have to make a house call. I don't do delivery."

Ted watched with amusement. "Maybe you could establish some kind of signaling system with her—a bell or something, like Pavlov used with his slobbering dogs."

"That's a good idea," Walter said as he stood up. "I bought some music at an Islamic Center in California, and maybe I can condition her to come over to the cabin when I play it."

"Might be fun to try, but don't play it too loud. Lottie has some rather negative associations with Muslims, so it might set her off."

Walter stifled his surprise. "If you think it could create a problem, I'll get some different music."

"No, don't do that. She's got to dig herself out of that hole anyhow if we expect to live any kind of normal life. Just don't come on too strong, too fast. I'll monitor her a little more closely for a while, just in case." *I wonder what her problem is,* Walter thought. *Maybe I can ask Mac about it next week. He ought to have some theories, or some possible explanations.*

After lunch, Walter went for a short bike ride, and as he was returning up the gravel driveway to his cabin, he met Ted, headed outbound in his Toyota sedan. Lottie was seated in back, barely visible behind the Camry's darkly tinted windows. She was wearing a headscarf, which partially hid her face, but Walter's fleeting glimpse of her matched something deep in his memory. *I've seen her somewhere before—more than a year ago, but less than five. Her name doesn't ring a bell, but she could easily have changed it. Who is she—or rather, who was she?* He put it out of his mind for the time being and spent the rest of the afternoon sifting and storing things he had brought from California. *Yes, it was sort of like Christmas, but it was only May 29.*

His afternoon nap was shortened and punctuated by growing anticipation of the first test of the new cell phone booster, and once he had finished his evening meal, impatience finally won out. He sat himself down in the easy chair, retrieved Susan's number from the cell phone memory, and hit 'Send.' He immediately noticed was the static that had previously interfered with comprehension was totally gone, and the 'ring' signal was loud and clear. And when Susan answered, she sounded like was standing right next to him. "Hi, Susan. It's Walter. Can you hear me OK?"

"Oh my, yes! It's almost too loud. Wait a minute while I figure out how to turn down the volume.... There. Say something so I can check it."

"I just called to say I love you / I just called to say how much I care," Walter crooned the 1984 Stevie Wonder hit song with enthusiasm, but not much finesse. *"I just called to say I love you, and I mean it from the bottom of my heart.* Whaddaya think?"

"Well, the audio quality is great, and the sentiment is wonderful, but I wouldn't say you have a promising future in show business." She added her own special giggle.

"Damn," he said in mock anger, "I was hoping to get a gig at one of the big casinos in Vegas. Must you always be so honest and direct in expressing your opinions?"

"Let's stick with the audio and the sentiment, and not worry about the rest. Two out of three ain't bad."

"I can live with that. Now let's try one more test. We'll both hang up and you try to call me. If you don't get through after three tries, stop. I'll call you back after five minutes if I haven't heard from you."

Walter punched the 'End' key on his phone and waited. His phone rang within seconds, and when he answered, Susan started singing 'You Are the Sunshine of My Life,' a 1973 Number One hit by Stevie Wonder. Her rendition was considerably better than Walter's, maybe not quite good enough for the big-time in Vegas, but certainly more than adequate for a local cabaret if she wanted to make that scene. "Wow!" he said. "You're revealing an aspect of yourself I hadn't seen before."

"You ain't seen nuttin' yet," she replied, now trying to imitate Jimmy Durante.

"I can hardly wait," Walter countered. "When do we start?"

"Tomorrow afternoon, at my place. Are you ready?" she asked.

"As ready as I'll ever be."

"Well, before you get too lathered up in anticipation, there is something I have to tell you." *Oh-oh,* he thought, his heart sinking. *Here it comes.* "I share my living quarters with another being." Walter's heart dropped a few more fathoms. "I have a dog"—heart back up halfway—"an eight-year old Basset hound"—almost all the way up—"named Moses"—up and over the top. "I hope you're not afraid of dogs or allergic to them or anything like that. If you are, we'll have to limit our time at my house to 'touch and go,' as I think you aviators call it. Moses' presence permeates my place: his smell, his dander, his toys. It's probably all over me too. Perhaps you've noticed, and you've been too polite to say anything."

"Oh, yes," Walter seized the opening, "I did notice something unusual about you, several things in fact: the sad eyes, the long nose, the big paws, the wonderfully soft long ears that keep dangling in your food...."

Susan's giggles grew into outright laughter. "I've heard it said that people grow to resemble their pets or they choose pets they aspire to emulate in some way. Perhaps we can explore those theories once you've gotten to meet Moses," she suggested.

"Excuse me for being blunt, but I'd rather explore them directly with you. Is Moses a mandatory participant in your foreplay?"

More laughter. When she recovered, Susan said, "I hope not. However, he has been the principal male energy in my life during the past several years, so some readjustment will be required."

"I think I can handle that," Walter said. "I'm even looking forward to it."

"I thought that would be your reaction, but I just wanted to warn you. And I want you to know Moses is *not* the reason I was reluctant to invite you to my house. I worked through that matter a week ago, and I'll share it with you tomorrow."

"I'm looking forward to that too—very much," Walter admitted.

Getting on to more prosaic details, Susan explained she would be working until 2:00 PM, so Walter shouldn't arrive until 2:30 to give her time to get home and eat a sandwich. "That will also give Moses time to calm down. He's always excited to see me after I've been away for a few hours."

"I can relate to that," Walter joked. "It will be interesting to see how you balance his energies and mine."

"It depends upon his bladder control—and yours as well." Susan evened the repartee score—but neither of them was keeping score, because it was an 'infinite game.' When they ended the call after a few more snippets of chitchat, Walter was overjoyed with how well things were going and what the next day promised. *Quite a contrast with how things were earlier*, he thought.

35.

Again Walter awoke full of energy and optimism, as he had every day since he made up with Susan. He sailed through his meditation, breakfast, and Three-'SH' routine—*should I trim my beard, or get a dog license?*—and was preparing to drive into Bonanza to do his laundry when he was startled by a knock at his cabin door. He spun around to find Ted peering through the screen, a smile on his face. "Come in," Walter called. "Is this a business call or a social visit?"

"I dunno. Maybe both," Ted replied. "I just wanted to tell you I got a positive report on your friend Susan. You can bring her over any time you want, although I ask that you tell her about my need for confidentiality and privacy. I'm sure she'll understand."

Walter was thunderstruck. Susan's background check had come thru in just 24 hours, which indicated whoever was doing the investigation already knew of her. *But why? How? Apparently there was quite a bit about Susan's past she hasn't told me. Ted said she would understand about his need for confidentiality,* which reminded Walter of Susan's statement, just the previous weekend, about her own need to keep the location of her residence from being widely known, and her promise to explain all that to him. *Was there some connection between Susan and Ted?* Walter was still reeling from this one-two punch, when Ted asked how his cell phone booster had checked out. "It works like a champ," Walter crowed, pointing to the unit. "My tests last evening showed I can call out and receive incoming calls with good signal strength and excellent audio quality. If you want to do the same thing, I'm sure you could get similar results."

"How much did it cost?" Ted asked.

"I paid three-fifty plus tax in California. For a bigger house like yours, you might need a more powerful unit. Some of them cost as much as six hundred bucks. The company I bought it from has a store up near Portland, or you could order it by mail."

"I think I'll hold off for the time being," Ted said, "but I will reimburse you for what you paid."

"No need for that," Walter objected. "I bought it without checking with you."

"True, but it increases the value of my property, and your improved ability to communicate reliably is more important to me than you might have realized."

Ted reached in his shirt pocket to extract a business card and handed it to Walter. "Since you've got my back, so to speak, in this living arrangement—my house and your cabin in relative proximity—I want you to know what to do in the event of a major emergency." Walter looked at the card: it was blank except for a telephone number with an 800 area code. Ted continued, "That's the 'Mayday' number. If you call it and give them my name, help will come, not the local sheriff or the fire department but *serious* help: at least a couple Suburbans and probably a chopper or two. It will take them fifteen minutes to an hour to get here, but they will come no matter what the time of day, in any kind of weather. They may ask for your name for verification, but that's all they will need. They already know where we are and that you are associated with me, for better or for worse. Any questions?"

Again Walter was stunned. He certainly understood the meaning of a 'Mayday' call and what response it is intended to evoke: it is to be used only as a last resort in situations of dire emergency, because all who hear the call are expected to drop everything else and do whatever is necessary to help. All that had been indelibly etched into his consciousness in his pilot training many years ago. Now he was too shocked to ask any questions; he could only grunt to indicate he understood. Ted waited a few more seconds to see if Walter could find any words. "If you've still got the bill for the booster, give it to me and deduct the amount from next month's rent. And thanks for taking the initiative on this. I should have thought of it long ago." Still somewhat dazed, Walter picked up the bill, which was lying on the kitchen table, and gave it to Ted. Ted glanced at it, then stuck it in his shirt pocket, and walked out the door. "See you later."

Another grunt was the only response Walter could muster. He sat down at the small dinner table and tried to collect his wits. Images of choppers, Suburbans, Susan, and Ted whirled around and intermingled in his mind, then coalesced into a large black meteorite that seemed to crash down into the middle of the table, blowing everything to smithereens and leaving him standing alone in a wasteland of smoldering debris. What little he had learned from meditation kicked in, enabling him to just stay there in the chaos without trying to escape it or clean it up. He closed his eyes and concentrated on his breathing for several minutes, eventually drifting into a neutral muddle that was not uncomfortable.

Abandoning the idea of doing his laundry, he went out onto the porch, hoping the fresh morning air would restore his energy. Abigail was waiting for him when he got there, so he fetched her a handful of mash before he sat down. Then he made one more trip inside to put the *Yusuf* CD on the stereo system and cue it to play the final track, the 'Call to Prayer.' The music helped him clear and calm his mind, and he remained quiet and motionless in his porch chair for nearly an hour. When he stood up afterward, Abigail fluttered off the porch and waddled away, leaving a beautiful, fresh egg in the middle of her nesting place. Walter's first reaction was to take it over to Ted, but a second thought said, *Give it to Susan.* He wrapped the egg in a paper towel and plastic grocery bag, and carefully placed it in his truck so it would not roll off onto the floor if he had to brake suddenly or went around a turn too fast. He collected his keys, phone, and billfold, and off he went, smiling in anticipation of Susan's surprise at his—and Abigail's—special gift.

In KFalls, Walter had a number of errands to run: get cash at the bank, drop off his suits and dress shirts at the cleaners, buy some ammunition, get an Oregon driver's license for himself and Oregon license plates for his truck. While buying the ammo, he also picked up an information sheet on obtaining an Oregon 'Carry and Conceal Weapon (CCW)' permit to replace the California permit left over from his airline job. He knew a training course would be required, but he welcomed it because his shooting skills were rusty. After lunch he found a barber shop in the Fred Meyer shopping center that included beard trims in their 'List of Services' and booked an appointment for the following week. He was eager to surprise Susan by showing up all beautified at her June 6 graduation.

At 2:30 sharp Walter pulled up in front of Susan's house on Wantland Avenue. It was a typical Klamath Falls residential neighborhood, with mostly one-story houses, all of them dating back to the 1950s or even late 1940s. Susan's was of average size, about 2000 square feet, with an attached one-car garage. It appeared to be well-maintained. He got out of the truck, then reached back in to carefully retrieve the bag containing Abigail's egg. Cradling it in both hands he walked toward the front door, wondering how he would protect it during his first encounter with Susan's dog. He was thankful Susan had warned him about Moses, and he became doubly thankful a split second after he rang the doorbell. From inside the house came a loud howl followed by a cacophony of barks and baying, which constituted Basset-speak for "I see him! There he is! I've got him cornered (or treed)!" and was intended to intimidate whoever or whatever it was on Walter's side of the door.

The door opened, and Susan and Moses simultaneous propelled themselves at Walter, the former hitting him high and the latter low. Walter had somewhat anticipated the assault and had formulated his priorities accordingly. First, he gave Susan a quick kiss while continuing to protect the bag/egg with both hands. Next he thrust the egg into her hands, saying, "Here, take this. Be careful. It's very fragile." Finally, he leaned down to pet Moses who had abandoned his bark/bay tactics in favor of frantically trying to climb Walter's leg to lick his face. Within seconds Walter was down on his knees, bestowing on Moses the hug he had intended for Susan and receiving the wettest, sloppiest doggy kiss he had ever experienced. Meanwhile, the bag/egg had pre-empted Susan from intervening to separate Moses and Walter, so all she could do was stand there and try to call off Moses orally. Initially, this had negligible effect on the dog and only slightly more on Walter, but the torrent of mutual affection gradually subsided to a trickle over the span of a minute.

Susan retreated to the kitchen, carefully laid the bag/egg at the back of a counter, and returned to Walter with some paper towels to mop off his doggy-drool-drenched face. By then he was standing again, laughing heartily, and trying to calm Moses. When he had finished drying himself, Walter wrapped his arms around Susan and gave her another kiss, this one of more appropriate duration, while Moses cheered them on with a series of barks. Susan, being well-practiced in Basset-speak, made no attempt to quell Moses' expression of approval, but turned her attention to Walter instead. "Are you OK? I had hoped to keep Moses under more control, but when you handed me whatever that was and told me it was fragile, I was completely stymied."

"Yes, I'm fine," Walter assured her, "but I don't know what would have happened if you hadn't warned me about Moses in advance. If either of us had dropped the item I gave you, we would have had quite a mess. Speaking of which, what did you do with it?"

Susan took Walter's hand and led him into the kitchen, where she gingerly placed the bag in the center of the table and opened it ever-so-slowly, as if it might explode like a jack-in-the-box. Unfolding the paper towel, she took its contents in her hand and pulled it out. "It's an egg!" she exclaimed.

"It's a *duck* egg," Walter clarified, "and it was laid only two or three hours ago."

"Yes, it's still warm. Where did you get it?"

"My landlord, Ted, has a Pekin duck—her name is Abigail. She seems to have taken a liking to me, so she waddles over to my cabin every day and sits there while I meditate on the front porch. I bought some duck mash at the feed store in Dairy so I can give her an occasional treat, and I folded an old towel to make a nesting spot for her on the corner of the porch. In response, she lays an egg for me from time to time, whenever the spirit moves her. This is Egg Number Three."

Susan's smile had become a giggle crescendoing into full laughter. "What did you do with Eggs Number One and Two?"

"I took them over to Ted and gave them to him."

"But why? The duck gave the eggs to *you*," she protested.

"I went all through that with Ted. He said the same thing, but I told him I couldn't bear to eat them myself."

"You sentimental, old softy! You ate the fish you caught, didn't you?"

"Yes, but eggs are different somehow."

"Some farmer you'd make!" she laughed. "What do you expect me to do with the egg?"

"Anything you want. I gave it to you. In fact, I think Abigail *meant* for me to bring it to you."

Susan was laughing harder now. "She also *talks* to you? Do you *quack* back? I'd like to hear that. Can you *quack* for me, too?"

Walter was turning red, but he was also laughing. He chose his words carefully, "No, it's nothing like that, but I do think there's some kind of communication going on between us, just like there is between you and Moses. I'm not going to say more, because I'm still trying to figure it out."

Susan put her arms around him. "Well, I think it's wonderful, and I look forward to hearing about future episodes in the '*Tales of Walter and Abigail.*' Thank you for sharing this with me—and the egg too."

"I'll be sure to convey your appreciation to Abigail," Walter said somberly, "although I hope the day will soon come when you will be able to say your thanks directly." Seizing the opportunity to ease into one of the issues that had been troubling him, he added, "If you can arrange to get the afternoon off in June 12, I'd like you to come out to the cabin, to see where I live, to sit on the porch with me—I bought two chairs—and then go have dinner in Bonanza. I would have liked to do that even sooner, but I couldn't rush it because of Ted's need to maintain privacy—more than that, *secrecy*—about where he lives. I don't know what his reasons are, but he assured me he has very good reasons, and they are legitimate. Anyhow, I've decided to trust him and take his word for it."

Susan replaced her smile with a serious countenance. "I can relate to that: what Ted's reasons might be, what his fears are, what he's doing about it. Unlike Ted, I'm ready to tell you my version of that story right now, so we can clear the air and not have any more misunderstandings like we did a week ago. I'm eager to do that, and I think you're eager to hear it, so why don't I make us some tea and let's sit and talk."

"That would be good," Walter agreed.

When they went into the living room with mugs of tea in hand, Walter saw that the room was relatively small and there was only one upholstered chair besides the sofa. He surmised that the chair was *Susan's*, so he astutely chose the sofa for himself. *This is Susan's space, and I have to be careful not to give the impression I'm going to invade and take it over from her*, he thought. As they sat down, Moses came over to the sofa and appeared ready to jump up in his lap. Susan read the sign, however, and ordered Moses to go lie down. Obediently, he retreated to a folded blanket in a corner of the room and curled himself on it, his head on his paws. "You know I wouldn't mind if Moses came up here and put his head in my lap," he said.

Moses lifted his head when his name was mentioned, then put it down again as Susan replied, "Yes, I can see you two are kindred spirits. I expected that, and I really wouldn't want it any other way. But I've taught him 'the house rules,' and I have to be consistent in enforcing them or he'll become confused and get into all sorts of mischief."

"And I'd better hurry up and learn 'the house rules' myself before I destroy everything you've established." Walter was half-serious, half-joking.

"Yes, that's what I've been afraid of," Susan responded. "Maybe that's why I haven't had any serious relationships with men since my husband was killed almost twenty years ago. Not that there weren't opportunities—there were an overwhelming number of them, especially at first—but I wasn't ready. I had to go through a period of mourning, which lasted a couple years. By the time it was over, I was completely turned-off by male aggressiveness, men who were insensitive to what I was going through and who seemed interested only in satisfying their own needs, which were primarily sexual. I swore off men altogether. I hope you can understand that."

"Yes. I've been on the other side of that, and my friend Tom whom I met up with in California is still there. A lot of men are. I think the comedian Robin Williams was spot-on when he observed that 'God gave men both a penis and a brain, but unfortunately not enough blood supply to run both at the same time.'"

Susan laughed. "The empirical evidence tends to support that conclusion, as I can personally testify. On several occasions I was forced to move to a different apartment because the advances were so insistent and persistent, but I learned. When I finally could afford to buy a house, I built a shell of security around me. I couldn't afford to live in an exclusive gated neighborhood, so I used privacy and anonymity. From what you've told me, your landlord Ted is doing the same thing, although he seems to have much better financial means than I ever did." Walter nodded his head to indicate his understanding and agreement but said nothing so as not to disrupt Susan's growing momentum.

"Now let's 'Fast Forward' to two years ago, when my daughter completed high school and left for a career in the US Army. That was a transition point for me as well as her. Just as you are doing now, I did a reassessment of my situation. I set some new career goals and developed an educational plan to realize them, taking advantage of the small financial windfall from not having to support her. I also looked at my personal life, my social life, my nonexistent sex life—and concluded I still have a few good years left. I also realized time was slipping away and nobody was knocking at my door, literally or figuratively, whether because of my age or because of my security net. Moreover, what few men I did meet in my job, my classes, and the few groups I had joined were either already 'taken' or rather unattractive. And then one month ago yesterday, you walked through the door of the Welcome Center."

"... and the rest, as they say, is history," Walter couldn't help interjecting.

"Well, you did sort of knock me off my feet, although I doubt that was on your mind when you first came in. It certainly wasn't on mine, but I was flabbergasted by how quickly that changed. Then you went off to Odell Lake for a week, and I began to have second thoughts. Sure, you were attractive and you were eligible—at least, you said you were—but I knew nothing about you and had very little way of checking up on you. More than being threatened by all that, I was surprised at how quickly and easily I had opened myself to you, making myself vulnerable, and when I saw what I had done, it scared me. I realized my physical privacy was the only line of defense I had left, so if you turned out to be a good-for-nothing scum-bag, my only recourse would be to hide out in this house..."

"... and that's why you didn't want to tell me where you live," Walter finished the sentence for her, then added, "Now I understand. I would probably have done the same thing in those circumstances. However, I was getting mixed signals from your ambivalence, and I couldn't sort it out. Your privacy and security issues got all twisted up and exaggerated by what I was hearing from Ted, creating some bad emotions for me as I was trying to figure out whether to rent his cabin or look for something else."

"Ironically, privacy and security was a central theme in our relationship right from the get-go," Susan added. "Your questions about 'weirdos' was what took us to Peet's that very first day."

"Yes, and I owe you a confession—and probably an apology—about that. As I began to learn more about the history of 'weirdo groups' in this area from persons other than you—especially from Mac, who told me about the Japanese balloon-bombs in World War II and the more recent Muslim *jihad* training center near

Bly—I wondered why you hadn't told me about them. I was sure you knew of them, so I felt you were intentionally hiding some parts of the story, and I began to question your motives."

Susan let out a big sigh. "Your intuition was right on target, because that's exactly what I was doing, and it all fits with what Mac probably told you. Now let me give you another piece of the story. At about the same time the Muslims were trying to get their Bly operation underway, I happened to take Lucy out to the Mitchell Monument for a Sunday afternoon picnic. When I stopped at the convenience store in Bly to pick up some cold drinks and check on directions, I overheard conversations between other customers and the store clerks regarding the arrival of '*furriners*' at the Frisco Ranch. Of course, this was two years before '9/11,' so nobody was expressing any fear, just curiosity. I thought nothing more of it either, until a few weeks later when a succession of Middle Easterners began trickling through the Welcome Center, asking for directions to Bly. After it went on for several weeks and seemed to be more than just a series of random events, I said something about it to Virginia Cox. The next thing I knew I was being interviewed by Federal agents—I think it was the FBI, but that might have been later. Again, I didn't make much of it, although they did ask me to send in a monthly activity report via email and immediately call a 'hot line' if I got wind of anything unusual.

"After '9/11,' however, the Feds suddenly became intensely interested in what had happened at the Frisco Ranch and whether there was any lingering activity. They regarded my situation at the Center as an important intelligence-gathering post, 'near the front lines' as one agent put it, and they considered using me as a key witness when they sought indictments and convictions for the handful of terrorists, would-be terrorists, or terrorist sympathizers who had been associated with the Bly operation. To protect me and the information I could provide about past activities, they wanted to put me into the Federal witness protection program, known as 'WitSec,' operated by the US Marshals Service. That would have meant a whole new life—a new name, a new identity, and a new location—for me *and* for Lucy—but I didn't want to do that. It would have been difficult enough for me, and I just couldn't believe it would work for her. Even if it 'worked' superficially, it would leave internal scars that would come back to haunt her at some later time, so I said, 'No' and stuck to my guns.

After lots of arm-twisting, more than a little fear-mongering, and hours of butt-numbing negotiation, they agreed to let me hunker down right here in Klamath Falls—'in plain sight' as the TV series hyped it—to keep up the vigilance at the Welcome Center. In lieu of blowing a wad of money in creating a new identity for me and Lucy, WitSec gave me a modest cash grant to make the down payment on this house and set up the privacy and security regimen—including Moses—that I've lived with ever since. And now you know the rest of the story, which, if you think about it, will explain my actions and apprehensions as you innocently fell into my life." Susan finished her tale with a slight 'so there' edge on her tone, which Walter immediately excused as understandable given the enormity of the emotional baggage she had just unloaded.

"I had no idea..." Walter stammered, "... but what you've just told me may clarify something else I've been puzzled about. Yesterday I gave Ted the information on your birthplace and date, so he could get a background check on you like he did on me before he would show me the cabin. It took him nearly a week to check on me—which is why I had to kill time at Odell Lake—but this morning he told me you had checked out OK. That was less than 24 hours, causing me to suspect he hadn't done a check on you at all. But if you've been in the WitSec system, even in your present low-key role, it would explain the almost-instant approval."

"... and more than that," Susan completed Walter's sentence, "it could explain whom he asked to do the background check on you."

Now Walter picked up the thread again, "But why would WitSec be willing to do that unless..."

"*Ted himself is also in the WitSec program!*" Susan finished the inference with a shout.

"There's more!" Walter joined her excitement. "He also gave me *this*"—he fished the business card out of his billfold—"and told me to call this number if there was a real '*Mayday*-level' emergency. He said doing so would bring '*serious* help,' which he characterized as Suburbans and helicopters on a scale beyond what local law enforcement can normally muster."

Susan eyeballed the card and handed it back. "I know that number. It's the same one WitSec gave me."

"... which *confirms* that Ted is indeed in the WitSec program!" they said in unison.

"*Whoosh!*" Walter collapsed backward into a sprawl on the sofa. Moses jumped up into a full-alert stance and let out a loud bay. Susan got up to calm him, but she broke into helpless laughter after two steps. Walter joined her, while Moses stood motionless, confused. As Susan and Walter quieted down, Moses' tail began to wag. Walter had been around dogs enough to know what that meant. "I think he wants to go for a walk," he said.

"Shhh!" scolded Susan. "You can't use the 'W-word.' He knows what it means, even when strangers say it. Yes, I think it would do all of us good to take a W-A-L-K." She opened a closet near the front door and took a long leash off the shelf. Moses began moaning and fidgeting with excitement as she clipped the leash to his collar. With her free hand she grabbed her jacket out of the closet, slipped it over one arm, and opened the front door. Moses charged out with Susan in tow. As she passed Walter, she tossed him a ring of keys. "It's the big silver key next to the whistle," she said. Walter knew the drill from his childhood days when he had a dog, albeit not a Basset. He closed and locked the door while Susan struggled to keep Moses under control and put on her jacket at the same time. After his initial surge of energy and a short search to find just the right spot to pee, Moses settled down into a sedate stroll, punctuated by frequent stops investigate a newly discovered smell or perhaps commune with an old favorite.

At first Susan took Walter's hand but gave up on that after she and Walter got wound up in Moses' leash several times. She directed their threesome to Reclamation Avenue, the next street north, and along it to Mills-Kiwanis Park, which occupied a full city block, about two acres. There were only a few people in the park, so she unsnapped the leash from Moses' collar to let him run free. When he strayed too far, she called him back, and he obeyed perfectly—a point that was not lost on Walter.

Walter elected to resume the discussion they had been having back at her house. "I also want to apologize for my reaction—my *overreaction*—in the bicycle shop last week. I thought about it while I was driving to California, and I think I understand what happened. At the Air Force Academy I was required to abide by a strict Honor Code that states very simply "We Will Not Lie, Steal or Cheat, Nor Tolerate Among Us Anyone Who Does." It was a formative time of my life, so that code of conduct has stayed with me ever since, although most of the time I am now the 'judge and jury' of my own conduct and as such I can make exceptions for myself or others whenever I wish. When we met a week ago, I was already struggling with inner turmoil over whether you were telling me the full story about 'weirdos,' and when you admitted you had lied, my old zero-tolerance Honor Code conditioning cut in, powered by the built-up emotion inside me, and I just lost it. It was completely unfair to you. It was all *my* baggage, *my* emotion, and I had no right to take it out on you. Anyhow, I'm very sorry. I would like to think it won't ever happen again, but the truth is I can't guarantee it. In any event, I hope you'll understand and be able to forgive."

Susan mulled that over in her mind before responding. "I *do* understand, and I *do* forgive you—not only now but also in the future. Yes, I was shocked by your reaction, and I was even more shaken by my own reaction. Like yours, it also came from the past, from an incident I thought I had processed and buried but which, as it turned out, I hadn't. I've already told you I was raised by foster parents, three different sets of them. After I had been with the first pair of foster parents about three years, they decided to get a divorce. Blame and guilt stemming from their inability to have children of their own probably had something to do with that, but it doesn't matter. What did matter is that I got put back into an institution. It wasn't my fault, but that wasn't what I felt. After almost a year of wallowing in my own guilt and shame, I was placed with another foster family. That went fairly well and I was able to get myself back on track. My second pair of foster parents was very loving, but also very strict. I forget what the circumstance was, but one day I told a lie—a little lie of almost no consequence—to my foster father, and he knew instantly it was a lie. I don't know what was happening inside his head, but he immediately sent me back to the institution, the last place in the world I wanted to be, even though I admitted my lie and apologized repeatedly and profusely.

"This all happened when I was in my early teens, going through the transitions all kids go through, and consequently being vulnerable in all sorts of ways. Of course, it was very traumatic for me, but I survived, thanks to a third pair of foster parents who were very understanding and forgiving and to a boyfriend who entered my life at that time and eventually became my husband. Anyhow, your reaction to my lie about the bicycle flung me back into that pit with my second foster father. I hung on by my fingernails long enough to get through my final exam at KCC—and by the way, I did manage to salvage an 'A' after all, so you can release any guilt you've been harboring about that—and then, when the pressure was off, I kind of lost it too. Virginia, God bless her, was most kind and generous, even though she didn't understand what was going on. For some reason I didn't feel comfortable in sharing the details with her. Besides, she had to cover for me at the Welcome Center since she had ordered me to take the day off. So I toodled up to Odell Lake and got my counseling there."

"With Mac?" Walter inferred.

"Yes, and that reveals another matter where I haven't been completely forthright with you. Mac has been something of a friend, mentor, and advisor for some fifteen years, especially since Lucy left and I was figuring out who I wanted to be when I grow up. I first met him when he did a psychological evaluation of me for WitSec."

That explains why she didn't tell me the full story, Walter thought. *My, what a wonderful tangle of relationships and secrets!* "It all makes sense now," he said, "but just like with the 'weirdo' stuff, your buried hurts and my old scars lined up and interacted hypergolically."

"Hypergolically?" she frowned. "What does that mean?"

"A 'hypergolic' reaction is one in which a substance ignites spontaneously upon mixing with another substance, like when a fuel comes together with an oxidizer in a rocket engine," he explained.

"Oh. I might have expected you to use a metaphor like that. I prefer 'monsters under the bed.' Your 'monsters' and mine had a battle."

"I'm not sure whose 'monsters' won," Walter laughed. "but it would be great if all of yours and all of mine got together and killed each other off, while you and I were safe and sound, loving each other in some other part of the universe."

"My house or your cabin? My place or yours," she asked—or suggested.

"Be careful what you ask for," he joked. "As Billy Crystal said, 'Women need a reason to have sex; men just need a place.'"

"That's the second time you've told a joke about sex today," she observed. "Is that what's on your mind?"

"Not especially—but I did wonder if the reason you had stalled off telling me where you live is that you were afraid I'd corner you and assault you."

"Once upon a time, it would have been a concern for me," she said, "but now it isn't. It has been completely overshadowed by the prospect of 'weirdos' invading the neighborhood."

"More 'monsters under the bed?'"

"Yes, but they seem to be under everybody's beds: Ted's, mine, yours…"

"… but not Moses' or Abigail's."

"Ah, yes. I guess we should try to emulate Moses and Abigail," she agreed.

"So when are you going to lay an egg for me?" he asked.

"Not today. It's the wrong time of the month." They both laughed, but Walter noted it was a very clever and tactful way of telling him where to direct his blood supply for the rest of the day.

Their stroll was now coming to an end; Susan's house was just ahead. Walter looked at his watch and said, "It's getting on toward five o'clock, probably too late for a decent bike ride, especially if we have to go out to Dairy to begin. Would you mind if we saved bicycling for another day and just hang out? I brought a CD I'd like to listen to with you, and I'm sure we can think of lots of things to discuss while we take turns fondling Moses."

Susan was still amused by the instant bonding between Walter and the dog, and she wasn't threatened by it, which surprised her a little. *He's OK as long as he doesn't try to move in or take over my life, at least not yet,* she thought. *I'll try to extend the same courtesy to him.* "You'll spoil Moses beyond redemption, but it's already too late to turn back from that. An evening of domestic tranquility really appeals to me right now. Did you bring your pipe and slippers?"

"No, I'm not moving in. I've still got some things I need to work on alone, and I've got a place to do it. We've got to know each other better before we seriously consider merging our households."

"Yeah, you're right," she agreed, "but I keep coming back to that because it just feels so good when I'm with you." She put her arms around Walter and kissed him. Moses gave a bark of approval—*just like Abigail's 'Quack,'* Walter thought.

Walter feigned shock at the kiss. "What will the neighbors think?"

"They can think anything they want," Susan said. "They'll do it anyway, no matter what we do. I hope you'll get to meet some of them at my post-graduation party next week, but if you're concerned about keeping up appearances, you can make a lot of noise when you drive off in your truck later. That way the neighbors will know you're not spending the night here."

Susan opened the door of her house, detached Moses' leash, and put it away in the closet. Moses headed for the kitchen and could soon be heard chugaluging water from his bowl. Then he reappeared, with long ears dripping, and plopped down on his bed in the corner of the living room. "Last Sunday you mentioned getting some carryout food for dinner. What did you have in mind?" Walter asked.

"How about Chinese? It's still a bit early, but we can beat the Friday night rush. Or do you have some more shopping to do first?"

"Chinese is good with me too," he said, "and no, I don't have any more shopping to do. I did it all earlier—although...."

"Yes?"

"I'm very happy I've straightened out my cell phone situation at the cabin and even happier you want us to connect by phone every evening, but there's one thing more I'd like to add, something I sorely needed when I was trying to call you last week: I'd like you to have an answering machine, so I don't have to keep track of your constantly changing schedule at the Welcome Center whenever I want to contact you. It wouldn't compromise your security because most of the machines on the market have optional prerecorded answering messages that maintain your anonymity. If you think it would work for you, I'll buy the answering machine today, as your graduation present."

Susan agreed with Walter's logic, and her present telephone was showing signs of aging, so she accepted his proposal. "There's a Radio Shack store on 6th Avenue and a Chinese restaurant just beyond it. Let's go have a look." Forty-five minutes later they returned with a new answering machine, selected by Walter, and a double helping of Susan's dinner choice, 'Wor Wonton Noodle Soup' with chunks of beef, pork, chicken, and seafood. As they slurped the noodles, the *Yusuf* CD Walter had bought in California transported their consciousness to a very different part of the world.

Later, while Susan cleared the empty bowls and tidied up the kitchen, Walter busied himself with setting up the new answering machine. This gave him an opportunity to check out her house—two bedrooms, just one bath, but a full basement—all decorated tastefully but modestly, in keeping with Susan's limited budget. Although everything seemed to be in working order, Walter's expert eye spotted a number of things that could use some preventive maintenance, some 'tuning up' to be put into tiptop condition—*a man's touch*, he thought. The second bedroom had obviously been Lucy's, and it was basically as she had left it two years earlier. A collection of framed pictures in Susan's bedroom documented her growth from infancy, but there was no trace of Susan's late husband.

Their conversation resumed over mugs of tea in the living room. Walter gave Susan a detailed account of his visit to the Islamic Center and left Disk One and Disk Two of Deepak Chopra's audiobook on *Muhammad* for her to listen to later. He also told her of Mac's forthcoming talk, which she marked on her calendar, and he showed her his letter of acceptance for the Insight Meditation Course in August, leading to a general discussion of their plans for the rest of the summer. If Walter combined the trip for that course with some subsequent vacation time with his kids, he would be gone for about three weeks. Susan wasn't happy about it, although she graciously tried to mask her feelings.

When Moses went to the kitchen door and whined to be let out to water the flowers in the back yard, Walter got the message it was time for him to go home. Besides, it was past his usual bedtime, and Susan had to get up for work the next day. Their usual goodnight kiss, an osculation that had become an oscillation between the final stage of parting and the first stage of foreplay, was replaced by a succession of less intense embraces, interlaced with slurps from Moses, who was campaigning for another walk. Without explicitly saying anything, Susan and Walter collaborated to induce several loud barks from him to draw the neighbors' attention to Walter's departure.

36.

Walter was reading on his porch at midmorning the next day when Ted sauntered into view. As usual, he came right to the point. "Now that you've recovered your work clothes from your old residence, I'd like you to give me a hand in scavenging some firewood before the weather gets too hot. Could you find time for that in your busy schedule next week, any day but Thursday?"

"Tuesday is booked for me," Walter answered. "Let's do it Monday and get it over with."

"Well, there's more than enough wood for us to handle in just one day, but Monday would be a good start. We can come back to it later, preferably before the end of June."

"OK with me," Walter said. "I'm not planning to go anywhere until August, but it looks like I'll be gone most of that month, taking a class in California and then a short vacation with my kids."

"August is a good time not to be here. Too damned hot. I hope you're headed to someplace cooler." What time do we start Monday?"

"Any time after eight AM. Just come down the path when you're ready."

37.

Walter was well rested by Monday morning. His weekend had been quiet— reading, listening to Chopra's audiobook, evening phone calls to Susan— and he had given up on further exploration of churches until he talked with Mac. He skipped his SHower and ate a bigger-than-usual breakfast laden with protein. Dressed in battered work clothes and boots, with a goofy old hat on his head, he set off for Ted's shortly after 8:00 AM. Ted was already out and about, loading equipment into a garden cart. As Walter approached, he started giving orders, albeit in the most non-directive tone he could manage. "The first thing we should do is re-stack what's left in the woodpiles, yours and mine, so whatever we collect today doesn't have to go on top. That should get us limbered up." He motioned for Walter to follow him and led the way around to the back of his house. This was new territory for Walter, and he took advantage of the opportunity to learn what was there, taking special note of three paths leading off into the trees in various directions. They worked in silence for about half an hour, finishing the job there, then moved to Walter's woodpile, and spent another thirty minutes re-stacking. The morning air was cool, but Walter took off his jacket when they had finished. "How about something to drink?" he asked Ted. "I don't have any beer, but I do have some fruit juice."

"Plain old water is fine for me," Ted replied. "It's too early for beer."

They sat on the edge of the porch, sipping from the large glasses Walter brought out. Ted outlined the next tasks in the day's work agenda while Walter listened. That didn't take long, and conversation lagged with the glasses still half full. Neither man rushed to fill the vacuum, but eventually Ted spoke up. "You seem to have wasted no time in getting yourself some female companionship and establishing a level of trust. I'm not objecting, mind you, but I am a little surprised you're inviting her out to the cabin so soon."

Once again Walter noticed how quickly Ted came to the point. *Diplomacy sure isn't his strong suit,* he thought. "I'm surprised too when I step back to consider what has happened. That's not to say there haven't been any glitches along the way—there have, but we seem to have settled all that a week ago. Last night I went to her house in KFalls for the first time, and I think that was also a good bit faster than she had expected." Then Walter decided to match Ted's style in homing in on the crux of the matter. "I was even more surprised by how quickly she passed muster with you, or whoever you had do the background check on her, but she explained all that to me last night."

That got Ted's immediate attention. "How so?" he asked.

"She said she thinks you're in the Federal witness protection program." Walter gave it to him straight on and watched for the reaction. Ted flinched like somebody had punched him in the stomach. Without waiting for him to say anything, Walter added the *coup de grace.* "She was given the same phone number you gave me last Friday morning."

Ted looked at Walter as if he were trying to see *through* him. Walter read this as indication Ted was rapidly sifting through his freeze/flight/fight options. He chose 'none of the above.' "That kind of nails it, I guess," he sighed. "I too was surprised by how quickly I got the green light on your friend—Susan, isn't it?—

but I hadn't connected the dots. I just thought her file was in the system because of some other work she was doing, perhaps a government job that requires a security clearance."

"No, she works at the Travel Klamath Welcome Center. She's seen a lot of stuff come and go in the past fifteen years."

"Well, that could explain why they gave her the phone number," Ted said.

"The curious part about all this is how I got involved with her in the first place. It was *you* who suggested I go to the Welcome Center for assistance in finding something to do and someplace to go while you got the background check on me. I did that, and while I was there I asked her about the 'weirdos' you had mentioned in our initial meeting. Little did I know how well situated she was to tell me all sorts of hush-hush stuff about that. I've been able to unravel a surprising amount of the story in the past month, although I doubt that I know everything. Maybe I never will. Maybe I'll never need to."

Ted pondered that for a moment. "I think that's where we should leave it for now. I won't dispute anything you've told me, but I'm not going to reveal any more about my situation unless and until I think it's absolutely necessary."

"That works for me," Walter concurred. "I won't ask, and you won't tell."

Ted was actually smiling as he got up from the porch, signaling it was time to get back to work. However, both of them continued to process what they had just learned as they cut, chopped, and stacked for the next two hours. When they reached a stopping point, Ted invited Walter to his house for lunch. "Lottie agreed to make some sandwiches for us—she actually *volunteered* to do that, which may be something of a milestone. She still isn't up to joining us, so we'll eat on the patio."

Lottie had everything ready for them, so all Ted had to do was pick up a large tray of food from the kitchen while she ducked out of Walter's view. The food was plain but good, not quite up to the standard of elegance Susan had gone to some length to achieve in her Stevenson Park picnic with Walter, but Walter was gratified to be admitted a little farther into Ted's circle of trust. Ted must have been on the same wavelength. Between bites of food, he expressed some further reaction to their earlier conversation. "After thinking about it, I'm kind of pleased you have learned more about my status with WitSec. As I said to you last Friday, you've sort of 'got my back' in living near me as you do, and what you now know will enable you to make more intelligent decisions if, God forbid, things ever come unglued. I've become increasingly comfortable with having you in that position, and knowing that your friend Susan has had some involvement with WitSec will add to my sense of well-being."

"Thank you. That's reassuring to hear," Walter replied. "I don't want to press my luck, but there are two more things I'd like to resolve with you while we're discussing your WitSec relationship. The first is that there's another person I would like to invite to the cabin in due course. I know WitSec engaged him to help out on a couple matters with Susan, so I wouldn't be surprised if you also know of him. I know him as 'Mac,' my fishing buddy, but his name is Dr. Delbert McCarter."

Ted brightened to the edge of a smile. "I'd say you're on a roll. You can bring him here any time you want, to your place *and* to mine as well. I wouldn't mind going fishing with him myself if the occasion ever presents itself, although I'm reluctant to leave Lottie alone any more than necessary. I'll even volunteer another piece of information about McCarter: he's Lottie's counselor too. I take her into town for a session with him every Thursday afternoon."

That came as no surprise to Walter, although he hadn't made the connection in the veritable flood of revelations he had received since the preceding Friday. He followed up: "The second thing is that I rediscovered my pistol in the stuff I had in storage in California. It's a 9mm *Beretta*, standard government issue. I had a concealed weapon permit for it in California, and I'd like to get one in Oregon too, just in case I want to go back to flying professionally out of KFalls or Medford. To do that I have to take some kind of training course authorized by the local sheriff—I don't know the specifics yet—and I was wondering if there is any place here on your property where I could do some target practice."

Ted thought about the request before answering. "Yes, I can make a place for you to do that, and I might even join in when you do, but give me a couple days to figure out where would be best. We need to be somewhat circumspect about it because the sound of gunfire tends to upset Lottie."

"OK, I understand," Walter said—*but I really don't understand*, he thought. *The missing piece in this puzzle concerns Lottie: is she the reason Ted is in the WitSec program or is it Ted? Either way, why is she so afraid?*

"I also suggest you exercise with extreme discretion as you explore the training program," Ted added. "People you meet will ask all sorts of questions, regardless of whether they have a legitimate 'need to know.' And you will likely rub elbows with some of the local 'weirdos.' They seem to have infiltrated just about everything connected with law enforcement at the local level. They haven't penetrated WitSec yet, and I hope they never will, but they would sure like to. If they get the slightest hint you know anything about it, they'll use every trick in the book to get information out of you."

"That's good advice," Walter agreed. "I'll be extra cautious, and if I have any doubts or if I run across anything that doesn't feel right, I'll check back with you before proceeding."

"You could also check with McCarter," Ted suggested. "He's got a much better view of 'the big picture' than I do."

Hmm, thought Walter. *This is indeed a bizarre tangle of relationships I've stumbled into, and Mac is emerging as the linchpin. Tomorrow should bring some interesting discussions with him. I wonder if we'll get around to fishing.*

38.

Walter was right on time, 8:00 AM, as he pulled into the parking area at the Dairy trailhead of the OC&E State Trail. Mac was already there, engine idling in his Ford Ranger pickup. He handed Walter a paper cup of hot coffee as he climbed into the passenger seat. "Hi, Walter. How are you doing?"

"I'm doing fine, finer than frog hair split four ways," Walter gushed.

"Full of piss and vinegar, I see." Mac chuckled. "Things must be going well for you these days."

"They're going a helluva lot better than they were the last time I saw you, Dr. McCarter, and I think you know exactly what I'm talking about. Thank you for helping Susan work through her problems, which in turn helped me deal with mine. It was pretty rough for a few days, but we got ourselves and our relationship back on track, and we probably wouldn't have been able to do it without your help. I want to express my appreciation, but I don't know whether to hug you or salute you."

Mac laughed harder. "I suggest you do neither, seeing as how we're in the truck and I'm trying to drive and you're trying to drink coffee."

"I don't know why I didn't recognize you as ex-military when I first met you," Walter said. "Maybe it was your fishing guide disguise, or maybe your psychiatric training modified your military comportment."

"I would hope it softened my demeanor as compared with the typical officer or noncom," Mac agreed. "It's hard to counsel anybody if he's standing in a full brace. However, I never went through the Air Force Academy like you. I was stationed there a few years, doing some teaching as well as counseling, but by then my medical training had shaped my professional behavior." He turned and smiled at Walter. "And in mid-life I took up fishing and transformed myself into a troll."

"Into *Yoda*," Walter suggested, recalling the incredibly powerful Jedi Master in *Star Wars*.

"But my ears are too small, and Yoda is much better looking," Mac protested.

Walter rode in silence a few minutes, trying to determine which matter he wanted to bring up next and how to introduce it tactfully, eventually returning to where they had left off with Susan. "In retrospect, I find it enlightening to look at how Susan and I got over our spat. It seems we each looked at the alternative of breaking off the relationship and decided independently we didn't want to go there. We got back in touch with that intention clearly in mind, putting the emotions—the 'monsters under the bed,' she calls them—to rest so we could meet and talk it out like civilized people. When we did that, we learned that the unexpressed fears behind our behavior were based on something rational— namely, things that had actually happened to us in the past—but we had allowed our imaginations to run wild and inflate the fears way out of proportion."

"That's typical," Mac said, "and when it happens, you've got to find a way to release all the emotional energy without doing any damage to the other person or to yourself. That's a basic part of counseling, because it usually takes a neutral third party who is not emotionally involved to guide and referee the process. That's not to say, however, that 'ordinary people' can't learn to do it for themselves. They can and sometimes do, but the odds are against it, because it isn't easy for people to look critically at themselves, resolve to make some changes, and then stick with it until the changes have become new habits. It's like trying to push a rope."

"I think Susan has a better understanding of that sort of thing than I do," Walter said, "but I'm learning by observing her and following her lead. After having clarified our intentions and shared them with each other the day after Susan came to you, we met at her house last Friday night and talked through everything. Although my out-of-control imagination had gotten me into trouble the week before, I could have never imagined what Susan told me about her past, including how she first came to meet you through the WitSec program." Walter paused to see if his mention of WitSec would evoke any reaction in Mac. It didn't—or if it did, Mac hid it well. *That's what one would expect of a psychiatrist, right? Now let's drop the other shoe and see what happens.* "As if that wasn't a big enough surprise for me, when we put our facts together we also deduced some things about Ted, my neighbor and landlord—namely, that he too is in the WitSec program, which he confirmed when I confronted him with the evidence yesterday."

"Ted who?" Mac asked. "You've told me a little about your neighbor and his obsession with security and secrecy, but I'm not sure I know him."

"Oh, but you do," Walter replied, "because his wife Lottie is your patient. Ted said he brings her to you for counseling every Thursday afternoon."

That managed to penetrate Mac's cool professional facade, and Walter could see it had, but if it had upset Mac, he got over it almost instantly. "Oh," he said, buying a little time to think about his reply. "I didn't know *that* is who your neighbor is. It's an interesting twist."

"Yes, I think so too," Walter agreed. "It sort of ties everything together in a big convoluted knot, but there are some loose ends sticking out that I still can't understand. I don't know *why* Ted and Lottie are in WitSec—I may never know that, because I have no need to. However, Ted made it clear yesterday he would tell me more if he felt it would maintain or improve his safety and security. Meanwhile, I gather from several comments he made earlier that Lottie has some kind of 'phobia' about Muslims, based upon something that happened to her in the not-too-distant past. I might guess *that* is why she and Ted are in WitSec, and from what you told me about the Muslim activities in Bly, I might even conjecture that could be part of the picture."

Mac thought a bit before answering. "Professionally and for security reasons I am very limited in what I can tell you. I'm sure you understand that. But I can safely say this much: (1) You are correct in your deduction that incidents involving Muslims in the past few years are directly connected to all this; but (2) there is no direct connection with the Muslims who are now in Bly, *insofar as I know*. However, things change over time, and everything is ultimately connected to everything else in the larger scheme of things." They both rode in silence a minute or so, each absorbed in his own thoughts, until Mac continued, "It helps me to learn of your relationship with Ted. I only know him peripherally, and you barely know Lottie at all. That could change because I have already noticed some changes in her—slight, but positive—since you moved in. Things you've said and done, even just your presence, have apparently improved Ted's outlook on life, which helps her. You've changed the tension on one end of the rope, and that affects the other end. Good job!" He smiled.

"Thank you," Walter smiled back. "I hadn't been aware of making any contributions to my neighbors other than paying my rent on time. On the other hand, when I told Ted yesterday I was going fly fishing with you today, he expressed interest in joining us sometime. However, he's presently very reluctant to leave Lottie alone."

"That presents an interesting opening which could greatly improve the situation," Mac said. "Let's see if we can find a way to give her some company. Of course, it would have to be company she can accept."

Walter steered the discussion in a new direction. "Meanwhile, I have developed an interest in Islam in a more positive vein. While I was in California, I stopped by one of the Islamic Centers in the Bay Area and bought a couple books and CDs. I also got to observe the Islamic midday prayer."

"What did you think of it?" Mac asked.

"It surprised me with its low-key simplicity and humility, which was a sharp contrast to what I had witnessed at the Bonanza Bible Church on Memorial Day weekend. I was really turned off by the sermon at the Bible Church, especially the hate-mongering directed not only at Islam but also, by implication, at anybody and everybody who disagrees in the slightest with the minister's version of Christianity. Moreover, I found the minister's interpretation troubling, being centered around a mean, vengeful old God rather than a loving, forgiving, peace-promoting Jesus."

Mac rolled his eyes. "Don't get me started. You already know what I think of most ministers. It's all about power. When Jesus was alive, the Jews—who were his primary if not sole audience—had very little power and were all bent out of shape about it. They wanted and expected a Messiah who would restore their power and give them freedom from the Romans and the other nations and tribes that had enslaved them historically. However, Jesus didn't fit their expectations, neither in his person nor his teaching, so most Jews rejected him. After his death and resurrection, which the Muslims reject, there was a great deal of confusion and disagreement about who and what Jesus really was. And after a few hundred years of disputation, the Roman emperor Constantine forced the Christians to pick just one interpretation and jettison the rest. That was all about power too: Constantine's political power and the power of the bishops who sucked up to him. The decisions made then have haunted us ever since.

"This has all become clearer with the archeological discoveries and historical scholarship since the nineteenth century. They say 'history is written by the winners, *their* way,' but we've learned a lot about what the losers thought and believed. Much of it is more appealing than orthodoxy, and what is more important, it may be closer to what Jesus actually thought and taught as well. That doesn't sway the conservative churches, however, except to cause them to 'circle the wagons' to 'protect the faith,' which really means to 'protect and preserve their wealth and power.' They trot out their tried-and-true Trojan horse, *fear*, and they doll it up in hell-and-damnation rhetoric featuring a mean *sonofabitch* as God to keep the troops in line. That's what you got at the Bible Church, and you'll get it at any church that puts the *written* Word of God ahead of everything else. In effect, they make an idol of the Bible, and the Muslims do the same with the Koran. There are exceptions to this idiocy in both Christianity and Islam, and you can find them if you dig a little bit. In Islam they're called *Sufis*."

"I may have heard of them," Walter said, "but I don't know anything about them."

"You probably won't find any around here; you'd have to go to Eugene or Portland. Many Orthodox Muslims tend to regard them as *infidels* because they're too liberal in their beliefs and practices."

"Perhaps I can find some *Sufi* groups in the Bay Area when I go back down in August for the Insight Meditation course. After I do a ten-day 'sit' in Sonoma, I hope to spend a week reconnecting with my kids, maybe somewhere near Yosemite or along the Central Coast."

"I'm glad you'll be doing the meditation course. It should make a big improvement in your practice, which you've struggled to get established here. It makes a huge difference if you are meditating with others in an appropriate setting and if you don't have to be concerned with preparing meals and such. However, the meditation course will also give your kaleidoscope a pretty good shake, so to speak, so if you're going to go off with your kids afterward, I strongly recommend you first allow a few days to reorient yourself. Make the reentry slow and easy, with as little stress as possible."

They were approaching the turnoff for Mac's favorite fishing spot on the Sprague River, so the conversation lagged as they mentally shifted gears. Rather than continue the tutorial on fly fishing he had begun in their previous outing, Mac simply led Walter along the stream bank, stopping frequently to scan the water surface for any telltale signs of fish. About a half-mile downstream, they saw a couple trout leap into the air, causing Mac to holler, "Here!" Over the next two hours, using a variety of lures and casting into or around numerous nearby holes that promised to harbor at least one trout, they caught several: Mac five and Walter two. They threw back the smaller ones, leaving four good-sized rainbows to divide between them.

They returned to the truck, put their catch in the cooler, and stowed their gear. As they were getting into the cab, Mac said, "I hope you don't mind going back to the Coyote Café again for an early lunch. I'd like to follow up on our reconnaissance of two weeks ago, but this time I'd like to *provide* a little information as well as collect it, mainly to build trust with the locals. If the opportunity presents itself, share a little bit about what we're doing there—namely, fly fishing in the Sprague River. If they ask about who we are or where we come from, tell them we're both from KFalls, you're a newcomer and I'm an old-timer who's taken you under his wing, and we were both formerly career officers in the Air Force. That should be enough to satisfy their curiosity, and if it doesn't nudge them into sharing much local news with us today, it will definitely pay dividends at in the future." Walter nodded his understanding. *I'm beginning to enjoy this*, he thought. *It's a pleasure to watch Mac penetrate people's defenses and get them to open up to him. Of course, he ought to be good at it, considering he's been practicing psychiatry for some thirty years. I can learn a lot from him if I pay attention.*

As soon as they sat down at a table in the Café, Walter could sense an undercurrent of tension among the patrons. At first he thought he and Mac were the cause, but as he sat and watched and listened, he sensed that 'the problem' had been there before they arrived. He turned up the gain on his intuition, looking for something that seemed out of place and eventually homed in on a man sitting by himself at the counter. Slender, younger than most of the men in the room, probably in his mid-to-late-twenties, dressed in tight black jeans and a black leather jacket, he seemed to be intensely observing everything and everyone from his vantage point on the raised counter stools. What made him stand out was his hair, cut short and bleached to a bright blonde even though its natural color was obviously black. Thus he resembled a punk rock musician, *à la* Mick Jagger, or a movie actor, *à la* James Dean, but certainly not a typical sheep rancher from Bly.

Despite the muted energy, both Mac and Walter were able to engage in sporadic bursts of conversation with the men at adjacent tables, thereby planting seeds of their authenticity as Mac had suggested. They ate their sandwiches and downed their beers unhurriedly, but James Mick Jagger-Dean was still swigging a Coke and taking it all in when they paid their bill and left. *I wonder what kind of impression we made on the guy*, Walter mused as they walked to the truck. *Hopefully, none whatsoever.* Once they were down the road a few miles, he gave Mac his assessment.

"I agree that the character at the counter was putting some kind of kibosh on the place," Mac responded. "He definitely didn't fit in there, although his clothing and hairdo indicated he was trying very hard to fit in somewhere." That was as far as Mac seemed willing to go, and he redirected the conversation elsewhere. "Is there anything else you want to lay on me today?" he asked. "We've got about twenty minutes before I drop you off and go back to saving the world from itself."

Walter briefly savored Mac's self-deprecating humor, then plunged ahead. "It must be awfully hard being *Superman*."

Mac chuckled. "Yes, it's a tough job, but somebody's gotta do it."

Walter considered his options another minute or two and decided that now was the time to tell Mac about Abigail. He described their interaction and how it had developed, building to the key facet of his near-obsession with her—the fact that she seemed to be able to discern his thoughts and moods, as indicated by her reactions and responses, albeit from a limited repertoire: staying or leaving, emitting a well-timed '*Quack*,' and of course, laying an egg. Mac suppressed his laughter as Walter related it all, but he was clearly enjoying it. When it came time for him to render an opinion, he said, "First of all, I'd say you are showing exceptional discernment in noting the duck's behavior and correlating it with your own actions and thoughts. The tricky part comes when you ascribe meaning to it. The normal tendency is to start from the world as you think you understand it, which is mostly what you have been told or taught or what you have read somewhere, and then superimpose that on what you've observed. Where they don't match, people tend to give precedence to the former—sort of like 'my mind is made up, so don't confuse me with the facts.' But if you look at most of the great scientific discoveries throughout history, they resulted from somebody doing the opposite—for example, Copernicus insisting that the earth revolves around the sun, despite what the Church said.

"Getting back to your relationship with the duck, it strikes me as an instance of 'animal communication,' which is an element of *shamanism*—that is, the beliefs and practices of so-called 'indigenous groups,' such as Native Americans or Australian aborigines. I'm not all well versed in that, so I won't attempt to analyze how your experience fits in, but if you want to delve into it, I can point you at some of the so-called experts."

They were approaching the place where Walter had left his truck. As Mac pulled into the parking area, he had some final words for Walter. "Now that we're past Memorial Day, my busy season as a fishing guide has begun. I won't be able to meet with you as often until after Labor Day, but I do want to see you at least once before you head off to your meditation course, preferably a week before you go. Meanwhile, if you happen to be going over to Bly for any reason, stop by the Coyote Café for a cup of coffee, just to check up on what's going on. If you pick up anything unusual, give me a call. I'm sure you know how to exercise appropriate caution in all that." As Mac opened the cooler to give Walter two of the trout they had caught, he added, "When we go fishing the next time, remind me to give you some pointers on equipment, so you can buy some for yourself. That way you'll have a credible cover, and I can send you on reconnaissance missions alone." Walter gave Mac an informal salute. *He just gave me an order.*

Mac drove off, but Walter stood there going over in his mind what Mac had said in the last two minutes. *It seems Mac has recruited me into something—something he's a part of and maybe even leading. I don't know the whole story yet, but it appears to have something to do with 'weirdos.'*

Walter spent the afternoon immersed in Islam, listening to another of the CDs in Deepak Chopra's audiobook on *Muhammad* and reading in Huston Smith's book on *Islam*. In the book he skipped ahead to the penultimate chapter, which was on *Sufism*, and the mystical version of Islam he found there contrasted dramatically with Chopra's account of the rough-and-tumble of seventh-century Arabia. Instead of the conflict, violence, and intrigue of the latter, *Sufism* presented a peaceful panorama filled with love and ecstasy radiating from an infinitely compassionate God. Moreover, the intuitive mysticism of the *Sufis* envisioned God as a force, an energy that permeates and interconnects all things rather than a cranky old man who issues stern judgments and metes out harsh punishments. Thus, Walter reasoned, the positive teachings of *Sufism* were far better in drawing him closer to God than the fear-filled fulminations of Thunder Ray and his ilk.

Later that evening he shared some of these feelings with Susan in their nightly phone conversation. Her reaction was one of agreement, empathy, and gentle amusement, and she promised to share some of the poetry of the 13th Century Persian Sufi *Jalāl ad-Dīn Rumi* when they got together again. Walter was not in the least surprised by her familiarity with *Sufism*, although he lapsed back into his curiosity about how many more delightful facets of her being she had yet to reveal to him. This time, however, he was not threatened by his lack of total knowledge but rather enchanted by the prospect of discovering her heretofore hidden charms little by little. Somewhere from a dark corner of his tangled memory came an erotic line from Theodore Roethke, "She'd more sides than a seal," and he filed it a more accessible place for easy recall at a propitious face-to-face moment.

As their chitchat skittered along, it occurred to Walter to ask Susan whether she had intentionally sent him to Odell Lake so he would meet Mac. "No," she said. "I knew he was a fishing guide there, and of course I knew him as a counselor, but I didn't know *you* that well. I didn't say to myself, 'Here's a dude who's trying to get his head straightened out, and Mac is just the guy to help him do it.' On the other hand, that may be exactly what I did *on the intuitive level*. I doubt we'll ever know for certain; it will be one of life's little mysteries we can go nuts trying to unravel—or we can just accept and savor it as we keep muddling along." Then she asked, "Are you getting comfortable with muddling, or are you still going nuts?"

It took several seconds for Walter to stop laughing and get himself together enough to answer, "I've come to prefer muddling, but I still need practice."

39.

'Day 30,' a.k.a. Friday, June 6, was Susan's graduation day. In anticipation, Walter had gotten a haircut and beard trim on 'Day 28.' He looked forward to dazzling Susan with his spiffy new appearance, but on the other hand he was sure the Coyote Café crowd in Bly would not be impressed. *I'll have to get really dirty before I go back there,* he thought. *Otherwise I'll scare them into silence just like the guy with the fake blonde hairdo.*

The graduation ceremony was to begin at 2:00 PM, allowing Walter plenty of time to check his mail and do some laundry in the morning. Back at the cabin, he shined his dress shoes and put on his freshly dry-cleaned suit. His tie collection left something to be desired, however: it consisted of a lone, solid-black tie left over from his airline uniform, and it was visibly frayed around the edges. He decided to buy a more presentable tie for the graduation ceremony, but lacking any knowledge of haberdashery shops in KFalls and not wanting to spend much money on an item he might wear only once or twice, he went to Goodwill. Their tie selection was meager and most of it was unstylishly wide or narrow or had hideous patterns and colors, but after picking through everything three times and spending ten minutes in agonizing indecision, Walter came away with something acceptable: a muted check pattern, dark red. He put it on in his truck, using the rearview mirror as a guide, and it took him only four tries to 'get it right.'

The Community College parking lot was almost full, so he parked in a remote corner and followed the stream of people into a central building known as 'The Commons.' Susan had instructed him where to rendezvous with Virginia Cox and her husband, so he soon spotted Virginia standing next to a large graying man in a sport jacket. She lit up in a big smile when she saw Walter. "I hardly recognized you. You're all dressed up!" she gushed.

"Yeah, I felt it was inappropriate to show up at such an auspicious event looking like a wild mountain man."

"You cleaned up far better than I could have imagined. I expected you to wear something a little more earthy," she kidded. Walter couldn't help blushing as she introduced her companion. "This is my husband, Darrell. Darrell, this is Walter, Walter...?"

"Baker. Walter Baker." When they shook hands, Darrell's firm grip and piercing eye contact shouted 'ex-military,' but Walter opted not to get into that just yet. They found some vacant chairs, sat down, and began leafing through the programs. Almost immediately Walter recognized a familiar name among the KCC Board of Trustees: Delbert McCarter, MD. *Why am I not surprised?* he thought.

The graduation ceremony itself was unremarkable, except in one respect: the Commencement Address was on '*Peace,*' a topic that seemed appropriate for a large university or an elite liberal-arts college, but not for a plebeian junior college giving two-year degrees in office administration and automotive technology. The speaker was a professor of religious studies at the University of Oregon, just three hours up the road toward Portland. He was apparently rather well-known in his field, but not outside it—certainly Walter had never heard of him before. "I've come to speak to you today in the most popular idiom of our time," he began, "the 'infomercial.' Accordingly, I'll be giving you lots of information, probably more than you can comfortably handle, or at least more than you cared to know. That last point is important—the information is about something that probably doesn't interest you very much to begin with, but it interests *me* and I hope it will also interest *you* by the time I get done. I know you're familiar with this kind of situation, because it's the essence of what we in academia call 'required courses'—and you wouldn't be sitting here now unless you had already endured a few of them and paid attention long enough to get a passing grade. So think of this as one last Required Course, but one that will be short—no more than thirty minutes, my contract says—and in which there will *not* be a 'pop quiz' at the end." The audience laughed appreciatively, a few graduating students even cheered, and the speaker acknowledged them with a bow.

"It should come as no surprise that I want to talk to you about religion," he continued. "After all, religion is what I teach. The 'good news' is I *teach*, not *preach*, so your salvation is not at stake here. Whether or not you go to heaven after you die does not depend upon whether you abide by what I say today. Nevertheless I am trying to sell you something, and the degree to which you accept it may determine whether your life—*this* life—will be heaven or hell. So pay attention, please. This is more important than you might think." Some polite laughter rippled through the audience, and recollections of Thunder Ray echoed in Walter's mind.

"We could spend all day arguing about heaven. Every religion, every church, every believer or nonbeliever has some idea of what it is, or is not, or might be. But I submit there is one thing included as an essential element of everybody's conception of heaven, and that thing is *peace*." He went on to mention the dubious relationship between peace and religion, saying "much of the arrogance and intolerance and violence in the world is, and always has been, promulgated in the name of religion. However, the prophets whose teachings are the basis for almost all religions have invariably proclaimed peace as their goal.

"So where is the disconnect between what is preached and what is practiced? It occurs when the message of peace gets corrupted and eventually overshadowed by the desire for *power*, and the process by which that happens is very insidious. First, somebody somewhere receives an inspiration, has an idea, about how to achieve peace, as he/she understands it. Naturally, that person wants to share that idea with friends in the expectation it will help them in their lives. But the friends may have different conceptions of peace, or may simply feel what has worked for some prophet or teacher can't work for them. Inevitably it seems, egos get involved and arguments ensue—and we've started down the 'slippery slope' that ends in violence. In some cases, we may even feel violence is justified, believing that God is on *my* side or *our* side, not on yours or theirs, and in extreme cases that God will reward us for punishing 'infidels' who disagree with us, even to the point of killing them!"

The speaker knew he was getting dangerously close to sermonizing, so he backed off. "Suppose," he said sweetly, "just suppose we inject a little *humility* into this, at the point where we first learn that somebody else has an idea that is different from ours. Suppose that instead of insisting that our idea takes precedence, we *listen* to what others have to say. Suppose that we abandon the pretension we are the sole possessors of truth and instead entertain the possibility that 'truths are many and all make the whole richer,' as Mahatma Gandhi put it. Suppose that we accept our own imperfection and acknowledge we are not omniscient, that as finite beings we cannot hope to completely comprehend the Infinite—that is, anything that might be worthy of being called 'God.' Suppose that we stop making ourselves and our religions into idols."

Walter's interest was engaged now. He found the contrast with Thunder Ray's approach refreshing, although he was sure a 'commercial message' was soon to follow. "It is my conviction," the speaker proclaimed, "that the study of religion is where we need to go." Stepping out of character, he added, "You knew that was coming, didn't you?" The audience laughed and he continued. "I am convinced *the study of religions can be an act of peacemaking IF—[pause for effect]*—if it is done with 'the right attitude.'

"And what is the 'right attitude?' Note that I said '*religions*,' not 'religion.' We've got to be willing to look beyond our own conditioning, our own culture"— *our own bullshit*, thought Walter—"to accept and honor truth wherever it may be found. We do this by seeking to understand religions outside our own—any and all of them—and by seeking to *learn* from them. This does not mean giving up our present religion, but it does mean possibly embracing beliefs, ways of thinking, and ways of living from other religions alongside our primary religion. Has it ever occurred to you a person can be a Christian and a Muslim at the same time? Or a Taoist and a Jew? Most Japanese practice both Buddhism and Shinto, observing the festivals of both, going to temples and shrines. And I know of one famous religious scholar, born and raised in China by Methodist missionary parents, who claims to be primarily Christian but also Buddhist, Hindu, and Muslim and who incorporates elements from all of these in his daily religious practice." *That sounds familiar*, Walter thought. *It's Huston Smith!* He gave himself a little pat on the back for having learned that in the past six weeks.

The speaker was now starting down the home stretch. "I suggest we start thinking of religion like jazz, especially as it's played in small combos, where each individual's talents are showcased while the ensemble as a whole offers support. Allow me to quote from the great jazz drummer Max Roach who worked with many of the top jazz musicians, such as Dizzy Gillespie, Charlie Parker, Miles Davis, Charles Mingus, and Duke Ellington:

> When a piece is performed, everybody in the group has the opportunity to speak on it, to comment on it through their performance. It's a democratic process, as opposed to most European classical music in which the two most important people are the composer and the conductor. They are like the king and the queen. In a sense, the conductor is also like the military official who's there to see that the wishes of the masters—the composers—are adhered to, and as a musician your job may depend on how you conform to the conductor's interpretation of the composer's wishes. However, in a jazz performance, everyone has an opportunity to create a thing of beauty collectively, based on his or her own musical approaches.

"Peace is like that. At its deepest level, it has a musical quality similar to an improvisational jazz performance. There is an element of risk involved, because the improvisation cannot be completely rehearsed—if it were, it wouldn't be improvisation. Sometimes things threaten to fall apart, but the musicians forgive one another for the mistakes they might make. 'There are no wrong notes,' said Miles Davis. Peace can be unpredictable too, filled with creative tensions that sometimes lead to sad and mournful moments, but it is cooperative and creative, surprising and sometimes joyful, and its competitive dimensions do not degenerate into violence.

"We can flourish on this planet only if we learn to listen—listen to the call of compassion which invites us to seek sources for respect and care within our heritages—listen to the call of honesty which invites us to acknowledge limitations within our traditions, and grow by seeking new ways of thinking and living." Again breaking character, he concluded, "There, that wasn't so bad, was it? We don't have time for questions now, but I'll hang around in case you want to talk to me later. Class dismissed!"

After the ceremony was over, Walter, Virginia, and Darrell went to the spot where they were to meet up with Susan. She arrived still attired in cap and gown, hugged Virginia, shook Darrell's hand, and then without the slightest hesitation embraced Walter in a passionate kiss. "Wow!" was Walter's surprised reaction as they separated.

"See what happens when you dress up?" Susan teased. "I've got to assert my claim on you before some bimbo comes along and tries to snatch you away."

"But I saw him first—at least today," Virginia joined in the fun.

Darrell, not to be left out, protested, "But I saw *you* before that."

They were all enjoying the laugh when up walked Mac, looking almost as dapper as Walter and ever so more distinguished in a grey business suit. "Good afternoon, Major," he greeted Walter.

"Good afternoon, Colonel," Walter replied.

Susan introduced Mac to Virginia and Darrell, who was not to be outdone—after she pronounced his name, Darrell added, "Lieutenant Commander."

Another group laugh resulted, and when it subsided Mac asked, "What did you think of the Commencement Address?"

"I thought it was wonderful," Susan replied, and Virginia agreed.

Darrell equivocated. "It was good, but a bit too liberal, especially for this community."

"I liked it," Walter said assertively. "It was certainly beyond my expectations, and I'd like to discuss it with you after I've had more time to think about it."

"You'll get the chance, but not today," Mac responded. "I've got to get back to Odell Lake for an important conference tomorrow morning." He winked at

Walter, then turned to Susan. "I'm sorry I can't get to your party this afternoon, but I hope we can get together soon to toast your success and plot your future—maybe the next time I get back to KFalls, which should be the middle of next week." He gave Susan a discrete hug and said good-bye to the others.

As Mac walked away, Susan began organizing the migration to the party at her house. "I came over with Virginia and Darrell, but I'll ride back with Walter. You all know where I live, so I'll see you there in fifteen minutes."

Moses was thrilled to see Walter again and seemed disappointed when Walter didn't get down on his knees to have his face bathed in doggy drool like he did at their first meeting. Naturally, Walter's clean suit and neatly trimmed hair and beard meant nothing to Moses. Walter, on the other hand, really didn't care whether Moses slobbered on his suit, because it had served its purpose and he didn't expect to be wearing it again any time soon. Susan, of course, regarded Moses' behavior as a 'lost cause,' and she was beginning to lump Walter in the same category. By the time Darrell and Virginia arrived, the Susan/Moses/Walter greeting pandemonium had run its course, and Moses was content to perfunctorily sniff their shoes and retire to his blanket in the corner of the living room. Besides, they were 'old news,' having visited there many times before.

Susan summoned Walter to the kitchen and handed him the chilled bottle of champagne from the refrigerator. Walter managed to open it without spraying most of the contents on the wall, and soon the four of them—Virginia, Darrell, Susan, and Walter—were lifting glasses in a joyful toast to Susan's accomplishment. Graciously enjoining everybody to 'sit and eat,' Susan placed a large tray of munchies on the coffee table. Walter found himself positioned next to Darrell at one end of the sofa, so he followed Darrell's earlier cue to open the conversation. "Lieutenant Commander, eh? Navy or Coast Guard?"

"United States Navy, twenty years," Darrell said proudly. "And you?"

Walter chose to give him his résumé short and sweet. "Air Force Academy, class of '91, then thirteen more years before a buddy talked me into flying for Alaska Airlines. Got downsized out of a job a few months ago, so here I am, trying to figure out what to do with the rest of my life."

Darrell's face lit up. He reached into his jacket pocket and pulled out his business card. Handing it to Walter, he said, "When you're ready to go back to work, come talk to me." The card identified Darrell as General Manager of a private aviation company operating out of Kingsley Field. "We're always on the lookout for mature, experienced pilots. You can work as much or as little as you want."

"I've only been here a month," Walter replied, "and I'm still getting settled. I've got some loose ends to wrap up in California in August, but after that I might be getting the itch to fly again."

The doorbell rang. Moses let out a mighty bay, suspending all conversation until he and the humans in the living room could inspect the intruders and 'take appropriate action.' The 'intruders' turned out to be a couple that lived next door, so Moses quickly lost interest. However, he was gratified that one of them gave him a brief scratch behind his ears before he went back to lie down. So the next hour went—five more neighbors arrived to offer congratulations to Susan. Some stayed for polite conversation, but two soon left, claiming 'other commitments.'

The hour approached five o'clock, and Susan began putting out a buffet dinner on the kitchen table. Darrell and Walter joined the line to fill their plates, and as they waited their turn, Walter took the opportunity to talk more with Darrell while Susan's attention was focused elsewhere. "There is something you might help me with," he said to Darrell in a low voice. "Susan told me she's never been up in a plane. She has a birthday in October, so I'm thinking of giving her a ride as a surprise birthday present. I'll need to rent a small plane and make a checkout flight in advance, because it's been years since I've been in anything smaller than a 737."

Ah-ha! thought Darrell. *He's more interested in getting back into the air than he lets on. Maybe I can reel him in faster than he expects.* "Why don't you give me a call next week and we can arrange a time for the two of us to take a ride. I've got a perfectly good Cessna 172 sitting around without much use."

Back to basics, Walter thought. *Should be fun.* For a second he considered giving Darrell his cell phone number but thought better of it. *That would be tipping my hand too much,* but he was surprised at how quickly Darrell had aroused his interest.

The party began to break up after dessert was served. Having finished their second cups of coffee, Darrell and Virginia called it a day, leaving just Susan and Walter—and, of course, Moses, who jumped up from his nap thinking they were going for a walk. Seeing that, Susan looked at Walter and Walter looked at Susan and they nodded their heads up and down in agreement. "OK, Moses," Susan said. "Let's go."

After a slow hand-in-hand stroll around the block with Moses, they returned to the house and cleaned up the dirty dishes: Walter with sleeves rolled up past his elbows, washing the items Susan didn't want to run through the dishwasher; Susan at his side with dish towel in hand, waiting to dry and put away whatever

Walter handed to her; and Moses sitting at her feet, looking up expectantly for a leftover tidbit—a classic *Norman Rockwell* scene of domesticity. When the chores were done, they retired to the living room: Moses to his bed, Susan and Walter to the sofa. Walter had thought to bring a bottle of good sherry in case it might be needed for the party, and he poured two small glasses for Susan and himself. Settling in beside her on the sofa, he asked, "So what did you really think of the Commencement Address?"

As she frequently did, Susan thought a few seconds before answering. "It was different—not what I expected, as you said before—but I liked it—which is to say it made me want to learn more, but there's no place in KFalls to do that. I doubt there's anything at Southern Oregon University in Ashland either, and besides it's an hour-and-a-half away, over a mountain road people try to avoid except when they're on vacation. So we'd have to go to Eugene."

It was Walter's turn to think before answering. "I wonder if that's why Mac seemed eager to sample our opinions after the address. Do you think he's trying to promote something locally, maybe even hire the speaker into KCC or, better, OIT?"

"There's no place, no program, at either institution for him to go into, so something like that would have to be created first. Then, he'd have to be lured away from the University of Oregon, the top school in the state. All that would take money, a large amount of it. Where would it come from?"

"I dunno," Walter said. "Maybe Mac has a few million squirreled away—you know, from all his moonlighting as a fishing guide."

"Fat chance," Susan dismissed him. "The odds would be better for you to make the millions as a singer in Vegas, doing your old songs."

"Now *that's* a thought," Walter brightened, "but it would have to be a duo. You've got a great voice. I could tell that from when you sang '*You Are the Sunshine of My Life*,' to me on the phone a week ago. Can you dance too?"

"No, we'll have to leave that to Moses," she suggested. The dog, having heard his name, peeked out from his slumber with one eye, then closed it again and let out a belch resembling the sound of a tire going flat.

"On that note," Walter said, "I think we should call it a night."

40.

Walter parked his truck in front of the one-story metal building at Kingsley Field. He would never have found it without Darrell's precise directions, because it was as nondescript as one could make it, with only a large building number painted above the door and a 12-by-18-inch sign to the right of the door announcing the name of the company. Inside, a young woman who multitasked as secretary, receptionist, and all-around 'gopher' sat behind a grungy metal desk. "My name is Walter Baker," he told her. "I have an appointment with Darrell Cox."

"Please have a seat. I'll tell him you're here." She barely stopped chewing gum to speak.

Walter sat on one of the two bare metal folding chairs along the wall. There were no magazines or newspapers to read while he waited, but it didn't matter. Darrell opened the conspicuously locked interior door from within and extended his hand as he approached. "Hello, Walter. Good to see you again. Looks like a good day to go flying." He led the way down a dark corridor to the back of the building and into an office just to the right of the rear exit door. The room was decorated with military austerity: painted concrete floor; large window with venetian blinds but no curtains, looking out on several planes parked on the apron beyond; numerous diplomas and pictures on the wall, all featuring a much younger Darrell Cox posing with various colleagues and aircraft from his past. Walter did a quick scan of the pictures as Darrell walked to his chair behind the large metal executive-style desk. "Looks like you were a helicopter pilot at some point in your career," he observed.

"Yes, but not since I got out of the Navy twenty years ago. That's a young man's job,' Darrell replied. "Did you every try your hand at choppers?"

"Only for about ten minutes, which was enough to convince me I didn't want to go there. I put in about seven years in fighters, which was fun, then moved on the bigger stuff, all the way up to the *C-5 Galaxy*. I recognized even then that my future was in flying multiengine planes for an airline or shipping company."

"We all end up there eventually, or behind a desk." Darrell waved at the pile of papers in front of him.

"I brought along all the tickets from my previous job at Alaska Airlines, to verify that I'm legit," Walter said, opening a large envelope and sliding its contents onto the desk.

Darrell smiled. "I have no doubt you're legit, but I'll take a look at this anyhow, just to keep the insurance company happy." He quickly leafed through the documents, then put them all back in the envelope and handed it to Walter. "Looks fine to me. Let's go for a ride." He led Walter out the door to the apron and over to a Cessna 172. Walter estimated it was ten years old, but it appeared to have been meticulously maintained. Darrell motioned for Walter to get into the left-hand seat, and he took the right. He spent the next twenty minutes going through everything, almost as if this were Walter's first flight, but Walter wasn't in the least offended. He appreciated Darrell's thoroughness and concern for safety—it told him a lot about the man. Darrell finished his tutorial and asked, "Any questions?" Walter nodded 'no.' "OK, then let's go. You do it all, as if I'm not here, but if at any time you want me to take over, just say the word."

Walter went down the preflight checklist, just as he would have done without Darrell's preceding instruction, then put on his headphones and established communication with the control tower. He looked at Darrell and said, "If it's OK with you, I'd like to head over toward Bly, following the OC&E Trail. Susan and I have hiked part of it, and we expect to cover all of it on bicycles by the end of summer, so I want to see where it goes and what I'm getting myself into." Darrell gave 'thumbs up,' and within minutes they were off the ground. Walter climbed to 3,100 feet and leveled off, all the while making a wide sweeping clockwise turn over Klamath Falls. As they neared Olene, he caught clear sight of the Trail and began following it, keeping it in view out the window to his left.

At Dairy, it occurred to him to check out the roads around his cabin, so he told Darrell he was going to make a small detour. He followed Highway 70 all the way to Bonanza, made a wide 180-degree turn, and started back. About two miles west of town, he turned due north to parallel Haskins Road and flew past his cabin to see how visible it was from the air. He was about to resume following the OC&E Trail when something just beyond Ted's house caught his eye. "I want you to take control so I can look at something," he told Darrell. "Go north another half-mile, then make a one-eighty and fly back south directly over Haskins Road. And if you're comfortable doing it at 1,000 feet, please do." Darrell nodded and put the plane into a gradual descent. Almost as an afterthought, but actually to hide his true purpose, Walter added, "I'm interested in some property down there." *That wasn't a lie*, he thought. *It just wasn't the* whole *truth*.

On the return pass above Haskins Road Walter pressed his nose against the glass as they neared Ted's place. The house, the outbuildings, and the clearing were easy to see, but the lane into the clearing was obscured by trees. What really interested Walter was faint evidence of a lane out of the *other* side of the clearing, leading north toward what was probably the northeast extremity of Ted's property. He caught sight of a power line strung along the lane, from the house toward that point, and as he followed it with his eyes, he saw a small windsock on a power pole next to another clearing. In the clearing itself were some small, low marker lights arranged in a specific pattern: it was a rudimentary helipad! To anybody other than an experienced pilot it was not discernible, but if you knew what to look for and had a general idea of where to look, you couldn't miss it, especially if those lights were turned on. Walter made no mention of it to Darrell, who probably couldn't see it anyhow because he was seated on the other side of the plane.

When they got to the intersection of Haskins Road and Highway 70, Walter took control again, swinging west to Dairy and climbing to 2,000 feet to follow the OC&E Trail as before. About ten miles north of Dairy, he turned northwest toward Switchback Flat to go past Round Mountain on the west side, and as they approached Sprague River, both the town and the stream, he turned east to follow the river and the Trail to Beatty.

Just beyond Beatty the OC&E Trail split. At Darrell's suggestion, Walter turned northeast to explore the 'Woods Line' portion, which zigs and zags thirty-five miles north into the Fremont National Forest, ending at Sycan Marsh. The marsh was unmistakable, a broad flat splash of bright green in an otherwise rough and mostly barren landscape. They made a wide turn over the marsh and flew south toward Bly, some twenty miles away. As they approached the town, Darrell suggested they turn east to follow the highway to Mitchell Monument, where the Japanese balloon-bomb had exploded in 1945. There wasn't much to be seen from the air, but at least Walter got some idea of where it was. As they started back toward Bly, Walter asked Darrell, "Where is the Frisco Ranch?"

A dour expression crossed Darrell's face, which Walter read as indication he was wondering why Walter had asked and how much he should divulge in answering. Apparently deciding in favor of not challenging Walter's 'need to know,' he said, "I'll show you." Taking the controls, Darrell dropped the plane to 1,000 feet and cut their speed. About halfway to town, he pointed to the left and said, "Down there."

Walter again pressed his nose to the glass of the side window, as they began a slow circle to the left. At first he saw nothing but rocks and scrub trees, reminding him of what Mac had told him about the terrain resembling Afghanistan. Then he picked out several low buildings, some of them single-wide trailers, with a few vehicles parked nearby. One of them stood out enough to command Walter's attention: a large white van with a gimbaled dish antenna (GDA)—dark gray, about three feet in diameter—mounted on top. He was studying it carefully, trying to discern any distinctive markings, when a man stepped out of one of the trailers and began waving an automatic weapon in the air. "He's got a gun!" Walter shouted. "Let's get out of here!"

Darrell punched the throttle and banked the plane sharply to the right. The engine noise was more than enough to drown out the sound of any gunfire, but Walter thought he saw a cluster of bullets whizzing past them. Within a few seconds, they were headed west again, climbing back to 2,000 feet, well out of the shooter's range. "Thank God the AK-47 doesn't shoot very straight and has lousy range," Darrell said with a grin.

"At 600 rounds a minute, it doesn't need to do anything else," Walter said. *So Darrell must have seen the bullets too,* he thought. On further consideration, it seemed to him the shooter wasn't trying to hit them, just scare them away. *He certainly succeeded in that,* Walter concluded.

A few miles west of Bly Walter got a new perspective on the segment of the Sprague River he and Mac had fished. He identified a few spots he would like to try on a future outing—that is, if he could remember them and find them again from ground level. He took the controls again and headed back to Kingsley Field. His landing was incredibly soft, reflecting Walter's considerable piloting skills, even in a plane unfamiliar to him. As the wheels touched the runway, Darrell started laughing. "If I hadn't known you were an Air Force pilot, that landing would surely have told me."

"Howzat?" Walter asked. *I thought it was a damned good landing—nearly perfect.*

"It was smooth as silk, but you were halfway down the runway. A Navy pilot would have put it down in the first fifty feet, and probably jarred your upper molars loose in the process." Walter was now laughing too. Darrell had nailed the stereotypes.

As they got out of the plane, Walter checked the fuel gauge and asked how much he owed for the gasoline. "Nothing at all," Darrell replied. "This was your qualification ride, part of your job interview, so it's all on my nickel. Let's go inside and talk." They went to his office, and Darrell phoned the receptionist to request some coffee. Walter settled into an arm chair, not knowing what to expect.

"First things first," said Darrell. "I like your flying style—smooth and safe—not that a Cessna 172 gives you much to show off with. As I said before, any time you want to come to work, we've got a place for you, full or part time. We've got six planes, all Cessnas, ranging from the one you just flew, up to the Citation Sovereign (a mid-size business jet with transcontinental range), which is where I need you most. There's plenty of demand for executive flying in this town, but we're limited by the number and experience of the available pilots. With your 737 experience, especially flying out of the Bay Area, I could keep you as busy as you could ever want." He pushed some sheets of paper across the desk to Walter. "Here's a description of our pay scales and benefits package. Take it home and read it, then call me if you have any questions."

He's put his cards on the table, Walter thought. *Now it's time for me to do the same.* "Thank you. I appreciate your interest in hiring me, and I'm definitely interested in working for you, but not just yet. I've gone to a good bit of trouble to set myself up in a situation where I can take some time off and sort out my life—sort of a sabbatical. As you probably know, I've recently been through a divorce and I've still got some adjustments to make, mostly with my kids, who are living with their mother in California. I've started making plans to vacation with the kids in August, and I have a couple other personal things I want to do as well. Consequently, the earliest I could be available is October, and I might even want to wait until next year."

"I understand what you're saying," Darrell said. "I think we could work that out quite handily." He leaned forward and put another card on the table. "However, I do have a slight sense of urgency that you should know about. My flying days are numbered because of my age, and once I get to where I can retire, I sure don't want to put in much time at a desk job. I need to find a successor and start grooming him to take over from me in two or three years." He paused to let that sink in. "From what I've seen and learned about you, I think you could be that person."

That certainly took Walter by surprise, not just the senior rank of the position being dangled in front of him, but also how quickly Darrell had chosen to reveal it. *I'll figure out that part of it in due course,* he thought. *Right now, the main priority is to not get stampeded into making a commitment I might regret later on.* "That's very attractive," he said in what he hoped was a diplomatic voice, "and I thank you very much for entertaining the notion I might be qualified, or become qualified, for such a position. I'll certainly keep it in mind as I consider my career options over the next few months. For the time being, however, I'll regard these discussions as strictly preliminary, with neither of us making any guarantees about what the situation will be next year."

Darrell considered that briefly, concealing any disappointment he might have felt over failing to make a quick sale. "That's fair, and I can live with it. I'm sure we'll be seeing one another at least a few times before winter, especially if you want to take Susan flying on her birthday, so we can keep each other apprised of our respective needs and wants." He stood up and extended his hand. As Walter shook it, he added, "Virginia is almost ecstatic about your relationship with Susan. She thinks you two make a great couple, and I agree." He gave Walter's hand an extra squeeze before he released it.

As he drove into KFalls from the airport, Walter's head was still spinning from Darrell's surprising job offer, but that faded into the background when he remembered what he had seen at the Frisco Ranch. He decided he should let Mac know about it ASAP. He went to the KFalls Library, logged onto the Internet, and sent an email message:

Hi, Mac:

This AM I made a checkout flight with Darrell Cox, out to Sycan Marsh and back via Bly. At my request, Darrell made a low, slow pass over Frisco Ranch, where I saw a large white van with a gray three-foot GDA mounted on top. I'm no expert on this, but I think such an antenna can be used for communications intercept, a.k.a. eavesdropping.

Our overflight drew attention from a resident at the Ranch, who shook his AK-47 at us. He may have fired off a few rounds, but we were already skedaddling.

Just thought you ought to know.

Best,

Walter

41.

The next day, Thursday, June 12, was Walter's birthday. According to prior arrangement, he met Susan at her house at 11 o'clock. After a good slobbering by Moses, he loaded her bicycle into the back of his pickup and they set off for an early lunch at a local Mexican restaurant. Next they drove to the parking area at Dairy, unloaded the bikes, and rode south and west to Olene on the OC&E Trail. For the most part, the Trail surface was fine gravel, so the 19.6-mile round trip took almost three hours. They returned to Susan's house to unload her bicycle and allow her to shower and put on dressier going-out-to-dinner clothes while Walter played with Moses on the living room floor. Susan came out of her bedroom looking like a fashion model and found them lying side-by-side, Moses sprawled on his back and Walter scratching the dog's long tummy. "*Humph!*" she said. "The saying is 'Love me, love my dog,' not the other way 'round."

"Well," said Walter, "if you want to come lie down here beside me, I'll be happy to rub your tummy too, but you should take off your clothes first, so you don't get dog hair all over them."

Neither smiling nor scowling, she looked at him for fifteen seconds but couldn't think of an appropriate rejoinder. Sensing her quandary, Walter began to chuckle. "Soon," she said quietly. Walter wanted to take her in his arms and kiss her passionately, but he was all sweaty and flecked with dog hair, so all he could do was give her a rather chaste kiss on the cheek as she walked toward the door. Before going out, she turned and handed him a key. "I almost forgot," she said. "Here's a birthday present."

It took Walter a few seconds to realize what it was: a key to her house! The significance of her action moved him so that he could only stammer, "Thank you, thank you" and make a mental note to get her a key to his cabin—'soon.'

They drove directly to the cabin, with Susan's interest growing as they advanced into territory unfamiliar to her: southeast on Highway 70 from Dairy toward Bonanza, north on Haskins Road to where Walter turned off on the narrow lane to his cabin, then a half-mile through the thickening trees. "Here we are!" he shouted as they pulled into the clearing. He parked, unloaded his bicycle and stored it in the shed, then led Susan up the porch steps, and unlocked the front door. "I'd carry you across the threshold," he said, holding the door open for her, "but I'd get you all dirty."

"Soon," she said again as she stepped inside. After a quick tour of the interior, she rendered her opinion: "It's bigger than I expected, and nicer too, not as rough and primitive as I pictured it. And it's cleaner than I had feared it would be. You're not too bad as a housekeeper." Walter was glad he had spent most of the previous evening cleaning and straightening up the place.

He poured her a glass of lemonade and led her to one of the chairs on the porch, the one he had designated as 'Her Chair,' next to the small table that separated it from 'His Chair.' Pointing to the latter, he said, "That's where I do most of my meditation, and the folded towel behind it is where Abigail sits whenever she decides to join me."

"Can you call her?" Susan asked. "I'd like to meet her."

"She's not as gregarious as Moses," Walter replied, "but I've made an effort to train her to come when I play certain music. Usually that's part of our morning routine, so I don't know if it will work this late in the day. Why don't you sit here and enjoy the quiet while I get myself cleaned up, and then we'll try it."

Susan spent the next fifteen minutes sensing out the spirit of the place: watching, listening, smelling, feeling, and communing with the trees surrounding the clearing. She was almost into a meditative state when a musical cry from the stereo inside the cabin startled her out of her reverie. A freshly showered and nattily attired Walter stepped onto the porch and sat down in His Chair as *Yusuf's* rendition of the *Adhan*, the Muslim 'Call to Prayer,' wafted past them and up the path toward Ted's house. Susan recalled having heard snippets of the *Adhan* in her not-too-recent past, but it was not in a setting like the present one where the music could penetrate her being and wrap itself around her soul.

Hay ala salat! (Come to prayer!)
Hay alal-falah! (Come to success!)
Allahu akbar. (God is most great.)
La ilaha illa Allah. (There is none worthy of worship except God.)

It lasted only two minutes, but it lifted her into a different world, a different dimension. She remained there, suspended, even after the music ended.

Another minute or two passed, then the mood gently receded when Walter whispered, "Here she comes." The duck had entered the clearing and was waddling straight toward them. Suddenly she stopped, apparently having noticed Walter was not alone. "It's OK, Abigail," Walter called softly. He quickly stepped inside and returned with a handful of mash, spreading it on the porch floor at the top of the steps, making sure to leave a small pile just in front of Susan's feet. Abigail took a few more steps forward and stopped. "It's OK, Abigail," Walter said again. A few more steps, another "OK"—two, three times, and she was at the base of the porch steps. Walter put the last of the mash, a bit he had held in reserve, on the first step in front of her, so she could eat it from where she stood. She quickly scarfed it up, then gave Walter a look that said, "Is that all I get?" Walter stuck his finger in some of the mash on the porch, to bring her attention to it. "It's OK, Abigail," he said again. With a push from her legs and a flap of her wings she was up, onto the porch. She ate the mash right in front of her, then advanced to the pile in front of Susan and looked up. Susan said nothing, but couldn't restrain her special gurgle-giggle of delight, which apparently satisfied Abigail. She bent down to eat some of the mash, waddled over to her place on the towel, and sat down.

Walter and Susan beamed in exultation. "What do we do now?" Susan asked.

"We could sit here in silence for an hour or so, and she would probably stay with us. I don't know what she will do if we talk quietly, but I suggest we try it for a few minutes. What do you want to talk about?"

Susan started to reply when she realized there was a man approaching them, following the path taken by Abigail. It was Ted. "I heard the music, and I saw Abigail set off in this direction, so I figured you were here," he said, mainly to Walter. "You said Susan would be coming for a visit, so I came over to meet her, to welcome her—oh, yes—and to wish you a happy birthday."

Everybody on the porch stood up—Walter, Susan, Abigail—and Susan stepped down to shake Ted's hand. "We don't have any birthday cake—we're going out to dinner in Bonanza—but we can offer you a glass of lemonade."

"I wasn't planning to stay long," Ted replied, "but lemonade would taste really good right about now." Walter invited Ted to take His Chair while he fetched the lemonade. Susan returned to Her Chair, and Abigail sat down too. Grabbing the brief opportunity to speak one-to-one with Susan, Ted said quietly, "I understand you and I have some matching pictures: run-ins with Muslim terrorists, protection under the Federal WitSec program, and counseling from the ubiquitous Doctor McCarter. Perhaps we can chat about it sometime when you're here again. It would help me to compare notes and gain some understanding of how unique my situation is."

As usual, Susan thought before answering. "I'm not sure what I can offer that you don't already know, but I'm willing to give it a go. I don't know when I'll be coming out here again, but it should be sometime in the next few weeks." Walter returned with the lemonade, and Susan turned to him. "Ted was asking whether I could spend a little time with him comparing our common experiences with WitSec and such—not today, but the next time I come out here."

"Sure, we can arrange that," was Walter's quick reply.

"What I also had in mind," Ted explained, "is that I might introduce Susan to Lottie—that being a woman and all, Susan might not threaten Lottie like most strangers, so maybe they could even talk for a while. Lottie has had almost no contact with anybody but McCarter and me since we moved here, essentially no relationship with another female, and I'm sure she misses that. I think it would help her to talk with Susan occasionally."

Recalling what Mac had said about the possibility of Ted joining himself and Mac for fly fishing, Walter immediately saw the potential benefit for Ted in periodic meetings between Lottie and Susan. "I think that's a good idea, but maybe we should run it by Mac first."

Ted smiled sheepishly. "I already did, after Lottie's counseling session this afternoon. He gave it his enthusiastic endorsement." *Thus our little knot of relationships expands, or gets even tighter,* Walter thought. *To Ted, Mac, Susan, and myself, we're adding Lottie—although Abigail has just now joined, ahead of her. I guess Moses will be next—but that can wait until we see how Susan and Lottie get along. Maybe I'll get to meet Lottie too—someday.* Walter and Susan greeted Ted's revelation with hearty laughter—to his relief. Having accomplished his mission for the day, he got up and started back toward his house, pausing halfway across the clearing to say 'Good evening' and to wish Walter a 'Happy Birthday' one more time. As he did so, Abigail stood up and fluttered down off the porch, hurrying to catch up with him. He waited until she was close, then resumed walking, but at a slower pace so she could easily keep up. Walter and Susan watched in great amusement, both struggling to keep from impolite laughter. When Ted and the duck were out of earshot, Walter whispered to Susan, "They make a great couple, don't they?"

Susan suppressed her laughter by busily gathering up the lemonade glasses and taking them inside. When she returned, Walter locked the cabin door, and they drove off to Bonanza. Walter had called ahead for reservations at the Longhorn Saloon & Restaurant, and he was looking forward to dinner there. It was clearly the best restaurant in Bonanza, at least in appearance—and probably, he feared, in price. That fear took a back seat as Walter and Susan walked in the door. There to greet them was the smiling hostess/waitress, none other than Nancy Norwood. "Hello, Walter!" she boomed. "Good to see ya' again. Where ya' been keepin' yourself?"

"Hello, Nancy," Walter stammered, fighting to maintain his cool. "Nancy, this is Susan, my very best friend." He wanted to say, 'my *fiancée*,' as a way of closing off any lingering hope of an assignation Nancy might be entertaining, but he doubted that Susan would be able to play along.

"Hello, Susan. Nice to meetcha,'" Nancy said sweetly as she looked Susan over from top to bottom.

To spare Susan any further discomfort in the situation, Walter intervened before she could answer. "We have reservations," he told Nancy.

"Of course," she said, looking slightly hurt because he had summarily ended the verbal sparring. "Walk this way." She fairly flounced as she led them to a booth. Walter couldn't decide whether that was her normal way of walking or whether she was exaggerating for his or Susan's benefit, a sort of 'in your face' gesture.

"Who the hell is she?" Susan demanded after they had sat down and Nancy had completed the standard ritual of presenting menus and a wine list and taking the beverage order. Walter couldn't miss the tone of irritation in her voice and her use of 'hell,' which he had witnessed only once or twice before.

"She's a local character," he explained defensively. "I met her at the town picnic on Memorial Day weekend." He wisely edited out the rest of the sentence, 'when we were having our spat,' and closed down the discussion with "I'll tell you about the whole thing later, when we're safely out the door." That seemed to satisfy Susan, and the rest of the dinner continued without incident. After they ordered, Walter commanded Susan's attention with an account of his post-flight discussion with Darrell Cox the day before. She too was blown away by Darrell's enticing, albeit tentative, job offer, and Walter could sense her 'connecting the dots' in its implications for his future and *their* future. The 'bottom line' was that Walter could be around Klamath Falls in a secure and somewhat prestigious position for as long as he wanted to be. Her mission, if she chose to accept, was to make him *want* to stick around.

The food came and a warm glow surrounded them as they ate and talked: their own private cocoon, just like their first dinner together barely a month earlier. Nancy was on her good behavior, serving them courteously and efficiently, but not *too* personally, so they were hardly aware she was even there. She had one more opportunity to give Walter a little jab before they left. He had paid the bill, leaving a generous but not outrageous tip, and they were almost out the door when she caught up with them, ostensibly to thank them for their patronage. However, she couldn't resist turning to Susan and saying, "Take good care of him, honey. You've got a real prize there, if you can hang onto him."

Susan managed to hold her silence until they were about twenty feet past the door, then she demanded in the same 'no bullshit' tone as before, "And what was that all about?"

Walter laughed nervously. "It's no big deal. She came on to me at the picnic, as I was going through the food line and she was serving me a piece of chicken. She made it obvious she wanted to jump my bones that very afternoon. I got the lowdown on her from the local real estate agent while I was eating. He said she wasn't in the habit of taking 'no' for an answer, so I simply disappeared after I finished my lunch: sneaked off to my truck and drove the back streets out of town. I haven't seen her since then, but I will admit to having taken some pains to avoid meeting her by accident. If I had known she worked at the Longhorn, we would have gone somewhere else for dinner. I hope she didn't ruin your evening."

"No, I wasn't about to let her do that—and besides, the evening isn't over yet," Susan replied in a calm voice. "Let's go back to my place and talk some more."

They rode in silence for about ten minutes. As they passed Olene, Walter had an idea. "If we can find a way to keep Moses distracted, we could lie side-by-side and I could rub your tummy like I did his earlier today."

"Maybe I should rub yours. After all you're the male, like Moses."

"I'm not so sure I want to go there. When I was rubbing Moses, I couldn't help but notice that parts of his—er—'equipment' had been surgically removed. Mine have been disconnected and I'm OK with that, but I don't want to lose them altogether."

"What are you saying?" Susan asked.

"I had a vasectomy, about eight years ago, after my son was born."

"*Arrrrgh!*" Susan emitted a sound that was half scream, half groan. "You rotten fink! I've been losing sleep for the past month trying to figure out how to handle birth control so we can have sex, and you've already taken care of that. Why didn't you tell me?"

"You didn't ask," Walter replied innocently.

"*Humph!*" said Susan. Walter could tell she really wasn't mad, just acting, and he sensed that 'soon' was about to happen. As they parked in front of Susan's house and walked to the front door, she seemed to exude an air of purpose and determination. Cutting short Moses' greeting ritual, she shooed him out the back door to pee in the yard rather than taking him for the walk he surely expected. Then she went into her bedroom and pulled down the bedcovers, leaving only the bottom sheet exposed. Returning to the kitchen, she dumped some food into Moses' bowl, then opened the back door and tapped her foot impatiently as she waited for him to return.

Walter observed all this with mild amusement mixed with puzzlement, eventually retreating to the living room to wait for Susan's attention to return to him. And when it did, it came with an intensity that took him by surprise. She almost tackled him into an embrace in the middle of the living room, flinging herself into an urgent, wet kiss. Their passion quickly erupted to a level of 'eleven' on a scale of ten. Moses was immediately caught up in the emotion and let out a sonorous bay of encouragement that managed to penetrate their awareness after several seconds, causing Walter to prematurely end their kiss in uncontrolled laughter.

Susan, however, was less than amused. Perhaps because her only previous sexual experience had been with her late husband when they were both barely beyond their teens, she had been conditioned to expect her partner to rush past the foreplay into the 'Main Event.' That and two decades of sexual abstinence now drove her to shed all inhibitions and become the aggressor. In contrast, Walter, the mature veteran of numerous trysts with lascivious stewardesses, had developed a talent and liking for a more deliberate crescendo of lovemaking, *adagio* rather than *vivace*. *Besides*, he reasoned, *Susan is most likely out of practice at this, so I shouldn't frighten her by coming on too strong.*

This mismatch created temporary confusion as to who was going to do what, with Susan finally taking the initiative by clawing at Walter's shirt, attempting to remove it like peeling a banana. He quickly caught on and began unbuttoning her blouse, but taking care not to damage what was obviously one of her most expensive items of clothing. He tossed it onto the coffee table and began trying to salvage his shirt, eventually opening it sufficiently to allow her to whisk it off his torso and vigorously plop it on the coffee table as well. They leaned into another passionate kiss, during which he reached around to expertly open the catch on her bra and she backed away just enough to let it slide off her arms. She flung it across the room in the general direction of the easy chair, but as luck would have it, it landed on Moses. He stopped his howling, mistaking the bra for some newfangled kind of leash. With perfect hound-dog logic, he inferred that they were about to go for a walk and began dancing excitedly around the room.

Meanwhile Walter and Susan were continuing their disjointed reciprocal striptease, he quickly unzipping and sliding her skirt down, she frantically picking at his belt buckle and fly zipper as he began fondling her bare breasts. At length, Walter's pants fell to his ankles, and he kicked them under the coffee table. Next he slid his hands down Susan's back, inserted his fingers inside the waistband of her now-damp panties, and slipped them down while caressing her *derrière* in the same smooth motion. No sooner had she stepped out of them than Moses pounced this new prize, noisily rooting his nose in the delightful smells it offered. Again Walter's attention was distracted from Susan's alluring body, and his delirious laughter resumed when he saw that the dog was now hopelessly entangled in the bra. Susan meanwhile was focused on trying to pull down Walter's boxer shorts without crimping the stiffening member within, and her annoyance with Moses boiled over when she discovered that Walter's mirth had temporarily diverted his blood supply from where it was needed most.

Muttering a most unladylike curse, she leaned over to pick up the boxers and snatch her panties from Moses' muzzle, then stood up, looking around the room for a place to stash the underwear safely out of the dog's reach. Noting Susan's frustration, Walter took charge—he bent down, picked her up in his arms, and tenderly carried her into the bedroom, forsaking their strange *ménage à trois* with the thoroughly befuddled Moses. He gently put her on the bed, went back to securely close the door, and returned smiling as his penis rose to the occasion once again. He paused next to the bed to gaze down at Susan's lovely naked body, savoring the voluptuous vista from her shapely breasts with small nipples now erect to her exuberant nut-brown bush. *She's even more beautiful than I imagined,* he marveled. *She hides it extremely well until the moment is right, which is* now! Filing the image in his memory for future reminiscence, he lay down beside her and continued his intimate exploration of her exquisiteness with his fingers, lips, and tongue. "Now," he whispered, "where were we?"

PART THREE

More Endings

Every journey has a secret destination
of which the traveler is unaware.

—Martin Buber (1878-1965)

42.

The next morning Walter was awakened by the sun streaming through the bedroom window. Susan was still sound asleep, curled up under his left armpit, her left arm draped across his chest. He didn't know how long she had been there, but his left arm was beginning to get numb. He could also hear Moses snuffling behind the closed bedroom door, where he had been exiled the night before. Now aware somebody in the bedroom was awake, the dog whined twice as if to say, "Please! I gotta go!" Slowly, Walter withdrew his left arm, trying not to awaken Susan. Buck-naked, he tiptoed to the door, expecting the usual joyous bath from Moses when he stepped out, but the dog's priorities were elsewhere. Walter continued to the back door and opened it for Moses, having observed Susan do the same instead of taking Moses for a walk the night before, when her priorities were also elsewhere. He paddled back to the bedroom to search for his underwear, forgetting that Susan had yanked them off him in the living room. He found her sitting up in bed, with the sheet wrapped around her torso. She began laughing when she saw his nudity, and his bravado hid behind a blush. "If you open the closet door, you'll find two pegs on the backside" she directed. "There's a bathrobe hanging on the left one. It's yours, your birthday present. I laundered it after I bought it, so it's all ready for you to wear. Of course, if you'd rather keep on walking around naked, that's fine with me, but you do so at your own risk."

Walter put on the robe. It fit perfectly. "When did you buy this?" he asked.

"Almost two weeks ago, after you came here the first time. I figured you'd need it sooner or later."

"So you planned this," Walter said.

Susan smiled demurely. "Sort of, but I didn't know when, because I was still stymied by the birth control issue. Yesterday all the pieces fell into place, and Nancy's parting 'advice' eliminated any hesitancy I might have had. Maybe we should go back to thank her."

"No, I think we should leave her out of this. What would you have done if I hadn't gotten a vasectomy?"

"I was thinking about that when we were riding back from Bonanza, before you told me. I was about to ask you to stop at a drug store to buy some condoms."

"Why didn't you buy some in advance like the bathrobe?"

"That's different," she explained. "I didn't know what type of condoms you prefer, or what size," she turned a bright shade of red. Walter was beginning to enjoy what Susan was revealing about herself, but a sharp bark from the back yard interrupted her confession. When he returned from letting Moses in, Susan was up and wrapped in her own bathrobe, which, he noted, matched his. *She sure does think things through and plan ahead,* he thought—with more than a little admiration.

"What time do you go to work today?" it occurred to him to ask.

"I don't," she said. "I've got the day off. I'm on ten-to-five tomorrow." *She even planned that too,* he thought.

Susan began instructing him in how to make coffee and how her kitchen was organized in general. She showed him where the dog food was stored and how much to feed Moses. *Coffee first, then Moses,* Walter filed the regimen in his mind. They discussed breakfast preferences and quickly found common ground. Then they sat down at the kitchen table and just looked into each other's eyes while they waited for the coffee to brew. Words were totally inadequate to express what both were feeling, so neither spoke for several minutes. Instead they basked in the afterglow of lovemaking as it returned to flood their consciousness with the spiritual connection they had achieved. It wasn't just that they had seen each other naked or that they had shared uncountable minutes of sexual ecstasy, but that their souls had touched and consequently things would never be the same between them. Walter now began to understand the deep hunger that had driven Susan the night before: a loneliness, an aching emptiness, a sense of having been abandoned when her husband was killed. He had experienced similar feelings in recent years, although they had come on gradually as his marriage died a slow death. It is what had led him to let go of everything, to back off and look at himself, to make a new start in a different direction.

It had been just over a month—37 days, to be exact—since Walter had moved into the cabin to begin his 'retreat.' It hadn't gone as he had expected—in truth, it almost never does—mainly because he hadn't counted on a Susan in his life—not yet, not so fast. Yet here they were, and she was obviously making room for him, maybe not to move in full-time—he knew better than to try that, not now and maybe never—but to spend a good bit of time there. Instead

209

of being sequestered in his cabin to read and meditate ten, twelve, fourteen hours per day as he had originally envisioned, he was now contemplating a life of commuting between his cabin and Susan's house on a schedule determined largely by her working hours. It would still leave him plenty of time for reading and meditation—his original expectations had been somewhat unrealistic, he had to admit, but he was somewhat surprised at how much and how quickly his plans had changed. Now there was the prospect of going to work for Darrell: full-time?—part-time?—when?—doing what? All things considered, his life was working out far better than he could have imagined.

"What are you thinking?" Susan asked. She had noticed his silence for—how long?—several minutes.

"I was thinking about how far you and I have come—and how fast—since that day I walked into the Welcome Center and asked you about 'weirdos.'"

"Tuesday, April 29," she said, "and as I recall, your original purpose in coming to the Center was not to ask about 'weirdos' but to find a place to stay until Ted got the background check on you."

"Yes, that's right. I was about to leave after you had made the reservation at Odell Lake Lodge, but something told me to prolong the conversation. All I could think of was to ask about 'weirdos.' So I did, which led to our meeting for coffee at Peet's..."

"... and the rest, as they say, is history," Susan finished the sentence. *That's becoming our mantra*, she thought.

"What are we going to do today?" he asked. "Have you planned that out too?"

"No, I didn't go that far. I wanted to leave a little room for your input."

" 'A little room.' Thanks a lot," he kidded.

"Well, since you asked," she countered, "I do expect you to stay here again tonight—that is, if you're up to it."

"Ha!" he snorted. "I'm not that old and feeble. We might even squeeze in a 'nooner'—that is, if you can handle it."

"A 'nooner'?" she mused. "I can't ever recall doing a 'nooner.' It would have been so far out of what my life was about it would have never entered my imagination. But now that you mention it, it does wake me up to how far we've come. I couldn't have imagined that either, but here it is, and it's wonderful." She got up to pour coffee for both of them. "However, getting back to the 'nooner,' I don't want to get too vigorous too quickly. Regardless of what kind of shape you're in, it's been years since I've had any sexual activity at all, so I'm probably not ready for sex five times a day and six on Sundays. Besides, I didn't attempt anything like that even when I was a young bride. We were too busy trying to survive."

"OK, I'll reduce your quota to three times a day and only two on Sundays, but you'd better get yourself together by the time you get past menopause," Walter joked.

"Dream on, dream on," she retorted.

Breakfast interrupted the banter, giving them both another pause to retreat into their own thoughts as they munched their toast and slurped their cereal. Then they cleared away the breakfast dishes and returned to sip their second cups of coffee, smiling across the table at each other in wonderment at the miracle that had occurred—at the whole string of miracles that was continuing right into the here and now. Moses, who had been waiting expectantly beneath the table for a tidbit to fall, finally realized that nothing would be forthcoming, so he got up and plodded to his blanket in the living room, nudging Walter and Susan out of their trance. She stood up, held out her hand, and began guiding Walter back to the bedroom. "It's not noon yet," he said in mock protest.

She closed the bedroom door behind them and turned to face Walter. Smiling seductively, she said, "Take off your clothes. I think I love you."

He loosened the tie to his bathrobe and let it fall to the floor as she followed suit. "I think I love you too," he said, taking her by the hand and leading her over to the bed. "Let's go find out how much."

43.

Physically, Walter and Susan welcomed the respite when she went off to work the next morning, but it was with mixed emotions. Spiritually, both would have rather spent another day in bed together, or just sitting at the kitchen table with cups of coffee, in silent communion. Poor Moses was thoroughly bewildered by all the changes that had invaded his territory, but Walter took him for a long slow walk before driving back to his cabin. He also stopped by the Klamath Falls Library to check his email. As expected, Mac had replied to his message:

Walter:

Thanks for the report on Bly. I don't know what to make of it, but it does remind me that you should be very careful what you talk about when you use your cell phone. Ditto wi-fi. Landline telephone and hardwire Internet access should be secure enough, however. You know what to do—just be aware.

I suggest you also mention this to Susan and perhaps your neighbor as well, although he should be well versed on this stuff.

I expect to see you and Susan at my lecture at OIT next Thursday night. No, there won't be a quiz afterward.

Regards,

Mac

Although Walter spent the day at his cabin, his schedule had been disrupted and his brain had been rattled by the recurring lapses in blood supply since Friday night. He tried meditation, then reading, and finally an early afternoon nap, which went best. After the nap he called Susan at work, just to see how she was doing. "I'm tired, but that's not surprising," she said. "I definitely want you to come back this evening after I get off work. Can you pick up some Chinese carryout on the way? Anything you get will be fine with me. And I think it would be better if you didn't stay over tonight, because I'm a little sore. If you stay tonight, it will be well nigh impossible for me to resist your advances or control my own urges."

"I understand what you're saying. Do you need to see a doctor?" Walter asked anxiously.

"No, not as things are now. I just need time to recover. If I'm not ready to rumble again by next Monday or Tuesday, I'll go to the clinic. You're coming in Thursday night so we can go to Mac's talk, aren't you?"

"That's the plan."

"Well, in anticipation of that I've scheduled myself to have next Friday off again, so you won't have to drive home in the dark," she said.

"That's very considerate of you," he teased. "Would you want to go meet my neighbor's wife on Friday afternoon as her husband suggested?" With Mac's warning in mind, he chose his words carefully so as not to mention names.

"If that works for her, I'm OK with that. Try to make it mid-to-late afternoon, so we'll have time for another 'nooner,'" she answered. Walter couldn't tell whether she was joking or serious until she added, "Can we get one of those crazy clocks where every number is a '12'?"

"I'm glad to see you have your priorities in order," he replied. *Have I created a monster?* he wondered.

"Gotta go," Susan said. "A client just walked in. See you about 5:30."

Walter hung up and sauntered down to Ted's house, finding Ted splitting logs next to his woodpile. "I just talked with Susan about her work schedule for next week, and it looks like she'll be coming out to the cabin Friday afternoon late. Would that be a good time for her to meet Lottie?"

Ted thought for a minute, as if consulting an appointment calendar in his mind. "That's the 20th, isn't it? I think that should work for us. I'll double check it with Lottie and confirm it with you next week."

"Susan and I will be attending Mac's lecture at OIT Thursday evening, and we may not get back here until Friday afternoon. So unless you tell me otherwise before I leave Thursday, I'll assume Susan should come knocking on your door around 3:00 PM."

Ted gave him a look that said he had 'put two with two' to infer that Walter and Susan would be spending the night together in town. "I very much appreciate Susan being willing to do this. She seems to be a very intelligent and understanding person—and very attractive too. I'd say you've made a good choice in latching onto her."

"Thank you," said Walter. *I'm glad you approve,* he thought to himself. *I wonder what you'd have said if I had brought Nancy out here.* He put the orneriness out of his mind in order to move on to another cat-and-mouse game. "Not to change the subject, but I was wondering if you heard a small plane flying low overhead last Wednesday afternoon."

"Yes, I did, now that you mention it," Ted replied. "Do you have any idea what was going on?"

"Yes," Walter laughed. "I was making a check-out flight with a friend, Susan's boss's husband, as a matter of fact. I wanted to see how visible your house and my cabin are from the air." Seeing Ted's scowl, Walter hastened to cover his tracks. "Don't worry, my friend couldn't see anything because he was seated on the other side of the plane. I explained my interest by saying I was considering buying some property along Haskins Road." Ted looked relieved, but said nothing, so Walter continued. "However, I did make a couple discoveries in my reconnaissance. First, I saw what looks like a rudimentary helipad a few hundred yards north of here. I presume it's on your property." Discretion told Walter to omit the rest of the sentence: "... *because there's a power line connecting it to your house.*"

Ted's scowl returned, but not quite as intense. He sighed and said, "Yes, it's a helipad, and yes, it's mine. How visible was it? Did it stand out from the surroundings?"

"It didn't stand out at all. In fact, I would never have spotted it if I had been at the controls and if we hadn't been flying at low speed and very low altitude."

Ted was solicitous now. "Should I do anything else to hide it more?" he asked.

"I can't think of anything. If you had put it closer to the trees, it would be too difficult to get in and out of safely, and if you cut back on the lighting, it wouldn't be accessible at night or in bad weather. As I think about it now, I'd say you had some expert advice in setting it up."

"Yeah, it was WitSec's idea in the first place. They spent a good bit of time deciding what to put there and where to put it, and they made several test flights with a 'Black Hawk' before we moved in."

"They did a good job," Walter said—and again he didn't say the rest of what he thought: "... *and it leads me to wonder what other security features have been built into this place.*" Moving on to another topic, he added, "There's another thing I saw on our flight that might interest you—or maybe not. When we were out near Bly, we flew over the ranch where some Muslims had tried to set up a '*jihad* training center' about fifteen years ago. It looks like something is going on there again, although there was no way to tell whether Muslims are involved—for example, I didn't see a mosque, or prayer rugs hanging on the laundry line. What I did see was a van with a gimbaled dish antenna mounted on top, the sort of thing that could be used for electronic eavesdropping."

Yes, Ted was interested, but he seemed to be trying not to show how much. "Can you give me more of a description than that?"

"It was just a plain white van, relatively new and clean, with no distinctive markings other than that the antenna dish was dark gray. I didn't get much of a chance to look it over because one of the locals got riled up over how low and slow we were flying. I think he even fired a few shots at us, but he didn't hit anything."

Ted said, "I might have fired some shots too if you had come back for a second or third pass over here." He was laughing.

"That's understandable," Walter responded, " but you don't have an AK-47—or do you?" Ted just smiled, so Walter closed out the discussion. "Anyhow, I told Mac about all that, and he suggested that we—you, me, even Susan—exercise discretion about what we send over wireless—that is, cell phone or wi-fi. Maybe you're already doing that, but he told me to remind you to be aware."

"Ah, the good Doctor McCarter is watching out for all of us, even trying to protect us from ourselves," Ted opined. They both laughed, but not too heartily. There had been a serious, even sinister, undercurrent to their discussion.

Shortly before five o'clock, Walter hopped into his pickup and drove to the Chinese restaurant where he and Susan had enjoyed big bowls of delicious noodles a week earlier. He ordered 'Kung Pao Chicken' and 'Beef with Broccoli,' along with spring rolls and steamed rice. He was unsure how spicy the chicken should be, but decided to 'damn the torpedoes' and request 'four stars out of five,' which was his preference. *If it's too hot for Susan, she can load up on the mild beef dish while I pig out on the chicken,* he rationalized.

Susan opened the door even before he could ring the doorbell. She took the bag of food and put it on the kitchen table, then returned to give Walter a long wet kiss. She had already changed from her work clothes into lounging pajamas, and Walter could feel her warm body through the flimsy material. Unable to detect any bra straps, he started moving his hands down her back to see if she was wearing panties. "Easy, you silly oversexed Sasquatch," she protested with a smile. "I told you we're taking the night off."

"Oh," Walter said, trying to look disappointed, "I thought you might have had a miraculous recovery since we talked on the phone a few hours ago."

"Don't I wish," she said.

Only then did Walter notice Moses wasn't dancing around his feet, clamoring for attention. "Where's Moses?" he asked.

"In the back yard," Susan replied. "I put him out as soon as I got home because I'm not up to taking him for a walk tonight. Besides, I wanted your undivided attention for a change."

"Are you sure you're OK?"

"Yes, I'm fine—just a little tired and tender, like I told you. If I seem to be sending mixed signals, it's because I don't want you to think I'm rejecting you, even for a minute."

"Oh. I think you're confusing me with those inconsiderate horny men who were harassing you after your husband was killed."

"Yeah, maybe so," she agreed. "This is all new for me. Twenty years ago my husband and I were barely out of our teens, so our energies were very different from what you and I are feeling now. You're a different person—kind, considerate, gentle—and I'm still getting to know you."

"You needn't rush," he said, "because I plan to give you a long time to learn all about me. And just when you think you've got me all figured out, I plan to invent something new about myself, just to keep you interested."

"You go right ahead and do that, and I'll do the same. We can keep studying one another until I get a PhD in 'Walter' and you get a PhD in 'Susan.'"

"What will we do after that?" he asked.

"Postdoctoral study, of course—focusing on geriatrics."

Walter had no comeback for that, so he kissed her—and again—and again, until they both began to breathe hard. His hands started exploring the contours of her back one more, slowly moving downward. When he got to her *sacrum*, she pushed him away and said, "Enough! That feels heavenly, but I'm hungry. Let's eat." She ate ravenously, even the spicy Kung Pao Chicken, and after the meal, they took cups of tea to the living room, where she sprawled on the sofa with her bare feet in his lap. Walter hadn't given much attention to her feet before—his priorities had been elsewhere, 'farther north'—but they were what was now being offered. He soon became fascinated with rubbing them, somewhere between a massage and a caress. After a few minutes, she started giggling. "Are you ticklish?" he asked.

"No, I just remembered something I learned from one of the other girls at work. She and her husband are Catholic, so they use the 'rhythm method' for birth control. Their priest told them that if they feel strong sexual urges during times of the month when it isn't 'safe' to copulate, they should rub one another's feet instead. Here we are with you rubbing my feet when I'm sure your hands would rather be somewhere upstream."

He laughed. "You're right about that, but I love your feet too, just as much as I love the rest of you."

"That's the first time you've said that," she observed. "You've never come right out told me you love me until now."

"No, I haven't," he admitted. "I've thought it many times, and I came very close to saying it on several occasions, but I was waiting for the right time and the right place. Whatever that was supposed to be, I didn't envision it like this: rubbing your feet."

They laughed again. "I'll cherish this moment, and write it down in my diary so I can tell our grandchildren someday." The word 'grandchildren' startled him. Seeing that, she quickly added, "No, I'm not saying I want you and me to make our own baby, although it does have some appeal. I'm counting on Lucy and your children to provide us with grandkids—but not any time soon, I hope."

Walter nodded agreement and they drifted back into shared silence while he continued rubbing and Moses watched jealously from his spot in the corner. After a bit, Walter said, "I was thinking ..."

"Yes?"

"I was thinking maybe I should bring in a set of underwear and some socks and stash them here for when I might need them, and maybe you should do likewise by bringing some of your things out to the cabin."

"That would probably be a good idea," she agreed, "but I doubt I'll be staying overnight at the cabin because I don't want to leave Moses alone all night."

"We can take him out to the cabin too. I should probably clear it with Ted first, although I doubt he'll object. He may even like the idea of having a watchdog around. I wonder how Abigail and Moses will get along."

"Let's wait until we see how things work out in my meeting with Lottie. Next Friday, right?"

"Yes, tentatively set for 3:00 PM," he confirmed. Walter went on to tell Susan about what he saw in his flight with Darrell and his subsequent exchange of emails with Mac. He ended by repeating Mac's caution about being discreet in what they discussed on cell phones or sent in email messages via wi-fi.

"I hadn't thought about that," Susan said. "I was all concerned about how admitting you into my household would affect my security, and I forgot that we might give access to others—'weirdos,' you called them—in the process." She paused. "Our life is getting rather complicated, isn't it?"

"So it seems. I hope it doesn't get so busy we don't have time to rub each other's feet."

"I haven't rubbed yours yet," she said.

"You're the one who's tired," he replied. "You can rub me next time."

"*Rub-a-dub-dub*," she giggled.

44.

Susan and Walter arrived at the OIT lecture hall just before 7:00 Thursday evening. Mac was already standing at the podium, reviewing his notes. When the hour arrived, he stepped a few paces to the side and the director of the Klamath County Mental Health Department made the introduction:

Doctor Delbert McCarter, better known as 'Mac,' is a local boy made good. Most of you already know his background, but for the few who don't, I'll tell you a little about him. He was born here in Klamath Falls and raised on a farm near Bonanza. After graduating at the top of his high school class, he went to the University of Oregon for his undergraduate and medical training and to the Oregon Health & Science University for advanced training in psychiatry. He entered the US Air Force and served twenty-five years, culminating in a leadership role in the flight surgeon school at Kingsley Field. Since his military retirement he has maintained an active counseling and consulting practice and joined the OIT faculty as an adjunct professor. Despite those many laudable accomplishments, he is best known throughout the region as a fishing guide par excellence. Tonight he will speak to us on 'Transitions: The Contributions of William Bridges.'

Mac stepped to the podium, glanced at his notes, and began, "There is a strong affinity between Zen Buddhism and fly fishing...Oh, sorry—wrong speech." Much laughter. "If you've ever met me before, you've probably already heard that one anyhow." He made a show of reshuffling his notes and starting over in earnest, explaining first that William Bridges is an American author, speaker, and organizational consultant who at age 40 abandoned a career as Professor of American Literature at Mills College in Oakland, CA, to develop and lead highly successful seminars on 'transitions.' Since then he has written ten books and served as President of the Association for Humanistic Psychology where, Mac implied, he had met and worked with Bridges.

Having given this background, Mac launched into his talk proper. "According to Ralph Waldo Emerson, 'Man is great not in his goals, but in his transitions.' According to Bill Bridges, *transitions*, are different from *changes*, although they are related. 'Changes' are shifts in external situations, like getting a new boss, moving to a new home, having a new child, or losing a loved one. They can be associated with *events* that can be readily be identified by 'outsiders' as well as those who are involved or affected. 'Transitions,' on the other hand, are *processes*, more internal than external, by which we, persons and/or organizations, come to terms with change. They consist of three steps or phases, starting with letting go of the way things used to be and ending with embracing the way things subsequently become. In between, there is a middle phase, a 'neutral zone' when things aren't the old way, but aren't really the new way either. This neutral zone is chaotic but potentially creative and is sometimes characterized as a 'wilderness.' Transitions are essential to successful change. If the transition doesn't occur or is aborted, people end up back where they started, at least mentally and emotionally, and the change doesn't work."

Next Mac briefly explained how people defeat change by resisting one or more of the phases of the associated transition. Then he talked about 'developmental transitions' which are not triggered by an external change but produced "by a natural, inner unfolding of those aspects of ourselves that are built right into who we are and how we are made"—what some people 'growth.' He spent a few minutes explaining the 'developmental model': a conceptual framework in which progressive change is seen as a sequence of 'stages' or 'levels,' each building in some way on the preceding one, with the proviso that it is not possible to skip over a stage—for example, to go from 'Stage 2' directly to 'Stage 4' (whatever those might be) without passing through 'Stage 3.' "Because any profound shift to a new way of experiencing the world is a developmental transition, life itself can be viewed as a sequence of such transitions, including early childhood, adolescence, the so-called 'midlife transition,' and old age or 'maturity.' Thus, it is important to understand these concepts, especially the three phases of transition, in order to make sense of life. Put another way, problems can arise if we lack such a proper understanding.

"A common problem, at least in Western culture, is that we tend to think in terms of a 'beginning-middle-ending' progression, whereas *transitions actually start with an ending.* The reason behind this is that we see each stage of progress or 'growth' as *adding* something, building on top of what was learned in the previous stage. Bridges insists many of life's most difficult and crucial lessons require *unlearning*, giving up or letting go of old outlooks, attitudes, values, and illusions (which we call 'realities'). Only when we have done that—'emptying' ourselves— is there 'room' in us for new ways of thinking and being. This is not a two-step process, however; it is a *transition*, with a 'neutral zone'—mixed signals, false starts, backtracking, and just plain emptiness—between the old and the new. It can be a very difficult time, like grieving over someone or something that has been lost, but it can also be a very creative time because everything is up for grabs and anything is possible. Eventually, however, we take hold of and identify with some new outlook and some new reality, as well as new attitudes and a new self-image. And when we have done this, we feel we are finally starting a new chapter in our lives."

The light was beginning to dawn in Walter's mind. He could see the past year of his life, perhaps even farther back, in a new perspective, one that cleared away some of the confusion, or at least allowed him to accept it, to 'pay his dues' by putting in his time in 'the wilderness.' He had been in similar situations before in his life, notably in his early weeks at the Air Force Academy, and he had made it through, although not without some wounds and scars. His attention shifted back to Mac, who was discoursing on how we avoid or delay transitions. "*Changes* tend to signal that we are in, or about to enter, a transition, especially if they are endings or losses: things that have always gone well in the past suddenly go badly, persons or organizations you have always trusted prove to be untrustworthy, and inexplicable or unforeseen problems crop up and disrupt your life. Ironically, people view these situations or events as disasters to be averted, mistakes to be corrected, or problems to be solved. In reality they are signals that the transition process has started, so making them go away is like turning off the alarm that woke you up. What we should do instead is pay attention to the alarm, but regard it as no more than an alarm—that is, 'a wake-up call.' We shouldn't ask *why* it is happening, but simply focus on *what* is happening, and most of all we should avoid making judgments, especially negative ones that reject or deny the importance of our old lives. All we have to do is *let go of the past.*

"Some people, however, actually use external changes to distract them from the harder business of letting go of their subjective realities and identities—their *illusions*, as the Buddhists label them. This is like rearranging the deck chairs on the *Titanic* as it heads for the iceberg. They make changes so they won't have to make transitions, and then they delude themselves by thinking they are *always* in transition, whereas in actuality they *never* are. The world's literature is full of stories about that, for example, Goethe's *Faust* or Tolstoy's novels. Of course, letting go—unlearning—is not something we are taught to do, at least not in our formal schooling, although life always seems to find a way to provide remedial instruction. Consequently, we come to fear endings and, perhaps even more, the emptiness and loneliness of the subsequent neutral zone. We see the glass as half-empty and the empty glass as worse, instead of entertaining the possibility it might be a *positive* step that takes us closer to a new beginning. We try to make a fresh start by an act of will, formulating an elaborate plan with a whole sequence of actions that we will take to transform ourselves or our worlds." *Was it a coincidence Mac looked at me as he said that?* Walter wondered. "When the plans don't work out, we say there was a defect in them or their implementation, but the problem may have been that we tried to make a *change* do the work of a *transition.* Maybe then, we will come to realize, with Pogo, that 'we have met the enemy and they is us.' And maybe then, we can accept the truth, articulated by Robert Frost, that 'the only way out is through.'"

Mac was through, too. Not that he had said everything that could be said or answered all the listeners' questions—there were many of those in the half-hour that followed. Walter and Susan didn't join the fray, knowing they would have opportunities for private audiences with Mac in the coming months, but after the Q&A Mac made his way over to speak to Susan, "I know you will be meeting one of my patients tomorrow for the first time. You may have some difficult moments during that meeting and even afterward. However, I wouldn't have endorsed the meeting if I weren't confident you could handle it. If it will help you detach from the emotions that will almost certainly arise and think of it as a crash course in counseling. Yes, it might be comforting to have a few more classes under your belt and maybe some introductory clinical experience before going into a situation like this, but sometimes we have to jump off the pier to learn to swim."

Turning to Walter, he said, "You shouldn't go with Susan to this meeting, because that would raise the ante to a level your neighbor probably can't handle just yet. Your job is to counsel the counselor—that is, help Susan process it all after the meeting is over." Then speaking to both of them, he said, "The goal here is to bring your neighbor to where she can handle a meeting with both of you and her husband as well. So visualize the four of you eventually sitting down to a social dinner together like so-called 'normal folk' do. Understood?"

Susan and Walter both nodded, and Walter said, "I think so."

Mac added, "I'd like to call you afterward to see how it went, but I don't want the call to go through Walter's cell phone or mine either. Is there a place and time where I can call you on an old-fashioned land line?"

Susan responded, "Yes, we plan to go back to my house afterward. You can reach us there in the evening. I think you already have my home number, but just in case, here it is again." She pulled a scrap of paper out of her pocketbook, scribbled on it, and gave it to him.

Mac shook their hands. "Good luck with all this. I greatly appreciate your willingness to undertake such a difficult task." As he walked away, Susan and Walter looked at each other in bewilderment. *What are we getting ourselves into?* they were asking. They rode back to Susan's house in silence, each lost in his/her own thoughts, trying to put their apprehension out of their minds so they could become totally absorbed in lovemaking.

45.

Lovemaking remained at the top of their agenda throughout much of the next morning. Susan insisted they eat an early, light lunch and meditate together in the living room in lieu of a 'nooner.' Walter readily acquiesced because he was having second thoughts about the 'nooner' anyhow. The meditation calmed them, dissolving the vague sense of dread that had been threatening to sabotage their passion.

They arrived at the cabin just after 2:00 PM and decided to fill the time by sitting quietly on the porch, not necessarily meditating, but letting go of all their fears and worries and visualizing the goal Mac had described the night before. At 2:55 Walter took Susan by the hand and led her down the path to Ted's house. At the edge of the clearing they kissed and he turned back while she continued onward to the front door. Scarcely a half-hour later, Susan returned to find Walter nervously pacing back and forth in front of the cabin. He stopped and wrapped his arms around her in a big, tender hug. She just stayed there, head on his shoulder, for several minutes. He thought she might be crying, but when they separated enough that he could see her eyes, they were dry. "Let's go somewhere else," she requested. "Stevenson Park."

Walter stopped some distance away from other vehicles at the park, but Susan asked that they stay in the truck. At last the words came tumbling out of her. "The biggest shock was when I first saw her and recognized who she is, and the hardest part was suppressing my reaction so as not to offend her." Walter's mouth and lips started to form the word "Who?" but Susan gave the answer before he could get it all out. "*She's Charlotte Hahn!*" Now Walter was speechless as his mind raced to fill in the rest. Charlotte Hahn had been Governor of Texas a few years earlier when an enclave of about twenty Muslims homesteading in the flat West Texas scrub came to public attention. He couldn't recall all the details, but he did remember that rumors had begun flying fast and furious, quickly coalescing into an 'official opinion' that the Muslims were a terrorist sleeper cell and hence a 'threat to national security.' Governor Hahn had taken 'prompt and decisive action,' just as she had promised during her extremely contentious and controversial election campaign. As commander-in-chief of the Texas National Guard, she had called in an MQ-1 'Predator' unmanned aircraft assigned to patrol the border with Mexico. Most Predators doing reconnaissance in that era were unarmed, but somehow it 'just happened' that the plane sent to the 'terrorist camp' was equipped with two Hellfire missiles. And it 'just happened' that information supplied to the Governor's Office—it was never released to the public in the follow-up investigation—convinced Hahn the group in West Texas constituted 'a clear and present danger' to the state and the nation. Accordingly, she gave the order to fire both missiles, and the Muslim enclave was obliterated twice over.

A big ruckus ensued, with an official investigation and all that rigamarole. The 'liberal Left' called for Hahn's impeachment and criminal prosecution, but they were vastly outnumbered by hard-line conservatives. Moderates, meanwhile, withheld their support of a joint resolution in the Texas legislature that would have exonerated her, so she finally resigned, saying she wanted to write a book and explore running for President in the next election. She went off to New York for a round of high-profile television interviews, leaving her husband and three kids behind in their family home in a small town west of Austin. While she was gone, another group of alleged 'terrorists'—who have never been apprehended— invaded her Texas home and massacred her family. She immediately went into hiding, not only to grieve her loss but also for her safety, because it was presumed she had been the primary target of the massacre and there might be further attempts on her life. Eventually, word got out that a Wall Street billionaire had taken her under his wing: they had married and disappeared together from public view. Walter's memory couldn't supply the billionaire's name, but he was all but certain it was now 'Ted Wilson.' He recounted all this to Susan, ending with the observation that 'Lottie' is a common nickname for 'Charlotte' in European countries. Realizing he might have added to Susan's 'overload,' he apologized for his little history lesson. "No problem," she replied. "It helps me sort out my own recollections of who she was."

"What happened after you got over your initial shock?" Walter asked.

"Not a lot. I told her I was a friend of Mac's, having been introduced to him when WitSec was trying to figure out how to protect me from the Muslims in Bly. That set her off into a diatribe about Muslims in general, the gist of which was 'the only good Muslims are dead Muslims.' I just listened, and when she was finished, I steered the discussion back to Mac's endorsement of the idea I should meet with her—not just once, but perhaps on a regular basis—for 'sociable women's conversation.' He apparently had talked with her about it yesterday afternoon, and she was willing to try it. But she wouldn't come right out and admit she missed social interaction with other women. She seems to have constructed a very hard, thick shell of defense around her self-image, one that doesn't allow the slightest admission of weakness or vulnerability. Anyhow, we agreed I would come back in two weeks and stay longer, perhaps an hour or so."

Walter considered this a moment and asked, "And how are you? Are you going to be able to sleep tonight?"

"I think so, but you may have to give me a long, sensual massage to help me empty my mind."

"With pleasure," he said. "That's what I'm here for."

"And a few other things," she shot back. Walter was relieved to see the 'old Susan' re-emerging from her encounter with Lottie. His mind leaped ahead to envision an established regimen whereby he helped her decompress, or detox, from each future session, his intuition telling him the future of his love life might depend on it.

Coming back to the 'here and now,' he suggested they take a walk in Moore Park, at the south end of Upper Klamath Lake, then pick up a pizza, and eat it at her house while they awaited Mac's call. It was after 6:30 when her phone finally rang. Mac was apologetic, saying he had gotten hung up with a fishing group and that had forced him to call via cell phone. Consequently, the conversation was brief and cryptic. "How did it go?" he asked.

"OK, I think. We talked for about half-an-hour," Susan reported, "and at the end we agreed to meet again in two weeks. I think it was largely due to your influence on her, your suggestion we do that."

"Good. And what was your impression?"

"I was really shocked when I recognized her, but I got myself together enough to be polite. She got a little excited when I mentioned how I came to meet you—I think I'll steer clear of that topic in the future—but I let her have her tizzy and it was all over in a couple minutes. In spite of her attractive appearance, she impressed me as being hard as nails underneath. I sure wouldn't want her to get mad at me."

"You did very well. I think you got a good picture of the situation and what you'll be dealing with. If you wish, we can talk about it some more—face-to-face—before you meet with her again. Maybe you'll also have some follow-up questions from my lecture. If so, bring Walter along." Walter was gratified to hear Mac would include him in such a confidential meeting, but on second thought, it troubled him slightly. *He obviously thinks I have a 'need to know,' but I don't understand why. What else is lurking underneath all this?* After the phone call, Susan and Walter returned to sharing what they could remember about Lottie's past. They found, however, that most of their unanswered questions pertained to Ted, so they resolved to dig deeper into that the next day.

46.

Susan was scheduled to open the Welcome Center at 10:00 AM the next morning, but she arrived at 9:00, with Walter right behind her. They powered up a computer and crowded around it while Walter logged into the Internet and Googled on 'Charlotte Hahn.' A secondary search through the several-hundred-thousand 'hits' quickly revealed the identity of her billionaire savior: B. Edward Wainwright. In twenty-five years on Wall Street, Wainwright had amassed a huge personal fortune as a principal in one of the top investment banks. However, he apparently had had a change of heart—reason unknown—at about the same time Lottie entered his life; he had suddenly resigned from the firm and begun 'spilling his guts' to Federal agents who were investigating securities fraud. Of course, it was imperative that Wainwright vanish into the WitSec program along with his new wife, who was being stalked by Muslim terrorist assassins. *How convenient!* Walter thought. He and Susan read several of the many different versions of the information the Google search had found, but they all amounted to the same story, with the same salient points and the same unanswered questions. After some thirty minutes of exploring, they knew where to go if they wanted to learn more: right down the path from Walter's cabin.

Walter drove home and settled into his somewhat-revised routine of meditating and reading. He summoned Abigail with the music he had selected for conditioning her, and they sat together on the porch until lunchtime. Walter was just finishing his sandwich when Ted knocked at his door. "I came by to see if Susan has survived her introduction to Lottie yesterday. What was her reaction?" As Walter had observed, Ted was not one to beat around the bush.

Walter, on the other hand, felt this was definitely a time for him to tread softly. "Susan is just fine. She was surprised by what she learned, which is understandable, but she's willing to continue the process through another meeting and beyond that, if it seems to be helping. I don't think anybody expects miracles, however."

"No, no miracles," Ted replied. "How about you? Now that you know what you know, do you have any problems? Any questions?"

"No, no questions. I think I know all I need to, and maybe even a little more. I'm OK with it." *He's asking whether I'm going to bail out, now that I know who and what he and Lottie are,* Walter thought to himself.

"It's been a tough couple of years," Ted began to open up, "tougher than we expected. The isolation has been the hardest part—no outside friends, just the two of us cooped up together. I had expected—or hoped—Lottie would eventually let go of her past, so we could build some kind of life together. Not that I thought we could ever return to the lives we had in the past—politics for her, business for me—but something new that would nourish us both: nature, perhaps. That's why I agreed to move out here to the boonies. When Lottie didn't pick up on it,

I talked her into letting me rent this cabin. I thought somebody living here might set an example we could follow."

So that's what I'm here for, and now Susan too, Walter thought, beginning to see how the pieces might fit together. *If Susan develops enough rapport with Lottie that the two of them can sit and chat for a few hours, Ted will be free to go fly fishing with Mac and me. Maybe Susan and Lottie will discover a common interest—like, say, cooking—they can pursue together. Maybe that will eventually coax Lottie out of her funk, so she and Ted can get on with jointly creating a new life.*

Ted felt the need to continue, to explain himself a little more. "You know, I didn't have to 'blow the whistle' on the shenanigans I saw going on in Wall Street. It wasn't my conscience that drove me to do it. I looked at Lottie's situation and saw I couldn't continue in my career and simultaneously provide the security and support she needs. After investigating several options, I decided WitSec was the best route, so I did something to get their attention and make them put me into their program along with her." *Just like I thought,* Walter congratulated himself. *Two for the price of one.*

"And here you are," Walter said noncommittally.

"It's not where I wanted to be, but I did make the decisions that put me here, for better or for worse. Now I've got to live with it."

"Susan says 'we are not punished *for* our sins, but *by* our sins.'" It wasn't much consolation, but it was the only thing Walter could think of.

Ted had said his piece, as much of it as he wanted to reveal now, so he bid a terse farewell. Walter's thoughts continued to pile up as he watched Ted trudge back toward his house. *I could be angry with him for leading me into this mess, so I would be justified in packing up and moving in with Susan, but that would be rushing things with her, and it might scuttle our whole relationship. Also, there's no way Ted could have been more forthcoming with me when I was considering the cabin rental, because it would have compromised his security intolerably. As it was, he took a significant risk in renting the cabin to me, and he has escalated that risk in the weeks since. He really doesn't have many other options. He's stuck in a tough situation, albeit one of his own making.* Later that evening, as he and Susan were eating supper, Walter shared these thoughts with her. She listened thoughtfully and said simply, "Ted must love Lottie very, very much."

47.

Life settled into a pleasant, not-too-exciting 'groove' for Susan and Walter over the next two weeks. They hiked and biked, read and talked, and divided their 'together time' between Susan's house and Walter's cabin, with overnights always at the former for Moses' sake. Susan's second meeting with Lottie landed on July 4, which was just like every other day for Ted and Lottie, and not much more than that for Susan and Walter. As before, Susan returned to the cabin drained and numb after an hour talking with Lottie. In truth, it was more 'listening to' than 'talking with,' because Lottie went into a rant no matter what subject Susan brought up. Moreover, most of her tirades ended up at the same point: she had been completely justified in ordering the bombing of the Muslim homestead in West Texas. "She's absolutely unrepentant," Susan grumbled to Walter as he sought to help her let go of the experience, "and when she put the force of her personality behind it, I felt like she was attacking me, that if I voiced the slightest disagreement with her, she would assault me physically. I don't know how Ted puts up with it."

"Like you said, he must love her very much," Walter reminded her.

"Yes," she said, "and that is extraordinary. I guess we could learn something from it. Maybe that's why the universe put us here."

"Well, I'm coming to believe that things don't just happen by chance. Every time I look at what has happened to me since I set foot in Oregon two months ago, I marvel at my good fortune. It's like the opposite of being punished by my sins."

"Keep thinking like that," she said, smiling weakly, " and remind me when I get confused, especially with Lottie."

"You're going to continue with it?" he asked.

"Yes, until somebody tells me to stop: you, Mac, Ted, or even Lottie herself. You told me Ted said he doesn't expect any miracles."

"That's right, but the way he said it suggests he would like to see a *little* change—for the better."

"I'm beginning to think even that is a tall order," she said unhappily.

48.

A week and one day later—July 12, to be exact—Walter was up and out the door much earlier than usual after spending the night with Susan. He had signed up for the Firearms Training class that was a prerequisite for getting an 'Oregon License to Carry a Concealed Handgun.' The class was held at the Klamath County Fairgrounds, almost within walking distance of Susan's house, but Walter drove because he had other errands to run later. He went to the registration table, paid his forty dollars, and filled in his name (Walter Patton Baker), city (Bonanza), occupation (pilot), and cell phone number on the sign-up sheet.

He helped himself to coffee from the urn at the back of the room and took a seat in the second row of tables. He was casually surveying the room and the other registrants when in walked the punk-blonde young man he had seen at the Coyote Café. Walter studied him as he registered and then looked away, but the man walked straight toward him and sat down in the chair next to his. Walter introduced himself. "Hello, my name's Walter Baker."

"Hi, I'm Al—Al Fath. I see you before?" He didn't smile, and he spoke with a slight accent.

Faced with making a quick decision, Walter chose honesty because he knew he wasn't good at lying. "I think I saw you in the restaurant in Bly about a month ago."

"Oh," he said. "Maybe so." Walter was impressed the man remembered him out of all the strange faces in the Coyote Café—and that was five weeks ago. Al continued in less-than-perfect English, "Registration list say you are pilot." Walter was even more impressed—*he's really observant*, he thought. "What type plane you fly?"

"At one time or another, I've flown just about everything from small single-engine propeller planes all the way up to the largest multiengine jets," Walter replied, "but recently it's been just Boeing 737s."

"For airline?"

"I flew for Alaska Airlines until the recent merger. Now I'm out of a job."

Walter's sixth sense told him that 'observant Al,' as he now thought of him, liked that answer because it gave him some kind of opening. "Can you fly helicopter?"

"No. I tried it, but I didn't like it."

Al seemed disappointed, but his interest didn't vanish altogether. "Too bad. I thought I might could offer you work. Maybe I still do. What is your phone number?" He pushed his notepad over, and Walter wrote down his name and cell phone number.

Now it was Walter's turn to ask questions, and he had just been given a legitimate reason. "What kind of work do you do?"

"Security guard."

Walter feigned confusion in the hope of extracting more information. "Where do you work?"

"Near Bly. At ranch."

Seeing his opportunity, Walter pressed his luck. "Why would a ranch need a helicopter, or a security guard?"

Al kept his head down so Walter couldn't see into his eyes. "People steal sheep." There was a tone of finality in his answer that said, "the interrogation is finished."

Nevertheless, Walter had one more question. "What is your phone number?"

Al turned his head to give Walter a piercing look. "I have no phone. If I need you, I call you." It sounded more like a threat than an offer, and the look added an exclamation point. Walter got the message.

The instructor was walking toward the front of the classroom, allowing Walter to turn away from Al without appearing to have been intimidated. The class focused mostly on gun safety, which always justified a refresher course, even for experienced military and law enforcement personnel, but there was to be no actual shooting practice. When the lunch break was announced, Walter turned to Al and asked, "Want to join me for lunch? There are several restaurants nearby."

"I no eat now." Al turned his back and hurried out the door. The curtness of his reply caused Walter to stop and think. *Al didn't drink any coffee when he arrived or at the midmorning coffee break. No water either, and he says he's not eating 'now.' I wonder if it's Ramadan.* Walter recalled from his reading of Huston Smith's book that Muslims observe thirty days of fasting each year, which requires them to abstain from food, drink, sex, tobacco, and who-knows-what-else during daylight hours. *If Al is a Muslim, it would explain his behavior,* he thought. Seeking further confirmation, Walter followed Al at a 'safe' distance to see if he would observe the Islamic requirement of noonday prayer. Al got into a battered old black Chevy sedan in the parking lot and leaned the seat back as if he were going to take a nap. *That proves nothing,* Walter thought, *because Smith's book quotes the Koran as saying explicitly 'when you journey about the earth, it is no crime that you come short in prayer if you fear that those who disbelieve will attack you.'*

When he returned from lunch, Walter again cast a surreptitious glance at Al's car. Al was still there, but he wasn't napping—he was talking on a cell phone! When he saw Walter, he turned his head to hide the phone, prompting Walter to deliberately look in the opposite direction as he walked on past. There was no further exchange between them in the short afternoon session, not even a good-bye when the course ended at two o'clock. Al again hustled out the door and into his car, but then he just sat there as if waiting for something, or someone. Walter decided to postpone his errands in order to return to Susan's house and use her phone to call Mac about his chance meeting. His attention was on the multilane traffic on 6th Street and Washburn Way, so he didn't notice Al's black sedan following about a half-block behind until he had parked his truck right in front of Susan's house. When he was halfway to the door, something told him to look back toward the street, just in time to see the Chevy whizzing by with Al hunkered down behind the wheel as if trying to hide.

Mac didn't answer his home phone—*of course! he's off doing his fishing guide act at Odell Lake*—so Walter left a message on his answering machine calling his attention to the email Walter now planned to send from the Library within the hour. The phone call lasted only a minute, and turning Moses out into the back yard and retrieving him again took only a couple more, but that was sufficient time for Al Fath to loop around the block and make another pass to get the house number before Walter returned to his truck.

At the Library, Walter first checked on the dates for Ramadan—June 28 to July 27 that year —, which added to the circumstantial evidence that Fath was a Muslim. Walter included it in his email report to Mac, but decided not to say anything about Al to Susan, lest she become alarmed. Nevertheless, Mac's email reply the next day recommended that Walter work out contingency plans for Susan to take refuge at the cabin in an emergency. As Walter analyzed the options in his mind before consulting with Susan, he identified only two significant complications: (1) what to do with Moses, and (2) telephone access for Susan if she were alone at the cabin. Thinking ahead to August, when he would be *incommunicado* for ten days at the meditation course before spending another week or two with his kids somewhere in California, he was most unhappy that Fath now knew the location of Susan's house. *He doesn't know about her yet,* he thought, *but that doesn't help matters much.* Walter briefly considered canceling out on the meditation course, but it didn't resolve the problem of the vacation with his kids, which he felt he absolutely *must* do. *Besides,* he thought, *I can't let my life be ruled by fear. If I start down that 'slippery slope,' I could end up like Lottie.*

49.

Mac's email also proposed another fly fishing expedition, and Walter immediately replied with his agreement. When they met the following Tuesday, the first thing on Mac's mind was Walter's upcoming meditation course. "I hope you realize," he said, "that this course will be more of a 'fresh start'—in computer terms, a 'total system reset'—than anything else you've done since you came here and probably more than anything else you've done since you left home and enrolled in the Air Force Academy." *No, I hadn't really thought of it that way,* Walter mused, but he shook his head up and down as if he understood. "In one of the more cogent pieces of advice in *The Bible*, Romans 12:2 says, 'Do not conform any longer to the pattern of this world, but be transformed by the renewing of your mind.' That's what it's all about. To renew your mind you've got to clean it out first, to purify it. All religions teach that purification and cleansing is the first step toward salvation, but you can't just take their word for it—you've got to find out for yourself. 'Know thyself' is how the Greeks expressed it, and the Christians, the Buddhists, the Hindus, and all the others simply elaborate on that, usually to the point where you get so much background the foreground goes underground."

Mac paused. "Anyhow, I expect your meditation course will trigger some *transitions* for you. I can't predict what they will be, and neither can you, but the experience of others indicates it's likely to be life-changing. However, the transitions may take months to manifest, or even years. I think you understand that, based on my lecture last month." They rode a few miles in silence before Mac decided it was time to move on to another topic. "What's on your mind today? I know your life has stabilized considerably in recent weeks, but you've also learned some things that were probably rather disturbing."

"That's certainly true," Walter concurred, "but I got over it quickly—surprisingly fast, in retrospect. Nevertheless, I find myself wondering what I still don't know that could come along to blindside me."

"Satchel Paige, the famous Negro baseball pitcher in the 1950s, said, 'It ain't what you don't know that will hurt you, it's what you think you know that ain't so.'" Mac joked.

"Yeah," Walter retorted, "he also said, 'Don't look back. Something might be gaining on you.'"

"Good point," Mac conceded.

Walter pressed ahead. "Most if not all the surprises that have caught up with me since I came here had something to do with Muslims. I'm most concerned about what I still don't know about them *and* what I think I know that's erroneous. That applies at the 'cosmic' level, meaning Islam in general, and it also applies locally, especially to what's going on in Bly. I've been doing a good bit of reading on the first of these, but I'd like you to tell me more about the latter."

Mac nodded. "I could see that coming. You know, of course, I'm limited by government security regulations and the rules of professional ethics as to what I can divulge, even if I personally think you have plenty of 'need to know.' That's why I've tried to create circumstances in which you've been able to discover or infer some very sensitive things through other means and other sources. But maybe if I back off to the ten-thousand-foot level, I can give you some information that will be helpful."

He paused to organize his thoughts. "First, what is going on in Bly seems to be very recent. It seems to have no connection to what happened there ten years ago, other than the possibility that whoever owns Frisco Ranch is a Muslim or is sympathetic toward Islam. Second, the Muslims now in Bly now seem less militant and fanatical than the earlier bunch. They are also stronger financially. The previous gang was outright poor, to the point where they were actually scamming the terrorist ringleader in England. Now they seem to have a modest amount of money, but the source is well hidden. Third, the current folk seem more competent, even professional, whereas the earlier bunch couldn't tell shit from applesauce.

"It's these last two points that are most troubling, however. It's as though the people now at Frisco Ranch are here for a specific purpose, a mission of some kind. Curiously enough, whatever it is seems to have driven out them of the seclusion that characterized the 1999 operation. The present group seems more willing to communicate with, maybe even engage, other people in the community. The bleached blond we saw in the Coyote Café last month is a case in point. Not only did he dare to set foot in the local hangout but, from what you said, he came very close to hiring you last Saturday. All this suggests that the global *jihad* between Islam and the West is *not* why these guys are in Bly—at least it's not the main reason. Their agenda is less grandiose, more focused. I get the impression that, once they accomplish their goal—or screw it up so badly they get kicked out of the country—they'll quietly go away, leaving as few tracks as they can. However, it doesn't make them any less dangerous to whoever or whatever their target is." They were approaching the turnoff for their fishing spot, so Mac cut short his comments. "We can talk about this more on the way back. We may even pick up some juicy tidbits when we stop at the Coyote Café, and I don't mean the edible kind."

As they unloaded their gear, Mac took a few minutes to coach Walter in what to look for when he bought equipment of his own. Then they both wandered off in different directions, each in his own little world. Walter tried to recall and find the 'promising spots' he had seen from the air, but without much success. Nevertheless, he caught three decent-sized rainbows, and Mac caught two plus a big brown. Both were quite happy with their success when they converged on Mac's truck two hours later.

The Coyote Café was doing its usual brisk business when they arrived. Several of the patrons recognized them and nodded 'hello' as they made their way to an empty table. As usual Mac positioned himself so he could strike up a conversation with three of 'the regulars' seated at an adjacent table, and soon he was chatting away with them while Walter silently scanned the room. Back on the road again after lunch, he asked Mac, "What did you get?"

"Not much," was the reply. "I learned there are about a dozen newcomers at the Ranch, along with the couple living there as caretakers. Several trailers were brought in for housing about three months ago, right before the new guys arrived. They are all under forty, and a few of them appear to be somewhat educated, judging from their interactions with folk at the local stores. They are apparently building fences and other structures to expand the sheep ranching operation, but there's no way it takes up all their time. It seems to be some kind of 'cover activity' so the presence of that many people doesn't arouse too much suspicion. They all appear to be well fed, although they certainly don't squander their money on drinking and carousing in the town. They seem intent on being model neighbors."

"All of that fits with what you told me earlier," Walter observed, "although I wouldn't consider the shots they fired at my plane as being very neighborly. For that matter, Al Fath didn't act like he wanted a close friendship with me last Saturday. He was all business, and none too cordial at that."

"I wouldn't read too much into it," Mac warned. "The locals around Bly, and other parts of the county as well, aren't very cordial either. Most are suspicious of strangers, if not outright hostile, and it takes a while for them to accept a newcomer, as you yourself have experienced at the Coyote Café. The main reason I'm doing better than you is because I've been around a while and they know I grew up here. There are still some areas I haven't penetrated either—for instance, the Jefferson State Militia. I know it's strong in certain parts of the county, like the Malin area, and I suspect most of the Coyote Café clientele are at least loosely affiliated as well, but they are very close-lipped about it. I can ask them about the Muslims without raising their hackles, and now that I've gained their trust, they'll readily share information about that, because the Muslims are 'the opposition.' But they are very, very careful not to expose their own activities to anybody but those who have been admitted to their inner circle."

Ranch & Rural Real EstateWalter remembered what he had learned about the JSM when he was digging around on the Internet nearly three months ago, in particular the article posted cautioning against trusting anyone who *asks* to join, "*including your own mother.*" Mac continued, "It's the tension between the JSM and the Muslims that worries me most. If it ever escalated into outright confrontation, there's no telling where it would end. There's been enough bad blood between the Militia and local law enforcement it's hard to imagine them being on the same page, and the JSM guys are almost certainly armed to the teeth, so local law enforcement would be outgunned as well as outmanned. The worst case scenario, involving intervention by the National Guard and/or Federal agencies, is all too plausible—and that's scary."

"So what's your role in all this? What are you trying to do?"Walter hoped he wasn't being too audacious.

Mac considered his reply, then said, "Pretty much what you would expect if you think about it. However, there is one thing that might not come to mind even though the clues are there and I know you've seen them. I'm trying to get a different message out to counter the confrontational, militant, violent, intolerant culture that pervades the entire country and the whole world and seems especially intense right here in Klamath County. Education is obviously the way to do it, but it involves *unlearning* more than learning, and we just aren't used to thinking in those terms."

"Aha!" exclaimed Walter. "That's what was behind the Commencement Address at KCC and also your lecture on Transitions."

Mac smiled. "You catch on real fast, and you connect the dots very well—which is why I recruited you for my team."Walter's mind raced back through his history with Mac and Susan and how the two of them had seemingly conspired to capture first his interest and now his commitment. Not that he felt they had been dishonest, but rather that he had been eager, perhaps too eager, to trust them.

When they got back to Walter's truck, he asked Mac to follow him to the cabin, explaining that he wanted him to know precisely where it was in case of an 'unforeseen emergency.' Mac was a little pressed for time, but agreed since Walter said it was part of the 'contingency plan' for Susan that he (Mac) had recommended. At the cabin, Walter waved in the direction of Ted's house and pointed out the path leading to it, then took Mac inside for a quick walk-thru. Along the way, Mac spied the *Science of Mind* magazine Walter had bought in California. "This looks interesting," he said as he picked it up and began leafing through it until something caught his attention. He read for half-a-minute, then handed the magazine to Walter saying, "Read page 34 before you go to your meditation course. It's good stuff." In deference to Mac's busy schedule, Walter skipped any further conversation, except to say that Mac should come back again to meet Abigail. "Ah yes, the duck," Mac grinned. "Where would you be without the duck?" *What the hell did he mean by that?* Walter stood scratching his head as Mac drove off.

50.

Susan's third meeting with Lottie came three days later, as Walter was firming up his August schedule in California. His meditation course was to begin in two weeks, on Friday afternoon in a retreat center north of San Francisco. From then until the course ended at Sunday noon nine days later, he would be *incommunicado*, with no telephone or Internet access. Only in an emergency would Susan be able to call the center and have a message relayed to him. Walter would pick up his kids the following Sunday and head off to Bass Lake, where he had rented a cottage for the week. His plan was for a low-key vacation, with a day trip to Yosemite National Park and lots of simple 'hanging out' to rebuild relationships with his son Ryan and daughter Katie.

That left the intervening week, immediately following the meditation 'sit,' unscheduled, and there was some uncertainty about what he would do then. He could, of course, return to Bonanza, only to drive back to California a few days later, but Mac had cautioned that he would need time to reenter and readjust to 'normal' life, and it was imperative he get his head on straight before vacationing with his kids. Most likely, then, Walter would not get back to Oregon until the fourth (but not last) Sunday in August. At least he would have telephone and Internet communication during the last two weeks of that period, but neither he nor Susan were looking forward to twenty-four days of physical separation.

Now they were making contingency plans, as Mac had suggested, in case any problems came up. Mostly they centered on Susan, who was being thrown back into her 'pre-Walter' lifestyle, but with a new 'wild card': biweekly sessions with Lottie. The 'good news' was that she could borrow Ted's cell phone if she needed to, but her overall communications capabilities at the cabin left much to be desired. The remaining contingency issue was Moses, and they had already discussed bringing him to the cabin to pave the way toward Susan spending the night there occasionally. Thus, today was the day to hoist Moses into the jump seats in Walter's truck, along with his bed, food and water bowls, and a long chain to tether him to a tree. Although the truck was new and strange to him, the dog liked being the center of attention, and he always enjoyed going for a ride. The cabin and surrounding grounds became a veritable amusement park for him, with new sights, sounds, and (especially) smells. For more than an hour he ran to-and-fro, taking it all in and getting his chain wrapped around several trees before plopping down on his blanket, which Walter had positioned on the porch corner opposite 'Abigail's spot.'

Walter and Susan missed the instant of initial encounter between Abigail and Moses, being themselves preoccupied with their own encounter in Walter's bedroom. They were vaguely aware, at some point, of a single '*Woof*' followed by a lone '*Quack,*' but the moment passed quickly and by the time they had gotten dressed and gone outside again, they found both the dog and the duck on their respective beds, sleepily basking in the afternoon sun. "*The Peaceable Kingdom,*" was Susan's pronouncement.

"If only it were that simple and easy between Christians and Muslims," Walter sighed.

"Maybe I should have Abigail and Moses accompany me to my sessions with Lottie, to set an example for her," Susan suggested.

"Do you think she would get the message?" Walter asked.

51.

On Friday, the first day of August, Walter was off to an early start. It was a six-hour drive from Klamath Falls to San Rafael, and sign-in for the Insight Meditation course began at 3:00 PM. The course itself didn't officially begin until 5:30, but he wanted to have some time to walk around and get himself out of 'Interstate mentality.' He had no trouble finding the retreat center—the directions and maps he downloaded from the Internet were excellent—and the sign-in process was quick and simple because he had already completed the registration forms and paid his fees on-line. All that remained was for him to sign up for his 'work meditation,' a daily duty intended to help him 'learn how to bring the spirit of wakefulness to the activities of our life.' Walter elected to assist in the kitchen during lunch preparation.

His lodging was a double room, to be shared with another person, but there was a *shoji* screen positioned down the middle to provide a modicum of visual privacy. The furnishings were Spartan: a bed, nightstand, reading light, folding chair, shelving, and hangers for each occupant, plus a shared sink and mirror. Showers and toilets were down the hall. Walter had opted to rent bed linens and towels for a modest fee, and he found those items neatly stacked on one of the beds, so he adopted that as *his* bed in *his* side of the room.

He was about halfway through unloading his duffel bag when his roommate walked in. Walter recognized him immediately—it was Hussein, who had been his host and guide at the Islamic Center in Livermore two months before. Walter finished unpacking and organizing his things, then engaged Hussein in conversation. "Is this your first time at a meditation course?"

"No, it's my second," Hussein replied. "I did a similar course here about two years ago."

"I'm completely new at this, although I have been trying to meditate regularly for about three months. What I'm doing is based upon what I read in a book, and I'm sure I have a lot to learn. So that's why I'm here."

"There's always something more to be learned, and that's why I'm here," Hussein smiled.

"Excuse me for asking, but I'm surprised that you, a Muslim, would come to a course such as this, which is primarily grounded in Buddhist teachings."

Hussein's smile broadened into a full grin. "I see no problem in that, although I admit some of the more conservative Muslims probably would. But I'm a *Sufi*, and many conservative Muslims have problems with that as well. It doesn't bother me nearly as much as it seems to bother them."

"You may be just the person I'm looking for, although I didn't expect to find you here at this course," Walter said. "I've gone through the books I bought at the Islamic Center—plus the one you recommended I buy elsewhere—and I want to learn more, not only about *Sufism* but Islam in general. Could we talk further after this course is over?"

"Sure, although my experience indicates we may be in no mood to do that for a few days afterward. Could you possibly come to the Islamic Center again, but later?"

"Yes, I could," Walter replied. "I have to be in the Livermore area about a week after this course ends, and it would be easy for me to visit the Center on Saturday, August 17. Of course, that depends upon whether you and I have recovered from this course by then."

"We can sort that out before we leave here on the 10th," Hussein suggested.

Walter saw that Hussein had finished unpacking. "I'd like to take a walk around the Retreat Center before the course begins, just to get oriented. Would you like to join me?"

"Yes, a walk would be good," Hussein said. "We'll soon be doing lots of sitting."

They strolled around for the next half hour, with Hussein occasionally pointing out the various buildings, all of them relatively new. The Center itself was situated in a gorgeous secluded valley with warm tan grassy slopes that turn to lush green in winter months. Scattered clumps of trees, mostly *California live oak*, offered restful shade. The ambience expressed peace and tranquility, a perfect setting in which to retreat from the hectic pace and infringing materialism of the modern Western world. At the Dining Hall, they picked a quiet spot to sit, and Walter used the opportunity to ask what advice Hussein might offer a novice taking the course. Hussein thought briefly and replied, "Everyone's experience is different, which is as it should be, and yet there is much in common among all of them, which is also as it should be. The initial task is to strike a balance between those two. For instance, we will all sit together in the Meditation Hall, each on his or her own 'mat,' which will be assigned. Some will sit cross-legged directly on the mat, a few may choose the 'lotus position,' although far fewer will be able to stay in that position for an hour at a time. Most will select some kind of cushion or stool for support, and elderly persons may even sit upright in a chair. There are no rigid requirements except that once the meditation begins, stillness should prevail.

"Nevertheless, there will be much fidgeting at first as each person searches for a position and the 'right' cushion or stool that will help them remain motionless for an hour. The experimentation will continue throughout the first day or two, but eventually people will settle on something. While that is going on, it's very important for you to 'stay on your own mat'—that is, to pay no attention to what the person in front of you is doing, or the person behind you, or on either side. Don't be distracted by what clothes he is wearing, what cushions or blankets he is using, and especially what changes he makes to these during the meditation. Don't allow yourself to become judgmental of anybody else or emotionally involved in what others are doing. Keep your focus on yourself and what *you* are doing. That will be challenging enough.

"And what should you do to avoid disturbing those around you? Certainly you will not be able, or *should not* be able, to sit through a full hour without experiencing any physical discomfort, even at the end of the course. The issue is what to do when the discomfort begins and intensifies. My personal experience is that if you yield to the pain by shifting your position or your cushion, the pain will return, or a new one will appear, within a rather short time. So my approach," he concluded, smiling, "is to start with the simplest seating that seems comfortable, make a few adjustments during the first day, and then learn to *sit through the pain*. After all, it's only an illusion." Walter nodded. The idea of enduring the pain was similar to what he had learned to do in the military drills at the Air Force Academy, so he was confident he could make the adjustment. What was new and different in his present situation was the idea that the discomfort is 'only an illusion.'

The evening meal marked the beginning of the course. The food was vegetarian, which Walter had never been able to work up much enthusiasm about, but it was surprisingly attractive and tasty; he even went back for 'seconds.' After the meal, the course staff introduced themselves and collaborated to give an orientation lecture. The basic rules, called 'The Five Precepts,' were simple enough—no killing or violence, no stealing, no sexual activity, no lying, and no intoxicants—and those rules would be strictly enforced. All other religious/spiritual and health practices were to be suspended, including yoga and physical exercise. There was to be no outside communication (letters, phone calls, or visitors), no reading or writing, and no music/radio/TV during the course. And finally, once the course began all participants were to observe 'noble silence,' which meant no talking, no gestures, no 'meaningful glances' or physical contact with anyone else, including spouses, friends, and relatives. It was to be as if you were there all by yourself, even though your eyes told you that you were one of about eighty participants who sometimes gathered as a group. All of this had been described in the advance material sent to course registrants, and every registrant had signed a statement agreeing to abide by these rules.

Following orientation, the retreatants, now segregated by gender, were led to the Meditation Hall, where the staff assisted them in finding their assigned places in the grid of lightly padded mats, each 30-by-30 inches, arranged in rows on the polished wood floor. Many retreatants brought additional cushions or stools, as Hussein had said, and light shawls or blankets. Others made their selections from the ample community supply of 'accessories' at the rear of the hall. Walter had his own blanket, a 'Goodwill special,' but he eschewed the other 'toys,' as Hussein had disdainfully called them. The meditation leader entered and sat down amidst an assortment of pillows and blankets, the quantity of which amused Walter, on a low platform at the front of the hall, and several of the staff took seats on mats off to the side. The leader rang a large gong to bring the session to order and gave a short talk on the origin and purpose of *vipassana*, a.k.a. 'Insight Meditation.'

"It is an ancient technique, thought to have been *rediscovered* by the Buddha some 2,500 years ago," he began. "It is a process of *self-purification* by means of *self-observation*—the word *vipassana* means 'seeing things as they really are.' It begins by observing the natural breath to concentrate the mind and sharpen awareness and proceeds to observing the changing nature of body and mind. This leads one to experience the 'Three Universal Truths' about life that were realized and clarified by the Buddha. The first, *dukkha*, usually translated 'suffering,' means that pain is unavoidable: birth, sickness, old age, death." *I can certainly attest to the inevitability of pain,* Walter thought. "Pain also results from being separated from what one loves, which leads us to the second truth, *anicca*, the 'impermanence' of all things and separation from our own essence, in particular our ego, which takes us to the third truth, *anatta*—translated 'egolessness.'" *This is beginning to sound a lot like Joel Goldsmith,* was Walter's reaction.

The leader went on to explain that the direct experience of these truths is the process of purification. Thus the ultimate aim of *vipassana* is the ending of suffering. Because all human beings share these fundamental problems, this remedy is universal: it can be practiced freely by everyone, at any time, in any place, without conflict to race, community, or religion. Nevertheless, it is grounded in Buddhism, so it is helpful to understand the basic concepts and teachings of the Buddha. These will be explained, the leader said, in evening lectures over the remainder of the course. Next he gave some basic instruction in observing the breath: not breathing in any 'special' way but simply focusing attention on the breath and *only* on the breath. Inevitably one's attention will wander, he said, distracted by thoughts and sensations. When that happens, one should simply begin again. Don't worry, don't judge, don't analyze. "The act of beginning again is the essential art of meditation practice—over and over, we begin again."

After a short break, the group reconvened and the actual meditation started. It was somewhat familiar to Walter because it echoed what he had read in Goldsmith's book and had attempted to practice on his own during the preceding three months. This gave him some confidence, but it by no means assured his success in maintaining his focus on breathing for more than thirty seconds at a time. After what seemed an eternity—actually about twenty minutes—his pains kicked in, growing out of barely discernible itches into more insistent sensations that became increasingly difficult to ignore. Finally, he shifted his weight, just a smidgen to stop the hurt, and put his attention back into his breathing. Within a minute another pain intruded, and after mentally wrangling with it for who-knows-how-long, he moved his right foot a fraction of an inch. He was now going down the 'slippery slope,' past the point of no return, and for the remainder of the hour-long session, most of his attention went into fidgeting. Even when he was able to keep his mind on breathing for fifteen seconds, he found himself so easily distracted by the sounds created by the fidgets of others nearby that he gave up any hope of getting back into genuine 'meditation.' *Hussein warned me about this,* Walter thought as he sat there, occasionally sneaking peeks at his watch and waiting somewhat impatiently for the session to end. *I'll do better tomorrow, after a good night's sleep.*

52.

Walter did sleep well, but not long. His alarm went off at 4:30 AM, and although he quickly shut it off, Hussein's alarm acknowledged the dim dawn only seconds later. Walter stretched, stood up, stretched some more, and shuffled over to the sink, washing quickly so as to clear out of the way for Hussein. Thus began the regimen that extended over the next eight days. Meditation started at 5:00 AM, with breakfast afterward, at 6:30. The half-hour from 6:00 to 6:30 was for 'walking meditation,' but on the first day the time was spent in instruction. 'Walking meditation' was new to Walter, but he quickly caught on to the process of shifting his weight to one foot, next slowly lifting the other foot, moving it forward, and gently putting it down—and then repeating the sequence on the other side, all the while concentrating on first the feet, then the legs, and continuing through the rest of the body. Not that it was easy for him to keep his mind focused on the actual sensations of movement, but the whole experience sent his mind back to his days at the Air Force Academy, and he wished he had learned about walking meditation before he had been required to do any marching as a Cadet.

After breakfast, the daily schedule consisted of seven 'sets' of one-hour sitting meditation followed by forty-five minutes of walking meditation: one 'set' before breakfast, two after, two more in the afternoon, and two in the evening. Lunch came at 11:30 AM and was the principal meal of the day. It was followed by an hour-long 'rest period,' during which Walter took a nap. There was no dinner as such, just a break for tea at 5:00 PM, but there were also bowls of fruit provided for persons who needed an 'energy snack.' Walter was one of them.

The one-hour 'dharma talks' in the evening provided an informative introduction to Buddhism as retreatants sprawled in rather UN-meditative positions on their mats. Some even moved to places along the walls of the room to support their backs, but when anybody lay down on the floor, the staff quickly and quietly suggested that was not acceptable. Walter rather enjoyed the talks, but his interest was dampened somewhat by the realization that Buddhism was yet another religion he ought to learn much more about.

On 'Day Two' through 'Day Nine' some of the sitting meditation sessions were done as a group in the Meditation Hall, and others were designated for individual meditation in the dorm rooms. Interviews, both voluntary and mandatory, were substituted for some of the afternoon sittings so every retreatant had at least two brief face-to-face meetings with one of the teachers during the course. 'Day Three' and 'Day Four,' Monday and Tuesday, were the toughest for Walter. He didn't seem able to hold his concentration for even a minute, and despite the welcome relief of walking meditation, the onset of pain seemed to come earlier and earlier in each hour of sitting. He began to doubt his ability to continue, although he knew full well that retreatants were not permitted to drop out except under the most extreme conditions, and he had signed a written statement acknowledging his commitment to that policy. Again he drew on his past experience with similar feelings as a fledgling Cadet—he resolved to 'tough it out' and made no mention of his anxiety at his first interview with a teacher.

By Thursday, 'Day Seven,' things were going much better. *I'm going to make it,* Walter thought as he soldiered through the day's agenda. Not that his aches and pains were in remission, but they no longer seemed to have the upper hand. Instead, he was making headway in resisting, even dismissing, them—barely acknowledging them as they appeared, and noting to his mild surprise they didn't stick around long when he ignored them. A similar scenario was playing out with his concentration, as indicated by substantial reduction in how often he had to 'start again.' He was vaguely aware of these indications of 'progress' but still too intensely engaged in the whole process to be able to step back and survey how far he had come.

53.

On 'Day Nine,' the last full day, the course itself began to 'shift gears,' largely to help prepare the retreatants for what might be the most difficult hurdle: integrating their *vipassana* experience with the 'real world' they had forsaken a week ago. Although they hadn't yet realized it, most of them had become different persons through the learning and especially the *unlearning* they had undergone, and many were about to discover they were unwilling—even unable—to resume being the persons they had been before. But if they were going to let go of being those 'old' persons, who—or what—were they going to be? It came as no surprise to Walter that the recommendation of the course teachers was to continue the practice of *vipassana* indefinitely, with an hour of meditation every morning and another every evening, plus a ten-day 'sit' once a year. That was the bare minimum. 'Spare time' should be spent in short courses and in five-or-ten-minute 'work breaks' throughout the day.

Last but not least, the teachers devoted a couple '*dharma* talks' to the practice of *dāna*, which means 'generosity.' This included not only monetary donations to the Retreat Center to enable others to take courses there but also the much broader concept of 'giving of oneself' in all aspects of life. In the latter, particular emphasis was given to *metta*, which means 'loving-kindness, friendliness, benevolence, amity, friendship, good will, kindness, love, sympathy, close mental union (on same mental wavelength), and active interest in others.' A final meditation session was given to introducing this form of Buddhist meditation, cultivating loving-kindness toward yourself, then your loved ones, friends, teachers, strangers, enemies, and finally toward all sentient beings (in that order).

In the midst of this, during the afternoon of 'Day Nine,' 'noble silence' was broken, meaning that retreatants were permitted to talk. Walter was rather amazed at the explosion of pent-up verbosity, as if everyone felt compelled to share with someone—anyone—what he/she had experienced during the preceding days. Strangely, Walter felt no such compulsion, although he did seek out Hussein, who also was content to sit quietly with him and just watch, listen, and feel what was happening without and (especially) within.

There were a few more meditation periods and lectures that evening and the next morning, during which 'noble silence' was again invoked, and then the course was over. While packing up and cleaning their room, Walter and Hussein agreed to meet the following Saturday at the Islamic Center near Livermore, "*inshallah* (God willing)," as Hussein put it. Walter *schlepped* his belongings to his truck and locked them inside, then returned to the bookstore to shop for books on Buddhism and make a monetary donation to the Center. Thus began his reentry. His thoughts began to shift toward Susan and Mac and Ted and .... As a somewhat hesitant first step in practicing *metta*, he wondered what had been happening in their lives during the past ten days. Little did he expect how quickly the events of those ten days would conspire to command his attention.

54.

While Walter was struggling to find his way in the meditation course, Al Fath was struggling to find Walter. On four consecutive days he called the cell phone number Walter had given him, but there was no answer. On the third and fourth he even dared to leave a 'call back' message and number, but he got no response. Now driven by a growing sense of desperation, he went to Walter's house—what he *thought* was Walter's house—on Wantland Avenue. He waited anxiously until 6:00 PM, thinking it would be the time when Walter would most likely be home. Walter's truck was nowhere in sight when Al parked his tired old Chevy in front of the house. *Maybe it's around back*, he thought, *or inside the garage, hiding behind the closed windowless door*. Despite his uncertainty, he strode courageously up to the front door to ring the doorbell. Within milliseconds after his finger touched the button, a blast of baying and barking burst behind the door, barely a foot away, and engulfed him in commotion such as he had never before experienced. He recoiled a step to collect his wits and, as the racket seemed to subside, reached out to push the button again, triggering a second salvo from within, no less intense than the first, but accompanied by a woman's voice straining to be audible over the bloodthirsty howls of the monster writhing at her feet, "Who is it? What do you want?"

Now the uncomfortable prospect of having to confront a *woman* was piled on top of his fear of the raucous monster. All of his negative impressions of Western femininity combined to unnerve him completely: assertive almost to the point of shrewishness, inhospitable, mean-spirited and vindictive, perhaps even armed with a handgun she was incapable of controlling. Al turned tail and ran back to his car, started it, and spun the tires accelerating away from the curb, stopping a half-block down the street to figure out his next course of action.

Susan, meanwhile, having caught a glimpse of this foreign-looking stranger through the peephole, was caught up in her own panic. He hadn't said a word, but her imagination told her he was a Muslim, most likely from Bly, and whatever had brought him to her door was somehow sinister. She tried to calm herself, but her instincts said her best choice from the 'freeze/fight/flight' trichotomy was the third one. She gathered a few groceries and some clothes and tossed them onto the passenger seat of her car, which—thank God!—was parked in the garage. As she began collecting Moses' bed, food dishes, and tether, Moses immediately caught on to the situation and started his anticipatory dance. Then she remembered the bag of dog food and his leash, the sight of which ratcheted up his excitement several notches. Lest he urinate all over the floor or the car, she opened the kitchen door and chased him outside, giving her time to catch her breath and rethink what she was about.

Knowing that she had tomorrow off, she called Virginia to leave a trail for somebody to follow in case she was abducted and failed to show up for work as scheduled. Unfortunately, neither Virginia nor Darrell were at home, so all Susan could do was leave a terse message on the answering machine in the calmest voice she could muster: "I've decided to spend tonight and tomorrow at Walter's cabin. There's no way you can contact me there, but if I can borrow his neighbor's cell phone, I'll call you at work tomorrow. In any event, I'll see you at the Center on Saturday." She put the remaining 'Moses items' into the car, retrieved him from the back yard, and lifted him onto the back seat. After doing a final walk-thru of the house to make sure all the doors and windows were closed and locked, she got in the car, opened the garage door, and backed out. In her haste to verify that the garage door had closed behind her, she failed to notice Al Fath's car parked no more than fifty yards away. Nor did she notice his black sedan following her, two or three car-lengths behind, all the way out of town, past Olene, onto Highway 70 at Dairy, and northward onto Haskins Road. Only after she turned into the gravel lane to the cabin and faded out of sight amidst the trees did Al Fath accelerate to see the exact location of the driveway, make a mental note of it, and then turn around to go on to Bly.

55.

After he completed all his business at the Retreat Center, Walter went to his truck and took out his cell phone. He wasn't scheduled to call Susan until 1:00 PM, but he was anxious to see if there were any messages. There were: two of them from the same number, plus two earlier calls without messages from that number, one he didn't recognize except to note it was a satellite phone. He listened to the first message. It was from Al Fath: "Walter, please call me at this number." The second message, also from Al, provided more information: "Walter, this is Al Fath. I have job assignment for you, if you can. Please call right away." Walter checked the date and time on the calls. The first and second, without a message, came on the previous Monday and Tuesday; the two messages were left on Wednesday and Thursday. He pushed the keys to 'Call Back.' The answer was prompt, on the second ring. "Hello." That was all, but Walter recognized the voice.

"Hello, this is Walter Baker. I'm returning a call from Al Fath."

"Hello, this is Al. I try call you all week. After four times no answer, I go to your house, but no find you."

You went to my house?! Walter winced, barely able to avoid saying it aloud. He quickly calmed himself and replied in an even voice. "I'm sorry. I'm in California. I've been taking a course all week, and I haven't been able to use the telephone."

"No matter. Is still time. I want you fly plane to Seattle and back. Take two people."

"OK," Walter said. "When?"

"When you return?" Al asked.

"I expect to be back Sunday evening, August 24."

There was a pause while Al talked with somebody at his end. "We go Tuesday, August 26. Fly to Seattle in morning. Two hours meeting, then return. You rent plane, we pay fifty-thousand dollars for rental, gas, and you piloting."

Fifty-thousand dollars! Walter was incredulous. "How much was that? Say again."

"Fifty-thousand dollars. Five-zero, zero-zero-zero," was the answer. "All cash. American money. But everything must be confidential."

"OK," Walter agreed. "I'll have to locate a plane to rent. I'll get busy on it and call you back to confirm, say, by Friday."

"Small plane is good. Slow and safe. No exciting, so confidential."

"I'll get back to you as soon as I can," Walter repeated. "If you need to call sooner, I should have my cell phone in operation from now on."

"OK." Al hung up.

Walter shut off his phone and took a deep breath. It wasn't one-o'clock yet, but he was in no mood to wait any longer to call Susan.

"Hello. Walter?" She sounded anxious.

"Hello, Susan. Are you OK?"

"I am now," she replied, "but...."

"But what? What happened?" he was almost shouting.

"Somebody came to my house—a man—at dinner time Thursday evening."

"Did he have short bleached-blonde hair?" Walter asked, his voice lower.

"Yes, as a matter of fact he did. How did you know?"

"I just got off the phone with him. He said he had been trying to reach me by phone since last Monday. He's a guy I met at the Firearms Training class."

"Why didn't you tell me about him?" Susan sounded a little miffed. "He scared me half to death."

"I'm sorry. I never expected him to contact me again, and I had no idea he knew where your house is. I still don't know how he got that information, but we'll figure it out later. You didn't let him in, did you?"

"No. Moses put up such a ruckus it frightened him away. By the time I could look through the peephole to see who it was, he was already running back to his car."

Walter laughed, as much with relief as amusement. "Sounds like Moses really did his job. Give him an extra hug for me. What did you do after Al—that's his name, Al Fath—after he left?"

"I was really shook up. I thought about it a minute and decided to gather up Moses and go to your cabin for the night—and the next day and night too, since I didn't have to go back to work until yesterday. I didn't try to contact you at the Retreat Center because I didn't want to ruin your meditation, and besides I knew there was nothing you could do from there. But I did invite Moses to sleep in your place next to me in bed. I hope you don't mind."

"That's OK," Walter laughed. "Just make sure he's back in *his* place by the time I get home. I appreciate his bravery, but that only goes so far."

"We moved back to my house last evening," she said. "Everything is OK now, especially if you're sure this Al Fath character is not out to get me, or you, or Moses." Walter was gratified to see he came in ahead of Moses in her list of concerns.

"I don't know who Al Fath is out to get," Walter said, choosing his words carefully, "but I'm sure it isn't any of us. He wants me to do some work for him, but there'll be no need for him to come to the house again. In the meantime, you can always hide away at the cabin again if you want to be sure." At that moment it didn't occur to Walter that Al might find the cabin too, much less that he already had.

With Susan thus reassured, Walter deferred any discussion of his meditation experience until he could figure out his plans for the next few days. He promised to call her again that evening for a more relaxed and soothing chat. As he shut off his cell phone, Walter shook his head, thinking '*so much for a slow, low-stress reentry into civilization.*' He wondered if most of the benefits he was supposed to realize from the meditation course had just been wiped out in the past half hour.

Walter drove slowly through San Rafael until he found a restaurant that promised better-than-fast-food at reasonable prices. Having subsisted on vegetarian fare for more than a week, he had expected that the first thing he would want to do is devour a piece of cow, a steak or a half-pound hamburger, but after scanning the menu he settled on a grilled cheese sandwich and a cup of tea. While waiting for the food to arrive, he attempted to clear his head by meditating with his eyes open, as the course teachers had suggested, and he found that it helped. Nevertheless he was dismayed at how much agitation he had absorbed in his brief exchanges with Al Fath and Susan. He ate his sandwich slowly, 'mindfully,' and spent another twenty minutes sipping his tea. As he stared into his teacup, something told him to head away from the urban sprawl and go into nature along the northern California coast, to go home, not to Bonanza or KFalls, but to Mendocino, where he had been born and raised.

He got in his truck, made his way to US 101, and turned north. As he got deeper into the wine country, a plan began to take shape in his mind. He would seek cheap lodging near one of the State Nature Reserves along the coast and spend time walking the many trails among the trees and rocks. Except for nightly calls to Susan, he would not make any phone arrangements with Al Fath until Thursday, which would give him three-and-a-half days of relative peace and quiet. Then he would drive to Livermore on Friday, meet Hussein on Saturday, and pick up his kids on Sunday. By the time he turned onto CA 128 some fifty miles up US 101, he had it all worked out; the main glitch was finding a place to stay, seeing as how it was the peak of tourist season. It had been some years since he had been back to Mendocino but he vaguely recalled some kind of visitor center on Highway 1 near Van Damme State Park. *Maybe I can get some help there.* However, that was sixty miles north, so he resolved to dismiss his worries by enjoying the beauty of the Anderson Valley along the way. He wished he had Abigail beside him to pass judgment on his unfolding plans, but alas, he would have to fly solo for the next two weeks. *Maybe that's why I went to the meditation course,* he mused: *to prepare myself for that.*

The Visitor Center was right where he thought it would be, and the gray-haired lady behind the counter was most helpful. "Yes, there is a nonprofit nature education center adjacent to the Jug Handle State Reserve, and there are overnight accommodations: nothing fancy, but comfortable and inexpensive." She called the center and learned that, thanks to a last-minute cancellation, they had a private room available in 'the Farmhouse' at a very reasonable rate. Walter snapped it up. He was so delighted when she handed him a one-page map with directions that he wanted to give the lady a hug, but thought better of it. *I'll save it for Susan and give her an extra hug on behalf of 'visitor center ladies' everywhere.* It was another fifteen miles to Jug Handle Farm, so Walter turned his attention to Mendocino. Much had changed since he lived there, but there were a few familiar landmarks. He decided against exploring his old hometown on this trip. *Better to bring Susan here sometime,* he thought.

56.

The next three days were an amorphous blur for Walter. He sought out places along the shore and in the woods that he had frequented in his youth, retracing paths he had walked more than twenty years earlier when he was making choices that had ultimately brought him to his present situation. The meditation course had given him 'new eyes'—albeit with less-than-perfect vision—to see what he might have done differently.

His interest in flying had begun sometime in middle school, when puberty invaded his awareness. Walter couldn't yet see how 'raging hormones' had led him to apply to the Air Force Academy, except that he was certainly motivated to find a way out of Mendocino, just as many adolescents can hardly wait to escape from the confines of their hometowns and their parents' control. He was only mediocre as an athlete, although he had played on the varsity basketball team; he had no special musical or artistic abilities; and he wasn't that smart, although hard work and self-discipline had put him in the top third of his class at the Academy.

What if he hadn't been admitted to the *Academy*? What other options had been eclipsed when he did get accepted? Where might those options have put him today? Nothing sprang to mind, but he looked at other male models who had influenced him. Tom Ketchum was first on the list. Walter had followed Tom's lead from the Academy to active Air Force duty to Alaska Airlines to divorce. Now, however, Walter had set a different course, as was evident from his aborted tryst with Nancy. Tom's career advice was in the back of Walter's mind when Darrell Cox put a job offer on the table, but Walter now realized *there is really no compelling reason why I have to follow through with Darrell Cox—or with Al Fath—or even with Susan. If I strip away the emotions—the 'cravings' and 'aversions,' as Buddhism characterizes them—these choices I'm now considering are not at all inevitable.*

He took out and read for the third or fourth time the *Science of Mind* article Mac had recommended:

An opportunity to start fresh is always available. To forge ahead in a new direction, you can make your past experiences stepping-stones into the future. The past is not precedent, and you are always free to make new choices; however, you can use the past as a foundation. You can call upon what you have learned in earlier stages of growth to guide your decisions and actions.

As you move forward in your life, you harvest the learning gained over the years through your experiences and activities. Nothing is wasted. No matter how unrelated a past experience may seem to what is presently unfolding in your life, something valuable has been gathered and stored for use now. You stand on new ground that has been tilled and seeded by all of the spiritual growth you have attained. Everything you go through in life produces spiritual growth—especially when you take time to reflect on experiences and consider their meaning for you. This process of reflection not only fosters your spiritual growth, but also supports you in moving gracefully and easily forward into the new beginning.

When the end of something comes in your life, start fresh by recognizing that renewal is a natural process and affirm the value of your past experiences. Trusting in the perfection of life, allow your unlimited divine potential to be more fully realized.

When he had finished, his eye moved to the epigraph at the top of the page, a quote from T.S. Eliot: "In my end is my beginning." It took his mind back to Mac's lecture on Transitions, especially the point about an 'ending' of some kind really being the *start* of a shift in life's direction. *That's where I am now,* Walter thought, *in the middle of a transition, in the 'wilderness.' What I learned in the meditation course about purifying my mind—clearing out the old thought patterns— will expedite the transition.* As he detached himself from serious reflection, a final playful benediction came to him: *Abigail would certainly agree.*

57.

On Tuesday evening, Walter's private retreat into nature to integrate the *vipassana* experience into his everyday life was again interrupted by a phone call. This time it was Mac. "I was talking with Susan today, and she mentioned that the Muslim guy had come to her house, apparently looking for you. She said he wants you to do some work for him."

"Yes, I was going to call you about it, but I was waiting until you were home from Odell Lake and had access to a more secure telephone." Walter recounted what Susan had told him about Al Fath's visit to her house and his subsequent telephone conversation with Fath. Mac expressed only minor concern about how Fath had learned where Susan lives, but his interest jumped a mile when Walter told him how much Fath would pay to be flown to Seattle and back. "The amount of money leads me to question how legit this gig would be," Walter said. "I'm not sure I should do it."

"Let me think about it, maybe talk to a few people, before you make a definite commitment," Mac requested. "When do you have to get back to Fath?"

"I promised to call him Friday, and I was planning to call Darrell Cox Thursday about renting the plane."

"OK, if I haven't called you back by Thursday morning, you call me at this number." Mac ended the call, leaving Walter wondering about his intention to 'talk to a few people.' Walter could guess who they might be, but he didn't want to think about it. Thursday would come soon enough.

58.

Walter's phone rang at 9:00 AM Thursday morning. It was Mac, and he was all business, which struck Walter as unusual. "We want you to go ahead with the gig for Al Fath," he said, setting Walter to speculating who 'we' was. "I've already talked to Darrell Cox about it, but you should call him too to make sure you're on the same page. I'll see you after this is all over, but if anything unusual should come up in the meantime, give me a call. Take care." Mac's final admonition was not lost on Walter. Again he wondered what Mac knew that he didn't.

He sighed as he retrieved Darrell's number on his cell phone and hit 'Send.' In contrast to Mac, Darrell seemed outright chatty. "Hi, Walter. I hear you got a flying assignment and you want to rent one of my planes."

"You heard right," Walter said, "but I hope you didn't get it from the KFalls newspaper."

"No," Darrell laughed, "I got it from an anonymous source whom you know. From what he told me of your client, I wouldn't want to send you out in a Cessna 172 though."

"My client says he wants to keep this inconspicuous. Actually, his English wasn't good enough to use that word, but I definitely got that message."

"I got that message too," Darrell replied, " so I'm only going to give you a 182. It's the Turbo model with a three-bladed constant-speed prop and the Garmin G1000 'glass cockpit' instrumentation, so it looks and feels a good bit different from the 172. In any event, the FAA rules require you to do a checkout flight, so I'd like you to come in a day ahead. I won't include that in the rental price, since I hear you're on a tight budget." He laughed again.

Walter agreed. "If you've got a spare set of navigation charts I can borrow, that would help. Mine are packed away in my stuff somewhere, and I don't want to stay up all night looking for them."

"Yeah, falling asleep at the controls is bad form," Darrell replied. "If you like, we can sit down and go over the charts when you come in for the check-out ride. Did your client tell you which Seattle airport you're going to?"

"No, not yet, but I'll insist on getting that information in advance. SeaTac is the only one I'm familiar with, but I would think he would want to go to Boeing Field since he wants to be inconspicuous. Anything else I should ask him?"

"Not that I can think of, but maybe you should brush up on your Arabic." Darrell was having great fun with this, Walter noted, but he wondered if it was a cover up.

"I might just do that," Walter playfully shot back.

After the call ended, Walter checked his body sensations as he had learned to do in the meditation course. He was surprised at how few 'problems' he could find. *Maybe I'm doing better than I expected*, he thought. *Were it not for* vipassana, *I would probably be feeling more than a little stress right now.* Nevertheless, he was happy to have another twenty-four hours of solitude before he had to call Al Fath.

59.

Walter had a sense of foreboding when he called Al the next morning, but he tried to maintain a positive attitude. "I've located a plane for our trip," he said cheerily, "a *good* airplane. I think you'll like it." There was no response from Fath, so Walter continued. "There is some information I need so I can prepare the necessary paperwork. First, what time do you want to leave Klamath Falls?"

"We leave 8:30 AM, but not Kingsley Field—Wilderness Airport," came the answer.

"*Wilderness Airport?*" Walter squeaked. "Where is it? I never heard of it."

"Small airport near Bly. Private. Good airport."

"OK, I'll check it out. If it doesn't work, I'll get back to you." Walter tried his second question. "Which Seattle airport do you want to fly into?"

"We tell you when we leave Wilderness Airport."

"*No!*" Walter strained to avoid shouting. "I am familiar with only one airport in the Seattle area, because my former employer, Alaska Airlines, operates only from SeaTac. I don't think you want to go there, because it's mostly commercial flights, not small planes, but if you want to go to a different airport, I need to know in advance so I can study the maps and navigation charts. It's a matter of safety."

There was some chatter, like Fath was talking to somebody else at his end. It went back and forth three times and then Fath said, "We go to Boeing Field."

"OK, that's good," Walter replied. He was encouraged to find that he could reason with Fath. "You said there would be two passengers. How much baggage? How much weight?"

More discussion at the other end, but not as heated. "Two, three, four bags. Total weight about 200 pounds," Fath said.

"OK." *Now for the potential show-stopper*, Walter thought. "I will need to know the name, age, weight, and citizenship of each passenger." Silence. Walter could feel the whole deal starting to go down the drain. "This is required by the insurance company, also the government. All I need to know *now* is how much weight. You can tell me the rest when I pick you up."

Another short exchange at the other end. "I am 160 pounds," Fath said. "Other passenger is 200 pounds."

Walter did some quick mental arithmetic on the total load. He was glad Darrell was giving him a more powerful plane than the Cessna 172. "Good," he said, trying to reassure his client. "We should have plenty of power to handle the weight. I was concerned that I might have to get a bigger plane."

"Anything else?" Walter could sense a growing impatience in Fath and/or his colleague.

"Do you have a formal written contract you want me to sign?"

"No," was the immediate answer. "No contract. Just speaking agreement."

"OK. I think that's all I need for now," Walter said in his best professional tone. "I'll check in with you to confirm everything Sunday evening, August 24. If you have any last-minute changes, you can tell me then. And if you have any other questions or concerns, call me anytime. Thank you very much."

Fath replied, but it was unintelligible, something like *"shock-run." Must be Arabic,* Walter thought.

He ended the call and put through another to Darrell. He wanted to know about this 'Wilderness Airport.' Darrell's reaction was a hearty laugh. "It doesn't surprise me that these guys want to fly out of someplace obscure. Wilderness Airport is about four miles east of Bly, set back a little from the highway on the south side. It's not that hard to get into or out of, but the runway is gravel. Looks like you're going to earn your pay."

"I'll be OK as long as I don't get shot at again," Walter said, "but I am glad you had the foresight to give me something better than the 172."

"There were other considerations that led me to give you the plane you'll be flying, but they don't concern you," Darrell said cryptically.

"Oh?" Walter's curiosity was aroused.

"I'll tell you about it someday, after this is long past. Have a good day." Darrell was obviously not in a chatty mood.

Walter loaded his bags into the truck and checked out of his room. Shortly after 3:00 PM he checked in at his favorite cheap motel in Livermore and paid for two nights.

60.

That night Walter had dream, a rather vivid dream. He was flying with Ted and Lottie, but he wasn't really piloting the plane because it wasn't a plane, it was a large white duck. They were being pursued by a blonde-haired coyote with the face of Al Fath, and they couldn't find a place to land. After a frantic unsuccessful search, they crashed, wiping out the duck on impact. Ted and Lottie were badly shaken up, but they were OK. Walter, however, was injured and unable to walk. So Ted and Lottie went for help, leaving Walter to observe his pain *à la vipassana* amidst the remains of the duck. After what seemed like an eternity, a rescue team arrived, led by Moses with Susan at the far end of his leash. She lovingly treated his wounds, picked him up, and carried him off to an emergency treatment center resembling the Coyote Café, where he was examined and given further treatment by a medical team consisting of Mac, Nancy, and Henry Parsons. Meanwhile, Thunder Ray led Darrell and Virginia Cox and Hussein in praying for Walter's recovery in the 'waiting room,' which was the Café's front patio. When he was released from the 'medical center' sometime later, Walter discovered that he could communicate directly with ducks, coyotes, dogs, and other animals as a consequence of his trauma. He was conversing in fluent *coyote* with Al Fath when the dream ended.

61.

In contrast with his premonition of conflict the previous morning and in spite of his dream overnight, Walter began the next day full of optimism. Not that he had any specific ideas about what the day would bring, but he looked forward to learning more about Islam under Hussein's guidance. After exchanging greetings, Walter plunged right into his reason for coming. "When I was here in May, I got Huston Smith's book on *Islam* and Deepak Chopra's audiobook on *Muhammad*, both of which I finished a month ago. I think I'm ready for something a little more advanced, in particular something that presents a different picture from the standard Western view of Islam. Do you have anything contradicting the popular conception of Islam as a religion of violence, one that cannot coexist peacefully with other religions or with modern Western society?"

Hussein began walking around the display tables, picking up this book and that, reading the descriptions and endorsements on the back covers, putting most of them back down, but giving a few to Walter for consideration. After extended discussion, Walter settled on two books, one a rather scholarly treatise by a professor of Islamic thought and the other a biography of Badshah Khan, a *Pashtun* Muslim who had been a longtime associate of Gandhi. Both books promised to enlarge Walter's perspective on Islam, but in quite different directions and styles. He was set for a few more months of 'bedtime reading.'

Next Walter asked about *Sufism*, which he knew Hussein practiced. Hussein's response was that *Sufism* was best understood *experientially*, through participation in *Sufi* rituals and interaction with *Sufi* teachers and students, but he did eventually assent to recommend a couple books, largely because there was no opportunity for Walter to participate in any *Sufi* activities during his current trip. As consolation, Hussein offered to research *Sufi* groups in Oregon and send Walter a short list of names, addresses, and phone numbers.

Last but not least, Walter said he was interested in learning a little Arabic. "You shouldn't learn from me, because I speak the Moroccan version," Hussein said, "which won't get you very far in the world. There are many dialects of Arabic, just as there are many dialects of English, but unlike English, there is a *Modern Standard* version of Arabic, which is taught in all the schools and universities and which should—I repeat, *should*—enable you to communicate with speakers of the various dialects. May I ask *why* you want to learn Arabic?"

Walter picked his words very carefully. "When I return to Oregon, I expect to have business dealings with some Muslims. Arabic may not be their native language, but I'm sure they have some facility in the language. On the other hand, their English is rather weak, and I'm eager to improve my communication with them."

"Do you know what country they are from?" Hussein asked.

"No, I have no idea," Walter answered. "All I know is the name of my principal contact, Al Fath. Does that give you any hint as to where he's from?"

Hussein frowned. " '*Al Fath*' is the title of one of the *surahs*—one of the chapters—in the *Holy Qur'an*—number 48, I believe. It means '*The Victory*.' I have to wonder if that's his true name."

Walter's heart sunk. "I don't know, nor do I know the exact nature of his business. I met him casually in a class last month, and he called last week to ask me to do a job for him." Walter discreetly avoided divulging what the job was and that he had already agreed to do it—or that the class was Firearms Training.

"I'd be very cautious if I were you," Hussein advised. "Whatever that is about may be entirely legitimate, but it could also be the complete opposite."

Walter thanked Hussein and then continued. "There's also another reason why I would like to learn a little Arabic. I don't know why, but I would like to be able to perform Muslim prayers, '*The Salaat*,' without embarrassing any devout Muslims who might be nearby."

Hussein's eyebrows lifted in surprise, but he was now smiling. "I can teach you that," he said enthusiastically, "or at least get you started." He walked over to a file cabinet in one corner of the room, opened a drawer, and extracted several sheets of paper stapled together. Handing the papers to Walter, he said, "Come with me, please" and led the way to a small room off the courtyard. With Walter reading from the instructions on the papers, Hussein went through the entire prayer ritual, coaching Walter in pronunciation, showing him how to stand, bow, sit, and prostrate himself, and explaining the meaning of each step. After they went through it a second time, Hussein led them back to the bookstore, where he went to the file cabinet again and took out a DVD. Giving it to Walter, he said, "This will repeat all I have just taught you, so you can continue to practice correctly. It's free; we don't charge for it when we feel the recipient is sincere. There are, however, two more items you should have. The first is a prayer rug, which is essential, and the second is a proper Muslim hat, which is optional." He steered Walter to a clothing display, and Walter tried on three different hats, one of them to his liking. Next they moved to a low stack of prayer rugs on a nearby table. As Walter picked through them, Hussein apologized profusely for the expense, all the while explaining that the prices were considerably cheaper than those in commercial shops and the proceeds from sales supported the Center's community work.

As if on cue, the 'Call to Prayer' began playing on the sound system, so they returned to the small room and went through *The Salaat* together, minus Hussein's coaching but with his solicitous patience for Walter to keep up. After the prayers, Hussein invited Walter to be his guest for lunch. With Hussein giving directions, Walter drove them to a nearby restaurant that specialized in *halal* cuisine, the Muslim equivalent of *kosher* food for Jews. Without even looking at the menu, Hussein ordered, and when the food arrived, he and Walter downed every last delicious molecule. They talked about their respective impressions of the meditation course they had just completed, then returned to the matter of Walter learning Arabic. Again apologizing for inducing Walter to spend so much money, Hussein recommended an introductory textbook that included a CD to teach pronunciation. As with Walter's previous visit to the Center, he suggested that Walter go to a nearby Barnes & Noble store to buy it.

After dropping off Hussein, Walter drove back to his motel and called his ex-wife Angela to confirm arrangements for him to pick up Katie and Ryan the next day. Angela was quite insistent that he be on time, saying she had another engagement to get to later. For his part, Walter was happy to get an early start. It would be a three-hour drive to Bass Lake—more if they got caught up in Sunday afternoon traffic.

62.

Shortly after 10:00 AM Sunday morning Walter arrived at his former home. Angela had Katie and Ryan ready to go, which aroused his suspicion. (She had habitually been late throughout their entire marriage, except when there was something *she* wanted to do.) His *vipassana* training cut in, and he stopped speculating about motives for her actions—besides it was really none of his business. As usual she had endless instructions for him to follow while the kids were in his care: not too much fast food, junk food, sweets—not too much TV or video games—use sun screen (not included)—brush teeth and bathe regularly—*blah, blah, blah.* Walter took it all in with no emotion, no reaction, noting it seemed to unnerve Angela, but not reacting to that either. *It's hard to have a duel if one of the parties is unarmed,* he thought. Having failed to provoke Walter with barely hidden aspersions on his competence as a parent, Angela went for a tried-and-true point of vulnerability, his wallet. "School begins in two weeks. It would be nice if you took the kids shopping for school supplies and some new clothes. They can tell you what they need."

"OK," Walter replied, keeping an even tone in his voice. With a fifty-thousand-dollar payday on the horizon, he could easily afford to blow a few hundred bucks on his children.

Now down by two strikes, Angela tried again. "I expect you to have them back here next Saturday, between four and five o'clock—if it's not too difficult for you." Walter stifled a smile at her final jibe. In the old days, he would have responded in like nastiness, but now he just nodded agreement. Finally, she had to bring up a matter that might give him an opening. "I'll be gone most of the time over the coming week. If you need to contact me, call my cell phone. I think you have the number, but if not, the kids know it." She hesitated, knowing she was about to lower her defenses even more. "I'd rather not be disturbed during this period, so please don't call me unless it's absolutely necessary. I've already given Katie and Ryan those orders, but you may have to reinforce them."

Again, Walter showed no emotion. Keeping his face blank, he said simply, "OK. Anything else?"

Angela could no longer hide her confusion over his non-confrontation. "No, I guess not," she muttered. Having run out of nastiness, all she could think to say was "Have a good time."

"Thank you. We will." Walter tried to say it sincerely, not gaining any satisfaction from having stymied her aggression, but truth be told, he had enjoyed the encounter. "Let's go, gang!" he hollered to the kids, who had been eavesdropping on the exchange between their parents from the next room.

As they gathered their bags and headed for the door, Walter paused to take stock of his children. He hadn't seen them in six months, and he was eager to reconnect with them. Katie was the spitting image of her mother, only an inch or two short of Angela's five-feet-six. Both were stylishly slender, not to say anorexic, and wore their hair long and straight, although Katie's was dark brown like Walter's and Angela was a blonde. Now 13 going on 29, Katie's body was beginning to fill out, and she didn't quite know what to make of it. That would come soon enough, and neither of her parents was very comfortable with that. Music was her primary interest, and she appeared to have talent. Ryan, on the other hand, was not quite 10 and still very much a boy, oblivious to the changes that would occur when his hormones cut in. A good foot shorter than his sister, he was more skinny than stout, but not really either. He wore his dishwater blonde hair in a crew cut, which contributed to his slightly nerdy aura, something he had inherited from his father. His interests were animals and quasi-mechanical things he could take apart and put back together. Like his father, he was not particularly athletic or artistic.

Walter put their bags under the pickup's tonneau cover along with his own and stowed their fragile items behind the front seats. "Katie, you get first choice on where to sit."

Predictably, Ryan fussed. "Why don't I get to choose first?"

"You'll get first choice next time, and we'll take turns after that," Walter said calmly.

Ryan wasn't satisfied with that. "Why don't I get first choice this time and Katie next time?"

Walter was ready. "Because Katie is older and bigger and her name comes before yours alphabetically. Besides, as a gentleman you should always let her go first."

"That's not fair!" Ryan protested.

"Life isn't fair," Walter explained, "and if you haven't yet learned how to live without always being *numero uno*, now is a good time to get started." Seeing that

Katie was getting settled in the right front seat, he asked Ryan, "Would you like to ride front and center, next to me, or would you rather enjoy the luxurious expanse of the balcony?"

"*Humph!*" Ryan climbed into the jump seats.

They rode in silence the first half hour, as Walter navigated eastward toward Manteca. Turning south on the Highway 99 'speedway,' he announced, "We'll be on this road about an hour. Then we'll stop for lunch." There was no sign of acknowledgement from Katie or Ryan; both were so absorbed in whatever music they had programmed into their iPods they probably hadn't heard him at all.

About 45 minutes later, Ryan removed his earbuds and asked, "When do we eat?"

"When we get to Merced, in about ten minutes. What kind of food do you want?"

"*McDonald's!*" Ryan shouted. He was loud enough to penetrate Katie's iPod fog, prompting her to remove her earbuds too.

"Your mother said you shouldn't eat too much fast food," Walter countered.

"Yeah, she would say that," Katie grumped.

"We haven't been to McDonald's all summer," Ryan whined. "We were out in the middle of nowhere in that stinkin' summer camp in Maine."

"Didn't you have a good time?" Walter asked.

"It was OK," Katie replied. "The best part was we didn't see much of Mom. She was in another part of the camp, and she checked on us once a week, but that was all."

The highway signs indicated their turnoff was just ahead, and Walter spotted some 'Golden Arches' in the distance. In five minutes, all three of them were unwrapping their Big Macs with gusto. When they had devoured all but the last few fries, Walter probed for information. "Your mom said not to call her this week, unless there was an emergency."

Katie took the bait immediately. "She's going down to Morro Bay with her boyfriend," she said scornfully. "She hasn't seen him all summer, and when we got back Friday she had 'the hots' so bad I couldn't stand to be around her."

Without waiting for his dad's reaction, Ryan chimed in. "His name is 'Festus—Festus Foster.' That isn't his real name, but it's what he uses with his band: 'Festus Foster and the Fremont Frogstompers.' His real name is 'George.'"

"The 'Fremont Frogstompers'—that's an unusual name," Walter said innocently, hoping to provide just enough reaction to sustain the tattling.

"It's a country band," Ryan said disdainfully, "and they're actually from Stockton. Festus plays the banjo and sings."

Katie added, "I hate country music. It's nothing but a lot of whining. Mom got hooked on it right after ... right after you two split up."

Walter sensed the building emotion and moved to cut it off. This wasn't the time or place to let it all out. "Yeah ... well," he mumbled. "Let's hit the road again."

Katie and Ryan traded places in the truck, and they headed eastward on Highway 140 through the flat, fertile farmland. In the distance ahead the snow-topped Sierras loomed like a solid wall, and within an hour the road was twisting and turning through the foothills around Mariposa. They continued another thirty miles at reduced speed on Highway 49 to the town of Oakhurst. At the main intersection, Walter turned left into the shopping mall to buy groceries at Raley's Supermarket. The kids surprised him with their maturity as they shopped; they didn't squabble over likes and dislikes, and they picked through the various brands to find the best values. As they got back into the truck, Walter explained they only had ten miles more to go, so it was 'fair' for Ryan to remain in the front seat. Katie accepted it without complaint, which pleased Walter. *So far, so good*, he thought. They drove up the hill through town, turned right on Road 222, went up another long, steep hill, and came to Bass Lake. Walter followed local roads to the real estate office, stopping briefly to pick up the key and a local map, which the kids shared—*a minor miracle!*—in navigating to their rental house. To determine who got first choice of bedroom, Walter used a guessing game: "I'm thinking of a number between 1 and 100. What is it?"

Katie's guess was closer than Ryan's. "Can I take *any* bedroom?" she asked.

"Sure," Walter replied. "Then Ryan will choose between the other two, and I'll take what's left." The significance of his not giving himself the first choice was not lost on the kids. Nevertheless, Katie did not pick the master bedroom, which had its own bathroom, and Ryan followed her generous example. Walter was moved.

The rest of the day was spent in walking around the area: 'The Pines Resort,' the small cluster of other businesses in 'the Village,' and the profusion of houses and cottages of all sizes and shapes crowded around the north shore of the 1,170-acre lake. In midsummer it was almost full, the water level near 3,376 feet, supporting fishing, swimming, water skiing, and boating. The kids begged Walter to let them try water skiing, but all he would commit to was renting a boat. He was more interested in devoting at least two days to exploring Yosemite National Park some fifty miles to the North. Katie and Ryan, having already spent most of the summer in rural Maine, had had their fill of nature and campaigned for a trip to the large amusement park at the south end of San Francisco Bay. "That's nearly 200 miles from here, so it's out of the question," Walter explained, but it gave him an idea: he could fly Susan to San Jose to celebrate her birthday, and they could stay over an extra day to take Katie and Ryan to the amusement park. That would be a good way to introduce her to the kids, and *vice versa*. He decided to try it out right then and there. "However, I was thinking…" he began. "I have a friend where I'm living in Oregon, a very lovely woman…"

"Your girlfriend," Katie interrupted, a look on her face that said, "*Aha*! I thought so!"

"Well, yes," Walter conceded, aware that he was blushing. "I'd like you to meet her, but getting you two up to Klamath Falls seems difficult since the cabin I'm renting is small. Susan—that's her name—has a birthday in October, and I want to bring her down to the Bay Area to celebrate. If we came on a weekend, we could all go to 'Great America' together."

"And mom could go spend the day in Stockton with Festus!" Ryan blurted out.

"Yeah, she'd agree to just about anything if she could get away for a toot with him," Katie added, summoning back Walter's blush.

"Er … well, … let's all think about it," he stammered, "and see if we can make it happen."

Later that evening, after they had eaten a supper of sandwiches, fruit salad, and lemonade and watched the two hours of TV Walter had established as their ration, he sent them off to bed. Before he turned out the lights in their rooms, he visited each of them to say a personal goodnight. Ryan was full of questions about what they would do the next day, but Katie was pensive. "What's Susan like?" she asked.

Walter was caught off-guard. He hadn't given any thought to what words he would use to describe Susan. "Well, she's very warm and gentle. I think you will like her. She's about my age and she works in the tourist information center in Klamath Falls."

"Is she divorced too? Does she have any kids?" Katie began to reveal her true interest.

"She has a daughter Lucy who is almost twenty, but I haven't met her yet. Susan's husband was killed in an accident when Lucy was three, so Susan raised her as a single mom."

"Are you sleeping with her? Are you two shacked up?"

"Susan has her own house in town, and my cabin is out in the woods more than twenty miles away. What we do when we get together is none of your business," Walter replied evenly, then added. "But yes, we are in love."

Katie considered this briefly, then went to the heart of her concern. "Do you plan to make babies with her?" *Is there any room in your life for me?* she was asking.

"Definitely not. Lucy is no longer living at home. She's in the Army. I will have you and Ryan to look after for at least the next ten years—for the rest of your and my lives, in fact."

Katie had heard what she wanted to hear, although Walter was sure that once would not be enough. She let out a sigh of relief and said, "I love you, Daddy."

"I love you too, Katie." Walter leaned over and kissed her on the forehead. There were tears in his eyes as he stood up.

<h1 style="text-align:center">63.</h1>

The week at Bass Lake was active, but slow-paced. On Monday they went to Yosemite to ride around and explore the options, and on Wednesday they did a six-hour, six-mile guided hike. Walter had doubts about Ryan's ability to go the distance, but he was pleasantly surprised when his son kept up the pace with nary a complaint. Tuesday afternoon they rented a powerboat so Katie and Ryan could get their first wave-boarding experience on Bass Lake. It proved to be great fun, and Walter even remembered to buy some sunscreen to slather all over the kids and himself. Thursday was a 'hang' day for all of them to rest up from the hike. They went out for dinner at a Chinese restaurant—the kids' choice—in Oakhurst to give everybody a break from Walter's limited culinary repertoire. Again he came away impressed at his children's maturity and good manners. *They sure didn't get it from me,* he thought. *Angela is doing a good job raising them, Festus notwithstanding.*

Monday bedtime was Ryan's turn to quiz Walter about his love life, as Katie had done the night before. It was clear that Katie had shared with her brother what she had learned. "Will you and Susan get married?" he asked.

"Probably," Walter said. "We've talked about it a little, but we're not in any hurry. We want to get you and Katie and Susan's daughter involved in sorting out which of you would live where. Most likely Lucy will continue her career in the Army, so she will come home to visit occasionally. At some point you and Katie can decide whether you want to continue living with your mother or come live with Susan and me. It's even possible that one of you will choose your mom and the other will choose me."

Walter realized he had probably said too much, pushing his son into unnecessary confusion and worry about details that could be worked out later. Ryan, however, had something more basic on his mind. "What if I don't like Susan? Or she doesn't like me?"

Walter thought this over before answering. The 'wrong words' could come back to haunt him. "I'm sure Susan will like you," he began. "She seems to like everybody. I think you will like her too, but you'll have to decide that for yourself after you've had a chance to meet her. If you don't like her much, you'll probably want to continue living with your mother. I might be disappointed at that, but it won't stop me from liking you—from loving you."

"Even if you love her more than me? What then?"

Now Walter could see where Ryan was coming from. He hadn't even reached puberty yet, but male competitiveness had already taken root. "It isn't a question of my loving Susan more than you or you more than her. Love doesn't work that way. If I love Susan, it doesn't mean I will love you any less. And if your mother loves Festus, she won't love you any less either, even if you don't like him."

Walter was sure his last comment went to the nexus of what was troubling Ryan, and his suspicion was confirmed when Ryan said, "It doesn't seem that way."

Again Walter thought before replying. "Sometimes we say or do things we don't really mean. I'm sure you occasionally make nasty remarks about your sister or play dirty tricks on her and she does the same to you, but that doesn't mean you don't love one another, deep down inside. Sometimes we interpret what others say or do as mean and nasty even when they didn't intend that at all." Walter resisted the temptation to launch into a mini-sermon on judgmentalism. *Maybe in eight or nine years*, he thought, *if we're still speaking to one another.*

On Friday afternoon they all piled into the truck and drove down to Fresno for shopping. Buying school supplies was the easy part, but picking out clothes was much more difficult and time-consuming. It had to be done serially, one person at a time, so Walter used the occasion to further educate Ryan in gentlemanly tolerance and forbearance regarding the female gender, all the while inwardly laughing at his own checkered history in that area. *Some men never learn,* he mused, thinking of his buddy 'Tomcat' in particular. He gently reprimanded himself for being judgmental of others—and for being judgmental of himself. *Damn! That takes all the fun out of being a man.*

When at last their stamina and blood sugar had dropped to the point where food took precedence over shopping, Walter found an inviting pizza restaurant. As they waited for their food, he reviewed the calendar for the rest of the year, hoping to gain his children's buy-in or at least to set expectations. Soon after returning to Oregon, he would initiate plans for Susan and himself to come down in early October and spend a day with Katie and Ryan at the 'Great America' theme park. As soon as he could nail that down, he would confirm it with Angela. After that, however, the future was a big question mark. Thanksgiving and/or Christmas would be the obvious times to arrange a get-together, but where? He promised to explore some options for venue and travel so they could discuss them at the 'Great America' outing, but otherwise he avoided specifics, feeling that he shouldn't raise expectations he might not be able to meet.

Back at the Bass Lake rental house, Katie and Ryan skipped their two-hour TV allocation in favor of lounging in deck chairs on the patio, listening to their iPods and watching the sunset light show on the water surface, while Walter attempted to read his book on 'Arabic for the feeble-minded.' No words needed to be spoken. It was 'good old family time' at its best.

64.

Everybody was lethargic Saturday morning. Nobody wanted to leave. It wasn't the place so much as the situation, the company. All three of them moped through breakfast and trudged off to their bedrooms to pack. When that took far less than the time available before Walter's announced noon departure, he rounded them up for another walk down to the Village and back. "You know," he said as they strolled along, "it's possible we could come back here for a week at Christmas. We wouldn't be able to do any boating because the lake is drained down to half-full and Yosemite operates on a reduced schedule in the winter, but at least we would be together."

"That's better than the other alternative," Katie responded.

Ryan was more definite. "I'd rather come see you in Oregon, even if I'd have to sleep in a sleeping bag on the floor."

Walter laughed at the ten-year-old determination. "I'm sure we can provide better accommodations than that, but you might have to share your space with a dog."

"A dog?!" Katie and Ryan exclaimed in unison. "You didn't say anything about a dog," Katie added, and wide-eyed Ryan asked, "Do you have a dog?"

"Susan has a dog," Walter answered, "an eight-year-old Basset hound. His name is 'Moses.'"

"Holy Moses!" Ryan shouted.

Walter and Katie laughed. "No, just Moses," he said.

"That settles it," Katie announced. "We want to come spend Thanksgiving or Christmas with you in Oregon."

"OK, I'll work on it, but we'll have to get your mother to agree. Maybe it would help if you suggested to her that she'd be able to have some more time alone with Festus." Walter felt a little guilty about conspiring with his children, but he excused it on the grounds that he was teaching them to see Angela's relationship with her boyfriend in a more positive light.

Back at the house again, they loaded the pickup and climbed in. They were still running ahead of schedule, but Walter had promised Katie and Ryan one last lunch at a McDonald's along the way, and the initial pangs of hunger were already noticeable. He returned the house key to the rental office and drove south through North Fork to Highway 41. About twenty miles north of Fresno, they turned west on Highway 145 brought them a McDonald's in the farming town of Madera. Everything went like clockwork, and they sat down to their Big Macs barely an hour after leaving Bass Lake. After lunch, Katie offered to relinquish her front seat to Ryan, but he declined. *Who sits where no longer seems to matter*, Walter noted with satisfaction. *The kids have learned to stick together and support one another through the upheaval of the divorce and now the uncertainty of their parents finding new partners.*

After another two hours of travel through the vast Central Valley farmland, they pulled into the driveway at the kids' home right on schedule—Angela's schedule, that is. The kids pitched in to carry their luggage inside, and Walter brought up the rear with their purchases, still in the store bags. Angela met them at the door, looking a little bleary-eyed from what Walter surmised was a succession of sleepless nights. He let go of those thoughts as he plopped the bags down at her feet, saying quietly, "We bought a few things, as you suggested. I hope they meet with your approval." He didn't give her a chance to reply, going on quickly to outline the tentative plans they had made for him and Susan to come down from Oregon for a day with the kids at Great America. "I'll research the dates and options and run it by you to see what you prefer," he said, edging toward the door. "Good-bye, Katie! Good-bye, Ryan!" he hollered. The kids came running for a final three-way hug. "See you in October," he said. For once, Angela was speechless.

65.

Impatient to get home to Susan after more than three weeks away, Walter was up and on the road by 7:00 AM the next morning. He opted for the shortest route, by way of Walnut Creek and Interstate 80, because it was Sunday and traffic would be light. Two hours out, he pulled off Interstate 5 at Williams for coffee—at Granzella's, of course. After tanking up at the food counter, he walked across the street to the Gift Shop to buy some Garlic Stuffed Olives for Susan, and Virginia and Darrell, and Ted and Lottie, and Mac, and .... *Oh, what the hell! I'll just get a case of six large jars.*

From there Walter drove nonstop past Red Bluff and Redding to Weed, where he paused for lunch. Shortly after one o'clock he left Weed on US 97, bound for KFalls, and just before three, he pulled up in front of Susan's house. He bounced out of the truck and almost sprinted up the walkway. Halfway to the door, he could hear Moses' welcoming bark, and Susan opened the door just as he was reaching for the bell. For once, Moses was outdone in enthusiasm, and maybe even saliva, as she leaped into his arms and covered his face, ears, and neck in wet kisses. Then Walter and Susan stood in the doorway grinning deliriously at each other as they caught their breath. It took them nearly a minute to realize that Moses had been cheering them on all the while and the whole neighborhood must be aware that *Walter had returned!*

They went inside and Susan made tea while Walter communed with Moses. When the tea was ready, Walter joined Susan on the sofa and began telling her about the meditation course, his post-course 'retreat' in Mendocino, his meeting with Hussein, and his week with Katie and Ryan. The mention of 'Festus Foster and the Fremont Frogstompers' drew a good laugh, but her interest peaked when Walter got to his prospective plans for an October outing to 'Great America' with her and his kids. He had originally intended to make the trip, especially the flight, a surprise for her, but now he wanted her participation in the planning.

She fetched a calendar and together they picked the date and roughed out the schedule: fly to San Jose on Friday, October 3; spend the next day at 'Great America'; and fly home Sunday afternoon, October 5.

Susan was clearly delighted with all this, but she expressed concern about the expense. Walter dismissed it by telling her of his lucrative flying job for Al Fath, which took them into a sobering discussion of how that would unfold over the next two days. Naturally, Susan was worried about Walter's safety, not so much from flying an unfamiliar plane into an unfamiliar airport, but from getting involved with persons—*foreigners*—worse yet, *Muslims*—whose trustworthiness was uncertain. Walter countered by pointing out that Mac had vetted the gig with 'undisclosed persons or agencies,' presumably affiliated with the United States Government. Rather than reassure Susan, it had the opposite effect. "We don't know whose those people are either. Even if they are in the Department of Homeland Security or something like that, can we trust them to come to your aid if problems arise?" she demanded. Walter conceded that there was risk involved, possibly substantial, which might explain the large amount of money he was to be paid. At the same time, he didn't want to be prejudiced by the fear mongering contaminating the media since '9/11.' Susan reluctantly accepted that, and they finally agreed that he could always back out of the deal right up until takeoff from Wilderness Airport if the situation looked fishy.

Both of them were now 'talked out,' so Walter used the hiatus to make his promised call to Al Fath. It went smoothly as he confirmed arrangements: 0830 departure from Wilderness Airport, arriving Boeing Field around 1100 hours; return departure around 1300 hours, arriving Wilderness approximately 1530; passenger information to be provided before initial takeoff; payment to be made upon return to Wilderness. Fath said all that was 'good.' Walter then injected a new element, telling Fath he would be making a checkout ride on Monday to familiarize himself with the aircraft and he wanted to make one of the three mandatory practice landings and takeoffs at Wilderness Airport, probably around noontime. Walter explained that this was to assure safety for their Tuesday flight and he would be accompanied by a flight instructor. Fath seemed to understand and raised no objection. Walter ended the call feeling relieved that everything was going well. He gathered up Susan, and they went off for some bowls of Chinese noodle soup, followed by a short walk with Moses, and then early to bed, albeit not necessarily to sleep.

66.

At 0955 hours Walter walked in the front door at Darrell's company. Even before he could give his name to the receptionist, she greeted him, "Good morning, Mr. Baker." She got up from her desk, keyed in the combination on the lock, and opened the door to the central hallway. "They are in the conference room—second door on the left." The word 'they' tipped off Walter that Darrell was not alone. Not that he was surprised—based upon Mac's reference to 'we' in their telephone conversation, Walter expected to be face-to-face with Federal agents of some stripe before or after his trip. He entered the conference room to find Darrell flanked by two 'suits' who flashed official IDs at him as Darrell introduced them. It happened so quickly Walter didn't get their names or their agency affiliation, but it really didn't matter.

Things immediately got down to business. The agents wanted to know how Walter had met Al Fath, so Walter briefly recounted seeing him in the Coyote Café in Bly, making sure to mention he was in the habit of going there after fishing expeditions with Dr. Delbert McCarter. He told of meeting Fath at the Firearms Training class, relating their conversation in some detail and adding that he thought Fath had taken the course for the same reason he did: to obtain an Oregon CCW permit. Therefore, Walter suggested, the Feds probably had records of Fath's mandatory background check in one of their systems, somewhere, "... but I doubt that 'Al Fath' is his true name."

"Yeah, we've got him, and we know who he is," came the response. To Walter's surprise, the agent volunteered additional information. "He and most of his buddies in Bly entered the US on student visas and got recruited into the Bly group when they ran out of money. We have reason to believe they're not fanatics, motivated by *jihad*, and they plan to go back to college when they've saved up enough cash. What we're most interested in is who recruited them and for what purpose. And who is supplying the money?"

The second agent spoke up. "What we hope to learn from your trip to Seattle is who they are meeting with. We don't intend to eavesdrop on their conversation, but we would like to get some pictures and, if we're lucky, follow their contacts after the meeting is over. What that means for you is that you don't have to do anything above and beyond getting them to the meeting and back again without arousing any suspicion."

"So the risks for you are minimal," Darrell interjected.

"On the other hand," the second agent continued, "whatever other information we can get will be a bonus, so pay close attention and try to remember any names, places, and dates they might mention. We'll be here to debrief you the minute you get back. Any questions?"

Walter thought it over and answered, "Nope. It sounds straightforward."

"See you tomorrow afternoon," one of the agents said as they headed toward the door.

For a millisecond, Walter thought of replying, "*Inshallah* (God willing)," but he wisely thought better of it and simply nodded. Darrell waited until the agents had gotten to the reception area and the door had closed behind them. "That wasn't so bad, was it?"

"It's much simpler than I expected. I'm very happy I won't have any distractions from flying the airplane. It will require enough concentration as it is, what with my lack of familiarity with the plane and the airports. Speaking of which, can we go over the charts and the FAA information sheets on BFI and this rinky-dink airport near Bly?"

"Here you go." Darrell slid a small stack of maps across the table and helped Walter unfold the top one. "Here's Wilderness Airport: it's a half-mile strip, 80 feet wide, gravel, totally unattended, with no services, no nothing except for a building barely big enough for one plane. That's all I can tell you about it."

"I'd like to do a landing and takeoff there when we do the check-out ride," Walter said. "I informed Fath of that when I confirmed everything with him last night, and he didn't object."

"Good idea. I'd rather not get shot at again," Darrell said. He slid a second map atop the first. "Here's Boeing Field, which should be more familiar territory for you."

"Oh, yes," Walter said. "It was an alternate for SeaTac, so I had to know about it in case of an emergency, but I never had to go there."

Darrell sat down and leaned back in the chair. "Something tells me you won't go there tomorrow either. I'm sure it has occurred to the Muslims that the Feds might be running some kind of surveillance, so your passengers might make a last-minute 'switcheroo' on your destination in an attempt to foil that."

"What do you suggest I do if they try it?" Walter asked.

"First, you insist on confirming everything before you take off. Since you have to get the passenger information anyhow, you can make it all seem like standard preflight procedure. You tell them you've got to radio the passenger info to me—'for insurance purposes,' of course—and if there's any change, you can ask me to file a modified flight plan with the FAA on your behalf. Then you delay your takeoff until I confirm I've done that, meaning I've alerted our 'friends in suits' to the change." Walter nodded his agreement, and Darrell continued. "If they try any other cute tricks during the flight, you tell them you've got to report in to me, that if you deviate from your flight plan without doing that, you'll soon have military jets escorting you. Then, in your communication with me, you indicate you've got problems by using 'Pig Latin.'"

"*Pig Latin?!*" Walter was incredulous.

"Yes. If these guys aren't good in English, they won't be able to understand it, and if you only use it for a few key words, they won't catch on to what you're doing. However, Pig Latin doesn't help if you want to say 'Mayday,' so as a backup we should also agree on a code word or phrase you can use to signal you're under duress. Any suggestions on that?"

Walter drew a blank until his recent dream flew into his consciousness. "A *duck!*" he said. "I'll say something about ducks." They both were still chuckling about that as they went out the door to the plane.

They spent the next fifteen minutes sitting in the cockpit while Darrell methodically went over the Cessna 182T's integrated instrument system, based upon two large LCD flat-panel displays. Walter adapted quickly because it was much closer to Boeing 737 instrumentation than the array of a dozen circular 'steam gauges' on the Cessna 172 he had flown earlier. After taking off and flying around in circles for about half an hour, Walter made the first of the three mandatory practice landings on Runway 25 at Kingsley. Next he took off again and flew out to Bly, where he made a slow, careful landing at Wilderness Airport. The runway was in good shape, and there were no obstructions near the approach path, so it was fairly easy, although Walter wasn't eager to go there in bad weather. Taking off from Wilderness, heading 260, he discovered that the west end of the runway was *less than a mile* southeast of Frisco Ranch.

67.

Walter was back at *Kingsley Field* at 7:00 AM the next morning. The plane was all gassed up and ready to go when he arrived, so all he had to do was complete the preflight check. As he strapped himself in, Darrell walked up to the right-hand door and opened it. He pointed to a toggle switch in the upper right corner of the instrument panel and said, "Flip this to the 'up' position just before you board your passengers and 'down' again after they get out."

Walter looked at Darrell. "Camera system?"

Darrell smiled. "That's one of the reasons I wanted you to fly this particular plane." He pointed to a sticker near the communications panel. "That's the frequency for the channel to my Operations Center. I'll monitor it for the first hour, after which you'll probably be out of range. After that I'll track you on the Internet if you use 'flight following.' Have a good day."

"When I get the passenger information at Wilderness, I'll call you so you can file a flight plan. I'll take care of 'flight following' after I'm airborne," Walter said. "See you this afternoon, *inshallah*." Darrell may not have known the precise meaning of the Arabic, but he got the joke.

At 0755 hours Walter took off from Kingsley Field (LMT) on Runway 25. He climbed to 3,100 feet, headed east-northeast, and landed at Wilderness (80OR) at 0820. As he taxied toward the west end of the runway, he saw Fath's old Chevy parked next to the lone building. He turned right on the taxiway, stopped in front of the building, and cut the engine, remembering to switch on the cockpit camera before he got out of the plane. Two men got out of the car and walked toward him: one was Al Fath, the other a larger, older man. "Good morning," Walter greeted them. "It's a great day to go flying. We should have perfect weather all the way to Seattle." Both men grunted acknowledgement and walked toward the plane. The older man had a small briefcase, but neither had any luggage. "No baggage?" Walter asked.

"We get in Seattle," Fath replied.

Walter shrugged and helped the men into the rear seats. Seeing that they seemed confused, he asked, "Have you ever flown in a small plane before?"

"No, only airline," Fath answered. His colleague nodded 'no.'

Walter pulled a barf bag from a seat-back pocket and opened it. "If you get sick, use this." He made a gagging sound and held his mouth over the bag. The older man seemed slightly affronted by the informality, but said nothing. Undaunted, Walter replaced the bag and pointed to a red plastic male urinal under the pilot's seat. "If you to have to pee, use that." The affront level went up several notches, but Al Fath giggled. Finally, Walter pointed to the fire extinguisher under the right front seat. "I hope there will be no need to use that, but you should know it's there in case we have an emergency." Fath and his colleague exchanged nervous glances.

Walter got into the pilot's seat, closed the door, and took out a clipboard. "I need your names, ages, and citizenship."

Al Fath responded first, as if to set an example. "My name is Al Fath. I am twenty-five years old, from Algeria." Walter noticed he said this in slow, perfect English, as if he had rehearsed it. *If so, it wasn't just to impress 'lil' ol' me,* he thought.

Fath nodded to the other man, who said in a low voice, "Ali Hazik, thirty-three, Syria."

"Thank you," Walter said. "I want to confirm we are going to Boeing Field. It will take a little more than two hours, depending upon the wind, but we should be there by 1100 hours."

Fath and Hazik exchanged glances, and then Fath said, "Not Boeing Field. We go Sanderson Field—Shelton, Washington."

Walter feigned surprise, then displeasure. "I don't know Sanderson Field," he said evenly. "I'll have to check on it." He switched the radio to Darrell's operations channel and called in. When Darrell answered, Walter said, "We have a change of destination—to Sanderson Field in Shelton, Washington. Where the hell is it, and what will I find when we get there?"

"I'll look it up on the computer. Give me a couple minutes," Darrell replied. While they waited, Walter pulled two bottles of water out of his bag and handed them to his passengers. He fetched a third bottle for himself and took a drink, displaying an attitude of 'business-as-usual' calm. The 'couple minutes' seemed like half-an-hour, but Darrell's voice was almost cheerful—*I told you so!* was the underlying message. "To get to Sanderson (SHN), turn left to heading 328 at Olympia, and go nineteen miles. It's unattended, but they've got a fine five-thousand-foot runway. As I recall, they even landed a retired 747 there some years ago—of course, it never took off again." He rattled off more information about runway direction and elevation, radio frequencies, etc., as Walter took notes on his clipboard. "You've got good weather and visibility all the way, so you shouldn't have any problems. Going north out of Olympia, Shelton is the first town you'll come to, and the airport is three miles northwest of the town, right alongside US 101. If you get to the Hood Canal, you've missed it—turn around and come back about eight miles."

"Got it," Walter said. He read off the passenger information to Darrell and requested, for the benefit of his passengers, that he file a flight plan with McMinnville FSS.

"Have a good day," Darrell replied, which Walter took to mean that the Feds were already on their way to Shelton.

Walter turned to his passengers. "OK, we're all set for Sanderson Field. It's about ten miles closer than Boeing Field, and there should be a lot less traffic, so I expect we'll get there a few minutes sooner—if I can find it." His passengers didn't seem to get his joke—or if they did, they weren't amused. "Please do not talk during takeoff and landing, so I can be sure to hear all communication from Air Traffic Control. At other times, it's OK if you talk to each other or even to me, but stop immediately if you hear incoming radio messages. And *never* use your cell phone at any time. If you need to call somebody to confirm our arrival time, do it now."

Fath looked at Hazik, and Hazik nodded 'yes.' Fath took out his cell phone and keyed in a number. The conversation was short, but in a language Walter did not understand. He did, however, recognize a few words like 'Sanderson' and '1100 hours' and '*inshallah.*' Fath closed the phone and put it in his pocket. "Let's go," he said.

Walter started the engine, set the radio to 124.200 MHz, the Seattle Air Route Traffic Control Center frequency, and taxied to the east end of the runway. He paused there and turned to check on his passengers again; Fath looked reasonably calm and relaxed, but Hazik was nervously fingering his prayer beads. Walter smiled, revved the engine, and said loudly, "*Allahu Akbar!* (God is Great!)" as he released the brakes. Climbing through 3,000 feet off the ground, Walter called Seattle ARTCC, gave his plane number and type, present position and altitude, and requested "flight following to Sanderson Field at Shelton, Washington." The Air Traffic Controller gave him a four-digit number that he dialed into the plane's transponder to allow their flight to be monitored on radar until just before they landed at Sanderson.

They continued climbing to 8,500 feet en route back to the Klamath Falls VORTAC, where they turned northwest, heading right up the center of Upper Klamath Lake. Minutes later they had a beautiful view of Crater Lake, just off to the right and only a few hundred feet below. At Eugene, they turned north toward Portland, and at the Battle Ground VORTAC just beyond, veered slightly left to heading 329. At Olympia, about 100 miles farther north, they again turned northwest, and began their descent. Fifteen minutes later they flew over Shelton, turned left, and landed on Runway 23. Once clear of the runway, Walter radioed Seattle Air Traffic Control and Flight Services of their arrival, then taxied to the Olympic Air maintenance facility on the north side of the airport, and parked in the line of other private planes on the ramp. When he cut the engine, Fath took out his cell phone and made a brief call.

As Walter was escorting Fath and Hazik toward the Olympic Air hangar, a rather rotund man in a black windbreaker got out of a car in the parking lot and waved to them. Hazik apparently recognized him and started walking in his direction, with Fath following close behind. Walter stopped and watched them shake hands before 'Windbreaker Fats' ushered them into his car. As they backed out of their parking space and pulled away, Walter noted the make, model, and color of the car, as well as four of the seven digits on the license plate. He followed the car with his eyes all the way out of the airport and onto the highway, heading north. Once they were out of sight, he called Darrell to report their successful arrival and give him the car information.

That done, Walter had nothing to do but wait for two hours, according to the schedule. He walked into the maintenance hangar, looking for a toilet, and learned that Skydive Kapowsin, in the next hangar north, operated a café. So instead of the peanut-butter-and-jelly sandwiches he brought along for his lunch, Walter treated himself to a big plate of fresh Hood Canal shrimp. After lunch, he took a walk around the airport, but there really wasn't much to see: one active runway (plus vestiges of a former north-south runway), the Olympic Air and Skydive Kapowsin hangars, and a number of smaller hangars for private planes. *An unlikely place for a covert rendezvous*, Walter thought.

Shortly after noon he retreated to his plane to sit and watch the grass grow. He would have liked to read or even take a nap, but he wanted to gather more information about the car when his passengers returned. Alas, it was not to be, because he didn't see the car approach, and it immediately turned around and sped off as soon Fath and Hazik got out. Instead of the four pieces of baggage Walter had expected, Fath was carrying one moderately sized suitcase and Hazik only his briefcase. Walter intercepted them on the ramp and explained that he needed to weigh the suitcase in order to properly balance the aircraft. However, Fath would not allow him to carry it, so they all paraded into the Olympic Air building where Walter had located a baggage scale. The suitcase weighed in at just under 50 pounds.

Once they were all settled in the plane, Walter made a phone call to Darrell to report his Estimated Time of Arrival at Wilderness, 1530 hours, and radioed Seattle Flight Services to activate the flight plan for his return flight. He started the engine, contacted Seattle ATC, and they were off. The flight back was uneventful, although Fath and Hazik were fidgety, not so much *nervous* as *excited*.

They were about ten minutes ahead of his ETA when Walter landed the plane at Wilderness. He taxied to the same spot where he had parked earlier and shut down the engine. As his passengers got out, Walter reached into his flight bag and brought out one of the jars of Garlic Stuffed Olives he had bought at Granzella's, then positioned himself between the plane and Fath's car so they couldn't get away without paying him. As Fath and Hazik approached, they saw the olives and got the hint. Fath set the suitcase on the ground and opened it, using his body to block Walter's view of its contents. Hazik put a latex glove on his right hand, reached into the suitcase, took something out, and Fath quickly closed the suitcase. The 'something' turned out to be a 'brick' about 2.5 by 6 by 2 inches, wrapped in light brown paper. Without touching it with his bare hand, Hazik gave it to Walter and said something like "*Shock-run.*" Walter took the 'brick' in one hand and gave the olives to Hazik with the other. "This is a little present for you. I bought it in California last week. I hope you like stuffed olives," he said, speaking more to Fath because he wasn't sure how much Hazik could understand. Then, guessing that Hazik had said 'thank you' in Arabic, he looked Hazik in the eye and added his own imitation of "*Shock-run,*" coming close enough to evoke smiles from both Hazik and Fath. As the pair hurried off to Fath's car, Walter went back to his plane, flipped the camera switch to the 'off' position, and got himself underway to Kingsley.

It was almost 1600 hours when he radioed ATC and Flight Services to report the termination of his flight. Grabbing his flight bag, water, charts, and clipboard, he walked to the Operations Center. Darrell was waiting just inside the door. "Welcome back," he said, flashing a broad grin. "The party's in the conference room. You go entertain the guests while I unload the camera." The same pair of Federal agents Walter had met a day earlier were there to greet him, but today they were in a better mood. In an offhand, almost collegial, sort of way they told him they had been able to scramble agents from Olympia in time to meet Walter's flight at Sanderson. They said their associates had tracked the car that picked up Fath and Hazik to an area of exclusive waterfront homes in Union, Washington, some eight miles north, and had taken numerous pictures of Fath, Hazik, the driver, and the car.

Walter contributed his piece of the 'show and tell' by putting his flight bag on the table. He suggested that the agents put on latex gloves before removing 'the brick' which he assumed was his payment. The agents set about delicately opening the wrapper as if they were performing brain surgery, an 'operation' taking several minutes, while Walter paced nervously, worried about whether he had gotten paid or stiffed. To his joyful relief, it was the former; the 'brick' consisted of five-hundred pristine $100 bills, just as they had come from the US Bureau of Printing and Engraving via the Federal Reserve Bank system. The agents explained that they were going to take the wrapper and all the money as evidence, giving Walter a signed receipt for same, and if he gave them the number of his bank account, they would have fifty-thousand dollars deposited to that account within three days. This inspired Darrell, who had returned with the disk drive from the camera system, to comment, "Isn't it wonderful to have the US Government launder this money for you? When it shows up in your bank account, please stop by and settle up your bill with me. I should have it figured out by then."

The Feds were also interested in the suitcase Fath and Hazik had picked up in Union and which supplied Walter's cash payment. Walter said it weighed about fifty pounds, causing them to guess it might have contained forty 'bricks': $2,000,000. "How big was it?" they wanted to know.

"It was relatively small, maybe 18 by 24 by 6 at the most," Walter estimated, and a brief flurry of calculation by 'the suits' confirmed that it was about the right size to hold forty 'bricks.' With that, Walter was free to go, although the Feds reassured him they would be happy to meet with him again if he had any subsequent recollections from the trip that might interest them. Walter was walking on air as he left the building. He glanced at his watch. *Susan should be home from work by now.*

Another joyous greeting awaited Walter at Susan's house, almost matching the passion two days earlier. Susan was relieved that the flight had gone well and Walter had not been abducted or shot and left to die on the tarmac. Walter tried to convince her that his passengers had been perfect gentlemen—docile, even timid about their first flight in a small plane—and his impromptu gift of Garlic Stuffed Olives had delighted them. His account of the suitcase full of money and his payment of a 'brick' of $100 bills brought a big smile to her face, especially when he explained it would enable him to continue living in the cabin another year if he wanted to. All this good news warranted some kind of celebration, so off they went to a local Italian eatery to pig out on lasagna.

Over dinner, the conversation turned to Susan's activities during Walter's California sojourn, in particular her biweekly meetings with Lottie. "I told you how unhappy I was over how our first two meetings went in June. I knew I had to do something different if I hoped to get different results, and I hit on the idea of asking Lottie to tell me about her childhood. She certainly didn't need any urging to talk about herself—she did that, and only that, right from the get-go—but I had to move her past the two major events that have shaped her life in the past several years—namely, the bombing of the Muslim enclave that she ordered when she was Governor of Texas, and the subsequent retaliation against her family. In our third meeting, in mid-July, she tried to keep doing what she had done in the first two, but with some gentle persistence I was able to get her to talk about how she came to be elected Governor. In the next two meetings, while you were in California, we continued with that, going into how she met her husband, where she went to college, and so on. Consequently, I'm beginning to get a picture of what her childhood interests were, and I hope to resurrect some of those interests to move her out of the funk and isolation she's wrapped herself into. It's way too early to declare success, but I think we're getting somewhere."

Walter was impressed, not only with Susan's insight and skill, but also with her patience and compassion, and he said so. He asked whether Susan might be able to persuade Lottie to have a two-or-three-hour meeting with her so Ted could go fishing with him and Mac. "Yes, I think so" Susan replied. "I'll bring it up when I meet with her this week. If she's receptive to the idea, you might even go fishing when I meet with her in September. But how do I arouse her receptivity and how do I sustain it long enough for her to allow Ted out of her sight all afternoon?"

Walter mulled this over and came up with a suggestion. "You might be able to get her really absorbed in telling her life history by asking her whether she has ever considered writing a book, an autobiography even, like many other political figures have done in recent years."

Susan wrinkled her nose. "That would certainly play to her enormous ego, but this woman definitely doesn't impress me as being highly literate. She's tough and shrewd, with lots of 'street smarts,' and she's certainly a good public speaker, but I doubt she ever wrote any of her own speeches after she got out of high school."

"The same could be said of several former Presidents," Walter countered, "yet they managed to inflict their memoirs on the public. There were thousands of 'ghostwriters' who were salivating to help them do it for a small cut on a book likely to sell a million copies or more. With the right agent, the right marketing,

I'm sure Lottie could get a lucrative contract from a major publisher—not that she needs the money—and the publisher or agent could find a skilled writer to shape the words from her mouth into acceptable prose."

Susan considered his idea, and the more she thought about it, the better she liked it. "Yes, I think that would work. Walter, you're a genius."

"Not really," he said, "but sometimes I do get inspired by certain people in certain situations. For example, I have this friend Susan ...."

68.

As usual, Susan had Friday off, so Walter stayed over at her house Thursday night. Before they went out to his cabin after Friday lunch, they stopped by his bank to see if the fifty 'large' had been deposited in his checking account. It had, so they drove out to Kingsley Field to settle his account with Darrell. Darrell had the bill ready, and the amount was very reasonable, less than $1,500, so Walter wrote a check right on the spot. Since Darrell was in a generous mood, Walter asked him what it would cost to rent the Cessna 182T for three days, October 3-5, to be flown to San Jose on Friday, parked all day Saturday, and flown back on Sunday. A peek out the window revealed that the Cessna was parked right outside, and Walter took Susan out to show her the plane while Darrell pecked at his calculator. Susan was duly impressed, or so she said, and when they came back to the office, Darrell told Walter his estimate of cost. Walter was more pleased than ever and gave his immediate acceptance, subject to confirmation after he checked with Angela about the kids' availability.

"Before you go," Darrell said, "I'd like you to see a segment of the video from the cockpit camera on Tuesday." He turned the monitor on his desk so Susan and Walter could see the screen and punched a few keys on his computer keyboard. The image on the screen showed Fath and Hazik in the rear seats of the Cessna as Walter taxied it to the end of the runway just before taking off from Wilderness Airport. Fath's bravado facade was starting to come apart, and Hazik's prayer beads were getting a sweaty workout. Then Walter's voice was heard to boom, "*Allahu Akbar!*" The look on both passengers' faces turned to abject horror and persisted for several seconds as the plane's engine came up to full power and they accelerated down the runway. Darrell broke into uncontrolled laughter, with Susan and Walter joining in. When they calmed down, Darrell asked, "Whatever inspired you to holler that?"

"I dunno," Walter answered. "It's how Muslims begin their prayer five times a day, so I thought it would be appropriate, especially after I saw the prayer beads. Later I remembered that the '9/11' terrorists were alleged to have shouted it just before their planes crashed into the Twin Towers and the Pentagon, and I was a little concerned I had gone overboard, that I had given the impression we were taking off on a suicide flight. Consequently, I didn't say anything when we took off at Sanderson, but I don't think Hazik was clutching his prayer beads then either."

"No, he was clutching his two million dollars," Darrell said.

"Well, I'm glad to see he got his priorities sorted out," Walter quipped.

Later that evening, when Walter and Susan were discussing the details of their planned trip to San Jose in October, Susan looked sternly at Walter and said, "Don't you *dare* shout *'Allahu Akbar'* or pull some other stunt like that on my first plane ride."

"OK," Walter replied, his devious mind already scheming ways to have a little fun at her expense. "I was thinking of giving you a set of prayer beads during the preflight briefing, but I guess I'll have to come up with something less obvious. Would you like me to have a priest come bless the plane before we go? Or maybe a shaman from the Klamath tribe?" Susan laughed, but only a little. "I know," Walter said. "I'll give you some diapers."

69.

Shortly after lunch two weeks later, Walter drove his pickup up the lane to Ted's. Susan got out and went in the house for a scheduled three-hour conversation with Lottie, while Ted put his fishing gear under the truck's tonneau cover and climbed into the passenger seat. Walter drove to Dairy to pick up Mac at their usual rendezvous spot, then headed toward Bly on Highway 140 while Mac engaged Ted in talk about fly fishing. It seemed Ted had done a good bit of it, that it had been his principal hobby when he was working his way up the ladder in the financial world. On the other hand, he hadn't touched a fishing rod, except to store it, since he had met Lottie. He had hoped to interest her in fishing, especially since it was not a spectator sport, but so far he'd had no success. Her fears of being abducted or murdered by Muslims had intensified to the point of obsession in the past year, despite Mac's best efforts and his as well. "I hope you don't take this as criticism, Dr. McCarter, because I know you are doing the best you or anybody else can do," Ted said. "It seems Lottie can't let go of her fears because she doesn't have anything else." Mac nodded agreement but said nothing, allowing Ted to steer the conversation back to fly fishing, in keeping with the reason he was there: to get a little respite from Lottie and his concerns about her.

Soon Ted and Mac were chattering about the various places they had fished. It was obvious that Ted's experience was much broader, because he had had the means to travel to the best fishing locales in the world and hire the top fishing guides. As Walter listened to Ted's muted boasting, he recalled an unguarded remark Mac had made to him in a moment of candor at Odell Lake: something to the effect that 'all relationships between males begin as a dick-measuring contest and most never advance beyond it.' That thought must also have come to Mac's mind again as he brought the discussion back to the 'here and now,' the Sprague River, which he unapologetically characterized as 'one of the best of the cheap and easily accessible places and by far one of the cheapest and most easily accessible of the best places.'

His timing was perfect—no sooner were the words out of his mouth than Walter turned off Highway 140 to the parking area for their favorite spot. As they unloaded their tackle, Mac gave a few suggestions regarding lures—"spinners work well here"—and wading versus bank fishing—"it's not that deep, but check for holes before each step." They went their separate ways, and for the next ninety minutes each was in his own world, inhabited only by the sky, the water, the fish, and himself. Then, as if their internal alarm clocks had been synchronized, they began to look around to see where the others were and to slowly migrate to a spot near the truck. Walter had two good-sized rainbows, "enough for tonight's dinner with Susan," Mac had three, and Ted had one, but he also had a *big* German Brown that could have fed all of them and their spouses as well. *Ted won that contest too*, Walter observed. As they put their catch in Mac's cooler and their tackle alongside it in the back of Walter's truck, Mac said, "I know time is short, but I'd like to go by the Coyote Café for a cup of coffee so Ted can experience some of the local color." Turning to Ted, he added, "When the revolution comes, it may well start there."

It was obvious from the dearth of vehicles in the parking lot that the Café was not busy. As they stepped inside, Walter saw that less than half the tables were occupied, but the one in the left front corner caught his immediate attention. Seated at it were Hazik and another man Walter had never seen before. Hazik looked in Walter's direction but didn't acknowledge him, so Walter looked away and followed Mac and Ted to a table toward the back. However, after they had ordered coffees, he saw Hazik's associate looking in their direction, as if Hazik had pointed them out. In a low voice, Walter said, "Don't turn around and look, but one of the passengers I flew to Seattle last month is sitting at the table in the front corner. He's the older one, facing the door, and his name is Ali Hazik."

Walter had told Ted he was going to fly two passengers to Seattle and back, but no further details about the gig, so it was 'new news' to Ted that they were Muslims. He looked surprised and shocked, and he hunkered down in his chair as if he did not want to be noticed. He couldn't hide, however; when Hazik and his friend got up to leave, Hazik came over to Walter and thanked him for the 'delicious olives from California.' In the process he got a good close-up look at Ted, leaving Walter and Mac to wonder if that was his real purpose in being sociable. After Hazik was out the door, Ted glared at Walter and growled, "You didn't tell me you were doing business with Muslims."

Speaking slowly and evenly, without emotion, Walter replied, "I chanced to sit next to another Muslim, the other passenger I flew to Seattle, at the Firearms Training class back in July. He called me while I was in California and contracted with me to rent a plane and fly it for him, which happened two days after I got back. I thought the whole thing was just a coincidence, and I never expected to see either of my passengers again. Today was just another coincidence, although Mac and I have learned that a group of Muslim men is living at a ranch less than two miles from here. We're sure both of my passengers are part of that group."

Ted looked at Mac for corroboration. Mac nodded his head up and down, saying nothing, but after a minute of silence to sort out how much he should divulge, he explained, "Whenever I come to Bly to fish, I like to stop by this Café because it's the main hangout for the over-forty men in town, and I can usually pick up some local gossip while I eat lunch. It's how I check the pulse and temperature of the 'good old boy' segment of the community. It's also how I keep track of the Muslim group because the 'good old boys' in Bly are well-connected into the Jefferson State Militia, and the JSM is watching Frisco Ranch like a wake of hungry vultures." Walter could see a smile starting to creep across Ted's face, and he seemed to relax, only to tense up again as Mac continued. "The problem with this surveillance is it's a two-way street, as I've just realized. This is now the second time we've seen one of the Muslims in here, so it appears they are coming to the Coyote Café to keep an eye on the JSM. Either they are very cocksure or very naïve."

They finished their coffees and got back in the truck. As Walter pulled out onto Highway 140, Mac said to Ted, "There's more I think you should know, but I didn't want to blab it while we were in the Café. When the Muslim guy contacted Walter about flying to Seattle, Walter immediately came to me and I ran it by my friends in one of the Federal agencies that maintain a presence hereabouts. The upshot was that they wanted Walter to accept the assignment so they could get some intelligence on who or what is behind the Muslims in Bly. The caper was successful and we now know—*we now have evidence that will stand up in court*—that the money behind this Muslim group is coming straight out of a bank vault owned by the company you used to work for."

Ted gasped, and so did Walter. After a pregnant pause, Ted stammered, "You're telling me my former business associates, the ones I testified against in the past and I will probably testify against several more times, have hired this bunch of Muslims to come after *me*?"

"You got it," Mac said. "The Feds have already checked far enough into the backgrounds of Hazik and his buddies to know they are not hard-core Muslim *jihadis*, but wannabe college students who are trying to earn enough money to go back to school. They are not terrorists, nor are they sympathetic with terrorist causes and tactics, insofar as we can tell. The Feds now believe the guys in Bly are not especially motivated to settle a score with Lottie. If they happen to do some damage to her when they take you out, that's just gravy."

Walter glanced over at Ted. He was white as a sheet, struggling to breathe. For a moment Walter thought he would have to pull over and administer CPR, but Mac was closely monitoring the situation. Nevertheless, Walter decided to head directly to Ted's house and get him lying down before taking Mac back to his truck. In their haste, none of them noticed the white van parked in the weeds several yards off Haskins Road, just south of where it met Highway 140. The large gray gimbaled dish antenna atop the van was aimed South-southeast, right at Ted's house and Walter's cabin.

At Ted's house Walter pulled up a few feet in front of the doorstep and sounded three insistent beeps on the horn. As Mac helped Ted out of the truck and up the steps, Susan opened the door. "Get him onto a bed, or a sofa, or something," Walter yelled to her. The trio disappeared into the house and Walter unloaded the truck, carrying the cooler into the kitchen. As he was lifting Ted's catch out of the cooler, Lottie came in. "Ted did very well at fishing today," Walter said, presenting the fish to her, "but he got very upset over what happened when we went for coffee. Mac or I can explain it to you later." It was his first—and, as it would turn out, his only—face-to-face meeting with Lottie. She grabbed a wad of paper towels, spread them on the counter, and plopped the rainbow and the big German Brown onto it. Then, without saying a word, she turned and hurried back to the bedroom where Mac had taken Ted. Susan came out and Walter handed her the two trout he had caught. "Here's our supper tonight. Take them back to the cabin and I'll clean them when I return from delivering Mac to his truck at Dairy."

"What happened to Ted?" she asked.

"He got more than a little disturbed by what Mac told him about the Muslims in Bly. I think he'll be OK if he rests a while."

Mac reappeared, trailed by Lottie who looked more confused than worried. "There's no need to call an ambulance unless he's had a history of heart trouble," he advised. Lottie nodded her head 'no.' "Susan, please stick around for a while to help everybody get back on track."

"See you at the cabin," Walter said to Susan as he picked up the cooler and returned to the truck. "If Lottie doesn't know how to clean Ted's fish, take them back to the cabin and I'll do it," he called back.

Riding back to Dairy, Mac reflected on what had happened. "That was mighty rough on Ted, and I'm sure it will unnerve Lottie when she talks with him. It might be a good idea for you or Susan to stay close through the weekend. I'm booked for Odell Lake tomorrow afternoon through Sunday evening, but you can always call me in an emergency."

"We'll handle it," Walter responded.

"Don't use cell phones if you can possibly avoid it. I think mine has been compromised recently, although the land line into my house is still relatively secure. Susan's home phone is probably OK, too."

"If all else fails, we can try 'Pig Latin.' That's what Darrell suggested I do on the flight to Seattle if I had to say something on the radio that might anger Fath and Hazik."

Mac laughed. "That's an old trick, but nobody knows for sure how well it works until it's too late. Maybe its greatest benefit is that you think it's a viable safety net." *Sort of like 'the placebo effect,'* Walter mused.

They were arriving at Dairy, and he had some parting words for Mac. "Thanks for covering my tracks with Ted at the Café. For a minute there, I thought he was going to strangle me for daring even to talk to Muslims. When he found out the greatest threat to him is not Muslim *jihad* but good old American revenge, it was quite a shock. All the same, I'm glad he knows it now because it puts him and me on the same page regarding who might invade his territory and what their primary objective is likely to be. That's important because Ted seems to regard my presence in the cabin as part of his line of defense."

"And so do I," Mac replied. "Keep up the good work."

"Yessir!" Walter saluted. Mac chuckled and returned the salute as he got out of the truck.

When Walter got back to the cabin, he found Susan sitting on the front porch along with Abigail. He gave her a long hug and kiss—Susan, that is—and asked, "What's with the duck?"

"She followed me back," Susan said. "I think she wants some of the fish. Speaking of which, you've got some work to do." They went inside and Walter cleaned the fish, both his and Ted's. When he was finished, Susan offered to return Ted's fish while Walter got started on supper. As he watched her head down the path, he saw Abigail following along once again. Susan didn't come back until twenty minutes later. "Ted is up and doing fine," she reported, "but he insisted I stay and listen while he told Lottie what had happened." She repeated what Ted had said, and Walter confirmed it was accurate.

"Mac wants me to stay here this weekend—you too, when you're not working—to keep an eye on Ted and Lottie. He thinks our presence will reassure them and calm them down."

"OK," Susan said, "but I've got to see that Moses is taken care of. My neighbor has a key to the back door of my house, and Moses recognizes her as a friend, so I'll call her." She took Walter's cell phone out to the front porch, returning in a couple minutes. "It's all set. She'll let Moses out to pee in the back yard and put some food in his dish. We can bring him out here tomorrow."

As they sat down to the supper of pan-fried trout Walter had prepared, he said, "You've heard all about my outing with Mac and Ted. How did your afternoon with Lottie go?"

"Very well," Susan replied. "I got her to start telling me her life story, and she didn't want to stop. I finally broke in and asked her if she had ever considered writing it all down in a book. At first she rejected the idea, saying she wasn't a good writer, but when I suggested she could work with a ghostwriter like other prominent political figures have done—I mentioned a few—it got her attention. I think she'd still be babbling about it if Ted hadn't come home all bent out of shape."

Walter chewed his food and pondered the day's happenings. "I think when we look back on all this in a month or so, we'll see that today marked a significant turning point for both Ted and Lottie."

Susan considered that and answered, "Yes, and it may be a turning point for us too."

70.

Susan was scheduled to work the next day, so Walter got up early and made breakfast. He dropped her off at her house, went grocery shopping, and then drove back to the cabin. As he was unloading groceries, Ted strolled into the clearing. "Good morning. How are you feeling?" Walter asked.

"Much better, thank you," Ted answered. "I want to thank you for cleaning the fish last evening. I could probably have done it, but it was considerate of you to handle that chore while I was discombobulated. We ate some of the fish for supper, and it was delicious."

"Susan and I also ate the two rainbows I caught. Fresh-caught trout tastes so much better than the frozen stuff they have at the supermarket."

Never one for small talk, Ted moved on to the real reason for his visit. "Now that I'm 'combobulated' again, I was wondering if you would like to join me in some target practice, as you mentioned a couple months back. We never got around to it, but what we learned yesterday has moved it up in priority, at least for me."

"OK," Walter said. "When do you want to do it?"

"How about now?"

Wow! Walter thought. *He certainly has moved it up in priority. Fear has a way of getting people's attention.* "Let me get these groceries into the house and grab my gun. I'll meet you at your place in five minutes."

As Walter walked down the path to Ted's, he recalled an earlier conversation in which he said something like, "you don't have an AK-47, do you?" and Ted had just smiled. Now Walter had the answer: it was, "No," but the smile meant, "I've got something better," in this case an Uzi-Pro submachine gun. *It's a funny-looking thing,* Walter thought, *not quite a foot long with the stock folded,* but he had no doubts about its capabilities.

Ted led the way northward up a broad path between the house and an outbuilding. Seeing the power line half-hidden in the trees alongside, Walter realized they were going to the helipad he had spotted from the air. When they got there, Ted propped up two 3x3-foot pieces of cardboard against trees on the east side so they would be shooting away from his house. "Try not to hit the landing lights," he said with a grin.

Walter shot first, from about thirty paces away. His first round missed the target altogether, his second caught an upper corner, and the third was far enough to the side it knocked the cardboard over. Aiming at the second target, he put all 13 bullets remaining in his magazine into a two-foot circle in the center. *Pretty damn good,* Walter thought, *considering how long it's been since I've fired this thing.* "Not bad," Ted said. "Now let's see what I can do." Firing at the second target from the same distance, he emptied the fifty-cartridge magazine in less than three seconds, shredding the cardboard into a gazillion pieces. Walter was astounded that a weapon so small could deliver so much firepower so quickly.

"Where did you get that thing?" he gasped. "I didn't know guns like that were sold to the public."

"They aren't," Ted said with a wink. "With enough money and the right connections, one can cease to be public." *Of course!* Walter thought. *That's the space Ted's been living in for however-many years, and I'm living right on the public/ nonpublic boundary.*

They put the first target back into place and retreated to a firing position about 90 yards away, well outside the effective range of Walter's Beretta and close to the Uzi's maximum. Walter decided not to waste his ammunition because anything he hit would be mostly luck. Ted fired intermittently, apparently trying to gain enough control to limit the bursts to a few shots. The cardboard held up through about thirty rounds, then collapsed. Ted shrugged and gave up.

On the way back to the house, he pointed to one of the outbuildings and said, "I think it's time you knew there's a secure, fireproof bunker underneath that, with enough provisions to last Lottie and me for a couple weeks. That's our third line of defense, this is our second"—he held up the Uzi—"and you're our first. WitSec's helicopters and US Marshals are the last."

Walter replied, "Actually, I don't see myself as the first, because I think there is a line of defense beyond your property based on local law enforcement and maybe the Jefferson State Militia too. And there may even be another line of defense beyond that, one consisting of relationships between people like you and me and 'outsiders' like the Muslim group at Bly. Mac is putting considerable effort into developing and maintaining it, and into connecting it with the investigative side of law enforcement through intelligence gathering. You got a small glimpse of it yesterday, which was why he took you to the Coyote Café. He's been taking me there ever since we started fishing the Sprague River four months ago, so I've been recruited into his network whether I want to be or not."

Ted thought this over and replied, "Yeah, I can see that now. I guess I also recruited you into my personal militia when I rented the cabin to you."

"That was intentional, wasn't it?" Walter said, consciously keeping an accusatory tone out of his voice. "That was why you fixed up the cabin and put it up for rent in the first place."

"Uh-huh." After a few seconds, Ted added. "It looks like we all got more than we bargained for—you, me, Susan, Lottie, and Mac—and it ain't over."

"No, it won't be over until we finally realize it's over, and we may be the last to know. In the meantime, I'm beginning to come around to Mac's point of view, based on the dictum 'an ounce of prevention is worth a pound of cure.' If we keep focusing on fear, we're going to need a helluva lot of cure."

71.

Mac had figured out Walter's schedule, at least to the point of knowing he spent most Thursday and Friday nights at Susan's house because Susan had Fridays off. He called there the following Thursday, after his weekly counseling session with Lottie, and asked both Susan and Walter to get on the line. "Lottie appears to be making some major changes in her attitude as a result of her discussion with Susan last week and what Ted learned from Walter and me. She's all hot-to-trot for writing a book about her life, which is the first sign of any genuine enthusiasm I've seen in her since she became my patient. She insisted that Ted get her a cell phone and install a cell phone booster system like the one at Walter's cabin. She's been contacting old friends and colleagues to network her way to prospective publishers and agents. She also had Ted dredge her old diaries and scrapbooks out of the barn, what few things she had salvaged from her past, and she's started going through them, making notes and an outline."

"How's Ted taking this?" Walter inquired.

"According to Lottie, he's being very supportive. He even made some calls to people he once knew in the publishing world. However, I can't help but think that he's nervous about the exposure, the possibility that more people will find out where they are. He probably wouldn't do it at all if it weren't for the fact that it's primarily Lottie who is getting exposed and they've learned that she's not being threatened nearly as much as they had thought. All the same, if Lottie goes through with this and reclaims some of her former fame in the process, it will certainly conflict with Ted's heightened fears for his own safety, fears that we validated big time in the past few weeks."

"What's your prognosis?" Susan asked.

"I don't know, and that's why I'm calling to get you two up to speed. At present, Lottie's ego is fully engaged, and her history is one of sudden, foolish, even self-destructive actions whenever that happens. She seems not to have learned a damned thing from her past, so I seriously doubt she will moderate her own ambition for Ted's sake."

"You're saying we probably can't save her from herself," Walter said.

"Right, but maybe we can save Ted," Mac replied.

"So what do we do that we haven't been doing already," Susan wanted to know.

"Nothing that I can think of, but just doing it more diligently and more thoroughly. Maybe you can think of something else."

"It's the opposite," Walter said. "We were planning to go to California for a three-day weekend next month. I want to celebrate Susan's birthday by taking her on her first plane ride, and I also want to introduce her to my kids. I think we should cancel the trip."

"No, don't do that," Mac answered. "You've got to live your lives too. We'll put an alternate safety net in place for that weekend. I'll make sure not to book any fishing guide activity so I can be on alert." He paused, then added, "I don't want to sound like a worrywart, but I have a feeling something's got to give sooner or later. In the past my premonitions about these things have usually been on target." He paused. "I'm sorry to bother you with this, but sometimes psychiatrists need counseling too." They all laughed, but it was a nervous laugh, not one of joy.

72.

Mac's premonition took a step closer to becoming history when Susan met with Lottie a week later. In contrast with her uptight aggressiveness in their early meetings, Lottie was lighthearted, almost carefree, revealing that she had found a big-name publisher for her proposed book and was on the verge of signing a contract that would net her a generous advance. However, she was vague, even evasive, when Susan asked her what Ted's reaction was to her new undertaking. It was as if Ted didn't figure into her future in any significant way and his feelings, therefore, didn't matter.

Susan, on the other hand, did matter, or so Lottie said at the conclusion of their hour together. It seemed like she was saying good-bye, but also promising to get back in touch once she got established in her new life. Susan recounted all this to Walter over dinner that evening. "I wish I had already completed the 'Basic Counseling Techniques' course I'll be starting at OIT next week," she said. "I'd be more confident that I'm handling this properly. Do you think we should call Mac about this? Or should you have a chat with Ted?"

"No to both," was Walter's response. "It's for Ted and Lottie to work out between the two of them. As long as they don't appear to be putting themselves or us in danger, we should stay out of it. However, I hope that Ted never finds out whose idea it was that Lottie write a book."

73.

On her birthday Susan got a surprise telephone call from her daughter. Not only did Lucy wish her mother a 'happy birthday,' but she also announced she would be arriving in two days—Saturday, October 4, to be exact—for two weeks of home leave. Susan's first reaction was to scrub the trip to California, but when Lucy heard that, she would have none of it. "Go ahead and make the trip,

Mom," she said. I'll need to sleep for 24 hours to recover from jet lag. I can get the house key from the neighbors to let myself in, and I can feed and walk Moses so the neighbors won't have to." Susan had to admit she was really excited about getting her first plane ride, meeting Walter's kids, and seeing part of the Bay Area, so she agreed to Lucy's proposal. Thus, it was all settled by the time Walter got to Susan's house Thursday evening, except that he had to put in a couple hours helping Susan get Lucy's room ready.

The next morning they were up and out the door to Kingsley Field by 0930 and in the air by 1100. Before Walter headed south toward San Francisco, he gave Susan a brief aerial tour: north over Upper Klamath Lake, then east over Chiloquin following the Sprague River to Beatty, turning sharply right just east of Bly Mountain to approach Bonanza from the North, and finally turning west to follow the highway past Dairy, Stevenson Park, and Olene back to the airport. Now at 7,500 feet he turned south over Susan's favorite bird-watching spot at the Lower Klamath National Wildlife Refuge and followed the western edge of Lower Klamath Lake into northern California. Mount Shasta loomed more than a mile above them and ten miles to the West as Walter set his course for the VORTAC at Red Bluff. South of that, he called Susan's attention to the town of Williams, home of Granzella's, promising to drive her there someday to personally sample their many varieties of olives and other deli delights.

As the low hills closed in from the West and they caught their first glimpse of San Pablo Bay, Walter focused his attention on flying. The dense air traffic generated by three major airports and more than a dozen minor ones in the Bay Area left him little spare time to play tour guide. They passed over Berkeley and Oakland, Susan craning her neck to see the San Francisco-Oakland Bay Bridge, the Golden Gate Bridge, and the much less impressive San Mateo Bridge. Gradually descending, they continued south-southeast some 30 miles past the southern tip of San Francisco Bay before turning at Gilroy and entering the approach pattern for Runway 29 at San Jose's Norman Y. Mineta International Airport (SJC). Susan was fascinated by the large commercial jets landing and taking off on the two 11,000-foot runways to their right, but slightly alarmed at their proximity. Walter, of course, had landed at this airport many times, so he was not bothered by the other aircraft. This time, however, he was landing a diminutive Cessna on the old 4,600-foot runway, and he was relieved that the approach had gone smoothly, with no urgent calls from Air Traffic Control for course or altitude 'adjustments.'

By two o'clock they were lounging by the pool at their hotel in Santa Clara, sipping lemonade, and lunching on plates of appetizers. For dinner Walter drove them back to the 94th Aero Squadron Restaurant located on the west side of the airport. Styled as a rural French farmhouse with a crashed WWI aircraft in the yard, it had a panoramic view of the SJC runways, making it the perfect place for a pilot to take his sweetheart for a romantic dinner. Susan might have preferred candlelight and a waterfront view, but she allowed as how the food was delicious and the service was good.

After breakfast the next morning they drove around the south end of the Bay and north on Interstate 880 and 680 to the Pleasanton-Livermore area where Walter used to live. Rather than confront Angela, Susan remained in the car while Walter went into the house to fetch Katie and Ryan. The kids' introduction to Susan went as Walter had expected: Katie looked her over from top to bottom and probably would have sniffed her like a dog if decorum had permitted, whereas Ryan was too excited about going to the amusement park to do anything more than mutter a halfhearted "Hi."

The day at Great America was an unqualified success for all of them. Ryan and Walter insisted on riding all eight of the roller coasters, even the oldest dating back to 1976, but Katie and Susan had their fill after two of the early-1990s-vintage rides. On the other hand, while the 'menfolk' were scrambling their vestibular systems, the 'womenfolk' were engaged in the delicate and sometimes deadly chess game of 'getting to know you,' wherein each 'move' reveals some part of oneself and/or attempts to entice the other into doing likewise, all the while avoiding emotional land mines whose existence is usually well hidden. Katie wanted to know all about Lucy and Susan's relationship with her, but Susan wisely limited her inquiries to Katie's school interests and aspirations. Consequently, there was no mention of Festus, in keeping with Angela's strict orders to Katie the night before.

The real success of the day was in bonding. By late afternoon, they were at ease with one another, laughing and joking, giving and accepting—*like a family*. Of course, it would take time, a good bit of time, before they were a 'closely knit' family, meaning that they were committed to each other in ways and degrees that would endure hardship as well as pleasure. But they had started down that road, consciously or consciously, and if they paused long enough to 'enter the stillness,' they could feel the connections that had started to form. They arrived back at Walter's former house minutes before Angela's decreed curfew of 9:00 PM. Katie and Ryan were tired but happy from their active day, so they burst through the door and disappeared into their bedrooms leaving Walter to face off with Angela in a nebulous discussion of arrangements for the Christmas holiday. The best that could be negotiated there and then was a mutual 'I'll get back to you' statement, because neither of them was certain where they would be and what they would be doing in December.

74.

Under their originally planned schedule, Susan and Walter would have been in no hurry to leave San Jose the next day, but Lucy's surprise visit to KFalls had changed that. Accordingly, they were underway by 1000 hours and on the ground at Kingsley by 1230. While Walter shut everything down on the plane, Susan called Lucy on his cell phone to tell her they would pick her up in 20 minutes and go out for brunch. Thus Walter's introduction to Lucy took place with Moses doing his customary welcoming dance, although slightly less exuberantly than usual because he was worn out from all the attention Lucy had lavished on him.

In any event, Walter was immediately charmed by Susan's daughter. She was an inch or two shorter than her mother, but more muscular, probably owing to the Army's physical conditioning program. Her hair was black and her skin was darker than Susan's, reflecting her father's coloring, which in turn came from his Spanish mother, as Susan had explained to him during their return flight. Piercing dark eyes completed the picture, giving Lucy a Mediterranean appearance the Army was attempting to exploit in her overseas assignments. At will, she could adopt a soft-and-seductive aura appropriate for the 'Dance of the Seven Veils' or she could put on a steely 'don't mess with me' demeanor along with her boots and camo fatigues. The Lucy that first shook Walter's hand and then lunged into an earnest hug was midway between these two extremes: 'Mama's little girl' in a grown-up Army uniform.

They rode off to Applebee's in Walter's pickup and had just finished ordering when Lucy exclaimed, "Oh! I almost forgot. You had a phone call this morning from a man who said his name was Mac. He wants you to call him ASAP." Walter and Susan exchanged looks that said "Uh-oh!" and Walter went outside to call from the privacy of his truck while Susan and Lucy reconnected after being separated more than eighteen months. When he returned, he had a strange look on his face, one that expressed amusement mixed with sorrow. Susan interrupted her discussion with Lucy to hear what he had to say.

"Lottie has left Ted. On Friday morning, she invented some *cockamamie* reason to send him into Klamath Falls, and while he was gone, she piled her stuff into the Toyota and took off. They found the abandoned car yesterday morning in Reno, Nevada. Last night she telephoned WitSec in Medford to tell them she was dropping out of the program and she would get back to them in a couple weeks. WitSec traced the call to somewhere in the vicinity of San Antonio, but she apparently turned her cell phone off right after that so they couldn't use the GPS feature to pinpoint her location."

"I can't say I'm surprised," Susan said. "I had a feeling she was going to do something like that. Not that I could have stopped her if I had tried."

"Anyhow," Walter continued, "Mac wants me to get back to the cabin after we eat. He said I should find Ted and give him whatever support and comfort he needs—to make sure he's OK and doesn't do anything dumb. So let's eat up, and then I'll take you two back to the house and be on my way. Once I track down Ted and assess the situation, I'll call you with a status report."

Susan turned to Lucy and explained that Lottie and Ted were Walter's neighbors and they were 'going though some transitions.' She promised to fill in the rest when they were back at the house. Both Susan and Walter tried to return their attention to Lucy and continue their conversation with her, but in the back of Walter's mind an alarm was sounding: "*Quack! Quack! Quack!*"

Rather than park his pickup under the carport next to the cabin, Walter drove down the narrow lane to Ted's house and pulled up right in front, just as he had done when he brought his distraught friend home from the Coyote Café. Today, however, Ted was already home, but no less distraught. He opened the front door almost before Walter had turned off the ignition, but he didn't have the energy to muster a greeting. Walter walked slowly around his truck and stood at the foot of the porch steps, waiting to see if Ted would invite him inside or come farther outside himself. "I hear you've become a bachelor again," Walter said, trying not to sound too cheery about it.

"So it seems," Ted replied, "and in more ways than one. Not only did Lottie take off with the car but she also wrung Abigail's neck and left her carcass right where you're standing now."

Walter was stunned, speechless. A jumble of intensifying emotions stampeded through him like a wild herd: first incredulity, then anger, then despair. He wanted to scream and cry at the same time, but he was too overwhelmed to make a single sound. He broke into a cold sweat and began shuddering as on the few occasions after he had had life-threatening 'close calls' in the cockpit. He put one hand on his truck for support and stared at the ground, the alleged spot where Abigail had met her end, seeking confirming evidence of the atrocity, but there was nothing: no signs of a struggle, no telltale drops of blood, no feathery remnant he might pick up and save as a relic. As his grief began to subside, his mind began to probe the symbolic significance of this senseless act. Abigail had been Ted's 'gift' to Lottie, an early attempt to kindle a new interest that would lift her out of her funk. Beyond that, Ted may have known that ducks represent faithfulness in marriage among some cultures, notably Japan and Korea. If Lottie knew that as well, her parting gesture was intended to express defiance and rejection rather than appreciation for Ted's love and devotion. In any event, Walter suddenly felt that he was transgressing on sacred ground that had been consecrated by the brutal murder of his dear companion and 'counselor.' "Let's get out of here," he exclaimed, "ride into town, or somewhere."

"You don't have to twist my arm," Ted answered, pulling the door closed behind him and striding toward the truck with sudden vitality.

Without giving much thought to where he was going or why, Walter drove into Bonanza. As they approached the main intersection, the Longhorn Restaurant & Saloon came into view, and his intuition told him to go there. It was mid-to-late afternoon and business was slow, recharging its batteries in the lull before the dinner hour onslaught. Nevertheless, Nancy was present and primed, and she pranced over to meet them as they came through the door.

"Hi, Walter! How's it hangin'?" she greeted him with a big grin.

"Like a beagle's tongue after a day-long fox hunt," he fired back, hoping to catch her off-guard.

He should have known better than to engage her in repartee. "Well, then, I'd say that hot dog needs a stiff drink!" she retorted. "Who's your friend?"

"This is my neighbor, Ted. Ted, meet Nancy."

"Nice to meetcha, Ted," she said, looking him up and down as though inspecting a steer at a cattle auction. "Would you like a drink too, or would you rather go for a dip in the pool?" she asked, running her hands invitingly down her body to smooth her dress. Poor Ted was speechless. His mind was already a wreck from Lottie's absquatulation, and even several years of sharing his household with her hadn't inured him to the brashness of Texas women. Satisfied that she had subdued both of the men before her, Nancy led them to a booth, wiggling her ass seductively all the way.

"I'm buying," Walter announced as they sat down. "Do you want something to eat?" he asked Ted, all the while leering at Nancy's bountiful body on display within arm's reach.

"It's too early," Ted managed to mumble, still intimidated by Nancy's *chutzpah*. "I'll just have a beer."

Nancy rattled off half-a-dozen brand names, and Ted picked one. Walter decided this wasn't the time to stick with his no-alcohol regimen and said, "I'll take the same."

After Nancy walked away, Ted wagged his head in her direction and asked, "Is she always like that?"

"From what I hear," Walter answered, "what you see is what you get."

"*Humph!*" Ted snorted.

Since he—or, more likely, Nancy—had succeeded in distracting Ted from his troubles for a few minutes, Walter hesitated to return to the subject of Lottie, but his curiosity got the best of him. "If you don't mind, could you take me through what happened on Friday? All I know is what I got from a brief phone conversation with Mac."

Ted sighed and began his sad tale. Over the next three hours—including three beers each, sandwiches, dessert, and coffee—Walter learned that Lottie had apparently been planning her escape for weeks, but somehow Ted had failed to read the signals. It was probably wishful thinking on his part that they could continue living together while she worked on her book. He had helped her set up her own business with her own cell phone, bank account, and credit cards. Meanwhile, she had started sifting through her old records and files to pick out the material she would need to refresh her memory, secretly packing it neatly away in a box she could lift into the car for a quick getaway. More recently, Lottie had also gone through her clothes, making like she was putting away the summer stuff and hauling out the winter items, when in fact she was packing her bags. Then on Friday morning she said she needed a particular kind of sherry for a dish she was making for supper, insisting that Ted go into Klamath Falls to get it right away. It didn't strike Ted as out of the ordinary, so off he went, giving her at least a half hour to put her things in the car, stuff her purse with a few thousand in cash they had lying around the house, dispatch Abigail, and split. She left him a note saying she would get in touch when she got her new life organized, that he shouldn't worry about her because she had lined up several old friends to help her. She said she just couldn't continue living in isolation, that she missed the fame and public attention of her former life. She *didn't* say she was sorry things hadn't worked out better between them, nor did she take any blame for it. That just wasn't her style.

When Ted got home and found the dead duck and the note, he called WitSec, who told him to call the police and ask them to put out a 'BOLO.' The police suggested he go on-line to check credit card charges for clues as to where she had gone. Because he didn't have Internet access at home, Ted had to go to the Library for that, and he didn't get around to it until midday Saturday. The credit card account showed she had bought gas in Lakeview, so Ted figured she was heading down US 395 to Reno or beyond. He called the Nevada Highway Patrol, and they tracked down the car in a parking lot at the Reno airport. After some further checking, they also learned she had chartered a private jet to fly her to San Antonio, making the reservation *a week in advance* and paying for it—$18,000— with the new 'business' credit card that Ted had gotten for her and for which he, not she, was financially liable. The outcome was that Lottie was now with her old friends somewhere in Texas, probably plotting some kind of political comeback or at least a return to public life and notoriety. Ted, on the other hand, had never known that kind of life and never wanted it. Moreover, he felt that since he now had a bounty on his head, he had to stay in the WitSec program.

Just before they started on their sandwiches and third round of beers, Walter ambled off to 'the Men's' to tap a kidney. Nancy nabbed him *en route* and inquired about Ted's availability. "You'll have to ask him yourself," Walter said. "All I know is that he's recently separated from his wife."

"I'd like you to ask him for me," Nancy pleaded. "The management here doesn't like it if I get too aggressive with customers."

"OK, I'll sound him out and let you know before we leave," Walter relented. Back at the table, he put Nancy's proposition in the most neutral terms he could think of. "The waitress thinks you're interesting and attractive and would like you to stop by her place to get better acquainted."

"When?" was Ted's terse reply.

"I dunno. Could be any time, I guess."

On Nancy's next trip to their table, Ted looked her in the eye and asked as nonchalantly as he could, "What time to you get off work tonight?"

She smiled. "Eight o-clock. And tomorrow is my day off."

Ted smiled back. "Please give me your name, address, and phone number before we go." *I wonder if he's going to get WitSec to do a full background check on her,* Walter mused.

Some time later, when Nancy brought their bill, Walter reached out for it, saying "I'll take it."

"OK, you can have it," she said sweetly, "but this is for *him.*" She handed Ted a small piece of paper, folded double. "In case you're wondering, there's no charge for my services outside this establishment. I don't even accept tips."

"I understand—strictly amateur," Ted said.

"The word 'amateur' comes from the Latin word for 'love,'" she cooed. "*Amateurs* do what they do because they *love* to do it." She was grinning lustily now, and Walter detected a hint of blush in Ted's face.

On the way out of town, Walter swung down a back street to point out Nancy's house. "How come you know that?" Ted asked suspiciously.

"She tried to put the make on me earlier this summer," Walter answered. "I almost bit, because I was having a spat with Susan at the time, but I chickened out on Nancy at the last minute."

"You made a good choice. I think Susan is more your type. On the other hand, I seem to be naturally attracted to Texas women."

"Well, if you decide to 'dip into Nancy's pool,' as she picturesquely phrased it, I hope it works out better for you than the previous woman from Texas," Walter joked. Later that evening, just after eight o'clock, he saw the truck headlights as Ted drove away from his house and down the lane to the main road.

75.

For Walter, Monday was a sharp contrast to the jam-packed activity and upheaval of the preceding three days. The change wasn't exactly welcome; it felt strange, empty. When he stepped out onto his front porch for his usual after-breakfast meditation, he saw Abigail's folded-towel nesting spot, reminding him that she was gone forever. Tears streamed down his cheeks as he picked up the towel and her water dish, carried them to the storage shed, and returned to his chair on the porch. His meditation didn't go very well, which came as no surprise, considering all that had happened, but he had learned to keep going despite the discomfort, to work through 'life's shitty little tragedies'—'defilements,' one of the meditation teachers called them—and to not deny their existence by attempting to run away from them. In reflecting on his own life and what he had observed in others, he came to a 'profound realization,' at least for him: *Whenever people get into trouble, they tend to react by repeating the behaviors and thought patterns which got them into that trouble, usually more compulsively than ever.* Now he applied that insight to what Lottie had done in recent days and weeks. Rather than change her behavior to return her husband's love and devotion, she had *intensified* her arrogance and self-centeredness, blithely throwing away her marriage and possibly her safety and security as well. Her outlandish execution of Abigail encapsulated it and added an exclamation point.

Next his thoughts turned to Ted. Walter wished he had been around to observe Ted's immediate reactions while his awareness of Lottie's truculence unfolded. Ted had had more than forty-eight hours to pull himself together by the time Walter got there, so Walter was dealing with 'embalmed information' as he tried to analyze actions and discern motives. *Sort of like measuring IQ with a proctoscope,* he thought. The absurdity of the metaphor was like a whack upside his head; it was futile to even attempt such analysis—that was what the meditation course had been trying to teach. Now backtracking to what he had observed, Walter saw that Ted was not attempting to chase after Lottie. He was letting her go and putting his energy into what was right in front of him: Nancy, at least for the moment. To confirm that, Walter strolled over to Ted's house. Ted's pickup was gone, so Ted wasn't there, Walter inferred. Had he spent the night with Nancy? Walter couldn't tell for sure, because the evidence at hand didn't rule out other alternatives. All Walter could do was bide his time and give his attention to more constructive thoughts and actions. It might not be as much fun as his old habits of speculation and fantasy, but it made life a helluva lot simpler and, in the long run, more gratifying.

If he had had a choice, Walter would have preferred to spend the day with Susan, getting on with grieving over his loss of Abigail, but she had to work, and when she wasn't working, she needed to spend time with Lucy. Although Walter longed to share his sorrow with Susan, he was reluctant to open himself to Lucy—not that much, not yet—so her presence was forcing him to 'suck it up' with time-honored military taciturnity. The compromise was for the three of them to spend the evening together, and when he called Susan the previous night to report on his rescue efforts with Ted, they had agreed that she would bring supper to the cabin after she got off work. That left Walter with little to do by way of preparation, other than a general tidying up, and he spent the rest of the day reading and practicing rudimentary Arabic, especially the Muslim *Salaat.* If Lucy's linguistic training included Arabic, as Susan suspected, perhaps she could help him with pronunciation.

76.

What a difference a day made! The 1934 song, revived many times over the years, was looping through Walter's brain as he awoke the next morning. He'd had a good visit with Susan and Lucy the night before, getting to know Lucy better and *vice versa*. Not that she was willing to divulge much about her career as an Army translator, but yes, she did speak Arabic, which hinted at why she wouldn't say much more than that. It also helped that Susan had brought Moses along. "I thought his presence might compensate for your loss of Abigail," she whispered when Lucy was out of hearing range. "If Lucy weren't visiting, I'd even suggest you keep him here at the cabin for a few days, but I'm carefully picking and choosing the ways I'm introducing her to the changes you have brought into my life. For instance, we had a woman-to-woman chat about you spending the night at my house Thursday night, in my bed as usual, and she's OK with that. You don't even have to worry about putting the toilet seat down. I hope that will repay you for giving Lucy maximum time with Moses while she's here."

"I love you" was the first response that came to Walter's mind, and then he added, "You seem to understand my needs and priorities even better than I do, and you solve problems even before I'm aware they exist. Lucy did a great job training you as a parent."

Susan punched him playfully in the stomach, then gave him a big kiss. Lucy noticed and called, "Hey, you two! Every time I turn my back you've got your hands all over each other. Do you need me to take a walk for a half-hour, or however long it takes for middle-aged half-geezers like you?"

"We're making up for lost time," Walter replied, smiling, "to remind you of the sacrifices your mother made raising you as a single parent."

"I heard all about that last night," Lucy replied. "I'm thankful for my mother's love, and I'm thankful you're here with her now, but guilt I don't need."

Walter laughed and turned to Susan. "I see your daughter inherited your quick wit and sharp tongue."

"Nature *and* nurture," Susan confirmed. "She learned well." Lucy smiled and made a deep bow.

Walter replayed the exchange in his mind, savoring it as he hauled himself out of bed and started the coffee maker. About an hour later, his phone rang. "Good morning," Mac said. "I hope I didn't wake you."

"No, I've been up more than an hour. What's up?"

"Would you be interested in a brief fishing trip this morning? I know it's short notice, but I could meet you at our usual spot at nine-thirty or ten."

"Let's do nine-thirty," Walter said. "See you there." He finished his breakfast, cleaned up the dishes, and got dressed. Then he walked over to Ted's house, just to check on things: no sign of Ted or his pickup. A molecule of worry crossed Walter's mind. *Maybe Ted isn't shacked up with Nancy—maybe he's been abducted, or worse—maybe* .... He shook himself to stop the fearful chatter. *Let's start with the simplest, most benign scenario: he's still at Nancy's. We can go by her place to check on the way to Bly.*

As usual, Mac was waiting with a cup of black coffee for Walter. As he fastened his seatbelt, Walter said, "Let's go through Bonanza. Ted's gone AWOL, but I think I know where to find him." In the six or seven minutes it took to drive to town, Walter gave Mac a quick synopsis of his Sunday afternoon commiseration with Ted at the Longhorn Saloon, ending with the fact that Ted had left his house at about the same time Nancy was getting off work that evening. When they got to Bonanza, he directed Mac down a side street toward Nancy's house, and as they turned to go past it, they saw Ted's dirty white pickup parked right in front.

"Bingo!" Walter hollered. "Either they're still at it or she's doing CPR to resuscitate him for another round."

Mac laughed heartily. "It comforts me to know he's in safe hands and if he dies, he'll go happily." He navigated to Big Springs Park, turned left, and pulled onto Bly Mountain Cutoff at the main intersection. *I forgot,* Walter thought. *Mac was born and raised around here.* As they left Bonanza behind, Mac explained why he had made a last-minute call to go fishing. "Since your trip to Seattle, there's been some chatter building about the Muslim group in Bly, and it's crescendoed in the past couple weeks. I want to hear what the customers at the Coyote Café are talking about, but we can get in an hour or so of fishing first, mainly for the sake of appearances."

With that understanding of the ulterior motive for their trip, they released everything they caught, which was more than usual. *What a shame,* Walter thought, but his anticipation had grown to a high level by the time they walked into the Café. The place was nearly full, with no vacant tables, but two men seated at a table for four motioned for Mac and Walter to join them. As they sat down, Walter recognized them as persons he and Mac had *schmoozed* with during their previous lunches there. Sensing that the stakes were much higher this time around, Walter let Mac take the lead in conversing while he concentrated on scanning the room to monitor the comings and goings and to see who was talking with whom. "Thanks for the seat. Crowded today, isn't it? Is there some special occasion?" Mac asked in a casual tone, sort of like "Gee, the walls are sure perpendicular today!"

"No special occasion," came the answer, "but something is in the wind. The Muslim guys out at Frisco Ranch seem to be getting ready to do something, although nobody outside of there knows what."

"How can you tell? What's happening at the Ranch that makes you think they're about to make a move?"

The reply was a slight retreat from certainty: "I don't have any direct personal knowledge, mind you, but I hear the Muslims are drilling like soldiers and training for some kind of military operation."

"Live weapons fire?" Mac probed.

"Can't tell if it's live, but there has been a good bit of small arms fire, some of it with automatic weapons. Nothing big, though: no grenades, bazookas, or artillery."

"How long has this been going on?" Mac asked.

"Ever since they came here last spring, we've been aware they are well-armed, because they'd take a few shots if somebody got too close or appeared to be snooping around. It seemed they weren't trying to really hit anybody though, just scare them off. Anyhow, about a month ago, they started shooting without anybody provoking them, as if they were practicing, and it's gotten more intense in the last week."

Satisfied with that information, Mac tried a new direction. "Is anybody doing anything about it? Has the Sheriff been notified?"

"I suppose the Sheriff knows, but nobody here has any confidence in his department's ability to do much, especially to respond quickly with enough manpower and firepower to be effective."

Mac backtracked: "How many people do the Muslims have over at the Ranch?"

"Ten or twelve, all of them young, in their twenties, except for their leader. They seem to be in good physical condition, based upon the exercise drill shouts we hear, plus what we've seen around town. A couple of them have even stopped by here now and then."

Scrambling his questions like a professional interrogator, Mac went back to the issue of response. "If people hereabouts feel the Sheriff's Department doesn't amount to a fart in a windstorm, aren't they worried?"

"Yes and no. People are concerned, but they don't know for sure that whatever the Muslims intend to do will happen *here*, in this immediate area. They could be planning to invade Portland, or Las Vegas, or someplace in California."

The second man at the table, who had been silent until then, chimed in, "Maybe they're going to Vegas to kidnap some of them sexy show girls." He grinned lecherously.

His partner gave him withering look and growled, "They'd have one helluva time finding any virgins in Vegas, much less seventy of them." Then in a normal tone, he picked up where he had left off. "The main thing that folk around here are worked up about is the possibility the Muslims will attempt some kind of military action right here in Klamath County. That possibility is why we have the Jefferson State Militia," he said, a tone of pride creeping into his voice. "It's why the JSM was formed in the first place and why a small group of dedicated and loyal citizens maintain it in a state of readiness, whether the Sheriff or any other local law enforcement agency likes it or not—or the Feds, for that matter." That last bit, delivered with a tone of defiance, seemed to have been especially for Mac's and Walter's benefit.

Mac might well have ended the interview at that point, while he was ahead information-wise, but he pressed on, as though there was some urgency in getting every last bit of intelligence. "I gather from what you've said you feel the JSM has adequate resources to match if not overwhelm whatever the Muslims might roll out. Can they deploy it quickly enough? Or to put it differently, how would a common citizen like me call out the Militia if he came into knowledge of an imminent attack? Have you infiltrated the 911 Call Center?"

Walter felt a tension across the table and a hesitancy to rush into divulging too much. In the end, however, pride—ego—prevailed, and the answer came dribbling out. "The Militia has its own intelligence network throughout the county, and that would probably suffice for most situations that might arise"—a sly smile began to appear on the speaker's face—"but a call to '9-1-1' would work too"—the smile became that of the 'cat that ate the mouse.' Now, at last, Mac was satisfied, and Walter could resume breathing normally. They leaned back in their chairs and turned their attention to the food and drink that had been quietly ordered and delivered as the discussion was going on. Their 'friends' meanwhile collected their check from the waitress and got up to leave, apparently confident they had made their day's contribution to Peace, Truth, and Justice.

After they ate, Walter suggested they go back the way they had come, so they could see if Ted's truck was still parked in front of Nancy's. Sure enough, it was, bringing Mac to say, "If Ted isn't back at his house by tomorrow noon, you'd better go yank him out of Nancy's clutches. He needs to be at least somewhat rested and fully alert before the weekend comes. I have a feeling the cork is going to pop real soon and he will be involved somehow." Walter immediately recalled Mac's phone call to him and Susan almost three weeks earlier. Mac's premonition had been right on the money, although the way things had eventually played out was quite different—more bizarre, in fact—than they had imagined at the time. That was only once, but given the stakes, Walter was not about to dismiss Mac's 'feeling' about the cork.

77.

When Walter woke up the next morning, he felt he was back in the military: a man with a mission. His mission, as events had conspired to define it, was to protect Ted from whatever the Muslims at Bly were up to. His orders, from Mac, were to bring Ted back into the security of his house. It wasn't clear how much Mac knew about Ted's bunker or his automatic weapons, but he surely knew WitSec had contingency plans to extract Ted via helicopter as a last resort. The 'first resort' was simply that very few people knew where Ted's house was and the supposition that none of the Muslims were among those very few people. Walter was positioned somewhere between the 'first' and 'last,' but his role there was ambiguous.

With all that buzzing around in his head, he walked over to Ted's house after breakfast; there was still nobody home and no sign of Ted's truck. Next he drove into Bonanza and cruised past Nancy's house; Ted's truck was still there. The problem, therefore, was how to wrest Ted out of Nancy's clutches, and as Walter's mind homed in on that, a rhyme began playing in his brain: *'Leave them alone and they'll come home / wagging their tails behind them.' After three nights and two days with Nancy, Ted's 'tail' is more likely to be dragging than wagging*, Walter thought.

He remembered Mac's 'orders' that Ted be home *by noon*. It was not quite ten o'clock, and *Nancy's workday begins no later than eleven, if she's going to work at all, so I might as well stick around to wait and watch. But where? Ah, the real estate office is right*

305

across the street from the Longhorn. I'll go have a chat with Henry Parsons. As usual, Henry had his feet propped up on the desk and was reading *Ranch & Rural Living Magazine* when Walter walked in. He put the magazine down but left his feet where they were. "Hi, Walter. I haven't seen you since Memorial Day. Been hiding from Nancy?"

"Not exactly, although I admit to staying away from the Longhorn Saloon except on two occasions. The first was when I had forgotten she works there, and the second was more recently when I had a friend I wanted to meet her."

Henry picked up the trail like a champion bloodhound. "That friend wouldn't drive an old white Ford pickup, would he?"

"Yes, as a matter of fact, he does," Walter answered, pretending to be ignorant. "Why do you ask?"

"It's been parked in front of Nancy's house all day Monday and all day yesterday. It was still there this morning when I drove by."

"No kidding?" Walter said innocently.

"They must really be gettin' it on," Henry continued. "Nancy called in 'sick' to the Longhorn yesterday, but nobody minded because Tuesday is a slow day. She hasn't pulled a stunt like that in a long time."

"Really?" Walter said, then tried to change the subject. "What else is news?"

"Not much is actually happening, but the rumor mill is going bonkers. Seems people are expecting the Muslims in Bly to do something real soon."

"Muslims in Bly?" Walter decided to play dumb a while longer to see how Henry's take on the situation lined up with what he'd heard at the Coyote Café.

"There's about a dozen of 'em camped out at the Frisco Ranch. They came last spring. They're pretending to be doing a little farming, building some things so the Ranch can handle a bigger flock of sheep, but they're also doing military training, especially in the past month or so. That's what's got folks all stirred up."

"Do people think they're terrorists?"

"That was the initial reaction, but this bunch of Muslims isn't anything like the genuine terrorists who tried to set up a *jihad* training center at the Ranch fifteen years ago. These guys aren't wild-eyed and crazy acting—they appear to be better educated and somewhat civilized—but that makes things all the more puzzling and frightening. If they aren't bat-shit crazy fanatics, what are they up to? Are they some kind of 'sleeper cell?'"

Walter popped the sixty-four-dollar question: "Is anybody doing anything about it?"

"The local law enforcement guys have their heads in very dark places, as usual. The Feds are nowhere to be seen, and if it's like what happened before, they won't show up until long after the shit hits the fan. But never fear, the Jefferson State Militia is carefully monitoring the situation and is prepared to do whatever is necessary to protect persons and property." *I've heard that line before,* Walter thought.

"What's the Jefferson State Militia?" he asked blithely. Walter was beginning to enjoy this.

"A private group of concerned citizens, patriots in the best sense of the word, who are willing to put their own butts on the line to keep the peace. They're the kind of people who made this nation great."

Following Mac's example, Walter decided to push the envelope. "I hope I never have need of their assistance, but if I did, how would I contact them? Smoke signals?"

Henry didn't laugh at Walter's joke. He put on his best 'official' countenance and said, "You can always call me." *Just as I suspected,* Walter thought. Something on the street out front caught Henry's attention. "Whoa! There she goes!" he exclaimed.

"What?"

"Nancy just drove by. She parks her car next to the park across the street to the east of us. Keep your eyes peeled. You'll see her walk over to the Longhorn in a minute or so." Walter did as Henry directed and soon Nancy slowly walked— 'hobbled' was more like it—diagonally across the intersection. "She's not moving at her usual pace today," Henry observed. "She's acting like she's been rode hard and put away wet." *I wonder what kind of shape the rider is in,* Walter mused, smiling.

He looked at his watch: 10:45 AM. "Gotta go. Thanks for the conversation."

"Stop in any time," Henry said, "especially if you'd like to see some of the properties I've got for sale."

"I might just do that," Walter replied, "after the first of the year." *Henry probably thinks I'm stringing him along,* he thought, *but this time I'm serious.*

Driving home, Walter was of two minds: one was to give Ted some time to get home, take a shower, eat something, and take a nap before Walter knocked on his door; the other was to get to Ted ASAP because he might sleep for several days once he got into bed alone. Walter decided on the second. He pulled up in front of the house and, seeing Ted's truck in the open garage, he beeped his horn several times. The front door opened to disclose an incredibly bedraggled, half-clothed body, but the aura told a different story: blissful happiness. Walter approached, unable to restrain a smile. "Signor Casanova, I presume—or is it the Marquis de Sade?"

Ted managed a weary smile. "I think I just set a new record for *coitus uninterruptus*. Show some respect."

"I can see you need some sleep and rest, as well as food and maybe a transfusion, but Mac insisted that I talk with you as soon as you could tear yourself out of Nancy's arms. We paid another visit to the Coyote Café yesterday, and the 'buzz' is that the natives are restless out at Frisco Ranch. Apparently they're feverishly preparing for some kind of escapade, and based upon what we learned about who's bankrolling them, we believe that you are the object of their intentions. Mac thinks it's all gonna come down soon, so he wants you to be rested and alert. Those were the exact words he used." Ted nodded slowly, as if his brain were unable to take in information at more than ten percent of its normal rate. Walter gave him a little time to catch up, then continued. "To complicate things, I'm planning to spend Thursday and Friday nights at Susan's house in KFalls and most of Friday riding around the county with Susan and her daughter. I'll be back Saturday morning, but if that isn't good enough to keep you feeling safe and secure, speak now or forever hold your peace."

It took Ted a few seconds to decipher what Walter meant by 'holding his piece,' but once he got the intended spelling of 'peace,' he understood. "If we knew for certain when they were coming, I'd insist that you be here, but I just checked my answering service and nobody has called for an appointment. Maybe I'll go hide out at Nancy's place—although I'd hate to make her miss more work."

"Your truck would be a dead giveaway," Walter objected, "and besides, your other layers of defense—your arsenal, your bunker, and the helipad—are all here."

"Yeah, you're right," Ted said somewhat glumly. "I guess I could have her come here. The Muslims could haul us off together."

"You didn't tell her where you live, did you?!" Walter almost shouted. "Or that you're in the WitSec program?!"

"No" came the answer, somewhat tentatively. "At least, I don't think I did."

Seeing Ted's uncertainty, Walter decided to take charge. "Let's plan on you staying here through the weekend—say, until Nancy gets off work Sunday evening. Don't even go out to get groceries. I'll come back over tomorrow morning to get your grocery list and go shopping for you. If you need gas in your truck, I'll drive it into town and leave mine here. OK?"

Not being accustomed to taking orders, Ted suggested some changes. "How about you let me sleep until noon tomorrow? Then come over and we'll drive into town together in your truck. We can eat lunch somewhere—my turn to buy—then get some groceries and I can pick up my car, which has been hauled back from Reno. You got your CCW license, didn't you?" Walter nodded 'yes.' "OK, bring your weapon with you. You can be my bodyguard. I'll leave my guns here because I don't have any kind of license whatsoever." *Fine time to become a law-abiding citizen,* Walter muttered under his breath.

78.

For Susan, Lucy, and Walter, Friday was the day of the big outing to the Mitchell Monument. Susan and Lucy hadn't been there since their fateful picnic beginning the chain of events that nearly propelled them both into the WitSec program fifteen years ago. Susan had ultimately taken a firm stand against totally reconstructing their lives, but her encounter with the Muslims had shaped her existence ever since. There was to be no picnic this time, however; Walter wanted eat at the Coyote Café, not only because of its important role in *his* brief history in Klamath County, but also because he wanted an update on the heightened tensions he and Mac had tuned in on earlier that week.

They arrived at the Monument at about 10:30 AM and spent the next hour poking around, bird watching, and admiring the fall foliage. Then they drove back to Bly for lunch. Walter was not surprised when a hush swept over the room as he walked in with two attractive women. He had harbored a few misgivings about taking Susan and Lucy into the favorite haunt of the local working-class males, so he told Lucy to wear her camo fatigues and Susan to 'dress down' into hiking clothes. Not that he needed it, but he was still carrying his handgun, as per Ted's request when they went into KFalls the day before.

They ordered sandwiches and were diving into a plate of 'coyote howlers' when one of the men from a group across the room walked over and sat down in the empty chair at their table. Walter recognized him as one of the two he and Mac had shared a table with on Tuesday. He pointed at the holster peeking out from under Walter's jacket and said, "I see you're ready for today's excitement."

"What do you mean?" Walter asked.

"Haven't you heard? The gang from Frisco Ranch is gonna make their move this afternoon."

Walter's jaw dropped. "No, I hadn't heard. Where? What time?"

"We don't know exactly, but we're ready. We've got a small group that will follow them when they leave the Ranch, but they won't engage. We'll stay out of sight until we can figure out what they are up to, then we'll call in a larger force, either as one platoon or as several small squads—whatever the situation requires."

"OK, thanks," Walter said. "We'll eat up and hit the road. I'd like to get these women safely home before all the excitement begins."

"Good idea. See ya later—somewhere."

As his 'friend' rejoined his colleagues, Walter turned to Susan and Lucy. "You heard what the man said. I think I should make some phone calls, first to WitSec to get them mobilized, then to Ted to warn him, but I can't do it now. If the guys across the room see me on the cell phone right after they've told me their plan, they might get upset. We've got to eat quickly, but not like we're panicked. When we're a couple miles out of town, I'll pull over and make my calls. We may lose fifteen minutes that way, but I'll be sure to get through to WitSec."

When the waitress brought their sandwiches, Susan asked for take-out boxes, saying they wanted to take part of the food home. That bought at least ten minutes and probably prevented indigestion. Once in the truck, Walter drove to the place west of town where he and Mac fished. After making his calls, he pulled back onto the highway and mashed the accelerator. "I'd like to take you two into town, but there isn't time for that. We'll drop me off at the cabin and then you can take the truck and go." He looked at Susan. "Do you think you can drive this thing?"

Before Susan could reply, Lucy spoke up. "If she can't, I sure as hell can!" *The apple doesn't fall far from the tree*, Walter marveled.

Driving up the gravel road toward his cabin a half-hour later, Walter saw that the narrow lane leading to Ted's house was blocked by a big, black Suburban bearing US Government plates. He pulled up in front of his porch steps and jumped out, making room for Susan to slide over into the driver's seat. As he turned to close the truck door, a figure in black stepped into the clearing. He wore a Kevlar vest and a baseball cap, both with 'US Marshal' printed on them, and he carried an automatic weapon. "Who are you? And what are you doing here?" he demanded.

"My name is Walter Baker, and I live in this cabin. I've been renting it from Ted Wilson, whose house is at the other end of that path. These women are my *fiancée* and her daughter."

The 'Man-in-Black' appeared to relax a little. "I'm Special Agent Robert Jeffries. We understand that a group of Muslims is headed this way with the intention of abducting or perhaps harming Mr. Wilson."

"That's my understanding as well. I found out about it when we were having lunch in Bly about an hour ago, and I'm the person who called WitSec. The best information I have is there are about ten or twelve men in the group, all relatively young, probably college students rather than professional soldiers or fanatic terrorists."

"That fits with what we've been told by other sources," Jeffries said.

"I see you've blocked the lane to the other house, so they will most likely end up here in this clearing," Walter said. "My arrangement with Ted—that's Mr. Wilson—is that I sort of slow them down, talk to them, whatever. I've probably met two of them before, but I can't say I've established much rapport with them. What's your plan of defense?"

"We've got five more agents and one more vehicle at the house. The chopper has already come and gone, so Wilson is safe, no matter what. Our main concern now is to protect the property, plus you, your women friends, and ourselves. I doubt that the women have time to get out of here without meeting the Muslims on the road, so I recommend that they go down to Mr. Wilson's house."

"We'd rather stay here with Walter," Susan called from the truck. "If things get dicey, we can go out the back door and through the woods."

"OK," said Jeffries. "I'm going to stay out of sight initially, back in the brush along the path, so as not to escalate the situation by my presence. If we can downplay confrontation and avoid violence, let's do it."

"Understood," Walter said. "Thank you."

"Good luck," Jeffries said as he faded back into the woods. Susan and Lucy got out of the truck and went into the cabin. Walter followed, taking off his handgun and giving it to Lucy. Then he picked up the *Yusuf* CD and put it in the stereo player. "I may want you to play this at some point," he said.

The sound of approaching vehicles grabbed their attention. Walter picked up a book off the table and stepped out on the porch in time to watch Al Fath's venerable Chevy pull into the clearing in front of the cabin, followed by an equally decrepit pickup. Hazik was riding shotgun in Fath's car, with three others in the back seat; the pickup had three men in the front seat and three more standing in the bed behind, two of them holding AK-47s. Hazik and Fath got out and walked toward Walter. He smiled and said in his best Arabic, which he had rehearsed with Lucy, "*As-salaam alaikum.*"

This clearly took them by surprise, but they managed to answer weakly, "*Wa alaikum.*"

"How may I help you?" Walter asked.

"We come for man who lives here," Fath answered.

"I live here," Walter said, trying to keep an even tone in his voice, neither aggressive nor defensive.

Hazik spoke up. "Not you—other man I see with you in Café—Wainwright."

"One of the men you saw with me in the Coyote Café lives in that house," he gestured toward Ted's, "but I don't know him as 'Wainwright.' He told me his name is 'Ted.'"

"No matter. We take him with us. Wife too," Hazik growled.

"Why?" Walter asked.

"Huh?" Hazik and Fath said in unison.

"Why do you want to take him? What has he done to offend you?" Silence. "I repeat," Walter said, his voice growing quietly assertive, "what has this man, my neighbor, done to offend either of you or any of your colleagues?" He gestured toward the others.

After what seemed like an eternity, Hazik said, "Nothing."

"Do you know of anything he has done to offend Muslims anywhere else in the world?"

"No—but his wife ..."

"We'll discuss her in just a minute," Walter cut Hazik off. "So if he has done nothing to offend any Muslims that you know of, why do you want to take him? Where does the *Holy Qur'an* say that *Allah* gives you the right to do that?" He paused, and when he saw no answer was forthcoming, he pressed on. "Perhaps you don't remember what the *Qur'an* says, but I can lend you my copy if you would like to look it up." He held out the book in his hand. "It has both Arabic and English, so you can choose."

Now Walter looked directly into Hazik's eyes, then into Fath's, then back to Hazik, then Fath again. Fath broke first. "*Qur'an* does not say that," he admitted.

"OK, what about the *hadith*? Did the *Prophet*, peace be unto him, ever take up the sword against any person, any nation, who had not directly offended him?"

Fath, apparently feeling he was on firm ground, responded more quickly. "The Prophet Muhammad, peace be unto him, fight to defend Islam."

"Has my neighbor threatened to attack Islam: the *umma* or the teachings and beliefs? Do you have any reliable evidence of that?"

Again a long pause, then Fath slowly nodded his head 'no.'

"OK, now let's consider my neighbor's wife. I concede that she made some decisions and gave some commands that resulted in injury and death to Muslims in Texas. Were any of those persons related to you, either as your family or your friends?"

Hazik and Fath began talking to one another in Arabic. As they did so, Lucy slid through the door to stand slightly behind Walter, prompting a brief ripple of comment among the Muslims in the vehicles. After a minute of intense discussion, Fath spoke on behalf of Hazik and himself. "Muslims in Texas not our family, not our close friends, but brothers in Islam."

"I accept that," Walter said. "And the *Holy Qur'an* says it is right and proper to avenge violence against other Muslims, but in the case of my neighbor's wife, it has already happened: her husband and her children were killed, brutally slaughtered in their own home. I admit that no proof has ever been offered that the persons who did that were Muslims, but certainly *Allah* has punished her, certainly she has suffered, and I can verify from my experience living as her neighbor that she continues to suffer. How can you justify adding to it? The *Qur'an* permits retribution only in measure to the offense committed."

Another flurry of conversation in Arabic ensued between Hazik and Fath. Lucy leaned forward slightly to hear what they were saying. Finally, Hazik spoke. "What you say is correct."

"Thank you," Walter said. "Therefore, I ask you to leave in peace. Do not make the mistake of committing violence where none is justified." He was about to say 'good-bye' in Arabic when another pickup charged into the scene, squeezing by the Muslims' vehicles and stopping on the opposite side of the clearing. Henry Parsons was driving, and there were four other men in the back of the truck. Walter saw their ill-concealed automatic weapons and stepped quickly off the porch and over to the truck. "Put your guns away!" he shouted. "Don't start a war!"

Henry got out of the truck and stood facing Walter, six feet away. "Hi, Henry," Walter said cheerily. "Thank you for coming. As you can see, I've been having a discussion with my Muslim visitors. I'd like you to meet their leaders." With one hand he signaled Henry to follow him and with the other he motioned to Hazik and Fath to approach. They all met in the middle, beside Walter's truck. Walter made introductions, then continued in his best 'master-of-ceremonies' manner. "As I was saying, we've been having a good, sincere discussion, and my Muslim friends have decided to abandon their mission and go in peace. The crisis is past, because my neighbors are now under US Government protection. There never was any real danger, because they were gone before my Muslim friends arrived." He paused to let this sink in, then went for the wrap-up. "I suggest, Henry, that you allow Mr. Hazik and Mr. Fath and their colleagues to leave and that you wait here at least ten minutes so as to assure them safe conduct back to the Frisco Ranch. If that course of action is acceptable to all of you, I think it would be wonderful to end this gathering by shaking hands." With that, he extended his hand to Hazik, who hesitated, then took it. Almost miraculously, Fath stepped toward Henry, who didn't hesitate. By the time Walter got to Fath, Henry and Hazik had all four of their hands interlocked and were managing faint smiles.

Hazik and Fath went back to their car, and Hazik shouted something in Arabic to the other driver, who started his truck, turned it around, and drove down the road. Fath started to follow, but as he was turning around, Lucy called to him in Arabic, surprising him so much that he almost backed into Walter's truck. Susan came out of the cabin and, together with Lucy, walked over to where Henry and Walter were standing. Again, Walter did the honors, and Lucy broke into a big grin when Walter introduced Susan as his *fiancée*. Several minutes of small talk ensued, with Henry obviously eager to get to know this woman who had sufficiently charmed Walter that he could turn his back on Nancy Norwood.

After Henry had finally driven off with his somewhat disappointed squad of would-be warriors, Special Agent Jeffries stepped out of his hiding place near the edge of the clearing. "That was *in-fucking-credible*," he said. "I would never have believed it if I hadn't seen it with my own eyes."

Walter assumed a Gary Cooper 'aw, shucks' pose, while both Susan and Lucy hugged him and peppered his face with kisses. With one arm around Susan and the other around Lucy, he asked Jeffries, "What happens now?"

"Mop up," was the answer. "That will be your reward for an outstanding performance. I'll go report in to my boss and come back with specific instructions." Walter, Susan, and Lucy retired to the front porch to wait, savoring glasses of lemonade Susan had prepared, thinking they might be needed as some kind of peacemaking gesture. Within minutes Jeffries returned to say that he and one of the other agents would remain in Ted's house overnight, in case anybody got the bright idea to come back and loot the place. They would be leaving the next morning and wanted Walter to return to receive the keys to the house, vehicles, etc. Jeffries handed Walter a business card bearing his cell phone number, and Walter reciprocated by reciting his cell phone and Susan's landline numbers, which Jeffries programmed into his cell phone.

With that, Walter, Susan, and Lucy were *out of there*, cruising toward KFalls where they gorged themselves on Italian food and drank a little too much wine over the course of the evening. The uneaten halves of their lunchtime sandwiches became Moses' treat, although he was puzzled by this radical departure from his usual fare.

314

PART FOUR

New Beginnings

Seize the moments of happiness,
love and be loved!
That is the only reality in the world,
all else is folly.”

—Leo Tolstoy (1828-1910)

79.

The next morning Walter delivered Susan to work shortly before 10:00 AM and then drove to the cabin. He walked over to Ted's house, finding the WitSec agents about to leave. As they handed him Ted's wad of keys, they said that Ted would *not* be returning to the house—*ever*—because too many people now knew his former identity and where he had been living. He would be staying in a 'safe house' in Medford until WitSec determined his future identity and place of residence, probably within a week. Walter, on the other hand, would be 'caretaker' of the property until further notice, and Special Agent Jeffries would be the intermediary for all future communications between Walter and Ted/WitSec. Further instructions for Walter would be forthcoming after the weekend, "thank you very much." They drove away, leaving Walter standing there in the very spot where Abigail had met her appalling end, suddenly feeling very much alone, as if he had been abandoned along with the house and property he was now in charge of. He called Lucy and asked her to drive Susan's car out to the cabin and keep him company until Susan got off work. "Please bring Moses along," he added.

No sooner had he hung up than he got a call on his cell phone. "Hello, this is Al Fath," said the voice at the other end. "Thank you much for meet us yesterday. Your advice very good, so we make no mistake. But what to do now? We receive money but we no complete assignment. Last night we have many prayer, long talk at Ranch, but no agree. Can you help us?"

Walter was momentarily speechless. He sensed that this was an extraordinary opportunity, but he had no idea what to do, and no authority either. He needed advice—at least another Abigail. "Yes, I'll help you, but I need to talk to my friends first. I'll call you back by five o'clock today. Until then, don't call anybody else, don't make any decisions, don't do anything except pray. Ask *Allah* to guide you—and me and my friends—like yesterday."

"OK," Fath said. "*Shock-run.*"

"*Salaam,*" said Walter. He dialed up Mac's cell phone.

"I hear you had quite a day yesterday," Mac said.

"It ain't over," Walter said. "The fat lady got called back for an encore." He repeated Fath's request, emphasizing that he had promised to get back to Fath within a few hours.

"It's Saturday, but I'll make some calls. Hang tight." Walter reminded Mac that he had only an unsecured cell phone. "That may not matter any longer in light of what happened yesterday, but I'll keep it in mind," Mac replied.

Lucy and Moses arrived soon thereafter, so Walter set about preparing lunch at the cabin. As they were eating, he expressed concern about his future residence. "I don't know how much longer I'll be allowed to stay here. I presume Ted will sell the house, although that could take months during which time I could probably persuade him to let me continue as caretaker."

Lucy was direct, like her mother. "I noticed you referred to Mom as your *fiancée* yesterday. I wasn't surprised, and I was certainly delighted with the idea, but she hasn't discussed it with me. I don't mean to pry, but it seems to me your residence question has some bearing upon when you get married and *vice versa*."

"Yes, indeed," Walter replied. "Truth is, I haven't actually gotten down on my knees and begged Susan to marry me. I called her my *fiancée* because it seemed to be the easiest way to describe our relationship to people who have a limited command of English. I was comfortable in doing that because I regard her as my *de facto fiancée*. In the discussions we've had about the future of our relationship, we've acknowledged that marriage is where we're headed but neither of us wants to rush things. I've taken a 'slow-and-easy' approach to how much time I spend at her house because I know there are some emotional issues involved for her. All that was predicated on the assumption I could live here for at least another six months, and now that that is uncertain, it will force us to reconsider the timing for our marriage."

"I understand," Lucy said. "Let me go on the record here and now that (a) I'm two-hundred-percent in favor of you and Mom getting married, and (b) it doesn't matter to me when and where you do it—meaning I don't have to be present at the wedding—because I don't know where the Army is going to put me next or when. That means (c) whatever decisions you make about where you live don't matter to me either. I've left home, physically and emotionally, and I don't intend to move back in—just visit as often as I can."

"That helps," Walter said. "Thank you."

"One thing more. I don't know how you feel about me calling you 'Dad,' but once you're married to Mom, I'd like to do that, if it's OK with you. I've missed having a father all these years, and I'm looking forward to making up for that—with you."

Walter thought he was going to cry. "I'd be honored if you called me 'Dad' and I could call you my daughter. You know, of course, you'll also be 'big sis' to my kids, which will give you a whole new array of rights and responsibilities."

"Ah, yes," Lucy smiled, "I can teach them all sorts of dreadful things, to keep you and Mom awake at night."

"It will probably unnerve my ex-wife terribly, but I'll try not to take too much pleasure from that."

Their conversation was interrupted by Walter's cell phone. "Hi, Walter. This is Mac again. I've talked to several of my friends in various Federal agencies. Both the FBI and the ICE—the US Immigration and Customs Enforcement—would like to meet with your Muslim friends. Can you arrange a meeting next Monday afternoon, say 1:30, with Hazik and Fath? It would include representatives from those two agencies, plus you and me."

"I'll give it a go, and I would like to include Lucy, my future daughter, who will be visiting for another week." He winked at her. "She's an Arabic translator for the Army, so she can help if there's a language problem."

"Excellent idea," Mac agreed. "Can we do this meeting at your cabin? It seems like a good setting: centrally located and politically neutral."

"It might be a little cramped for seven people, but everybody should be able to find it by now. I'll call Fath right away and get back to you with confirmation."

Walter immediately put in a call to Fath, who was initially surprised and skeptical about meeting with FBI and ICE agents. Walter patiently explained that these would be the people who had the authority to negotiate with him and Hazik and he (Walter) would *personally guarantee* they would not arrest him and Hazik after the meeting. To reinforce the point, he said that, in addition to the two Federal agents, he (Walter) would attend the meeting along with a government advisor, his friend Dr. McCarter, and also an Arabic translator.

"Translator is Army woman at your house yesterday?" Fath wanted to know.

"Yes. She is my daughter." Another wink at Lucy. "She is on home leave."

Fath was now more receptive. "Good. We meet Monday, 1:30 at your house."

After he hung up, Walter looked at Lucy. "I hope you got all that."

"Yes, it seems the wedding date just got miraculously moved up. Congratulations, Dad."

"Don't tell your mother. I want to surprise her," Walter said.

80.

During what remained of the weekend, Walter took some time to reflect on where he was and how far he had come since arriving in Oregon almost six months ago. His intention had been to 'retreat' from the cares of everyday life, but except for the ten-day meditation course and the ensuing five days at Mendocino, there had been far less seclusion than he had hoped. Right from the outset he had become entangled in Ted's own attempts to 'escape,' which had almost mushroomed into armed violence. At the same time, he had willingly—nay, eagerly—gotten involved with Susan and Mac, both of whom had prominently and permanently maneuvered themselves into his life. He had rather quickly come to assume that Ted and Lottie—and Abigail too—would also to be permanent players in his story, but now they had suddenly departed and were unlikely ever to return.

The frenzied comings and goings of the past week—the trip to San Jose, Ted's marathon 'sexcapade' with Nancy, and the Great Confrontation of US Marshals, Muslims, and the Jefferson State Militia in his front yard—had taken his mind off Abigail's grisly demise, but now his grieving resumed and a few more tears paid tribute to her memory. *Why should I be so broken up over a silly old duck?* he asked himself. Letting go of his judgmentalism and revisiting the warmth her presence had provided, he realized how much his front-porch interactions with her had broadened his awareness to include non-human *confidantes* and guides. Of course, he had instantly bonded with Moses, but that was different: he hadn't looked to the dog for counsel and validation. Abigail, however, had taught him something new, something he could, and should, explore at greater length in the future.

Walter had also learned from Ted—and from Lottie too, albeit indirectly— and now that they were gone, he reflected on what they had taught him. Ted's extreme devotion to Lottie came quickly to mind, and yet when Lottie insisted on severing the marriage, Ted seemed able to let her go with surprising ease. Walter recognized it as the *non-attachment* and *impermanence* that Buddhism teaches, but it was too much of a stretch for him to see Ted as a 'good' Buddhist even though there was nothing in Walter's experience of Ted to indicate otherwise. Lottie, on the other hand, seemed to epitomize most of the things Buddhism says *not* to do.

Walter chose not to dwell on that, to get caught up in more judgmentalism, but rather to be thankful to her for coming into his life to be learned from and even loved. He wished her well in her new life, and the same for 'Ted,' whatever his new identity might be.

81.

On Monday morning Walter and Lucy took Susan to work and did some grocery shopping before going to the cabin to prepare for their 1:30 meeting. Moses, alas, was left behind at Susan's house. At about 11:00, Walter got a phone call from Special Agent Jeffries with the promised 'further instructions' from Ted:

Walter was to go through the house to collect Ted's and Lottie's personal belongings, including clothing, pictures, jewelry, and the contents of drawers that seemed to contain personal records, etc. Lottie's clothing was to be donated to Goodwill, but Susan was welcome to take for herself anything she wanted. The other personal items were to be inventoried, wrapped, and packed in numbered boxes for shipment to Ted by way of WitSec within two weeks. Household items such as dishes, glassware, and linens were to be excluded from the inventory and would remain in the house. Ditto books, music, tools, and firearms. Walter would be reimbursed for his expenses and compensated for his time and effort at an unspecified rate.

Walter was to live in the house rent free through at least the end of the year. He should freely use up the food, beverages, and other consumables, but he would be responsible for future utility bills. He would be given at least thirty days advance 'move-out' notice when the house is sold. Instructions for sale/disposal of household furnishings, the car and truck, and other items would come at that time.

Jeffries said written confirmation of these instructions would be sent to Walter via email. After the call, Walter shared his instructions with Lucy. "Looks like I've got my work cut out for me for the next two weeks."

"I'll be glad to help you with collecting and packing all the stuff," she said. "I don't have to leave until Saturday morning."

They ate a quick lunch, after which Walter tidied up the cabin while Lucy did the dishes and prepared refreshments for the meeting participants. At about 1:15, a government SUV arrived, bringing Mac and the FBI and ICE agents, all in suit and tie. Walter recognized the FBI agent as one of the two men he had dealt with in Darrell's conference room. Ten minutes later Fath and Hazik drove up in Fath's dilapidated car. They were wearing not-very-stylish slacks and sport jackets but no ties. Walter walked out to their car to welcome them and escort them inside. There wasn't enough space for everybody to sit around the breakfast table, so Walter directed Fath and Hazik to the sofa, Mac to the easy chair, the agents to the two porch chairs he had carried inside, and Lucy and himself to straight chairs from the kitchen, all clustered around the coffee table in such a way that the Muslims were seated in the 'place of honor.' Walter and Lucy brought glasses of lemonade for everybody and put plates of dates and small pastries on the coffee table. (Lucy had assured Walter it was all *halal*.)

Walter introduced Mac, who introduced the agents, and then Walter introduced Fath and Hazik, Lucy, and himself. Mac took over the meeting, asking Hazik and Fath to explain why they had called Walter. The story that emerged was that the Muslims—Hazik, Fath, and nine others—had been hired to abduct Ted and his wife for a specified amount of money. That money had been delivered, "with the kind assistance of Mr. Baker who flew the plane to Seattle and back." Subsequently, the Muslims had completed their planning and training, culminating in their foray to Walter's cabin on the preceding Friday, where "Mr. Baker had met them and convinced them that carrying out their mission would be a serious mistake in the eyes of *Allah*." All this was conveyed in halting English by Fath, with occasional interjections in Arabic by Hazik and a few interventions by Lucy to get everything accurately expressed in decent English.

At that point, Mac began asking some questions intended to confirm or dispute what he knew to be the understanding of the Federal agents who had been tracking the Muslims at Frisco Ranch. He verified that Fath and his colleagues had all come to the US on student visas with the goal of returning to their own countries to apply what they had learned in order to improve living conditions there. Even Hazik, who was older, had been a graduate research assistant in the College of Agricultural Sciences at Oregon State University.

Thus, the present Frisco Ranch group was a very different breed from the Muslims who had attempted to establish a *jihad* training center in 1999: they had been recruited by word-of-mouth out of a common need to earn enough money to continue their education. Hazik and Fath were the key persons in this, not just as recruiters, but also as the sole contacts with the yet-to-be-identified persons who had defined and financed their mission. Mac made it plain it was *those persons* who were the target of the FBI investigation, not Hazik, Fath, and their colleagues. The FBI agent spoke up to confirm it, which opened the way for the ICE agent to say that his agency would grant amnesty for the visa violations the Muslims were technically guilty of—*if* the Muslims would cooperate in the FBI investigation, up to and including testifying in court as necessary. Again, Mac went over those points very slowly and carefully, with Lucy's assistance, to make sure Hazik and Fath understood. They apparently did, which led Fath to ask, "What we do now?"

Mac said, "Nothing," and the FBI and ICE agents nodded their agreement. Mac went on to explain, "It will take a while for your 'sponsors' to catch up with the fact that your group has abandoned its mission. The primary way they would learn that is directly from you, so please don't communicate with them. If they call you, delay them with vague answers or pretend that your English isn't good enough for you to understand them. Meanwhile, you have their money, and you can be sure they won't try to get it back from you because that would expose them. You can live on it for a while and ultimately divide what's left of it among your group so you can all go back to school. The outcome will be that your group will dissolve in such a way that your 'sponsors' cannot easily find any of you but the FBI will be able to contact you when and if necessary."

Mac paused to see if Hazik and Fath had any questions. None were forthcoming, so he went on to give them specific instructions. "Go back and discuss this with your group. It's important that all of them agree to this. When you have that agreement, call Walter and he will inform the rest of us. After that, various agents from the FBI and the ICE will come to Frisco Ranch to gather more information and provide further instructions. This will probably take two or three months, but the members of your group can begin thinking about resuming their studies early next year." *He didn't really give them any option of not agreeing,* Walter observed. *Good, tough negotiating tactics!*

Smiles lit up Hazik's and Fath's faces. They stood up, signifying that they were satisfied with what they had learned and willing to proceed as Mac had outlined. Mac spoke up with a final directive. "If questions or problems arise, contact Walter, at least until we give you different instructions. Thank you for meeting with us and for your magnanimous cooperation. *Salaam!*" Handshakes were exchanged all around. Fath contrived to come to Lucy last and start a conversation with her. They retreated to a corner of the room for a brief discussion in mixed Arabic and English, eliciting a smile of approval from Mac.

After everybody left, Walter and Lucy drove into KFalls and loaded up on packing boxes, wrapping paper, tape, and felt-tip markers at an office supply store.

Then they picked up Susan at work and Moses at Susan's house, and they all went back to the cabin for dinner. The meeting with Hazik and Fath occupied most of their table talk, but after dinner they walked down to Ted's house to check it out—Moses too. Walter was more curious about the bunker under the outbuilding than anything in the house, but he didn't mention it because he wanted to explore it on his own first.

82.

Expecting that Lucy would not arrive before 10:15 after driving Susan to work the next day, Walter went to explore the bunker. The first thing he had to do was find it. He knew which building it was—Ted had pointed that out—and that the bunker was underneath, but that was all. The fourth key he tried opened the padlock on the large outside door, and he swung it wide open to let in more light, leading him to discover a light switch just inside the door. The overhead fluorescents made it easy to discern Ted's filing system for his tools and equipment. The John Deere '2000 Series' tractor caught Walter's attention, but he didn't linger there. Looking around the interior space, searching for a stairwell but finding none, he saw that the right interior wall was about four feet *inside* the exterior wall beyond it and the space between the walls might not be the closet it appeared to be. Again there was a padlock on the 'closet' door, so Walter had to try several keys before he could gain entrance. Sure enough, there was a rather steep metal stairway going down, terminating in a 4x4-foot landing and another door, made of heavy steel. He located the light switch on the wall and went down. This time the padlock was larger and more formidable.

The heavy door opened inward, but Walter could see from its edge that it was several inches thick, constructed like the door of a bank vault with deadbolts that could be operated only from the inside. His groping hand found another switch, and the lights came on to expose a 10-by-16-foot room with walls and ceiling of poured concrete—well reinforced, Walter suspected. The room contained a double bed, two easy chairs, a desk, a small dining table, a TV, and a tiny kitchen. A shower and toilet were tucked under the stairway, with only a sliding door separating them from the main room. Built into the wall next to the toilet was a heavy-duty combination safe, about 14-by-20 inches. Walter's second pass around the room disclosed a ventilation system, a CB radio, an Uzi with quite a bit of ammunition, and a goodly stash of food and water, leading him to estimate that the place could withstand a siege of at least two weeks, as Ted had claimed. For the time being, the wall safe didn't challenge him, so he filed it away in the back of his mind expecting that he would learn the combination eventually. He backed out of the bunker, locking it down as he went, and returned to the house to begin his packing chore.

He decided to focus on Lottie's items first to give Lucy a chance to pick through them before she had to leave town, and by the time she arrived from KFalls he had all of Lottie's clothes sorted and stacked in neat piles on the beds. He put her to work setting up an 'MS Excel' file on his laptop computer so they could inventory everything that would go to Ted, and he began assembling the packing boxes. After lunch they started filling boxes with Ted's clothes, carefully sorting and tallying as they went. It was slow, tedious work, but they made good progress by dinnertime.

While Walter prepared dinner, Lucy drove into town to bring Susan and Moses back for the evening. They ate in the cabin, then took Moses for a walk, ending up at the house so Susan and Lucy could 'shop' for clothes at 'Lottie's Bargain Outlet.' It turned out that most of Lottie's things fit Lucy better than Susan, but Lucy had little need of anything beyond what the US Army was providing. Consequently, Susan claimed only casual items like exercise and work wear for which exact fit wasn't important, while Lucy walked away with some rather unmilitary lingerie and pajamas.

83.

Walter and Lucy continued packing and sorting over the next three days, with Susan joining in on the third, her day off from work. Walter hauled boxes of Lottie's clothes to the Goodwill on Wednesday, but the boxes of Ted's stuff took up most of the available space in the two smaller bedrooms by Friday. Walter's rule was 'If in doubt, pack it and get it out of here.' He wanted to delay moving himself from the cabin to the house until the clean-out was finished, but he looked forward to the convenience of the washer and dryer and the comfort of central heating in the approaching autumn.

On Thursday, Al Fath called Walter to say, after much discussion and prayer, the Muslims at Frisco Ranch had come to unanimous agreement to accept the terms and conditions the FBI and ICE agents had put on the table at Monday's meeting. Walter thanked him profusely and was about to hang up when Fath said, "For me one more question." *Oh-oh!* Walter thought. "Is about your daughter—have you find husband for her?" Walter was confused by the question until he remembered that Fath came from a culture in which most marriages are arranged by the parents of the bride and groom, often after long negotiation over dowries and such, and that *love,* in the Western sense of the word, has nothing to do with it. In his most fatherly manner, he explained to Fath that he and his 'wife' would not find and impose a husband on Lucy as it is done in many non-Western countries. Lucy would be free to marry whomever she chose, whenever she wanted—or to not marry at all, if she wished. Yes, she might consult with her parents when/if she herself found a prospect, and her parents might express an opinion, even exert some influence, but there would be no dowry or anything like that. In a tone of relief, Fath said, "I understand. Thank you very much," and ended the call.

As he returned to the packing task, Walter asked Lucy, "What did you and Al Fath talk about after the meeting ended on Monday?"

"He started telling me about himself and his plans to resume studying for a degree in agricultural engineering at OSU. We didn't have much time, so he had to hurry, but it almost sounded like a sales pitch."

"I think he's interested in you—as his future wife," Walter said. Lucy blushed, and Walter related the phone discussion he had just had with Fath.

Lucy responded, "Marrying somebody like Fath and following him back to live and work in his native country isn't very compatible with the Army career I've chosen, but I wouldn't rule it out. I don't think I'm violating security rules by telling you I'm involved in counterinsurgency, which means working with the local population to help them solve their problems and build better lives for themselves instead of joining the *Taliban* or *al-Qaeda* to fight the evil infidels. I'll even risk bending the rules by telling you I've spent some time in the *Pashtun* area along the border between Afghanistan and Pakistan and I speak *Pashto* as well as Arabic. Fath told me he's from that area."

"He claimed to be from Algeria when I flew him and Hazik to Seattle, but I suspected that wasn't true," Walter said. "I'm also fairly sure that 'Al Fath' isn't his real name."

"Yes, probably so," Lucy agreed. "I hope it doesn't get him into trouble with ICE, but it's not a show-stopper as far as his potential relationship with me is concerned." She paused and then delivered 'the bottom line': "If he brings up anything even remotely pertaining to marriage to me again, tell him to talk to me directly like a Western man, because that's who he'll have to compete with if he wants to me to accept him as my husband." That sent Walter's eyebrows skyward. The fact that Lucy would even consider a relationship with Fath had never crossed his mind. *Still*, he thought, *I do kind of like the guy, and he seems to be growing on me.*

Steering the conversation in a less precarious direction, Walter asked, "In your studies of *Pashtun* language and culture, have you ever come across the name 'Badshah Khan?'"

Lucy wrinkled her nose, like her mom did when she's puzzled. "I've heard the name, and I know he was a major figure in *Pashtun* history in the past fifty years, but that's all. Why do you ask?"

"I got a book on his life at the Islamic Center in California. He was apparently Gandhi's right-hand man, and he continued Gandhi's work in pacifism and nonviolent resistance long after Gandhi was assassinated. He stands out as a *Muslim pacifist* in sharp contrast to the warrior model that Muslim terrorists try to promote. If he interests you, you can take my book with you and I'll get myself another one." Lucy nodded 'yes.' "And now that I know that Al Fath is a *Pashtun*, I'll bring up Badshah Khan if I have any more fatherly conversations with him."

"Poor Al," Lucy laughed. "On the one hand, you're telling him he has to adopt the Western male model if he wants to partner with me, and on the other hand, you're promoting a *Pashtun Gandhi-protégé pacifist* as the kind of person he should emulate. He'll really be confused."

84.

Susan and Walter took Lucy out for a farewell dinner in KFalls Friday night. Walter had thought they might cook the dinner for themselves in Ted's house, but he wasn't moved in yet. Nevertheless, Walter's prospect of living in the house through the end of the year led Susan to suggest that Katie and Ryan could come for a few days at Christmas and they could have a 'family Christmas' there—with Moses too—instead of trying to squeeze everybody into her house and the cabin. Walter liked the idea, but raised an objection. "For a *real* family

Christmas we need Lucy here too." He turned to her. "Is there any chance you'll get more home leave soon?"

"Yes, there is. I won't know my next assignment until I report for duty next week, but I expect I'll be in the US rather than overseas, which makes home leave for holidays a possibility." Lucy paused and a twinkle appeared in her eyes. "In addition to holidays, there are other 'special occasions' that can be used to justify a weekend pass—like, for example, a wedding." Walter saw her looking at him as if to say, "*Well?!*" but he was caught by surprise.

Susan, meanwhile, was looking back and forth from Lucy to Walter to Lucy again, asking, "What's going on here?" In the startled silence, Lucy's youthful impatience took over. "Look, Walter, you've been introducing Mom as your *fiancée,* not just once, but several times in these past two weeks. I understand it's been a convenient way to explain your relationship to strangers, but we all know where this is headed, so why don't you get on with it?"

"Are you suggesting we get married at Christmas?" Walter sputtered.

"Of course!" Lucy exclaimed. "Your kids will be here, and I can use it as an excuse to come back for a day or two. You'll have Ted's house, which might not be available come January. What else do you need?"

A little courage, was the answer that came to Walter's mind. He turned to Susan. "Whaddya say, Toots? Do I have to get down on my knees right here in front of Lucy, God, and everybody else in this restaurant?"

"Er ... um ...." Susan mumbled.

"For Chrissake, Mom!" Lucy erupted. "Just say 'yes,' so we can get on with the planning."

With that, Susan found her voice. "OK, but may I kiss him first?"

Walter saw where this was leading, and he was ready. It was a little clumsy, because they were seated around a table, with plates of food to stick their elbows in and wine glasses to be knocked over, and he would have preferred to be standing up so their bodies could plaster themselves all over one another, but ... whatever. Afterward, Susan turned back to her daughter, "There! Are you satisfied now? Or do we have to start taking off our clothes and consummate the marriage right here and now?"

Lucy broke up with giggling. "That's a thought, but no, you can wait until we finish the meal and you get home to the bedroom."

Later that evening, after they had made love, Walter and Susan lay in bed and talked. Walter wanted to buy Susan an engagement ring, which Susan said she didn't need, but Walter insisted. Walter also wanted to start looking for a place to live after he moved out of Ted's house, and Susan said they could stay in her house for at least a few months. She also said that Oregon law requires the wedding be conducted by a minister or a judicial officer and that there be two adult witnesses. They agreed on asking Darrell and Virginia Cox to be the witnesses, but neither of them knew of a minister or a church they really liked. Walter wanted to fly Darrell's Cessna 182 to Livermore to pick up Katie and Ryan at Christmastime.... Susan began wondering about a wedding dress.... Walter began thinking about a honeymoon....

They were all up bright and early the next morning to get Lucy to the airport and Susan to work. When that was accomplished, Walter went to a jewelry store that Susan had recommended—after some arm-twisting. He spent an hour looking at all sorts of rings, eventually narrowing his choice down to three and promising to bring Susan in for a final decision that afternoon. Then he drove out to Bonanza to talk with Henry Parsons about buying a house. Henry greeted Walter with unusual enthusiasm, not because he had intuited that Walter was finally serious about buying something, but because of the 'non-confrontation' that had occurred at Walter's cabin a week earlier.

Walter expressed profound gratitude that the Jefferson State Militia had put in an appearance, even though it had turned out they weren't needed. "It's good to know that the JSM exists and is well organized and plugged into what's going on in the County," he said. Henry asked what was going to happen to the Muslim group at Frisco Ranch, but Walter was noncommittal, not wanting to spill the beans about their agreement with the FBI and the ICE until it was a done deal. Walter did explain that Ted had vanished into the WitSec program again, and that he (Walter) was now living in Ted's house as a caretaker until some decision was made about selling the property. "I know I can stay there through December at least, but I need to start looking for another place to live," he said.

"How about Nancy Norwood's house," Henry suggested. "It's up for sale."

"Huh?! What happened to Nancy?" Walter wanted to know.

"Gone. Either she's following your ex-neighbor into oblivion or she's bailed out for a hunting ground where the animal population is more to her liking. My money is on the former. Rumor has it she told her coworkers at the Longhorn that Ted might not be the greatest lover she ever met, but the fact that he could not only spell 'Wall Street' but had actually been there made up for a lot." Walter snickered, recalling Ted's bedraggled condition after his marathon bout in the sack with Nancy.

Henry went on to discuss other properties on the market, pointing out their location on a large county map tacked to his office wall and printing out data sheets on a few of them that interested Walter. Armed with that information, Walter promised to return with Susan to do some serious looking in a few weeks. Later that afternoon, when Susan got off work, Walter took her back to the jewelry store, where they decided on a ring.

85.

On Monday Walter called Special Agent Jeffries to inform him that Ted's belongings were all packed, inventoried, and ready to go. Jeffries instructed Walter where to email the inventory and told him a truck would come by Wednesday morning to pick up the boxes. He also asked Walter to send an email statement itemizing his time and expenses to date. He was uncertain how and when Walter would be paid, saying that the details of Walter's compensation "were being worked out as we speak" and promising to call back when he knew more.

Next Walter called Mac. "We need to talk. Any chance we can do some fishing sometime soon?"

"How about tomorrow, usual time and place?" Mac suggested.

"Done! See you there."

Walter spent the rest of the day moving his stuff from the cabin to the house, all the while chafing over the prospect of having to move again in a few months.

86.

At the 'usual time and place,' Walter got into Mac's pickup, fastened his seat belt, and accepted the customary cup of coffee from Mac, but he couldn't contain his enthusiasm very long. "The world sure looks different from what it did the last time we went fishing. It's been an interesting couple of weeks."

Mac laughed. "There's said to be an ancient Chinese curse, 'May you live in interesting times,' although its authenticity is questionable, because those who quote it are unable to supply the original Chinese. Supposedly it was the first of three curses of increasing severity, the second being 'May you come to the attention of powerful people' and the third 'May your wishes be granted.' So just because you've made it this far doesn't mean you can relax."

"I guess the meeting we had with the Muslims, the FBI, and the ICE a week ago, plus all the dealings I've had with WitSec in the past ten days, is evidence I've been on the radar screen of 'powerful people,' so I'm already into 'Curse Number Two.' But now that Ted and Lottie are out of the picture, maybe I can sink back into obscurity," Walter replied.

"I wouldn't count on it," Mac countered. "To quote another acclaimed commentator on the human condition, William Shakespeare, 'The evil that men do lives after them; the good is oft interred with their bones.' Ted and Lottie aren't even dead yet, and hopefully they won't be for a long time."

"*Inshallah*," Walter said, bringing a grin to Mac's face. "The only death has been Abigail, Lottie's duck, and I've been thinking about the good she brought to me."

"Don't let go of that," Mac advised. "Stick with it and see where it leads you. Meanwhile, I can tell you of another 'death' of sorts. The FBI has followed up on the leads you provided regarding who has been financing the Muslims at Bly, and some arrests have been made under 'RICO,' The Racketeer Influenced and Corrupt Organizations Act."

"Oh, great!" Walter said unhappily. "That could bring *me* to the attention of the guys Ted is helping send to jail. Next thing I'll be in the WitSec program too."

"You've only been involved peripherally, and you probably will never be called upon to testify in court, so I don't think you'll need government protection—but it's not entirely outside the realm of possibility either." *Mac's attempted reassurance isn't all that reassuring*, Walter groused.

"Well, in the short term, I seem to be moving into 'Curse Number Three' territory," he said, trying to shift the subject to something more pleasant. "Ted has informed me, through WitSec, that I should live in his house, rent free, for the remainder of the year. I've already moved in, but only after I complied with his request to pack up all of his and Lottie's personal stuff. The truck comes tomorrow to pick up Ted's things, and I took Lottie's abandoned clothes to Goodwill last week, as per Ted's instructions. He sure didn't waste any time getting her out of his life."

"No, and I think it indicates he always knew that she would eventually double-cross him. He had hoped she would change and become the gracious, forgiving person he saw buried deep inside her, but he didn't leave himself too vulnerable. From what I hear at WitSec, he had an airtight prenuptial agreement that cuts her off from everything because *she* left *him* and there's no evidence he drove her to do that—that he had abused her or anything like that. At least, that's what I'm prepared to testify if I'm ever called to do so."

Walter made another try at getting to the *positive* things he wanted to share with Mac. "Anyhow, because I'll have the house at my disposal through the Christmas holiday, I can bring my kids up from California to spend a few days here. *And* Lucy will try to get a weekend pass so we can all be together for the wedding. So my wishes are being granted."

"Congratulations!" Mac exclaimed. "What's the date?"

"We haven't set a date yet, because we have to find a minister first. We thought maybe you could help us, because we haven't found any local churches as liberal as we would like. Fundamentalism seems to have a lock on the religious scene in Klamath County."

"It's not quite that bad," Mac replied, "but it really doesn't matter. I can marry you, and I'd be delighted and honored to do it—that is, if I'm acceptable to you and Susan."

"You're certainly more than acceptable, but we had no idea you're a minister along with all your other qualifications."

"Well, I don't advertise that fact, but I got some ministerial training at a small theological school in central California some years ago. At that time I was working with a group of military chaplains whose primary training was in religion but who were doing a good bit of counseling, so I decided to 'mirror' them by getting a little religious training to go along with my counseling credentials."

"What church are you a minister of?" Walter asked.

"I was trained and ordained in a 'New Thought' church, which you probably never heard of. There are several New Thought denominations in the US, plus some independent churches, with a total membership of only a few hundred thousand. One of the denominations, Religious Science, publishes the *Science of Mind* magazine I saw in your cabin, so you've had more exposure to it than you might have realized. In any event, New Thought regards itself as having at least one foot in the Christian tradition, although certainly not in the Christian mainstream. The 'other foot' may be even farther afield, leading some adherents to characterize themselves as being '*more than Christian*.' That appealed to me, and it seemed to fit well with being a chaplain, where you get called upon to minister to all denominations of Christians, plus Jews, Muslims, Hindus, Buddhists, Taoists, and so on—and if the guy in front of you is a Rastafarian, your job is to help him be the best Rastafarian he can be, not convert him to your own particular faith. So I got ordained as an 'Interfaith Minister,' which gives me license to do pretty much whatever I damned well please."

Realizing he had given a ten-dollar answer to a fifty-cent question, Mac paused. "Sorry to go on a rant, but you already know how rabid I am about any person, any church, any religion that claims to have an exclusive franchise on 'Truth.' I agree with Ken Wilber, a contemporary writer and Renaissance man, who says that all religions have an element of Truth, *but only a piece of it*. Sometimes it's a very small piece, but that doesn't stop people from insisting it's the whole *megillah* and trying to impose it on others, by force if necessary."

"I get the picture," Walter said, wanting to ease Mac down off his soapbox. "I think you're exactly the kind of minister Susan and I have been looking for. What is your availability during the last two weeks of December?"

"I'll have to check my calendar," Mac said. "I'll call you later today."

They pulled off Highway 140 and parked at their usual fishing spot on the Sprague River. Walter knew the drill quite well by now—they walked off in different directions, took out their gear, and spent the next two hours in their own self-contained domains. The trout were hungry, and both Mac and Walter ended up with more than a dozen good-sized rainbows between them. As noon approached, the growling crescendo in their stomachs told them it was time to pack up and make for the Coyote Café.

Recalling the 'buzz' they had encountered two weeks earlier, Walter wondered what the atmosphere in the Café would be today. He expected something low-key, but it seemed like somebody rang a bell when they walked in the door. All eyes in the room followed them as they found their way to a table in the back corner, and the attention remained fixed on them even after they sat down. Within seconds, a tall, muscular, forty-ish man got up from one of the other tables and slowly walked over to stand smack dab in front of them, as if emulating Clint Eastwood in one of his 'spaghetti Westerns.' He looked briefly at Mac, then aimed his gaze squarely at Walter and spoke in his best Eastwoodian drawl, "Are you the feller who faced off the Muslims over on Haskins Road about ten days ago, the one who talked them out of completing their raid and into going back to the Frisco Ranch?"

Walter didn't know whether to shit or comb his hair. He glanced at Mac as if to ask "what the hell is happening here?" but Mac seemed to be perfectly relaxed and at peace with the world. Looking back into 'Clint's' steely stare, Walter answered, "Yes, I'm that person," using a tone of voice that (he hoped) conveyed neither fear nor aggression.

'Clint' stretched and plumped himself up to maximum proportions. "Well, then, I'd just like to shake your hand and, on behalf of the entire Jefferson State Militia, thank you for your courage and cool-headed action in defusing a potentially explosive situation. Henry Parsons tells me there would probably have been a nasty battle there if you hadn't done what you did. It was a miracle." He extended his hand.

Walter stood up and shook it, but he was too taken aback to say anything at first. Finally he came out with something like "I appreciate the readiness of the JSM to intervene in delicate situations in order to protect life and property, and I'm especially thankful they showed up in my front yard when they did."

'Clint' managed a crooked smile and replied, "The Militia can always use people like you. If you're ever interested in joining up, talk to Henry."

"Thank you. I will," Walter said, not willing to commit but also not wanting to insult 'Clint' by rejecting his offer outright.

'Clint' wasn't quite finished, however. "I also understand that you're a pilot."

"Yes, that was what I did in the Air Force and what I was doing at Alaska Airlines up until six months ago," Walter answered. Then, as if to pre-empt the next question, he added, "but I don't fly helicopters."

'Clint' said nothing, but his disappointed expression said 'Oh.' He turned and went back to his table. Thereupon, every other person in the room, including the Coyote Café staff, filed past Walter's table to shake his hand. Walter was clearly out of his element, but he made the best of it. Mac, meanwhile, was enjoying it all immensely, including Walter's modest discomfort. When Walter finally sat down, Mac leaned over and whispered to him. "I'd say you've definitely 'come to the attention of powerful people.' I hope you can handle it."

They ate their sandwiches in relative silence, and when Walter signaled to the waitress that he wanted the check, the Café's manager came over and said, "There's no charge. Your lunch is on the house today." Walter mumbled 'thanks' and slid a five-dollar tip under the edge of his plate.

As they were going out the door, 'Clint' motioned to Walter and asked, "Do you have any idea what the Muslims at Frisco Ranch are going to do next?"

Walter looked at Mac, who stepped forward to answer. "We believe that the group will be disbanding so they can all can go back to college. We expect they will be gone by the end of January." *Another miracle*, Walter thought, grateful that 'Clint' didn't ask for details. Once they were back in Mac's truck and tooling down the road, Mac turned to Walter and said with a grin, "OK, Mister Miracle-Worker, how *did* you persuade first the Muslims and then the Jefferson State Militia to 'fold their tents, like the Arabs, and as silently steal away,' as Longfellow put it? Did you plan it all out in advance, or did you make it up as you went along?"

"A little of both," Walter replied, "but mostly the former. My overall strategy was to 'win without fighting,' as the Chinese sage *Sun-tzu* taught more than 2,000 years ago, and my plan consisted of *surprise* and *deception* just as he advised. I actually started thinking about it several months ago, when I realized some kind of confrontation with the Muslims was a very real possibility. I started educating myself in Islam, expecting that religious belief would be at the core of their motivation. As it turned out, however, that wasn't the case, but I figured it out when I learned that Hazik and his crew aren't terrorist fanatics intent on *jihad*. By the time everybody showed up in front of my cabin, my plan had evolved to the point where I could *surprise* the Muslims with my knowledge and understanding of Islam and maybe *deceive* them into thinking it was equal to or even greater than theirs. So I had a copy of the *Qur'an* in my hand when I walked out onto my front porch and I greeted them in Arabic. Of course, it was fortuitous that Susan's daughter Lucy happened to be here to coach me on pronunciation and bail me out if I messed up. Anyhow, it worked, because I was able to convince them that taking action against Ted would be contrary to Islamic teaching, and then I was able to extend that idea to include Lottie—although it was a bit of a stretch."

"Well, it worked," Mac said, "but what would you have done if it hadn't?"

"That's where I would have had to make it up. I had prepared for that contingency by having some Islamic music ready on the CD player inside the cabin. The last track on the CD was the Islamic 'Call to Prayer,' and if the Muslims had gotten unruly, I would have had Susan play it at high volume in an attempt to quiet them down. I was even prepared to follow up by inviting them to pray with me—I had bought a prayer rug, I had marked the direction toward Mecca on the cabin wall, and I had learned to perform the *Salaat* myself—not perfectly, but well enough to surprise them. There would have been some logistical problems, however, because I doubt that they had brought their prayer rugs with them, and there are mandatory ablutions to be performed before Muslim prayer. I might have had to invite them all inside the cabin—but, fortunately, it didn't come to that.

"Lucy's presence was also an element of surprise that may have helped distract the Muslims from their own resolve, especially since they were not highly trained in military discipline. I saw them react when she came out on the porch, but I couldn't tell whether it was because she was a woman or because she was in an Army uniform. Her abilities in Arabic were my 'ace in the hole,' but we didn't have to use them."

"They sure came in handy in the meeting since," Mac observed.

"Perhaps more than you realize," Walter said. "Al Fath seems to have developed a crush on Lucy—or whatever it is Muslims feel toward women. I never regarded Army fatigues as a kind of 'camo burka,' but come to think of it ...." Mac chuckled and pushed on to ask about Walter's handling of the Jefferson State Militia. "First of all, it was dumb luck that the leader of the JSM squad at the cabin was somebody I knew and had developed some rapport with. Beyond that, my assessment of him was that he isn't a fighter, that he 'gets along by going along.' So when I led off with a nonviolent course of action, introducing Hazik and Fath and having everybody shake hands, he went for it like a fly to a turd. That was all it took."

Mac considered all this for a moment, then said, "For somebody who was trained in a military academy and served a number of years in the military, you seem to have come a long way."

Walter briefly weighed that as well. "Now that you mention it, I guess I have—but I don't think the *transition* is complete yet."

Later that evening, while Walter was having dinner with Susan, Mac called to indicate his availability to officiate at their wedding in December. Walter and Susan consulted their calendars and the three of them decided on Sunday, December 21, tentatively at 4:00 PM in Ted's house. A flurry of phone calls ensued. First, Walter called Angela and persuaded her to let Katie and Ryan spend a week in Oregon at Christmastime. Walter would pick them up at Livermore Municipal Airport (LVK) on December 20 and return them December 26, both times in the Cessna 182 with Susan flying copilot. He made no mention of the planned wedding. Next, Susan called Lucy and asked her to request home leave so that she could be present at the wedding. Lucy was confident she would be able to get at least a weekend pass, perhaps longer. Finally, Susan called Virginia Cox to enlist her and Darrell as the two marriage witnesses required by Oregon law.

Walter and Susan spent the next part of the evening discussing wedding details and speculating about a honeymoon in San Francisco after taking Katie and Ryan home on December 26. Walter was concerned that he might have to move out of Ted's house by January 1. Susan was worried about the expense of all they were planning. Eventually, they put their worries aside to walk Moses before bedding him down on his blanket in the living room. Then they went into the bedroom and closed the door behind them.

87.

For the next week, life settled into an uneventful 'groove' for Walter and Susan, which they both welcomed. Planning for the upcoming wedding and family holiday was uppermost in their minds, so Walter gave almost no attention to Special Agent Jeffries' phone call informing him that his reimbursement and compensation for sorting and packing Ted's and Lottie's personal effects would arrive via US Mail later in the week. Jeffries said there would be some papers to be signed and notarized, with one copy to be mailed back to WitSec, all of which sounded a little strange to Walter, but he dismissed it as bureaucratic red tape.

The papers were in Walter's box when he checked his mail at the Bonanza Post Office on Thursday. Recalling that Jeffries had said something had to be notarized and mailed back, Walter opted to read the mail over coffee at The Branding Iron Café rather than immediately return to the house. When he opened the large flat envelope from WitSec, he found a letter and two copies of another document, but it was certainly *not* 'bureaucratic red tape.' The document was a Legal Agreement transferring to Walter *total ownership* of Ted's house, the outbuildings (including the cabin), their entire contents, the forty acres of land, the vehicles, and "any and all other items remaining on the premises." It stated that the signatories acknowledged that this transfer was full compensation for "expenses incurred and services rendered to date" by Walter, and it was already signed by 'Ted Wilson,' with notarization. All Walter had to do was sign in the appropriate space, get it notarized, and the whole *kit-and-caboodle* was his!

It would be an understatement to say Walter was flabbergasted. It would be more accurate to say he was flabbergasted, flummoxed, and floored; confounded, dumbfounded, dumbstruck and thunderstruck; surprised, staggered, startled, stunned, and stupefied; astonished and astounded; amazed and dazed; and certainly openmouthed, speechless, nonplussed, and taken aback; as well as bowled over and blown away. Mostly, however, he felt an overwhelming sense of relief and gratitude. The cover letter also explained that when the signed agreement was returned to WitSec, their attorney would forward the appropriate paperwork to the various government agencies to record the transfers of property and issue deeds and titles. It cautioned there might be tax implications for Walter and advised, therefore, that he contact his own attorney and accountant. However, it also stated that WitSec's attorney would be available for consultation regarding the "special circumstances" of the transaction that might provide tax relief, and it gave his name, address, and phone number. None of this diminished Walter's emotion in the least, and a few tears began dribbling down his cheeks. He pulled out his cell phone and called WitSec. When Jeffries answered, Walter said, "I just got the papers you sent me. It boggles my mind. Is this for real?"

"You bet it is," Jeffries assured him. "I admit it's rather extraordinary, but I've seen some really weird stuff in my years here. Ted Wilson made quite a gift to you, but he also saved himself and this agency a huge amount of hassle by handing it over to you and walking away. I'd say you earned it too: you covered for him and helped him a lot during these past months, and you sure saved his chestnuts when those three truckloads of would-be warriors with automatic weapons wound up in your front yard." Walter asked how he could send a thank-you note to Ted. "Just write a card or letter like you usually would," Jeffries answered. "Send it to me with an attached note saying 'Please Forward,' and I'll see that he gets it. It may take a week or two, especially right now while he's still in transit, so don't expect a quick reply."

Walter thanked Jeffries for his help and ended the call. When he finally got himself pulled together and his face dried, he picked up the papers and ambled down the street to the real estate office. Henry Parsons, he figured, was a notary public or could tell him where to find one in Bonanza. Knowing Henry's well-deserved reputation as a rumormonger, Walter concealed the main text of the Legal Agreement by presenting only the signature spaces on the second page for Henry to witness. As Walter was stuffing one signed copy into the pre-addressed envelope provided by WitSec, Henry asked when Walter would be coming back to look at properties on the market. Walter was still too dazed to answer coherently, mumbling only "I dunno. This thing we just signed may turn everything upside-down. I've got to discuss it with Susan first, and maybe also a lawyer." Henry looked disappointed, but he didn't push for an explanation.

After stopping by the Post Office again to mail the signed agreement to WitSec, Walter retreated to the house—*his* house now—to sit and let it all sink in. He was tempted to call Susan at work to give her the news, but chose instead to wait until he could tell her face-to-face. He wanted to see her reaction, and of course, he looked forward to the big hug and kiss he knew would follow. He decided to pick her up at work and take her out to dinner.

Susan could sense something was up when Walter walked into the Welcome Center at 4:50 PM. Yes, they planned for him to stay at her place that night, as he customarily did on Thursdays, but he usually went to her house and waited there for her to come home from work, sometimes starting to cook supper. She gave him a questioning look—"Is something wrong?"—but he shrugged it off—"I'll tell you later." As they walked out into the parking lot, Walter said he wanted to go eat someplace quiet where they could talk "because I got some news regarding my housing situation today, and we probably need to make some changes in our wedding and Christmas vacation plans." He refused to say anything more about the 'news' other than "It was positive, *very* positive."

Susan played along with Walter's 'mystery' game until they had given the waitress their order at Applebee's, then she pounced. "OK, what is it with the house?"

"It's *mine!*" Walter said, "Which means it will be *ours.*"

"*What?!*"

"Ted is giving me the house, the cabin, the outbuildings, the land, and everything else that's left there, including the car, the truck, and the tractor."

"You're kidding!"

"Nope, not at all. Here's what I got from WitSec." He pulled the folded envelope out of his inside jacket pocket, extracted the letter and Legal Agreement, and spread them out on the table in front of her.

She read, half aloud, her voice going up half-an-octave with each succeeding paragraph, approaching *coloratura* level at the end. "This is incredible!" she squeaked.

Walter waited for the kiss, but he had to settle for a 'peck-and-a-half' *sans* hug because they were seated on opposite sides of a booth. As Susan settled back onto the seat, he said, "This means I don't have to move, which means I don't have to go to work for Darrell, at least not full-time, to earn enough money to buy a place where we can live together and maybe our kids too. So what are *you* going to do?"

Susan balked. "First of all, I'm not going to answer that within the next five minutes. You've had half the day to contemplate this, so please give me some time to get my head around it. Right now, my mind is spinning so fast I can barely talk."

"You seem to be making good sense to me," Walter said, "but I won't insist that you answer my question right away. If you like, we can wait and noodle it together in bed tonight."

"Yes, thank you," she said. She looked down at the letter again, then back at him, with tears starting to form in her eyes. Walter followed suit, and soon there were small puddles of tears on the place mats in front of them. They hadn't begun to mop up when the waitress arrived with their food. She put it down as quickly and discreetly as she could, apologized for the intrusion, and hurried away, hoping her untimely encroachment hadn't completely nullified her tip. Awash in feelings and devoid of lucid thoughts, Walter and Susan ate slowly, yet barely tasting the food. Dessert was pointless, ditto after-dinner coffee, so Walter paid the bill and left a generous tip to console the bewildered waitress. Rather than return to the Welcome Center to get Susan's car, they went directly to her house, took Moses on a perfunctory walk, and then settled into bed, but not to make love—not yet. As they had done two weeks before, after Lucy had induced them to 'commit marriage,' they just lay there touching, half-whispering in short 'stream-of-consciousness' phrases, whatever came to mind. Gradually, the touching became caressing until....

88.

Susan and Walter awoke the next morning with the remnants of the previous day's *'flabbergasm'*—her invented word—still jumbling their thoughts. As he let Moses out for his sunrise micturition, Walter's imagination played the scenario in a new venue, envisioning a fenced enclosure behind his new house to prevent the dog from following his nose all the way to Bonanza. A light snow had fallen overnight, so Moses piddled on the first blade of grass he came to and hustled back to whine at the back door, dissuading Walter from sliding back into bed to nuzzle Susan out of her slumber. Muttering to himself, he set to making coffee and put some dog food in Moses' dish. He was about to go into the bathroom when he realized that Susan was already there, sending him off into another vision of his new abode with its one, two, three bathrooms—maybe more. *'Curse Number Three: May your wishes be granted,'* popped into his head.

Minutes later, with Susan sitting across from him at the breakfast table, Walter related his discussion of the Chinese curses with Mac the week before. She readily agreed that his life had careened through all three of them in the past month, with her in tow. Her take on things, however, after a night of subconscious processing, was encapsulated in a Bible passage she said was quoted by President John F. Kennedy in one of his famous speeches. She jumped up to snatch a well-worn Bible off the bookshelf and began leafing through the pages. "Here it is," she said. "It's *Luke 12:48*—'From everyone to whom much has been given, much will be required; and from the one to whom much has been entrusted, even more will be asked.' I think that puts things into proper perspective."

"It's the same thing," Walter replied. "It's saying the same thing as the 'Chinese curses'—but I agree with you the Bible is saying it better, because viewed that way, they don't seem like curses at all—'challenges' maybe, but without malevolent intent."

"OK, Mr. Walter Baker," she replied with mock sternness, "much has just been given and entrusted to you—which is to say, a humongous challenge. What are you going to do about it?"

"What are *we* going to do?" he corrected. "Does this make you want to back out on our marriage plans? After all, there's no hurry now, because I don't have to move."

As usual when Susan was faced with a nontrivial question, she thought a while before answering. "Nooooo. I think we leave the wedding plans just as we have them, and the Christmas vacation too. It's what comes afterward that I think we need to reconsider."

"For instance?"

"For instance, I've been thinking for some time about how I could intensify and accelerate my studies at OIT, so I could complete my bachelor's degree sooner and maybe even get started on a master's, which is essential if I am to become the counselor I want to be. When you and Lucy began campaigning to set a wedding date in December, the pieces started falling into place in my mind. I began envisioning full-time study beginning in January, while cutting back my work at the Welcome Center to part-time—but I couldn't figure out how to manage all that with two houses, Moses, and of course you."

Walter was confused, but he put out signals saying 'keep going,' so Susan did. "The possibility that you might have to move in here with me was the sticking point. I kept seeing things in this house that would have to be changed, updated, replaced, and I couldn't figure out where the money would come from if I wasn't working full-time. I didn't want to dump a big financial burden into your lap, and I'm still concerned about that, since you haven't made a decision about whether you'll go to work full-time for Darrell. Or have you?"

"No, I haven't," Walter answered, "but before we go there, let's sort out the house thing and see how much money we'll need." His brain was revving up now, about to hit cruising speed. "Let's suppose you move in with me during the next month, so we're all set for the wedding and the Christmas vacation. And let's suppose you go ahead with your plan to work part-time and attend OIT full-time, starting in January. If you set up your schedule so your work and classes require you to come into town no more than three days a week, there would be little reason to keep this house. So you could rent it out or even sell it and use the money for your tuition."

"OK, I'm with you so far," Susan said. "What do you do?"

"I'm still not comfortable making a commitment to Darrell to join his company and work toward becoming his successor, attractive as it may be, but I could certainly tolerate working part-time for him. If we can survive on that, I'm ready to sign up."

"Let's make that our tentative plan and let it simmer a few days to see if any problems crawl out from under the bed," Susan said.

"Or better ideas," Walter replied. "I don't think we should assume that all the monsters under the bed are evil."

"Right," Susan agreed. "Given and received with the proper attitude, even the 'Chinese curses' are not really curses at all."

"And the proper attitude is?"

"Gratitude," she exclaimed. " 'Never look a gift horse in the mouth,' as the old saying goes."

"I buy that," Walter replied. "Whaddaya say we eat some breakfast and then go look at our gift house and feed our gratitude?"

They drove to what they were now calling 'Walter's house' and walked through it slowly, examining every feature and fixture, just as Walter had done before he agreed to rent the cabin. Susan focused her attention on the kitchen—the cookware, dinnerware, glassware, silverware, and assorted gadgets and utensils—and then moved on to the linen closets and the cleaning equipment. She soon concluded that she should inventory everything so she could match it against what was in her house to determine what should be kept in their merged household and what should be given or thrown away. Walter came to a similar determination when they got to the garage. His tools, Ted's tools, and maybe a few from Susan's house needed to be sorted through and integrated into the storage system obsessive-compulsive Ted had devised.

From there they went to the outbuilding with the John Deere tractor and some other tools and equipment. Susan wasn't much interested in all that, but she was impressed with the extensive collection of 'stuff'—she said it with a derogatory tone—which Ted had amassed. Then they came to the door leading down to the bunker. As Walter unlocked the first door, turned on the light, and led her down the stairway, Susan's mood swung from curiosity to incredulity.

Once in the room below, she stood in the middle, turning around slowly—once, twice—taking it all in. Walter pointed out the toilet and shower under the stairs and tapped on the wall safe, saying, "I don't know what's in there. Maybe I'll find the combination when I go through the files in the house." Finally, as the *pièce de résistance*, he opened a wall cabinet to reveal the Uzi, a couple pistols, and a ridiculous amount of ammunition. "I don't know what to do with this," he said, pointing to the Uzi. "I really don't want to keep it, but I want even less to see it in the hands of the so-called 'law-abiding citizens' I've met in this area, including the Jefferson State Militia. You wouldn't believe the demonstration Ted gave for me when we did a little target practice a month ago."

Susan rolled her eyes, but said nothing. "Speaking of which," Walter segued, "let's take a walk and I'll show you where we wasted the ammunition. It's an unusual feature of this property, and it came in real handy when the time came to pluck Ted out of here." They left the bunker, locking everything as they went, and followed the power line to the helipad. Susan lacked the technical expertise to fully appreciate what she was looking at, but she readily realized that (a) it was extraordinary and (b) it had been essential in evacuating Ted.

Returning to the house, Walter entered the garage and waved toward the Toyota Camry and the Ford pickup. "What do we do with these? We don't need two cars and two pickups for the two of us."

"This car is newer and nicer than mine," Susan said. "I could use it and give my car to Lucy."

"Good idea. On the other hand, my truck is nearly new, so we should sell this one or give it to somebody. It could use a paint job, but it still has plenty of good miles left in it."

"We could ask Lucy if she has a friend who needs it," Susan suggested.

A light bulb lit in Walter's head. "I can think of somebody who could probably use it, and he certainly wants to be Lucy's friend: Al Fath." A 'you've-got-to-be-kidding' look surfaced on Susan's face. "I gather that Lucy didn't mention that to you before she left," Walter said. "C'mon, let's go eat lunch, and I'll tell you about it."

Over lunch, Susan said that she wanted to invite Darrell and Virginia Cox to the house—which had now become '*our* house'—for Thanksgiving dinner, adding that Lucy had said she could come home then *in addition to* the weekend of the wedding. "In that case," Walter suggested, "let's invite Al Fath too. I'd enjoy sitting back and watching the intercultural interaction between him and Lucy. When it's all over, Lucy can drive back to Monterey in the Corolla and Fath can go back to the Frisco Ranch in the Ford pickup."

Their conversation drifted back to the subject of 'gratitude,' because Walter was curious to learn more of Susan's understanding of *Luke 12:48*. She started off by saying, "We like to declare that 'God is Love,' but there's a pervasive belief that God plays favorites—you know, 'God is on our side, not on yours'—or simply the belief we can influence God with our prayers and with our good or bad behavior. It's a false belief, because God is bigger than that. God does not sit up there in heaven dishing out rewards and punishments like Judge Judy. The troubles we experience in life are the natural consequences of what we say and do and *what we think*—but God's intervention is not required. That's what I meant when I told you that 'we are punished *by* our sins, not *for* our sins.'"

"It's like the old adage 'what goes around, comes around,'" Walter interjected.

"Right, and it works on the positive side too, which is where 'gratitude' comes in. But we make a mistake if we think that the good things we get in life are simply God's response to us, on a tit-for-tat basis. We don't make the first move, God does, and 'gratitude' is our response to Him, or Her, or It. God's nature is to give, and if we fail to get, it's because something in us—our thinking, usually—is not letting us receive. Consequently, the most common error is thinking there isn't enough 'good stuff' to go around—especially not enough love—which takes us back to the false idea that God plays favorites. If you believe in an abundant universe and a loving God, these false ideas disintegrate."

"OK, so you and I have received a huge gift—this house and property—that we really didn't earn. What should we do with it?" Walter asked.

"First, we accept it, and we don't quibble about details like the fact that the car is a Toyota when we really wanted a BMW. Next we pass it on, sharing our good fortune with others, not just our friends, but everybody. When we receive God's grace, regardless of our merit, we share it, regardless of our opinion of others' merit."

"This brings me back to another question that's related," Walter said. "We're going to share our good fortune with Lucy and Fath by giving them vehicles, and we're going to share our home with the Coxes at Thanksgiving, but what are we going to do for Mac? He's probably the person who most deserves our gratitude."

"I think we should ask him," was Susan's answer.

89.

Walter and Susan had an opportunity to do that a few days later, when they were meeting with Mac to plan their wedding. The planning was over quickly—the only thing Susan and Walter asked to include in the ceremony was *Psalm 23*, which they would recite together, changing the pronouns from singular to plural: 'The Lord is *our* shepherd ...' and so forth. The closing line— 'Surely goodness and mercy shall follow us all the days of our life, and we shall dwell in the house of the Lord forever'—provided a perfect *segue* into telling Mac about their *'flabbergasm*,' Susan's neologism for 'a flabbergasting event.' As they expected, Mac was delighted to learn that they would be living their new marriage in Ted's former house and that this would enable Susan to concentrate on her education. "What about you, Walter? What are your plans?" he inquired.

"In the near term, I want to get our two households integrated into one and fix up Susan's house so we can put it up for sale. I'll do some flying part-time for Darrell to pay the bills and maintain my proficiency, but apart from that I don't really know," Walter answered. "All I can say at this point is that I don't want to go back to a full-time job as a pilot—not if I can help it."

Mac shifted in his chair as if to indicate he was about to say something important. "I've enjoyed the relationship that has developed between us over these past few months," he said, "and I'd like to not only continue it but perhaps expand it. I haven't figured out yet how to do that—having you join me in the fly fishing biz is the only thing that has come to mind, but I don't think that's it. As you know, I would very much like to create a new program at OIT and KCC that would build upon their existing programs in criminal justice and applied psychology. It would complement those programs by focusing on *preventive*, rather than *remedial*, aspects of social balance— promoting and teaching understanding, tolerance, cooperation, and peace, rather than judgment, conflict, competition, and violence. It would include religion, but primarily in its practical aspects, rather than theology and doctrine, and it would emphasize what religion is *supposed* to do, which is to shelter us from the meanness of the world, rather than provide an institutional structure behind which people can hide their ambitions. Of necessity, it would be a multidisciplinary and interdisciplinary program, which poses a problem because no existing department will want to give it a home. However, I've succeeded in selling the idea to several local leaders, including some top people in the business community, and as a result, they have agreed to match whatever money I can raise from other sources. They've given me three years to get it all together, so I need to give it some serious attention."

He looked straight at Walter. "Something tells me you could help me do that. Call it a hunch, but that's the feeling I get, and it got a little louder and clearer when I heard about how you handled the near-confrontation between the Muslims and the Jefferson State Militia and still louder when I witnessed the subsequent meeting between the Muslims and the Feds in your cabin. At present, I don't have any money at all, so I can't offer you any kind of job, but if you're willing to build some 'sweat equity,' I think there could be something for you down the road. Have you ever thought of becoming an academician?"

90.

In the following days, Walter worked hard to organize and stabilize his new life. Moses moved in with him in a matter of hours, but it took Susan a week. Walter's meditation schedule had been completely upset by recent developments, so one of his first priorities was to reinstate it. Of course, he was no longer living in the cabin, and the weather was too cold for him to sit outside for any length of time, so he experimented with various places in the house, eventually settling on an easy chair in the office. He expected that, once the location issue was resolved, he would be able to pick up where he had left off at the cabin, but such was not the case. After some introspection, he concluded that he was missing Abigail and the rather strange rapport he had experienced with her.

Nevertheless, he pressed forward with his *vipassana* regimen, and it was there he had an epiphany of sorts. Abigail was gone, and that was that, but as he was grieving her loss, something new had come into his life: Lucy. He had lost a duck and gained a daughter. Not that his relationship with Lucy would be the same as it had been with Abigail, but that was exactly the point. It was time for him to integrate 'that still small voice within' that Abigail had externalized and to 'step up' to another level of maturity as Lucy's dad. Yes, the universe would still communicate with him as it had through Abigail but on a 'higher' level, and it was his responsibility to pass it along to Lucy, his own kids, Al Fath perhaps, and whoever else might come into his life. Walter couldn't articulate what the 'it' was, but he decided to think of it as 'grace.'

91.

Early in December, a Christmas card arrived in Walter's mail. Inside was a handwritten note:

Hi, Walter,

It occurs to me you may not have found the safe combination on a scrap of paper buried amidst the instruction manuals and such in the file cabinet. It's 29-62-8-47. In addition to what's in the safe, you'll also find a hidden storage area under the floor next to the sewer line to the toilet. If you take up the quarter-round in front of the shower, you'll see how to get into it.

Merry Christmas!

Ted (now 'Brad')

P.S.: Nancy (now 'Zsa Zsa') sends regards.

The handwritten return address on the envelope was 'B. Walters' and the postmark was Hawaii.

With a growing sense of excitement, Walter went out to the bunker and dialed the combination into the safe. It took him three tries to get it right, but when he was finally able to open the door, he found the interior space filled with 'bricks' like the one Hazik had paid him with after the August flight to Sanderson Field. He pulled one out and carefully opened the wrapper, just enough to verify that it contained brand-new $100 bills, presumably five-hundred of them. He closed the wrapper and started removing enough bricks from the safe to ascertain how many there were. They were stacked three across by four deep by six high, totaling seventy-two in all. He did the arithmetic in his head, three times to make sure he was correct: *72 times $50,000 per brick equals $3.6 million!* Walter felt the a huge wave, another *'flabbergasm,'* wash over him just as it had when he received the letter and Legal Agreement giving him ownership of the house.

He put the money back, closed the safe, went upstairs, and stumbled outside to get some fresh air. Then he went over to the house and drank a whole glass of water, somehow regaining enough presence of mind to stop on the way back to the bunker to pick up some tools to remove the quarter-round. Working carefully and deliberately, he took apart the flooring piece-by-piece, like dissecting a Japanese puzzle box, until he could see almost two feet of the sewer pipe underneath. Alongside it was a sturdy metal box about 12x12x8 inches. He tried to lift it out but it was much too heavy, so he tugged and pried on the lid tight-fitting lid until it finally opened.

Even in the dim light, the glint of three bars of solid gold dazzled him. Laid side by side, each was sealed in a polyethylene bag. With some effort, he took one out to examine it. He could see through the plastic that it was the standard 'Good Delivery' bar, weighing 400 troy ounces, about 27 pounds. Looking back into the box, he counted four layers of bars stacked crosswise. Again caught up in a full *flabbergasm*, he struggled to do the mental arithmetic: *four layers with three bars each equals 12 bars, and at 27 pounds per bar, that came to 324 pounds. No wonder I can't lift the box*, he thought.

Walter didn't know the current price of gold, but he vaguely recalled some mention of $1,600 per ounce in a recent newspaper article, so each bar was worth 400 times $1,600, or $640,000. He was now almost too flabbergasted to multiply that amount by the number of bars, but he was dimly aware it came to well over seven million dollars. So Ted had left him a 'Christmas present' of some *eleven million dollars* in cash and gold. Never mind the fact that it represented less than one percent of Ted's wealth, Walter had never dreamed of even *seeing* that much money!

He meticulously put the floor back together so there was no indication of anything hidden beneath it, but he decided to take one of the bars to the house, perhaps to remind himself that it wasn't a dream. He carried the gold from the bunker to the kitchen, put it down ever-so-gently in the middle of the kitchen table, sat down, and stared at it as he sipped another glass of water. In his muddled brain, he began thinking of how he would break the news to Susan when she got home from work, and what they would do with all that money, and what the tax consequences would be, and .... Walter couldn't stand any more of it. He carried the gold to his bedroom, hid it in the drawer of his nightstand, and took Moses for a long walk.

Susan got home shortly thereafter. Something in his hug and kiss told her things were out of kilter, but before she could ask, Walter took her by the hand and led her over to the sofa. "There's been another *flabbergasm*," he stammered, "and not just one, but *two*! *A double* flabbergasm!" He handed her the card from Ted. "Read this," he directed.

While she was reading, he retrieved the gold bar from his nightstand. As he sat down beside her again, she held up the card and said, "So?" Walter described what he had found in the bunker, his words tumbling out helter-skelter, and when he laid the gold bar in her lap and she felt its crushing weight on her thighs, Susan finally understood. "*Eleven million dollars?!*" she gasped.

Walter nodded toward the gold bar. "That's about 640,000 right there. The rest is still out in the bunker."

"What are we ever going to do with that much money?"

"I have no idea," Walter said. "We certainly don't need it. It's comforting to have a little extra, but even one million is hard to comprehend."

"From everyone to whom much has been given, much will be required; and from the one to whom much has been entrusted, even more will be asked." Susan said slowly and softly. The thought of Mac's vision of teaching peace sprung to Walter's mind once again. As it did so, Walter thought he heard an enthusiastic '*Quack!*' somewhere off in the distance—or was it inside himself?

There are only two ways to live your life.
One is as though nothing is a miracle.
The other is as if everything is.
—Albert Einstein (1879-1955)

As soon as you trust yourself,
you will know how to live.
—Johann Wolfgang von Goethe
(1749-1832)

Acknowledgements

I am deeply indebted to many persons who have assisted and encouraged me in the writing of this book:

For information that I incorporated into the story to make it factually accurate: Bob Berard, Jean Blaurock, Billy Cook, Steve Curtis, Bill Herrick, Todd Kepple, Ken Leuthold, Mike Merker, Ron Newton, Nadezhda Ovsyannikova, and Bonnie Vorvick.

For general advice and encouragement through the long ordeal of writing, editing, and publication: Jack Anderson, Mary-Alice Boulter, Cevin Brierman, Terri Bristow, Ken Burres, John Daniel, Betty Gowler, Geraldine Lesser, Janie Leuthold, Jennifer McCord, Brian McDonald, Angelo Pizelo, Resa Raven, Jim Rough, Elisabeth Ann Scarborough, and the Wednesday writing group (Gene Bradbury, Gwuinifer Carradine, Jim Fisher, Ruth Marcus, Terry Moore, and Carlyn Syvanen).

For specific expert guidance in editing my manuscript, Elizabeth Chowning and Sheryl Stebbins; in legal matters, Jacques Dulin, Esq.; and in formatting and generally getting it all together for publication, Magdalena Bassett.

For "being there" for me during this and other adventures: my family, Nina Powell, Brian Lindamood, and Elden Lindamood; their partners, Barry Shrewsbury, Sarah Lindamood, and Catherine Conover; and their children (my grandkids), Helen Lindamood, Sophia Powell, Allister Lindamood, Ian Lindamood, and Oliver Lindamood.

Most of all I thank my wife, Annette, for her loving support and understanding throughout the whole thing, without which it would never have happened.

Permissions

About *The Accidental Peacemaker*: A Conversation with George Lindamood

Why did you decide, at the age of 71, to write a novel, your first novel?

I did a lot of writing in my IT career. I was a much better writer than most techies—scientists, engineers, programmers—and that made a huge difference in getting me hired, recognized, and promoted. Nearly all of that writing was non-fiction, but there were a few notable occasions where I resorted to fiction or humorous essay to get my point(s) across. It was like sugar-coating a pill to help it go down, and it worked very well for me. So when, at age 71, I had some ideas I wanted the world to hear, I felt I would gain better acceptance if I wrapped them in an interesting story. Stories are found in every culture in the world and are the oldest teaching tools we have.

So your purpose in writing this book is to teach?

Yes. I've always been a teacher, and in seventy-some years on this planet I've accumulated some ideas and lessons I want to share with the world.

What are some of those ideas?

First, that life proceeds in stages, a series of distinct periods that are identifiable, at least in retrospect, and different from those which precede or follow. They are a normal aspect of human growth and development, both individually and collectively. Psychologists, sociologists, and anthropologists have studied them to the point that they are now regarded as predictable, although not necessarily inevitable—that is, some people or groups may choose to go only so far on life's journey and no farther, resisting any further change and growth.

Second, each stage builds upon the stages which precede it, and it's not possible to skip over a stage—for example, to go directly from 'Stage Two' to 'Stage Four,' whatever those may be. A more subtle point is that a person or group at any given stage may perceive rather clearly what the next stage may be, but they can't see or comprehend any of the stages after that.

Third, although each stage requires that a person go through the preceding one, the key to advancing to the next stage is letting go—that is, unlearning or abandoning ideas, beliefs, and/or behaviors from earlier stages. So transition from stage to stage requires radical change, which we sometimes embrace in our cultures—for example, being 'born again.' Adolescence and middle-age are recognized and even celebrated as normal transition periods, and in recent years as Baby Boomers have reached retirement there has been a growing interest in and understanding of the later stages of life.

How did you create a story about all that?

I invented a character—I named him Walter—who is encountering some common mid-life transitions. He's gone through a divorce, and he's been downsized out of a job. Somehow he has realized that the second half of his life—that is, the next stage, which is as far ahead as he can think—doesn't have to be a repeat of the first half, and he's entertaining the idea that the second half would be better if he made some major changes—if he 'reinvented' himself. So he decides to go off into seclusion—in 'the wilderness'—to reflect, to think, to sort out his 'unnecessary baggage' and let go of it.

It's a great idea—one that more people ought to try, or at least consider—but it's not all that simple, as Walter soon finds out.

Is the story autobiographical?

Yes and no. Many of the things in the story have happened to me. I've been downsized out of my job three times (once voluntarily) and divorced (just once). All of that pushed me into a lot of self-examination and reflection—psychology, anthropology, religious studies (Zen, Taoism, Islam, Judaism, Shinto, as well as several sects of Christianity ranging from fundamentalism through Greek Orthodoxy, to New Thought), and meditation. I've visited, traveled thru, or lived in all of the places in the story. But I've never been a pilot (I used to hate flying) or a fly-fisherman (although I've always wanted to get into it) or lived in an isolated primitive cabin. I never served in the military and I've never fired a gun.

So who is the intended audience for your book?

Anybody over 35, especially middle-class Americans, or anybody interested in human development. Also anybody who has ever been divorced, downsized, or otherwise depressed and discouraged by life's vicissitudes.

Will there be a sequel?

I've been thinking about a sequence of two sequels based upon "loose threads" I deliberately left in the present story. I'm also contemplating a screenplay based upon this story, but I have almost zero experience in that genre, so I have a great deal to learn (not that that frightens me). And I have some other projects in various stages of manifestation: a children's book, some short stories and essays, even a chapbook of poetry.

For further information and news updates about all of that, see my blog at www.accidentalpeacemaker.com

.

Author's Bio

George Lindamood was born and raised in Marietta, Ohio. Since retiring from a forty-two-year career in information technology, he has served as an AmeriCorps volunteer, taught English in China, completed a doctorate in religious studies, and played piano and trumpet in various jazz groups and for worship in Lutheran, Methodist, and Christian Science churches. Most recently, he has turned his attention to writing fiction and poetry. He and his wife Annette live on the Olympic Peninsula in Washington state.

16424157R00209

Made in the USA
Charleston, SC
19 December 2012